The camera never lies . . .

"You're very photogenic."

"I bet you say that to all the women you photograph."

"No," he said, "I don't. You also have a very photogenic house, and I think there's a lot more of your hard work and talent in this house than you give yourself credit for." Claire could feel him looking directly at her, even though she had her back to him as she took off her apron. She turned around and was struck all over again by how beautiful he was, with his strong features and tanned skin. There were laughter lines around his chocolate brown eyes, but also a deep groove between his eyebrows that she hadn't noticed until now. "I'm sure you could make anywhere you lived lovely."

Claire didn't say anything but started tidying the table.

"Now let me think. What else can I ask you?"

Would you like to kiss me? The words popped into Claire's head.

"Would you like . . ." Stefan began.

Yes, please, said Bad Claire in her head. *I'll just take my apron off and I'm yours for the rest of the day.*

A Perfect Home

KITTY GLANVILLE

BERKLEY BOOKS, NEW YORK

BERKLEY BOOKS
Published by the Penguin Group
Penguin Group (USA) Inc.
375 Hudson Street, New York, New York 10014, USA

Penguin Group (Canada), 90 Eglinton Avenue East, Suite 700, Toronto, Ontario M4P 2Y3, Canada
(a division of Pearson Penguin Canada Inc.) • Penguin Books Ltd., 80 Strand, London WC2R 0RL,
England • Penguin Group Ireland, 25 St. Stephen's Green, Dublin 2, Ireland (a division of Penguin
Books Ltd.) • Penguin Group (Australia), 250 Camberwell Road, Camberwell, Victoria 3124, Australia
(a division of Pearson Australia Group Pty. Ltd.) • Penguin Books India Pvt. Ltd., 11 Community
Centre, Panchsheel Park, New Delhi—110 017, India • Penguin Group (NZ), 67 Apollo Drive,
Rosedale, Auckland 0632, New Zealand (a division of Pearson New Zealand Ltd.) • Penguin Books
(South Africa) (Pty.) Ltd., 24 Sturdee Avenue, Rosebank, Johannesburg 2196, South Africa

Penguin Books Ltd., Registered Offices: 80 Strand, London WC2R 0RL, England

This is a work of fiction. Names, characters, places, and incidents either are the product of the author's
imagination or are used fictitiously, and any resemblance to actual persons, living or dead, business
establishments, events, or locales is entirely coincidental. The publisher does not have any control over
and does not assume any responsibility for author or third-party websites or their content.

PUBLISHING HISTORY
Berkey trade paperback edition / August 2012

Library of Congress Cataloging-in-Publication Data

Glanville, Kitty.
A perfect home / Kitty Glanville.
p.   cm.
ISBN 978-0-425-24777-8
1. Married people—Fiction.   2. Dwellings—Conservation and restoration—Fiction.
3. Values—Fiction.   4. Life change events—Fiction.   I. Title.
PR6107.L34P47 2012
823'.92—dc22
2011049765

PRINTED IN THE UNITED STATES OF AMERICA

10 9 8 7 6 5 4 3 2 1

To the memory of my beautiful friend Alex Locke,
who encouraged me to stop thinking about writing a novel
and actually sit down and do it!

A Perfect Home

CHAPTER 1

*Years of hard work and imagination
have created a stunning family home in the heart
of the English countryside.*

A butterfly settled briefly on the crisp, white washing, its wings quivering in the air. It looked so delicate, so exquisitely beautiful. Claire wanted to touch it, to feel the velvet fluttering in her palm. Unable to help herself, she reached out—but in that second it was gone. She looked around, shading her eyes with her hand against the late-afternoon sun. Then she saw it, flying in a haphazard zigzag across the flower beds, over the flagstones and toward the house. It looked as though it might fly through the open doors of the conservatory, but, as if pulled by an invisible string, it suddenly ascended until it was high above the steep pitch of yellow thatch, a dot against the cornflower sky before it vanished completely.

Claire took a deep breath and carried on working her way along the washing line. The scent of sage and lavender and cut grass mingled on the warm breeze, which brushed her cotton skirt against her legs and blew through the long strands of hair escaping from a clasp at the back of her neck.

She felt unusually calm as she unpegged the sheets and pillowcases and folded them into the wicker basket at her feet. The children had been fed and homework completed, a fish pie was cooking in the Aga for William's supper, she had packed up twenty cushion covers and thirty lavender hearts for Sally to collect for the gallery and cut out the fabric for an order of aprons for a local kitchenware shop. Claire looked at her watch; it wasn't even six o'clock. The washing was now done and she had deadheaded the roses around the porch to try to get a second flush of flowers before the photo shoot for *Idyllic Home* magazine in five weeks. All that was left was to make two dozen fairy cakes for the school fair tomorrow and put the children to bed, then she could pour herself a large glass of chilled Chardonnay and relax. For once she was in control.

Claire walked through the living room with the washing basket. She had designed a new range of cushion covers, appliquéd with patchwork houses and button-headed flowers, their leaves made out of antique ribbons. She had arranged them on a sofa to decide if she liked the design. Stopping, basket in her arms, she looked at them for the umpteenth time that day, trying to visualize how they might look as a display in one of the handful of gift shops and galleries that sold her work. The little houses depicted on the cushions were not unlike her own: symmetrical and square at the front, with a flower-covered central door. It was a child's idea of a house. A doll's house. A perfect house.

Claire's house had once been a farm, but the farmland was long gone, leaving only a garden and small orchard around the eighteenth-century building. Its neatly proportioned stone walls, painted in a rich buttermilk cream, sat beneath a dark, honey-colored thatch. The roof arched around two dormer windows on the second floor, which gave the effect of heavy-browed eyes staring out impassively.

In May, wisteria bloomed along the front in a blush of pink, and from late June lipstick-red roses blazed around the thatched porch. The back of the house rambled in a hodge-podge of extensions added over the previous two hundred years. The thatch clung to the additions in smooth, undulating curves, blanketing them like royal icing on a cake. The biggest extension was the large kitchen that William had built the year Oliver was born and next to it his latest project, a Victorian-style conservatory.

"It's so charming," visitors would enthuse when they first saw the house. But every time Claire pulled into the drive, she never got rid of the sense that it was watching her, judging her, making her feel she didn't quite deserve to live in a house so lovely.

Claire wasn't sure about the cushions—too twee perhaps? Too fussy? Something behind the sofa caught her eye—something wet and red and out of place. Claire picked up the dripping box of defrosted red mush. Her heart sank when she saw the pool of liquid on the floorboards. What would William say?

"Emily, Oliver, Ben!" she shouted. "Who's taken raspberries out of the freezer and left them on the new oak floor?"

"Not me," said Oliver from the other end of the room, where he lay draped across a leather armchair eating chocolate Hob-nobs straight from the package. He was wearing a battered fisherman's hat of his father's; it was much too big and fell la-zily over his eyes. From underneath it he watched animated cyber-warriors showing off their martial-arts skills in the de-fense of the universe.

"Not me," echoed Ben, sitting cross-legged much too close

to the cyber-warriors, naked apart from a bulging nappy and a smearing of melted chocolate around his mouth.

"Oliver, please could you find a more suitable program for Ben to watch?" Claire asked as she peeled a half-sucked cookie from the floor. "This will give him nightmares. And put those back in the cupboard."

"But, Mum," Oliver protested. "This is my favorite program and I *need* these, I'm starving."

"Ben did it." Emily appeared in the French windows, a long daisy-and-buttercup chain in her hands. "He must have put the raspberries there after I gave them to him yesterday. He was meant to put them in the fridge to defrost and tell you that they were there so we could have them on our cereal for breakfast."

"He's only two." Claire sighed.

"Nearly three," said Emily.

"Why were they out of the freezer in the first place?"

"The freezer was too full," replied Emily, shrugging her shoulders as she wrapped the floral chain around her thin wrist.

"But the freezer has lots of room in it."

"Not enough for the nasturtium-and-rose-petal ice cream that I made." Emily smiled at Claire, showing her missing front teeth. "I made it for Daddy. Milk, sugar, margarine, chocolate sauce, orange juice, and flower petals all mixed up in a cake tin. It's frozen now; I thought Daddy could have it for tea when he gets home."

"How many times have I told you, Emily, no cooking without me? And what am I going to do with the raspberries now? You've wasted a whole box of fruit." She shook it to emphasize her point.

"Careful, Mummy," Emily warned. "You're dripping raspberry juice all over the washing."

The phone rang. Claire thought about ignoring it. It was probably her mother, or it might be William telling her he was stopping off at Homebase to look for flathead screws or tile grout. Worst of all, it might be her mother-in-law. While she dithered, Emily jumped to answer it.

"It's a strange woman," she said in a stage whisper.

A loud, gushing voice greeted Claire as she took the handset.

"Claire, darling, how are you?" The woman on the other end of the line gave no time for Claire to answer. "Wonderful, wonderful . . ."

She realized it must be the journalist, Celia Howard, from the magazine. She took a tissue from Emily and mopped ineffectually at the stain on the floor as she held the receiver under her chin.

"Enjoying the sunshine in that lovely country home of yours? Not like us stuck here in stuffy London," Celia was saying. "*Super.* How lucky you are. Now, darling, about this photo shoot—we've been thinking about it in the office and we think your house would be just *perfect* for our Christmas issue. We're writing features for that now, so if we just change you to a festive shoot, it will fit in wonderfully."

"So you're not coming to photograph it at the end of August?" asked Claire, relieved at the idea of a postponement. She could put off all that cleaning now.

"That's right, darling; that date's all off now. We work four months in advance and the Christmas issue comes out in November, so the timing for this is fabulous. I've arranged it all; we'll be coming on Thursday."

Claire stifled a cry. It was Monday afternoon! Thursday gave her only two days to get ready.

"Celia, I don't think I can—"

"It's a two-day shoot, so the photographer will be with you on Friday as well," Celia interrupted. "Unfortunately, I'm up to my eyes this week, so I can't come to do the actual interview until next week. Now, of course we'll need to decorate the house in festive style. If you could get out a few decorations . . . just your usual ones. I don't want you to go to any trouble."

"You want me to put up Christmas decorations in July?"

"No, you don't have to put them up, dear. Leave that to the stylist," said Celia. "She'll bring a tree and decorate it herself."

"A tree?"

"Yes, she'll bring a Christmas tree. Unless you can get a tree locally—a good bushy one. You know, a silver Scotch pine or something like that."

"I think I'd better leave that to you." Finding the perfect Christmas tree in July would be difficult. Finding a good one in December was hard enough.

"And could you make some beautiful Christmas stockings to hang on the mantelpiece, in your lovely Emily Love style?" Celia went on. "Covered in your gorgeous pearly buttons? We could feature them as a reader offer—I'm sure you'll get lots of orders. Oh, and some mince pies would be lovely. We always have mince pies."

"Okay," said Claire, though it really wasn't okay. She felt a tight knot of anxiety forming in her stomach. Where was she going to find the time?

"Now, I told you about the *fabulous* photographer, Sienna Crabtree, that we were going to be using for the shoot?"

"Yes, she sounds great." Claire thought of all the things she was meant to be doing over the next few days and tried to rearrange them in her mind.

"She really is wonderful, but she can't do this week, so I'm sending a photographer called Stefan Kendrick. He's very good, recently back from working abroad. He's a *brilliant* photographer and a big hit with the female staff round here and some of the men are rather smitten too. You'll absolutely love him, darling."

Claire made a face at the phone. She didn't care how gorgeous he was; she just wanted someone to help her tidy the house from top to bottom, wipe the jam-smeared doorknobs, scrub the kitchen floor, dust the Cornishware on the dresser, and most of all help her get the raspberry juice out of the floorboards before William came home.

"Must dash," said Celia. "A million and one things to do. I wish I had your life in the heavenly countryside—*totally* stress-free, I'm sure. Lots of love."

Celia was gone before Claire had a chance to reply. She stayed squatting behind the sofa, staring at the soggy tissue and pink stain, trying to understand how she had suddenly found herself getting ready for Christmas during a July heat wave.

She was beginning to wish she'd never agreed to this whole thing in the first place.

It had been a month since Claire sent out images of her latest range of "Emily Love" cushions, appliquéd with hearts and flowers cut out of vintage fabric and decorated with ribbons, antique lace, and buttons. She had photographed them around the house—the light colors and simple antique furniture made a perfect backdrop for Claire's handmade designs.

Celia Howard, features editor for *Idyllic Home*, had phoned up two days later, saying her magazine adored the cushions ("recycling fabric is so *in* right now") but they also loved the

look of the house and could they see some more of it, prefer-
ably by the end of the day? Claire ran around taking snapshots
of all the rooms and the garden and e-mailed them to her.

"Exquisite!" Celia had enthused over the phone. "We'd love
to do a feature on your gorgeous house and your lovely little
rural craft business. Our readers just adore that sort of thing."

At first Claire had been nervous, but her best friend, Sally,
had soon talked her round.

"Just think about it as a wonderful opportunity for free advertising for Emily Love," she had said. "You always say how you
want to get your things featured in a magazine. Now you can
decorate the whole house with your work. You'll get loads of
orders and then you'll be able to expand beyond the spare
bedroom."

Claire had initially worried about William's reaction, but he
seemed quite pleased with the idea of showing off their home.

"I'll have to finish grouting the tiles on the conservatory
floor," he had said. "And then I'll have to repaint the hall. It's
covered in mucky handprints. I'm sure it's Ben. You've got to
stop him touching the walls, Claire."

He was keen to be there on the day of the shoot, though
Claire suspected that this was less to do with being in the photographs and more to do with making sure the stylist didn't
damage any paintwork or scratch the floors.

"They're not going to bang nails into the beams, are they?"
he asked as he touched up the paint on the banisters. He carefully dipped his brush in and out of a pot of Farrow & Ball
Shaded White, dabbing at dots of missing paint. "There are
enough holes and chips all over this house as it is."

"I can't see any holes or chips," said Claire, trying to squeeze
past him with a pile of ironing. "It looks fine to me." She stroked

his head affectionately as she passed; she liked the stubbly feel of his new haircut.

"That's the trouble," William answered. "You just don't notice the state this house is getting into." He jerked his head away from her hand.

Claire bit her lip and tried not to answer back. She couldn't face an argument when she still had the tea to make and the children to bathe.

"I think we'll have to forget about going away this summer. There are far too many jobs to do around the house and garden." He looked up at Claire. The disappointment must have shown on her face, because his expression softened. "I don't know why we need to go away anyway, darling. We've got it all here. People pay hundreds of pounds to stay a week in cottages not half as nice as this one. Why would we want to be anywhere else?"

At last the shock of Celia Howard's phone call began to lessen and Claire moved out from behind the sofa. She feared the raspberry stain was there for good and pushed the sofa back to hide it. As she did so she revealed something gray and lumpy, which could only have been regurgitated by Macavity the cat. She didn't know how long it had been there; it was encrusted onto the floor and in between the boards. On closer inspection, it looked as though it contained at least half of what had once been a bat. Claire shuddered. She'd deal with it later, she thought, and moved the sofa at an angle to cover it.

As she picked up the basket to wash the juice-splashed washing all over again, she thought about Celia's last words. *Stress-free life?* She had no idea.

* * *

Claire looked at the large clock on the kitchen wall: half-past nine. The fish pie looked sad and dry on top of the Aga.

Claire helped herself to a portion; she was used to eating alone. She contemplated having more wine but that would break her self-enforced rule of one glass a night. After a few minutes she poured an inch or two of Chardonnay into the large glass and mixed it with some soda water. Surely a spritzer didn't really count?

The table was half covered in fairy cakes. On reflection, Claire thought it had probably been a mistake to throw the de-frosted raspberries into the cake mixture; they looked soggy and unappealingly pink.

The phone rang and Claire leaped up to answer it before it woke Ben. She knew it would be her mother, Elizabeth.

"I'm not disturbing you, am I? You sound like you're eating."

"No, it's all right, Mum," Claire said, trying not to sigh.

"William not home yet, then?"

"I'm sure he's on his way. Actually I'm in a bit of a rush; the house is being photographed—"

"He's just like your father used to be . . ."

Claire wished she'd just pretended William was there.

" . . . Coming in whenever it suited him, no thought to me waiting for him after a hard day at work and looking after you. In the seventies we thought the next generation would be bet-ter, but they're all the same. Men! Better off without them, if you ask me. Honestly, Claire, I don't know why you don't put your foot down. You've got to stand up to him. That's what I used to do."

Claire could remember lying in bed with her hands over her ears trying not to hear her parents shouting downstairs.

"Of course your father was usually with another woman," her mother continued. "I always suspected that. I knew deep down but always forgave him. And look what he did in the end. Look where I ended up: dumped in a bedsit while he gallivanted off to California with his teenage bride."

Claire didn't dare remind her that the woman her father had finally left her for was nearly thirty. "It's a two-bedroom flat, Mum, not a bedsit. And it's been twenty-six years since he left. You could have moved house. You could have found someone else."

"And let someone do it to me all over again? No thank you, I'm not that stupid." Claire closed her eyes. She was used to this. She'd listened to her mother's tirades since she was thirteen years old and her assault on marriage hadn't lessened when Claire became a bride herself.

Elizabeth had been baffled by her daughter's wish to get married, especially to an accountant. Since Claire's father had left, she'd brought her daughter up to believe that marriage was a pointless institution that could only fail.

Claire had been determined to prove her wrong. Her marriage, unlike her parents', would work. Happily ever after, just like in the fairy tales—that's what she believed. That's what she wanted to believe.

"Nightmare evening," William said, suddenly seeming to fill the kitchen. "The train was late, then I went to get the wood for the living room shelves but they didn't have the right thickness. Can you believe it? It's a standard measurement. So I had to go miles out of my way to bloody B&Q." He thrust a bunch of yellow carnations at Claire and pulled loose his tie.

"I'd better go, Mum, William's home." Claire put down the phone and smiled up at her husband, wondering how she could incorporate the carnations into the Christmas decor. "Thank you for the flowers. Glass of wine?"

William was already opening a bottle of red, twisting the corkscrew down hard before pulling out the cork with a muffled pop. He poured himself a large glass.

"Let me guess," he said, nodding toward the phone. "Your mother ranting about her lot in life. She loves it, you know. Wallowing in her own misery."

"She's depressed. And lonely, especially since she retired."

"I'm not surprised." He was poking at the fish pie with the end of the corkscrew. "Who'd want to be with someone so grumpy?"

"Please don't be cruel, William," Claire said, pouring water into a glass vase. "She hasn't had it easy. It's not like it is for your parents. They've been lucky. They have each other and a lovely home and lots of things to keep them busy."

"That's right; you wouldn't find my mother moping about finding fault with her life."

That's because she's too busy finding fault with everybody else's, Claire wanted to say. But she held back.

"Fish pie?" she asked, putting on her brightest smile.

"I've eaten. Baguette at the station. What are these?" He picked up a fairy cake.

"Raspberry buns. Do you want one?"

"I'm not hungry," he said. "I'm going to put the new shelves up."

"It's nearly ten o'clock. Isn't it a bit late? You might wake the children."

"It's all right for you at home all day, Claire, but I've got to get things done when I can if you want this house to look perfect." He collected the keys for his toolshed and headed for the back door.

Claire longed to tell him that she didn't want it to be perfect, didn't *need* it to be perfect. She was happy with it how it was. If only William could sit back and enjoy it, enjoy his family. Enjoy her. She sighed and started arranging the carnations in the vase. William stopped, his hand on the door handle, and turned to look at her. He suddenly smiled and walked back across the room.

"Sorry, darling. I don't mean to sound so irritable. It's been a hard day and having to go to B&Q was the final straw."

Claire reached up to kiss his cheek and wrapped her arms around him. The muscles in his back felt tense.

"I could give you a massage," she offered.

"Maybe later." He gently stroked her hair. "Tell me how your day's been?"

"You won't believe what the magazine people want to do," she said, her cheek pressed against his pin-striped shirt. "They're going to come on—"

"Isn't that a bit tall for those flowers?" he interrupted her midflow. "I imagined you would put them in the Poole Pottery jug."

"I think I'll need that for the holly."

"Holly?" He disentangled himself from her embrace. "Why would you have holly at this time of year?"

"I was just trying to tell you." Claire bent down to search in the dresser cupboard for a tin to put the cakes into. "The magazine people are coming to photograph the house on Thursday and they want it to be a Christmas shoot. Christmas in July! I'm worried we'll never get the house ready in time."

She turned around to an empty room; he had disappeared to attend to yet another DIY project. The thought struck her that William didn't need to have an affair like her father had done—the house was already his mistress.

"Claire!"

William was back. The skin along his hairline had turned the sort of blotchy red that she always knew meant trouble.

"What the hell has been going on in the living room? Did you know that the cat's been sick and there's a huge stain on the floor?"

"Oh, that was an accident with Ben and some raspberries. And Macavity—"

"I've only just laid that at great expense—it took me weeks to sand and varnish. Now I'll have to do it all over again. I can't believe the trouble that child makes."

Claire took a deep breath. Why was it that William took Ben's sticky fingerprints on the walls and spilled juice as personal attacks on his own hard work?

"The stain is behind the sofa. No one will notice."

"I'll notice. Every time I walk in there, I'll see it. Why weren't you watching him? You're meant to be in charge of the children. That's why you gave up your job."

"I gave up my job to start my own business." Claire tried to keep her voice quiet and steady.

William's voice seemed to boom around the large kitchen. "Ten years I've spent working on this house, and you let a two-year-old and a cat destroy it. Can't you just try to look after the place?"

"I do, I really do but . . ." Claire began, but he held up his hand to stop her like a policeman holding up a line of traffic. He picked up his wineglass and left the room, leaving his angry words echoing around in her head.

A surge of rage welled up inside her, and picking up a fairy cake, she threw it toward the empty doorway. It fell short and rolled across the quarry tiles to where Macavity sat inelegantly licking his back leg. He sniffed it for a few seconds and wandered away toward the smell of fish pie on the Aga.

Claire sat down as the rage turned into a familiar lethargy. Why did she always seem to make William so cross these days? After all these years the house was finished. He had made them a beautiful home, but now Claire felt that he almost resented having to share it with her.

She looked at the flowers on the table and thought of her grandmother in her little florist shop. As a child, Claire would sit on the counter and watch her making sumptuous bouquets for weddings and elaborate wreaths for funerals. *All the flowers have something to tell us,* she used to say. *They all have their own special message, their very own language.* Claire tried to remember—red carnations were for longing and white for faithfulness, but what were yellow? She closed her eyes and could almost see the reels of shiny satin ribbon that her little fingers had longed to unravel and the rolls of pastel-colored wrapping paper hanging on the wall. Her grandmother's soft northern accent filtered into her mind: *You don't ever want to be given yellow carnations, Claire. Only disappointment comes with those.*

A single hot tear slipped down her cheek. She wiped it away with a tea towel and slowly put the fairy cakes, one by one, into the tin. She certainly felt as though she had become a disappointment to William. Every day there was a litany of things she had done wrong. Sometimes she wondered if he'd be happier if she and the children disappeared and he could have the house all to himself.

After a few minutes she heard drilling coming from the

living room and then the sound of Ben crying upstairs. Emily appeared in the doorway, her long toffee-colored hair tangled, her sleepy eyes half closed.

"Ben's awake," she mumbled.

"I know, darling," said Claire. "I'll be up in a minute. You go back to bed."

"Did Daddy have his ice cream?" Emily walked up to the table. She looked at Claire's face and then at the cupcakes. "Don't be upset, Mummy. I won't tell anyone you made them."

"I'm starving." Oliver stood beside them in his rumpled stripy pajamas, the fisherman's hat still on his head. "Is there anything to eat?"

"You've brushed your teeth. You'll have to wait till breakfast. Now go to bed, please."

"I'll brush them again, I promise. I'll never get back to sleep without some food." Oliver collapsed onto a kitchen chair as if weak with hunger, despite having eaten two helpings of fish pie and a bowl of ice cream for tea.

"Have one of these, then," she said, picking up a fairy cake.

"No, I mean proper food," he said, wrinkling up his nose in disgust. "You know, like real cakes from a shop."

Claire! There's chocolate all over the armchair. How did this happen?" William shouted from the living room. Claire looked up at the ceiling and tried to count to ten. She gave up at five.

"Come on," said Emily to her brother. "Let's go."

"I think I've trodden on a cake," said Oliver as he moved toward the door and flicked damp sponge off his bare foot in a spray of soggy crumbs. William stood in the doorway, still holding the drill, as he blocked the children's path. His eyes focused on the new mess in front of him. Oliver stared at the floor with his narrow shoulders hunched. Emily glanced at Claire and then at her father's face, meeting his glare with a radiant smile.

"Sorry, Daddy. It was me. But don't worry, I'll clear up the cake and I'll wipe the chocolate off the chair."

William's expression immediately softened.

"Thank you, sweetheart. Just don't eat in the living room again. You know the rules." He stepped forward and patted her head. Oliver squeezed behind him and disappeared upstairs. With a scowl directed at Claire, William returned to the living room.

"You don't have to do that, Emily," said Claire.

"What?"

"Take the blame for things that aren't your fault."

"I just don't want Daddy to be cross." Emily bent down to pick up bits of squashed cake. Claire gently pulled her daughter up and hugged her. It seemed like yesterday that she'd been a tiny baby; now, still just a little girl, she was taking responsibility for appeasing William's bad mood. Fresh tears threatened in the corners of Claire's eyes but she quickly blinked them back before Emily could see.

CHAPTER 2

*The pale blue Aga is the hub of
Claire's domestic routine.*

The day before the shoot Claire stood barefoot at the table on
the patio making mince pies. The Aga made the kitchen too
warm to work in on such a hot day. Ben sat under the table
playing with his own piece of pastry, every now and then sneak-
ing a little lump of it into his mouth. Macavity laid stretched
out beside them in the shade of a large pot of calla lilies.

It felt strange to be swatting away wasps as the familiar
smell of Christmas competed with the mingled summer smells
of the garden.

Claire had stopped answering the phone. All morning she
had had to field a constant stream of phone calls from Celia
Howard asking for *"just one more minuscule request"*—find holly,
put out candles, make a wreath for the door. She was waiting
for Celia to ask if she could lay on snow and arrange for a special appearance from Father Christmas himself. For the hundredth time she felt like canceling the whole thing, but the
thought of free advertising for Emily Love kept her complying
with all of Celia's requests. She remembered what Sally had

said at the school gates earlier that morning. "Just go for it, Claire. After all, what have you got to lose?"

The flagstones were hot on the soles of her feet. She meant to go and get her shoes but she was in a hurry to finish cooking so she could have lunch and vacuum the house before picking up Oliver and Emily. Cooking always made her hungry and she had to try very hard not to pick at the raw shortcrust pastry.

As she filled the pastry cases with mincemeat, topping each one with a fluted pastry lid, she could feel her white cotton blouse sticking to her back in the heat of the midday sun. She should have moved the table into the shade but it was too late now. She'd nearly finished.

Wiping a strand of hair away from her face with her flour-covered hand, she straightened up to admire her tray of finished pies. She smiled down at Ben and began singing "We Wish You a Merry Christmas."

"Merry Christmas to you too," a voice said.

Claire jumped and turned to see a tall man standing just a little way away from her on the garden path.

"I'm so sorry," he said. "I didn't mean to frighten you. I've been knocking at the front, but there was no reply, so I came round the side. I'm sorry, you were so absorbed in what you were doing. I tried coughing but . . . " He stopped and shrugged.

He smiled in a half-polite, half-amused way that revealed laughter lines at the corners of his dark eyes.

"I'm Stefan Kendrick." He stepped toward her and put out his hand. "I'm going to photograph your house for the magazine article."

"I'm sorry?"

"You are expecting us for a Christmas photo shoot, aren't

you?" He laughed and nodded toward the baking tray on the table. "Or do you always make mince pies in July?"

"I thought you were coming tomorrow?" *Please, please don't let it be today.*

"I am. I will be," Stefan said. "I was doing a small job for another magazine this morning. It was only a few miles away and I finished early. I thought I'd just come and take a look at your place so I'd know what to expect. I did try to ring, but no one answered. I like your house." He looked around him. "I can see why Celia's keen to feature it. It's lovely; very special."

He smiled at her and she noticed how thickly lashed his eyes were. Celia had been right, he was gorgeous, but even though his smile was kind and friendly, Claire decided he was much too beautiful to trust. He was probably arrogant and well aware of his handsome face, tanned skin, and broad shoulders.

"You've got flour on your face," he said, touching his own cheek to indicate where it was on hers. Claire rubbed it with her hand.

"You've smudged it now."

"It doesn't matter, does it?" Claire knew she sounded annoyed but she didn't like strange men scrutinizing her face, even if they were attractive.

Stefan ran a hand through his disheveled dark hair. "I'm sorry. I feel like I've got off to a bad start. I shouldn't have just turned up like this."

"It's okay," she said. "I just wasn't expecting anyone. I'm a bit hot, and busy, and, to tell you the truth, embarrassed. I don't usually sing in front of people over the age of five."

"Well, you should expand your audience age range—I'll be forty in October and I enjoyed it."

Claire smiled, she couldn't help it.

"Look, Mummy," said a voice from under the table. "Look at my heart."

Claire had completely forgotten about Ben in the last few minutes. He was still happily squatted on the flagstones, carefully rolling out his own chunk of pastry and cutting out shapes with a metal cutter, before squishing everything together to start again.

"Wow, that looks delicious," Stefan said as Ben rolled out his lump again. It was gray with bits of grit and moss flecked through it from the flagstones. Ben pressed his cutter down onto the pastry and, lifting out a rather wonky heart shape, handed it to Stefan.

"Cookie for you."

"Thank you. I'll ask Mum to cook it in the oven for me, shall I?"

"No." Ben looked indignant at the suggestion. "You eat it. Now!"

"Come on, Ben, don't get cross," said Claire, squatting down beside Stefan. "I'll take it and put it in the oven with the mince pies."

Ben's bottom lip began to wobble. Stefan looked at Claire, shrugged his shoulders, and quickly put the raw pastry into his mouth. He cautiously began chewing.

"Mmmm, very tasty," he said, in between mouthfuls. "You're a great cook."

Ben smiled proudly back at him.

"You're very kind to humor him like that," she said. "But you know there were squashed ants in that pastry?"

"It was rather crunchy." Stefan grimaced and ran his hand through his hair again. Claire noticed thin strands of gray at his temples, the only thing that could suggest his age.

"If you can wait for them to cook, you can have a mince pie as well." Claire picked up the baking tray and turned toward the kitchen door; she knew her attempts to dislike him were beginning to fail. Stefan picked up the nearly empty jar of mincemeat from the table.

"This looks suspiciously like a jar of squashed ants," he said, peering through the glass at the dark, slimy contents. "I think I might give the mince pies a miss—maybe wait till December like I usually do."

"Coward." Claire laughed. "You obviously don't appreciate our local delicacy."

"I'm afraid I've had enough ants for today. I'm more of a caramelized locust kind of man."

"How unadventurous you are." Claire was beginning to enjoy herself. She disappeared into the kitchen and Stefan followed her in, carrying the rest of the things from the garden table.

"Actually, I have been known to be very adventurous."

Macavity jumped up on the table between them. Stefan stroked the cat's orange back and Macavity purred, pushing himself against Stefan's hand.

"He doesn't usually like strangers. Do you have a cat?"

"No. Though I did as a child." He made a soft, clicking noise at Macavity, who gazed up at him with round green eyes.

"You are beautiful," Stefan said softly as he scratched Macavity under the chin. He looked up to meet Claire's eyes watching him. Feeling awkward, she quickly turned away.

"It's much too hot in here with the Aga on," she said. "We'll have a cup of tea in the garden and then I'll show you around."

Ben came in and stood beside Stefan with his arms up, wanting to be lifted. Stefan swung him onto his shoulders.

"Bet you can't touch the ceiling."

"I can, I can." Ben squealed as he reached out for the gnarled oak beams.

"You've got a friend for life, there," Claire said. "Do you have children?"

"No," Stefan replied as he walked the length of the kitchen letting Ben touch each of the four beams in turn. "No cat, no children. Not yet."

"Look, Mummy!" cried Ben excitedly. "I'm so big."

"You should have some; you'd make a great father," she said, immediately wanting to swallow her words. What a ridiculous thing to say—as if he might just go out and buy a ready-made family from his local Tesco.

"I've just got to find the right woman." He smiled at Claire across the room.

"Any cobwebs up there?" she asked, suddenly needing to change the subject. "I bet there are loads I've missed. I haven't had time to clean properly."

"You don't need to," Stefan said. "Dust and cobwebs never show up in photographs. It's a beautiful house, really unique."

"Thank you. Though all the credit should really go to my husband. He found it, renovated it, and frankly never stops working on it." She laughed rather too brightly.

"I think you're underestimating yourself." Stefan put Ben down on the floor. He looked around the large, sun-filled kitchen. "I bet you chose these colors. They're so fresh and light; they go so well with your work. I love the fabric combination on the armchair and these cushions. Although it's a bit too pretty for my bachelor flat, not quite the macho look I'm after!" He laughed. "Not that I haven't got a feminine side to get in touch with as well."

Claire smiled. Which mugs to use for their tea: floral ones, ones with hearts? No, the spotty ones would do. She dragged the kettle from the Aga as a splash of water hissed on the surface, almost scalding her.

"Your things are great; they have such a sense of fun and wit about them," Stefan went on. "Fantastic mixture of vintage and contemporary—I've really been looking forward to seeing your house."

"I hope it all lives up to your expectations," said Claire, ineptly opening a milk carton. His praise was making her feel self-conscious.

"It's all lovely so far," he replied, flashing another smile. "It will make a fantastic feature for the magazine. A shame it's going to be a Christmas issue, and we can't use the garden—it's beautiful. Who's responsible for that?"

"I'm responsible for the flowers and my husband is responsible for the very short grass."

A cell phone rang, the sound breaking the few seconds' silence that had settled between them. Stefan took a phone from his pocket and answered it. After a brief conversation, he snapped it shut.

"Unfortunately, I've got to go. I'd arranged to meet up with a friend for lunch nearby. I'm late and she's wondering where I am. I'd completely forgotten the time since I've been here." He ruffled Ben's hair. Ben beamed back up at him.

"Sorry about the cup of tea," he said to Claire. "I'd better rush or I'll be in trouble. See you in the morning."

He gave Macavity one last stroke and stepped out of the door into the sunshine. Claire could hear him whistling "We Wish You a Merry Christmas" as he disappeared down the path to the front of the house. A minute later she heard the crunch of wheels on gravel as a car pulled away from the drive.

"I'm hungry," said Ben, pulling at Claire's skirt.

Absentmindedly, she made him a sandwich and tried not to wonder who Stefan was having lunch with. She made herself a sandwich too, but as she sat down beside Ben at the table she found she wasn't very hungry after all.

CHAPTER 3

Claire fell in love with the picturesque property the first time she saw it. Although it was in need of some repair, she was quick to realize its potential.

"The photographer came today," Claire said, mixing salad dressing in a small blue jug as William went through the mail. He'd loosened his tie and undone the top buttons of his shirt.

"It's still so bloody hot, even at this time of night," he said. "Have we got any cold beer?"

"Yes. Can you get it yourself? I've still got loads to do after supper if I'm going to be ready for tomorrow." As William bent down to peer into the fridge, she noticed dark patches of sweat stained his back and armpits. Claire looked away and began chopping a cucumber.

"The photographer liked the house."

"What photographer?" he asked, still searching in the fridge. "There's something slimy on the bottom shelf in here. What is it?"

"The photographer who's photographing the house tomorrow," she replied. "You haven't forgotten the photo shoot, have you?"

William stood up, holding a dripping container of yogurt,

and sniffed the tiny plastic pot. "Uh! It smells ancient. How long has it been in there? Who opened it in the first place?"

"I don't know," Claire said, giving the end of the cucumber one final loud chop. "Please, could you just wipe away the mess without the accompanying interrogation?"

"Okay, okay." He backed toward the dustbin. "No need to attack the cucumber, Claire. I was just about to clear it up anyway."

Both of them were silent while he found a cloth and kitchen cleaner and slowly removed the contents of the bottom shelf before giving it all a thorough cleaning. Claire got on with preparing the salad for their supper. Looking up, she found William taking everything out of the fridge and putting half of it into a plastic bag.

"What are you doing?" she asked.

"Checking sell-by dates," he replied. "Did you realize how much of this stuff is out-of-date?"

"William!" she said in exasperation. "There is so much to do. If you really want to help, couldn't you go and vacuum the living room?"

"This needs defrosting too," said William, poking at a thick layer of ice descending from the roof of the freezer. "If you move all this stuff into the freezer in the garage, I'll do it to-night."

Claire thought of her best friend, Sally, who would be trying to get her two wild boys into bed while her husband, Gareth, lay on the sofa watching the enormous television he'd bought for her Christmas present last year. (Sally had told Claire that when he presented it to her, hidden beneath a blanket on Christmas morning, it was the closest she'd ever come to leaving him.) Claire knew she was lucky to have William, she really did. But sometimes . . .

"I'll sort out the fridge *and* the freezer over the weekend," she said, with strained patience. "After the magazine people have gone. It's just that it would be so helpful if you could do something that really needs doing right now."

"I had thought I might mow the grass after I've eaten. Before the light goes."

"William!" Claire tried not to raise her voice.

"What?"

"I've told you, it's supposed to be Christmas here. They're not going to photograph the garden. Mowing the grass is not a—"

"Don't shout, Claire." His interruption made her jump. "I've had one hell of a day at work to get things sorted so that I can be here tomorrow. I only want things to look smart when they come. It's just the same as you wanting your cushions and stuff to look nice in the pictures."

"The grass won't be in the pictures." She didn't usually answer back.

"It will show through the windows."

He took a bottle of beer from the fridge and took a long swig before pouring the rest into a glass. Claire watched him for a few seconds, trying to decide whether it was worth continuing the argument. She decided she didn't have the time.

"He was nice," she said after a little while.

"Who?"

"The photographer. He was lovely with Ben."

William muttered inaudibly and started opening the mail.

"This is the one," he exclaimed, suddenly enthusiastic. He thrust his latest copy of *Build It* magazine in between Claire and the chopping board. "This is what I'm going to make for us." He pointed at a picture of a wooden building, made up of tongue and groove, painted white, with a long veranda and a shingled roof. "What do you think?"

"A shed?" asked Claire. "Do we need another shed?"

"It's not a shed. It's a gazebo. You know, a summerhouse."

"Do we need a summerhouse?"

"Every English garden needs a summerhouse, Claire. Imagine—we could sit in it and drink wine in the evenings, read books, listen to music. We could have visitors to stay in it if we put in electricity, a little log burner in the corner. You and Sally could sit and drink coffee all day, or whatever it is you do together. Mix up witches' brew in a cauldron." He laughed.

Claire ignored his remark. She took the magazine from him and looked at the picture again. It was charming. It looked like something from the Scandinavian woods. An idea sprang into her mind. It certainly looked spacious enough.

"I could use it as a studio and then I wouldn't need to use the spare room anymore," Claire said, feeling a charge of excitement at the thought. A studio in the garden would be lovely. A space of her own for sewing and designing; perhaps a little showroom area to display her latest designs for customers to come and visit. A shop; she'd always wanted to have a shop. If they built it at the side of the drive, people could easily come and go. In her mind she already saw the Emily Love sign across the doorway, inside a sofa scattered with her cushions, bunting strewn across the ceiling, aprons hanging from hooks on the wall, a dresser piled high with stock. The other half could be her work area—a large table for cutting out patterns, glass bottles full of buttons and beads and rolls of multicolored ribbon on long shelves around the walls, cupboards full of fabrics. She smiled at William. "I'd love that—my own studio in the garden and a little shop. It would be wonderful."

"No, darling," he said, taking the magazine out of her hands. "It wouldn't be suitable for that. Perhaps if your business gets off the ground, we could think about converting the old woodshed for you."

Claire turned back to the chopping board and sliced a yellow pepper very thinly and then chopped it up fast, into little tiny pieces.

"I thought I'd build it at the bottom of the garden, cut down some of those old yew trees," William went on. "At the back it will look out over the hills to the sea."

"Can we afford it? Won't it take ages to build?" She didn't like the idea of cutting down the yew trees either. Wasn't that supposed to be unlucky?

"No, it won't take long at all. A few months of weekends and evenings. I'll put a patio area in front, looking out over the valley. Use up those extra flagstones we found in the corner of the orchard. Maybe you could make a couple of little flower beds beside it? Some lavender, a few hollyhocks—what do you think, darling?" He walked over to Claire and gave her a hug. Claire leaned into him and felt her anger seeping away.

He looked down into her face; his blue eyes sparkling, a familiar flush of DIY fervor coloring his cheeks.

"You'll love it, Claire. Wonder how we ever lived without it."

"It could be nice, I suppose," she said.

"That's my girl." He squeezed her just a little bit too tightly before untangling himself from her arms and picking up the magazine again to look at the picture of the summerhouse.

"Maybe your parents could stay in it when they come to visit?" said Claire.

"Oh no," he said dismissively. "I wasn't thinking about it for my parents. They like to be on hand to help you with the children. I was thinking of our friends from London."

"We don't have many weekend guests these days—apart from your parents." She sighed as she laid thickly sliced, home-cured ham on two plates. "You're always too busy when people ask if they can come."

"Don't get grumpy with me, Claire." William started sorting through the rest of the mail, ripping open the envelopes with a small, sharp knife. "And if you're trying to have a go at my parents, just remember how good they've been to us. We wouldn't have this house at all if it hadn't been for them."

Claire took a deep breath.

"I'm not having a go at your parents," she said, trying to keep her voice calm. "I know how grateful we are to them. They have been very kind." She forced a smile and he seemed to relax a little.

Claire could never forget how grateful she had to be to William's parents; she was never allowed to forget. It had been William's mother who found the advertisement for the semi-derelict farmhouse in the *Telegraph*'s property pages. She had persuaded William to view it while Claire had been on a girls' weekend in Marrakesh. Claire would always remember the utter disbelief and fury she had felt on discovering that William had made an offer and accepted a large financial gift for the deposit from his parents without consulting her.

She and William were newly married and had never discussed living anywhere other than the cozy two-bedroom flat overlooking Battersea Park. Claire had loved that flat. She liked to look out from their tiny balcony at the tops of London buses and across the park at people going in and out through the huge granite gateposts, jogging, riding bikes, pushing prams, lying in the sun. She liked to walk across the Albert

Bridge to shop on the King's Road with William during the weekends, see a film, meet up with friends for coffee, visit galleries, go out at night. She was young; she liked living in London. She hadn't finished with it yet; it still held excitement and opportunities for her. A dilapidated house with no neighbors in sight, in the damp, green depths of the countryside, was the last place she had wanted to be.

"I'll make it beautiful for you," William had said, nuzzling his face into her neck as she stood for the first time, numb with horror, on the overgrown driveway. "It will be the house of our dreams. The house of your dreams. I promise."

Claire had sighed. She didn't have a house she dreamed about. William was her dream. He was all she needed to be happy.

She had stared at the cracked gray shingles and the sagging thatch, and tried very hard to imagine how it could be. If it was painted, if the garden was cleared, maybe it could be tolerable. Maybe it could even be nice. A garden would be a novelty—she could plant vegetables, grow strawberries, have chickens, dogs, cats, even a goat or pigs. She could make jam for village fetes, wear an apron, bake bread. She suddenly had a picture in her head of lots of children running among wildflowers in the sun, golden-limbed with blond curls, like William's. Their children. The thought had felt nice.

"If this is what you really want," Claire had said to William, "I won't stop you. Maybe I'll get used to living in the country."

I f you really want to build a summerhouse, I won't stop you," she said now, pouring the thick yellow dressing onto the salad. "I suppose it could be something to think about for next year."

"No, not next year, darling," said William. "I want to do it this year. This summer. In fact, I'll go and phone that tree surgeon in the village now. As soon as he's cut down the yews, I can start to level the site and lay a concrete base." He started to walk out of the kitchen.

"I thought you said you'd be busy with other jobs on the house this summer?" Claire called crossly after him. "And supper is ready now."

There was no answer; only the sound of the latch on the study door clicking closed. Claire stood in the middle of the kitchen and resisted the urge to throw the ham and salad all over the room. She had to keep it clean for the morning.

Sitting down at the table, she ate three of the mince pies that she had made earlier on. She remembered Stefan joking about squashed ants in the mincemeat and smiled to herself.

The cat jumped onto the table with a soft thud and began to lick the ham on William's plate. She reached across and stroked the thick ginger fur. He arched his back and purred, dribbling onto the salad. Claire began to feel better.

"Did you say supper was ready?" asked William, coming back into the room.

CHAPTER 4

*In her blissful attic bathroom, Claire can relax
in her reclaimed Victorian rolltop bath and enjoy
an uninterrupted view of the sea.*

Claire woke up at dawn. It was already humid; no breeze blew through the wooden shutters of the bedroom window. There was no sound of birdsong; it seemed that even the birds were too hot to sing. The house was still and silent. Her cotton nightdress clung to her uncomfortably as she got out of bed and walked toward the shower.

As she let the cool water wash away the stickiness of the night, she thought about all the things she had to do before Stefan and the stylist arrived at nine. She felt nervous but strangely excited about the photo shoot; she was looking forward to it now. Stepping out of the shower cubicle, she hardly needed to dry herself—the warm air did it for her.

She stood naked at the window winding her long, dark, dripping hair into a towel. From up here she could see the woods at the bottom of the valley and fields and, far away in the distance, the sea. No need for frosted glass or curtains; there were no roads or houses, no one to see you for miles.

The sun was already flooding the room with soft yellow

light. She could remember when this room was cold and dark, the walls tiled in moldy cork and the floor covered in rotting carpet tiles. A chocolate-colored plastic bath had been squeezed into one corner, a thick white ring of scale permanently encrusted around it. Claire had hated that bath, refused to use it when they finally had hot water. She still remembered her happiness at seeing it disappear down the lane on the top of a Dumpster.

The bathroom was lovely now with its white cast-iron bath standing, claw-footed, on the checkered tiles. The cream walls were half paneled in pale blue tongue and groove; soft towels were piled high on a small pine table beside a ceramic bowl of smooth pink shells.

The shells reminded Claire of the holiday on a little Greek island the summer before she and William were married. She had collected them on the beach below their pretty villa on the edge of a fishing village. She and William had spent long lazy mornings in bed and afternoons swimming in the sea, exploring the hidden coves along the coast. Often they were the only people on the isolated beaches, and more than once they had made love on the soft, white sand with the hot Mediterranean sun shining down on their entangled limbs.

That seemed like another life to Claire. It seemed like another man.

Claire and William had first met at a Christmas party hosted by the City accountancy firm that he had worked for. It had been held in a fairy-lit, glass-fronted restaurant overlooking the Thames. A jazz band had played as the guests enjoyed the easy flowing champagne and a five-course dinner.

The week before, Claire had signed up as a waitress for a

catering agency. In her final year of art college, she was trying to make some sort of dent in her credit card debt. She already worked weekends in a shoe shop on Kensington High Street, but had found herself with more shoes than actual cash.

Her first job as a waitress had been for a television production company's launch party, serving canapés while dressed as a Tyrolean mountain girl with tiny lederhosen and a low-cut frilly blouse—on roller skates. *Nothing could be harder or more humiliating than that,* she had told herself as she queued up to put the check into her bank.

"This next one's silver service," the boss had told her over the phone. "You're fine with that, aren't you?"

"Oh yeah. No problem."

Putting down the phone, Claire had turned to her flat mate, Zoë.

"Help! What's silver service?"

"It's a bit like using chopsticks but with a large spoon and fork," Zoë had replied. "I once had a boyfriend who was trained in it. He used to serve me baked beans that way and expect me to be impressed enough to sleep with him."

"And were you?"

"No, I was more impressed by his brother, who was in a band, so I slept with him instead. Anyway silver service looked easy to me. You'll be fine, Claire. Just practice on me for a few days before the job."

"I haven't got a few days," she had said, sighing. "The job's tonight."

As Claire served the first course to a raucous table of men and women, she soon realized that silver service was not easy at all. The large, shiny spoons and forks refused to cooperate in her inexperienced hands. Smoked-salmon terrine slipped awkwardly back onto the serving platter and then slid onto the floor. The main course was worse. Miniature sweet corn and snow peas skittered out of her grasp and onto the table. Claire ended up inelegantly shoving slivers of roast beef and potatoes dauphine onto the plates of increasingly drunken customers.

The men were loud and crude. They threw bread rolls at one another and downed champagne as though they were drinking pints in a beer tent. Their girlfriends giggled and simpered at their partners' juvenile behavior. Claire wished she was somewhere else, where she didn't have to pretend to be polite to vulgar, spoiled, rich people, and where she didn't have to wrestle with oversize serving utensils.

Profiteroles for the dessert course seemed like the last straw. Claire emerged from the kitchen laden with a pyramid of golden pastry balls. As she approached her table, she could hear some of the men loudly debating the color of her bra beneath her white shirt. With a shaking hand and immense concentration, Claire successfully managed to pick up two profiteroles between the spoon and fork. She started to transfer them to one of the accountants' waiting plate. As her hand hovered above it, the accountant suddenly slapped Claire's bottom and the spoon and fork skidded apart, sending the profiteroles flying through the air and onto his lap. They rolled slowly down the inside of the man's thighs and nestled neatly in his crotch. He began to laugh lewdly, drawing the attention of the rest of the table. Leaning back in his chair, he demanded that Claire remove them herself—with her teeth. She heard laughter around her, and saw a woman watching her with a contemptuous smirk on her beautifully made-up face. Claire flushed red with humiliation and embarrassment, but then she felt anger taking over inside. She managed to smile calmly at the man, who looked at her with an expectant grin on his pink, puffy face.

"Yes, of course I will, sir. But I prefer chocolate sauce with my profiteroles." She picked up an accompanying jug of hot sauce from the table and swiftly poured it into his lap. He immediately leaped up from his chair, thick, scalding chocolate dripping down his expensive trousers.

Claire didn't wait to listen to the string of insults he shouted at her, just threw the rest of her pile of profiteroles into the middle of the table, from where they bounced and rolled onto the laps of the other diners. She quickly marched across the room, into the kitchen, picked up her bag and coat, and left through the back door, before any of the other waiters, or her boss, had a chance to realize what had happened.

Once outside in the freezing night, Claire walked around the corner and, leaning against a railing by the river, lit a cigarette.

"I'm so sorry about what happened in there."

Claire turned to see a tall, fair-haired man, whom she recognized as one of the quieter guests from the table.

"Sebastian was being his usual obnoxious self. He always gets like that when he's drunk. He deserved what you did to him. Well done." He grinned at her.

Claire said nothing but, blowing out a cloud of smoke, stared at the man through narrowed eyes. She wished he would go away. He looked uncomfortable with her silence.

"Someone should have told him he was going too far," he continued. "We should have stopped him." Claire looked at his pale, neatly cut hair. Tiny kinks in it suggested it would have been curly if he let it grow. "I should have said something, stopped him myself."

Claire still said nothing, but looked away, down into the oily water, where she threw her cigarette butt. It was cold. She shivered and wrapped her thin coat tightly around her.

"It's a freezing night," said the man. "Can I buy you a drink as an apology?"

Claire really didn't want to spend any more time with him, and didn't think he was the one who should be apologizing, but the thought of a drink was tempting. She had only enough money in her purse for her Tube fare home. The cash machines had stopped giving her anything from her account and she knew she had little chance of ever getting paid for the night's work.

"Okay."

The man smiled. Tiny lines fanned out from ice-blue eyes. He looked older than Claire and handsome in a Nordic, clean-cut sort of way—not Claire's usual type at all. "I know a little bar near here that's one of my favorites. My name's William, by the way."

Claire let herself be led across the road and down a small flight of steps into a warm, red room thick with smoke, people, and the smell of warm beer. Worn velvet sofas lined the room with black-and-white mosaic tables in front of them. The walls were covered in bright pictures of bullfighters and dark-eyed women posing with castanets.

"It's a Spanish bar," William said, his face close to her ear. It was hard to hear above the guitar music coming from the band in the corner.

"I thought there might be a theme," she replied, still reluctant to be in his company but longing for a drink. She liked to drink lager, but if someone else was paying . . .

"A double whiskey," she said as William left her at a table and started pushing his way to the bar. He raised his eyebrows. Claire smiled at him and lit another cigarette.

The whiskey and the womblike room warmed her. The band in the corner stopped playing and their guitars were replaced with softer Cuban music. William sat beside her and started to talk. He talked about his job, a new firm of accountants he was moving to, his flat, and his family in some Cotswold village that William said she really must visit one day and that Claire thought sounded deadly dull. She wasn't really listening to most of what he said. She was enjoying the warmth, the whiskey, the music, and watching the other people coming and going. She took more notice when he started to talk about the girl he'd been engaged to. They had recently split up.

"Irreconcilable differences," he explained when Claire asked what had gone wrong.

"Like what?"

"Like she wanted to take the job she was offered in New York and I didn't want to go with her."

Then he started asking her questions about her life. At first she was reluctant to tell him anything, but lulled by the mixture of alcohol and intimate surroundings, she found herself confiding in him. She told him things she hadn't talked to anyone about for years—about her father walking out on her thirteenth birthday, her mother's depression, a recent turbulent affair with an Italian sculpture student, and her ambition to set up her own textile business printing scarves when she left college.

William seemed genuinely interested. He asked more questions, probed deeper.

The guitar trio came back and started to play a frenzied song. A couple got up to dance in the tiny space in front of the stage; they were soon joined by another couple and a girl who danced on top of one of the mosaic tables.

Claire had had enough of talking.

"Come on," she said, pulling William up and leading him to the dance floor. He looked embarrassed. She pulled her white waitress's shirt loose from her short black skirt and tied it tight at her midriff, exposing a flat expanse of stomach. She saw shock and surprise in William's eyes, but she'd had three double whiskeys in a row and didn't care. Raising her hands above her head, she began to dance, slowly and rhythmically in time to the music, speeding up when the beat quickened. Twirling around William, she took his hand and made him spin her away and then back toward him.

"I don't really dance," he shouted into her ear above the noise of the band.

"I do," she said.

Another man approached and cut in, whisking her away from William, taking her in his arms in an improvised tango. He dipped her backward. Claire laughed. Her hair was falling out of the neat ponytail she'd tied it in for work. She was upright again and the stranger spun her around and around. She felt dizzy; her feet were slipping on the beer-soaked floor. The stranger let her go. She thought she would fall, but someone caught her. It was William.

"I think you need to sit down," he said, guiding her back to their table.

He ordered her a glass of water and she began to think how nice his eyes were and that she liked the chiseled look of his jaw. It crossed her mind to ask him home with her and then she knew it was time to leave—alone.

She tried to persuade him that she would be fine getting the Tube, but William insisted on hailing a black cab and asking her address so that he could pay the driver in advance. He hadn't asked her to come home with him or made any attempt to even kiss her. Claire was surprised; most men wanted something for the cost of a few drinks and even more for the cost of a cab.

He waved at her as the taxi pulled away. Claire sat back and began thinking about what she'd wear to a party she had been invited to the next night, and how she was going to get through another bleak, gray Christmas day with her mother and a small roast chicken in her lonely basement flat.

"The hall is full of roses," said Claire groggily as she shuffled, hungover, into the kitchen the following morning.

"They're all for you," said Zoë, sounding disgruntled.

Three dozen pink roses and a note.

I enjoyed our drink last night, would you like to do it again?
William x

And then a phone number.

Claire phoned him to say thank you. They met for dinner in a small French restaurant off the Strand. Then another dinner in Chinatown, and then a visit to the theater, and then a Sunday drive to Lewes for lunch beside a log fire in a pub. He constantly sent flowers.

"It's like living in a bloody florist's," said Zoë, peering at Claire through a vase of gladioli on the kitchen table.

For Christmas he gave her a charm bracelet with one tiny silver heart hanging from it. After a Hungarian meal on the King's Road, he took her back to his immaculately minimalist flat, undressed her very slowly, and told her she was beautiful. After that night she never left.

Within a week she had moved all her things into the bright top-floor rooms of the redbrick mansion block. She set about transforming it with 1950s vases, chintz cushions, and old furniture that she found in Dumpsters and junk shops. She painted a mural of mermaids on the tiny bathroom wall. In the evenings Claire cooked invented meals made from ingredients she found in the Turkish supermarket on the Fulham Road, played him Leonard Cohen, and took him to her favorite club in Brixton. William seemed constantly amazed and entranced by what he saw as her lack of inhibitions and unconventional attitude to life. He said he loved her bohemian, creative style.

He seemed to find Claire's comprehensive-school and art-college education exotic; it was so different from his own conventional private school experience. She made him laugh and he made her feel safe and secure. He was seven years older than her and seemed so sensible, so grown-up.

He took her away for long romantic weekends to Prague and Barcelona; walking hand in hand through the ancient streets, lingering over long meals and even longer mornings in bed. They spent Easter in Crete and a May bank holiday in Paris. Over thick black coffee on the Boulevard Saint-Germain, William told her that he loved her.

Claire had smiled at him through her cigarette smoke. She couldn't remember ever feeling so happy. "I love you too," she said.

He proposed on the steps of Sacré-Coeur and they bought a ring from a small jewelry shop on Rue des Francs-Bourgeois. Claire felt as though she was flying.

By the time she graduated, they had a date for their wedding and William had persuaded her to stop smoking, to stop wearing scarlet lipstick, to stop hennaing her hair bright auburn, and to drink white wine instead of lager. He gently told her that he found Leonard Cohen rather dreary (he much preferred Bruce Springsteen) and it became increasingly apparent that he wasn't enjoying the nights out in Brixton anymore. He suggested that Claire cut down on her clutter.

"Do we really need quite so many cushions in the flat, my

love?" And he painted over the mermaids in the bathroom. "The bare breasts might offend my mother."

Over the summer Claire and Zoë made plans to start printing silk and velvet scarves together in an archway studio in Balham. They had sheaves of flamboyant, brightly colored design ideas and Zoë had found a cheap printing table in the Free Ads.

"We're going to get a stall in Greenwich market every Saturday," Claire told William excitedly over dinner in their favorite tapas bar.

"It's really not a good time to start your own business, darling," said William, topping off her wine. "I met an old friend yesterday. He told me about an art teacher's position that's come up at his son's prep school. It sounds the ideal job for you."

"Sorry," Claire said to Zoë a week later. "But I've got to earn some regular money. I don't want William to think I'm scrounging off him all the time."

William didn't like Zoë.

"She's emotionally unstable," he said. "She gets too drunk. She's promiscuous. She flirts with me all the time. Haven't you noticed?"

Claire stopped seeing Zoë. She stopped seeing any of her friends from college, and spent evenings in restaurants and smart bars with William's old school friends and colleagues from his new job. If she found them dull and life monotonous, she told herself how lucky she was to have found William. He was the only man who had ever made her feel special or worthwhile. The thought of life without him terrified her. She remembered the grubby rented flats and doomed relationships she had seemed destined for and tried to remember to pick her clothes up off the floor and not to leave her empty coffee mugs on the kitchen table. She loved William; he loved her. Wasn't it what she had always dreamed of?

CHAPTER 5

It's the perfect home for celebrating an idyllic Christmas. Candles, holly, and warm mince pies around a blazing fire; what better way to keep out the winter chill?

Claire had wiped the last handprints and pencil scribbles off the walls and scraped out all the bits of Play-Doh from in between the floorboards. The house was unnaturally clean and tidy.

The children had the day off from school and were eating a breakfast of toast and chocolate spread. They sat on the patio steps so that they didn't make crumbs in the house. Behind them, William mowed the grass. It had gotten too late the night before.

Claire hastily scattered as many Emily Love cushions as she could around the living room and strung some of her bunting across the kitchen beams. Looking in the hallway mirror, she checked for lipstick on her teeth and smoothed down her hair. She had left it loose today, and newly washed, it shone as it fell in chestnut waves onto her shoulders. Her simple linen shift dress complemented her curves and suntanned limbs. Claire smiled at her reflection; for once she thought she looked quite nice.

At nine o'clock exactly, a small, bright orange hatchback pulled up on the drive. The back windows were obscured by green foliage. A skinny young woman with a mass of curly hair, dyed a shade of red that clashed dramatically with the car, jumped out of the driver's seat. She wore tiny denim shorts and a pink halter-neck top.

"Hi, I'm Babette. The stylist." Her accent was Scottish. "You must be Claire. Is Stefan here yet? He's always late. I'll never get this tree out by myself. Christmas shoots are always crazy." She spoke fast, with a very high voice; Claire could barely understand what she was saying.

"Love your house," Babette went on. "I love the oldie-worldy ones, but my flat is very modern. Sometimes I think I'd like to buy a cottage in the country like this, but I'd miss proper shops and I love my sushi bars and take-out coffees too much. Do you know what I mean?"

"I think so," said Claire.

"And I don't suppose there's much chance of getting a good spray tan in a twenty-mile radius of here?" Babette opened the back of her car and Christmas tree branches started springing out in all directions. She pulled ineffectively at a few bits of tree. "It's stuck. I'll have to wait for Stefan. I knew he'd be late. Could you get the box on the front seat? It's got the fairy lights and some dried orange decorations. I make them myself. It's very effective for old-style shoots like this one. I have a fake pink tree at home, but obviously that's not what would look good here. My boyfriend hates it."

Claire started to feel quite exhausted by Babette's incessant talking. Two days of this was going to be hard work. She took a large cardboard box from the passenger seat and asked Babette if she'd like a cup of tea.

"Do you have peppermint?"

"Yes, I'm sure I have."

Claire led Babette around the side of the house to the back garden.

"Actually, I'll have coffee," said Babette. "Strong and black with two sugars. Oh, look at your children, aren't they gorgeous! I'd love to have children but my boyfriend's not so sure. We've only been together for eight months. Hi, you guys, are you going to be in some pictures?" She waved energetically at the little group on the lawn.

The children stared, amazed by this lively newcomer. Ben's face was smeared in chocolate spread. He grinned widely.

"Is it Christmas now?" he asked.

"Looks like it," said Babette. "Are you excited?" She crouched down between the children. "I'm going to decorate your house with a tree and lights and I've got wrapped-up boxes in my car that are like presents, but they're actually just empty boxes."

"Oh!" the children groaned collectively.

"But," Babette went on, "I'll let you in on a secret: some of them have actually got tiny wee presents inside, so when we're all finished, maybe we'll open them and see if we can find anything for you?"

The children cheered, already enchanted.

"Who's going to show me their bedrooms?" asked Babette, jumping up from the grass. "Let me guess. I bet you've got a pink one," she said to Emily. "Pink is my favorite color."

"Do you like fossils?" asked Oliver.

"I love them," Babette said. "My boyfriend has an ammonite he once found on a beach."

"I've got nappies in my bedroom," said Ben.

"Bet you do," Babette said cheerily as Ben and Emily took her hands and led her inside, closely followed by Oliver.

"Which are your favorite kinds of fossils?" he asked as they climbed the stairs. "I've got ammonites and trilobites and a scorpion fossil from a desert in South America."

Claire left them to it; Babette was obviously a big hit.

She was just filling up the kettle when she heard footsteps.

"Hello again."

Stefan stood in the kitchen doorway. He wore a loose dark blue shirt and was carrying a small box of vegetables.

"I met a man in a van who gave me these," he said, smiling as he put the box on the kitchen table.

"Oh," said Claire, feeling inexplicably flustered. "It's our organic veg box. I thought it was coming tomorrow." She reached out to pull the box toward her, knocking a bag onto the floor. Yellow, orange, and red tomatoes in assorted shapes and sizes rolled across the kitchen in all directions. Claire bent down and started to pick them up.

"I'm surprised you don't grow them for yourselves," Stefan said.

She looked up to see him just a few inches away from her, collecting up stray tomatoes too.

"My husband isn't interested in vegetables. I mean, in growing them."

"Is that your husband on the riding mower?" Stefan looked at her, a half smile playing across his face. Their eyes met. She thought of William chugging across the green expanse of grass. The thought made her want to laugh.

"Yes," she said. "That's William."

"With all the space you have, you could easily have a vegetable patch," Stefan went on. "In my more wholesome moments I think about getting an allotment in London."

"I'd love to grow vegetables. I'm always saying to William it would be wonderful for the children to help grow their own. They might be happier about eating them, then."

"Can't you just go ahead and plant some?" he asked.

"William is very protective of his garden. They might make it look messy."

"You could have chickens too," Stefan carried on cheerfully. "I can imagine chickens pecking around, looking decorative."

"I would really like to have chickens," said Claire. "It would be so good to have our own eggs, but William has a great fear of bird flu. Oh, and the mess they might make!"

"And I'd have a dog. You haven't got a dog, have you?"

"I really want a dog," she said. "And so do the children."

"And your husband doesn't?"

"Smelly, dirty, expensive, dependent."

"Might make a mess on the lawn?"

Claire laughed.

"I love dogs," Stefan added.

"So do I." She suddenly realized they were both still crouched on the floor with tomatoes in their hands.

She stood up feeling that she had somehow been disloyal to William. In this short conversation with a man who was practically a stranger she had revealed more differences of opinion with her husband than she usually would with Sally. She hoped she hadn't made him sound too neurotic.

The cat greeted Stefan by entwining himself around his legs as though he remembered him from the day before. Stefan bent to stroke him.

"It's just that William loves this house," said Claire. "He likes it to look perfect."

Stefan looked around him. "I like a bit of mess, personally.

It adds character, makes a home a home. Sticky fingerprints, worn-out chair covers; it's all part of family life."

"Coffee?" she asked, suddenly remembering about Babette upstairs with the children.

"Tea would be lovely," replied Stefan. "I'll make it while you sort out your vegetables. What are you having? Tea? Coffee for Babette, I'm sure. I bet she asked for herbal first. She starts a new detox diet every day and stumbles at the first coffee hurdle each morning."

As Claire put away the carrots and potatoes in the larder, she caught a glimpse of her reflection in the large stainless-steel flour bin and grimaced. Compared to the coltish Babette, Claire looked frumpy and middle-aged; it was a long time since she'd been seen in cutoff shorts and a halter-neck top.

Back in the kitchen Claire found Stefan adding milk to heart-patterned mugs.

"Sugar?" he asked. She shook her head and he handed her a mug of tea. She felt like a guest; he seemed so comfortable and at home in her kitchen and it was Claire who felt slightly awkward and out of place. She glanced out of the window and saw a beautiful cream MG convertible parked on the drive. Its soft top was down, revealing dark red leather seats and a shining chrome-and-walnut dashboard.

"Is that gorgeous car yours?" she asked, opening the window and leaning out to get a better look.

"Yes," he said, coming to stand beside her. "It was made the same year I was born. I love old cars."

"I had a boyfriend with a Triumph Herald when I was at college. It was duck-egg blue and he called it Penelope. I've forgotten why."

"I call my car Claudia," offered Stefan.

"Can I ask why?"

"I'll tell you another time," he said, laughing.

"I hate the ugly minivan I have now. But it does the job of transporting three children, plus their friends and all the stuff that goes with them."

"My car's not very practical; she's always breaking down. But I'm very fond of her. Maybe I could take you for a drive later? Once round the village?" He paused and then added, "William too, if he'd like to go."

Claire felt flustered again. "I don't expect we'll have time," she muttered, busying herself with putting mince pies on a plate. She immediately wished she had sounded more enthusiastic.

Stefan turned away and, picking up Babette's mug of coffee, set off to start the shoot.

William and Stefan dragged the tree into the living room and the children helped Babette decorate it with her fairy lights and dried orange slices. It wasn't exactly as Claire would have decorated it herself (she liked to use a combination of spun-glass balls and brightly colored tin decorations) but she had to admit that it looked lovely. Large sprigs of holly adorned the fireplace and Babette hung on the mantelpiece the Emily Love stockings that Claire had made late the night before.

"Where do you get a Christmas tree in July?" asked Claire.

"I know a man who supplies me every year. I do about ten Christmas shoots for different publications in the summer," Babette explained.

"The trick is no shots showing windows," Stefan told them.

"Otherwise you'd see trees in leaf and blooming flower borders which would spoil that festive feel."

Claire looked at William; she knew that mowing the grass had been a waste of time. He was busy sliding cork coasters underneath the feet of the Christmas tree stand so that they wouldn't scratch the wooden floor.

"Now we need to get you all dressed up," said Babette. "No bare arms, no bare legs, and no feet. You've got to cover up."

"But it's going to be eighty degrees by midday," said Claire, already feeling uncomfortably hot in her thin dress.

"We need you in something wintry but glam. What did you wear on Christmas Day last year?" Babette asked Claire.

"I wore a Rachel Riley blue silk shirt," said Claire.

"She looked like Margaret Thatcher in her prime," William said, laughing. "It had a funny bow thing at the neck, very Tory party conference."

Claire winced. At the time he'd said she looked like a brunette Grace Kelly.

Babette looked slightly awkward. "Do you have anything else?"

"What about the cashmere twin set I bought you for your birthday?" said William. "You look nice in that."

"Sounds perfect," said Babette.

Thanks, William, thought Claire, her back already prickling at the thought of the hot wool.

"I know putting on a sweater seems unbearable in this heat," said Stefan, as though he'd read her mind. "But it's just for the pictures. We'll let you strip off completely in between shots if you want to." Claire laughed and felt herself blush.

"I'm sorry about this," he said. "It will be worth it in the end—I promise."

"The children need to put on some sweaters, and some tights for Emily," continued Babette. "Celia said that the children would be in traditional pajamas for some of the shots?"

"It was hard but I've managed to find two pairs of stripy flannel pajamas for the boys and a white Victorian-style nightdress for Emily. She looks gorgeous."

"Fantastic. You're truly wonderful," said Babette, giving Claire an unexpected hug. "William, do you have a sweater you can pull on over your shirt? And perhaps a jacket?"

He grunted unenthusiastically and Claire tried not to smile.

"Great," Babette said encouragingly. "You go and get changed, but if you could just light the fire first, that would be fab."

"Fire?" William asked incredulously.

"We'll need you sitting in front of a lovely cozy fire, opening your presents and looking happy," explained Babette.

Claire glanced at her husband's face. He certainly didn't look happy. He looked fed up.

"I'd better go and bring some logs in, then," he said.

"I'll come and give you a hand," Stefan offered.

"Wait while I get the woodshed key," William called over his shoulder, disappearing into the hall muttering, "I can't believe all this pretense is really necessary."

Stefan turned to Claire and smiled. "I know it's a long hot day for you all, but it's going to look beautiful. When you see the finished pictures, you'll forget the heat and the hassle. You'll have photographs you'll treasure forever."

"We could use one for our Christmas card this year," said Claire, laughing.

"Great idea," said Stefan. "Maybe I could Photoshop Santa hats onto you all?"

"Somewhere William has a Santa outfit he wore one Christmas when Oliver and Emily were tiny." Claire felt uncharacteristically giggly. "Shall I get it out?"

"Pretend to William that he has to wear it now."

"I'd love to see his face," she said. Stefan laughed.

"Excuse me, Stefan," cut in Babette. "Could you stop chatting her up and get on with the shoot?" She winked at Claire. "Watch him. He's a bit of a charmer."

For the second time Claire felt herself blush. It was ridiculous, she never blushed—it must be the heat.

The day passed quickly. It was more fun than Claire had imagined it would be. The children opened their empty boxes, squealing with delight when they found a sweet in each, two little bears for Ben and Emily, and a pack of Pokémon cards for Oliver. They smiled happily and obediently crept down the stairs in nightclothes, peeping through the banisters as if in awe of the magical scene below. Ben sat on the old dappled rocking horse, smiling to order, and Oliver and Emily pretended to eat mince pies, which they usually hated, eyes wide with appreciation. Claire stood beside them in her Emily Love apron holding Emily Love oven gloves as if she had just taken the pies from her Aga. Even Macavity the cat joined in and obediently lay in front of the fire beside the children.

At first Claire felt embarrassed posing in front of Stefan's lens, but he and Babette were so friendly and funny that she soon relaxed and got used to the constant clicking. Even William seemed to be enjoying himself. Claire couldn't remember when they'd last spent so much time together as a family.

"You could all be top-class models," Babette told the children at the end of the afternoon. "You'd make a fortune."

"Oh, could I, Mummy?" said Emily excitedly. "Could I be a real model?"

Claire shook her head firmly. "Definitely not. This is as far as your modeling career goes."

"These are fantastic," said Stefan as he looked back at the shots he'd taken on his camera. "The house looks great. What else are we doing today, Babette? Is that it?"

"I think we've got everything with the children and the tree, and we've done the kitchen from all the angles I can think of," she said. "We still need some pictures of Claire in her studio and the empty-room shots, but they can be done tomorrow. You won't need me for those."

"Where are you going?" he asked. "I thought you were booked into the hotel in town with me."

"Didn't I say? I've got to get back to London tonight," she said, taking orange slices off the tree. "I'm doing a shoot on a houseboat in Putney tomorrow first thing, but you don't need me anymore. I'd better get going because I've got a birthday dinner party at my boyfriend's best friend's girlfriend's flat tonight. It's an eighties fancy-dress do and I think it's going to be retro nouvelle cuisine, so I need to get home for a cheese-and-pickle sandwich and a bag of nachos first, otherwise I won't get enough to eat and I'll get so drunk I'll never get up for Putney tomorrow."

Babette unwrapped the lights from the tree, kissed and hugged the children as if she were their favorite aunt, and drove away in her orange car while Claire, the children, and Stefan stood at the front door waving happily. William had already left them and was busy measuring the space where the summer-house would stand.

"Iced lemonade on the lawn?" Claire asked Stefan, after she had put out the fire in the living room and he had packed away his cameras and lights. The heat was almost unbearable, even now at five o'clock.

"Perfect. I think that's enough hard work for today for everyone and we'll get a bit of peace and quiet now that Babette has gone."

"I don't think we'll get much peace and quiet with these three around." Claire laughed as the children suddenly appeared dressed in swimsuits. Emily had dressed Ben in an old pink shiny one of hers with a red-and-white frilly skirt. He was wearing it back to front, rather like an effeminate wrestler.

"Paddling pool, paddling pool!" they shouted together, hopping around her.

"We're so hot, I'm melting," said Oliver. "I'll soon be just a big wet blob."

"Wait till Daddy finishes what he's doing and then he'll put water in the paddling pool," said Claire, trying to get the jug of lemonade from the fridge as Ben pulled at her arm.

"Show me where everything is and we'll fill it up while your mum gets us all a cool drink," said Stefan to the children, shepherding them into the garden.

Five minutes later the children were happily splashing in the cool water and eating ice lollies. Meanwhile, Claire and Stefan sat a safe distance away on wrought-iron chairs. On the table a large glass jug of lemonade sparkled in the sunlight.

"I can't believe we've just had Christmas Day," said Claire, now happily changed back into her summer dress, her shoes kicked off, feet bare on the rough, dry grass.

"This is what it's like in Australia at Christmas," said Stefan.

"Have you ever been there?"

"I lived there for a few years a while ago. I spent three Christmases on the beach. Barbecued turkey drumsticks followed by an afternoon of surfing. It was fantastic."

"What brought you back?"

"I don't know really," he said, staring across the valley. "I missed frosty winter mornings and the snow, and there was a woman who broke my heart. I needed to come home." He was silent for a few seconds. Then he smiled at Claire, his dark eyes twinkling. "Maybe I just missed a good cup of tea and a Marmite sandwich."

"I thought you had Vegemite in Australia," said Claire. "Isn't that the same as Marmite?" She didn't want to know about the woman.

"No. The jars aren't as stylish."

"So it was packaging that brought you back to the rain and cold and congestion?"

"Yes, that was it. I like a nice display on my kitchen shelves." Stefan laughed, but then was serious. "I missed the British countryside. I wanted a life like this—old farmhouse, big garden, roses round the door, vegetable patch."

"Dog."

"Chickens," Stefan added.

Ben came over, arms outstretched, dripping with water and melted ice lolly. He gave Claire a hug and a kiss before running back and belly-flopping into the pool.

"You've got sticky ice lolly stuff on your skirt now," said Stefan. "Do you want me to get a cloth to wipe it?"

"You really don't have children, do you?" said Claire, laughing. "If you did you'd know that after a while you don't care about the sticky stuff all over you. It all goes in the wash at the end of the day. Though William struggles with the messier side of parenthood, he'd definitely be getting a cloth right now." She bit her lip; she'd revealed too much about William again.

"I always wanted to have children," Stefan went on. "But I think I'm getting a bit old now."

"Forty's not too old," she argued.

"How old are you?" Stefan asked, taking a sip of lemonade.

"I don't think you're meant to ask ladies their age."

"Sorry, I forgot. How rude of me." He grinned at her.

After a brief pause she said, "Thirty-seven."

"I thought you were older," he said.

"Thanks!"

"No, sorry. I didn't mean you look older; you look years younger, of course." He flashed a smile that immediately made Claire forgive him. "It's just you have so much, have achieved so much, when I feel I've hardly started. I've concentrated on my work and traveled for so long, but sometimes I look round at my flat in London and wonder what I've really achieved. What have I got to show for it all? Most of my friends are part of couples, some of them even on second marriages. Most of them have children, nice homes; they're settled. Like you."

"Are you with anyone at the moment?" Inexplicably she had found it very hard to ask that question but also impossible not to.

"No. Not really," he replied, then after a few seconds added, "Well, I'm sort of at the end of something casual that hasn't worked from the start."

Claire looked at him from the corner of her eye. Babette's comment about him being "a bit of a charmer" echoed in her head. She wondered how many casual relationships hadn't worked out for him in the past. How could someone so attractive still be single? He looked at her and she realized she'd been staring.

A silence fell between them; the sounds of the children

shrieking with laughter in the water filled the gap. Macavity jumped up onto Claire's knee and Stefan reached across to stroke his head.

William suddenly appeared with his notebook and tape measure. Claire felt a jolt of surprise. She'd forgotten that he was around. Stefan took his hand away from Macavity's head.

"I think the summerhouse is going to fit perfectly down there once the trees have gone," said William. "Any lemonade for me, darling?"

Claire realized she had forgotten to bring out a third glass.

"I think I ought to go to the hotel now," said Stefan, standing up. "I've got calls to make and e-mails to send. Can you recommend somewhere to eat in town?"

"There's a nice new little Italian on the High Street," said William.

"Come back and have supper with us," offered Claire, on an impulse. She felt her husband glaring at her.

"That would be great. If it's not too much trouble." He turned to William. "You can tell me all about the work you must have done to this place to make it so lovely." Claire thought she could see William's chest visibly expand with pride, his annoyance melting.

"I'll show you pictures of how it was when we first moved here," he said. "I'm sure you'll hardly recognize it. I took pictures of work in progress too. Every stage has been documented—seven albums so far."

"I'll look forward to seeing them later," said Stefan.

Claire pushed the cat from her lap and stood up to walk Stefan to his car.

"Don't worry," he said. "I'll see myself out. You go and get William his glass of lemonade."

CHAPTER 6

*There is nothing Claire enjoys more
than entertaining family and friends with a selection of
deliciously tempting meals from her beloved Aga.*

Stefan arrived on time, bearing wine and a bunch of red chrysanthemums. *Love and loyalty,* thought Claire.

"They're from the gas station, I'm afraid," he said apologetically. "The only place that was open."

"No twenty-four-hour shopping here," said William as he opened the wine. "It's the one drawback of living the rural dream."

"There's something I forgot to do today," said Stefan, bending down to pick up one of Ben's toy cars that he had just been about to step on. "The magazine needs a picture of both of you. It'll go in a small box in the corner of the article with some basic information about you. I'm sure you've seen the sort of thing I mean. Can we do it tomorrow?"

"I'll be at work," William put in quickly.

"That's what I was worried about," Stefan said. "We'd better do it now, then."

He posed Claire and William on the sofa in the living room.

"Could you put your arm around Claire's shoulder?" he asked. William dutifully obeyed. Claire felt awkward and embarrassed. She had lost the relaxed feel she had had earlier on in the day.

"Okay, maybe one without your arm round her. Just sit side by side. And could you both try to smile a little bit?"

Claire tried; her face felt stiff and uncomfortable. Beside her William sat upright, perched on the edge of the sofa as if longing to escape.

"I think that will be fine," said Stefan after a few minutes. He didn't look back through the shots and quickly zipped the camera back into its case. He smiled at William. "So, tell me about the house."

While Stefan looked through William's endless renovation photographs, Claire made dinner. She hastily put together a pasta dish with wild rocket from the garden, feta, and pine nuts and searched in the freezer for some leftover lemon ice cream she had made for a lunch party the month before. William's voice blurred into a gentle drone as Claire cooked. Occasionally a sentence would pierce her consciousness.

"And that was before I dug out the dry well for the septic tank . . . Of course, I had to paint the rotten timbers with wood hardener . . . Bats in the attic were the biggest problem."

She felt sure that Stefan must be bored. At one point he caught her eye. She dropped the packet she had in her hand and a shower of pine nuts bounced and rolled across the floor.

"Careful, Claire," said William, before turning back to the photograph album. "This one shows the stud partition wall I took down to make the dining room bigger."

They ate outside in the warm evening air.

"This is delicious," said Stefan, tucking into his dish of pasta.

"Yes, it's very nice, darling," said William, after tasting his first mouthful, then after a few seconds: "Have you put any salt in it?"

"Yes, of course," Claire replied.

"Well, I think it needs a little more." William took another mouthful. "Yes, it definitely needs more salt. I'll go and get some." He got up and left the table. Claire didn't know why but she had a sudden urge to cry. She resisted and stared hard at her plate of tagliatelle, stirring it round and round with her fork. Glancing up, she found Stefan watching her. He smiled.

"The salt mill's nearly empty," called William from the kitchen. "And there's no more rock salt in the cupboard." Stefan raised his eyebrows slightly and Claire felt a little better.

"I'll put it on the shopping list for tomorrow," she called back to William. He returned and immediately embarked on a long discourse about house prices.

Claire sat back in her chair, not feeling much like eating. She sipped her wine and watched the sun setting at the end of the valley. The sky changed from pink to orange to red and finally to navy. Moths came back and forth to the lights of the patio; the air was thick and perfectly still. Claire stretched out her bare arms on her lap. They looked smooth; fine golden hairs glistening in the light of a candle. She felt unusually aware of her body. Her skin seemed to tingle as if the night was softly stroking her.

As she cleared away the ice cream bowls, William suddenly took her hand and kissed it. She saw Stefan quickly look away.

Claire took the bowls into the kitchen and started loading the dishwasher.

"Shall I wash up these saucepans?"

She turned to see Stefan already standing at the Belfast sink turning on the taps.

"Do I use this?" he asked, holding up the dishwashing brush.

"No, that's for the cat's plate," she said, handing him another brush.

"You're a very good cook." He squeezed washing-up liquid into the sink. "That was a delicious meal. I couldn't taste the squashed ants at all and I thought the salt content was perfect."

"Thank you," said Claire, laughing. "Not all my culinary efforts turn out so well. I'm a bit hit-and-miss, with the emphasis usually on 'miss.' Do you like cooking?"

"I love it! I'm renowned for my Moroccan tagine among my friends."

"How exotic," said Claire. "I'm more of a roast-chicken-and-fairy-cake kind of a girl."

"That sounds good. I'm never happier than with a nice cup of tea and a fairy cake."

"I thought you'd be too macho for fairy cakes," she teased.

"I like to get in touch with my feminine side from time to time," he replied. "I told you that yesterday." He turned to grin at Claire over his shoulder, his hands deep in soapy bubbles.

She was putting knives away in the cutlery drawer; neat lines of wedding-present silver glinted up at her. Suddenly Stefan was standing beside her. She turned; only a few inches of space separated them. She desperately wanted to touch him, just to put out her hand and touch his arm, his chest, his face, to see what he felt like. She took a step back to stop herself.

"Is this where you keep your tea towels?" He pointed to the drawer below the cutlery drawer.

"Good guess," Claire said, opening the drawer and handing him one woven in blue and white checks.

There was a silence. She looked away and when she turned back he was beside the sink again, drying the saucepan.

"Any coffee yet, darling?"

William stood in the doorway. Claire wondered how long he'd been there.

"I'll put the kettle on," she said.

"I'd better be going," said Stefan. "I think I'm all done here." He hung the saucepan up above the Aga and folded the tea towel neatly over the oven rail.

"What time will you be back in the morning?" asked Claire.

"Is nine-thirty okay? I've only got to get a shot of you in your studio and a few more room shots. It should only take an hour or two at most, then I'll be out of your hair for good."

Claire closed the front door after Stefan had gone, and locked and bolted it for the night.

"Thank goodness for that," said William, taking off his shoes in the hall.

"Thank goodness for what?"

"Thank goodness he's gone. I thought he'd never leave."

"I thought you liked him," she said, surprised by William's sudden irritable tone.

"Thinks a bit too much of himself, if you ask me." He was pulling papers from his briefcase, looking for something.

"He was very helpful in the kitchen."

"I suppose you're going to start on me now, about how I should have washed up?" he said as he found the document he was looking for.

"I'm not going to start on you." Claire tried not to sound exasperated. "I thought you wanted coffee. I've just started making it."

"Changed my mind. It's too hot for coffee anyway. I'm going to bed to read this report for tomorrow."

William disappeared up the stairs. Claire sighed. He had seemed relaxed and cheerful, even affectionate earlier on, but now that they were on their own he was suddenly irritable and cross.

She went into the garden to clear the last of the glasses from the patio table and thought how nice it would have been to have sat out in the moonlight for a little while, drinking coffee with William. Years ago they would have done just that and talked for hours before going to bed. Now he always seemed to have something more important to do.

Claire heard a noise and Ben appeared in the doorway, red-cheeked, his yellow curls damp on his forehead. He had taken off his pajama bottoms and his nappy sagged between his chubby knees. He held up his arms and she picked him up, hugging his warm body close to her. She took him up to change him and as soon as she put him back in his bed he was asleep again.

She began to pick up toys from the floor of his room—wooden train track, farmyard animals, and knights stolen from Oliver's castle. As she turned to put them in the wicker toy basket, a sudden image of Stefan flashed into her mind. She froze in the middle of the room, her hands full of brightly colored medieval men.

She wondered what would have happened if she really had touched him when he had stood so close beside her in the kitchen. A series of possibilities flickered through her head: Stefan taking her in his arms, leaning down to touch her lips with his. A gentle kiss at first, then harder. Claire breathed in quickly. She was shocked at her thoughts—it was the heat, too much wine, she was tired—but as she went downstairs to turn out the lights she could still feel the imagined pressure of his kiss on her lips.

Later, upstairs in their bedroom, she lay on her side of the bed facing William's back; it radiated fiery heat. Remembering his affectionate kiss at dinner, she reached out and touched his bare skin, running her fingers lightly over his shoulder.

"It's really hot," he said, shifting away from her in the darkness. The window was open but there was no breeze.

Claire couldn't sleep, but it wasn't the heat. Something inside her ached. She turned over and over, wanting the dull pain to go away. She longed to sleep, but every time she let herself relax she saw the image of Stefan again, beside her, bending down to kiss her lips. Claire pushed her hands onto her closed eyes. What was wrong with her?

She must have slept at some point because she woke up to the sound of a bird singing outside. It was still hot, she was damp with sweat, and her head ached. She really must have had too much wine.

CHAPTER 7

*Claire has always been creative. After the birth of
her third child, she made her hobby into a successful
career, turning piles of hoarded vintage fabrics into
gorgeous cushion covers, tea cozies, and aprons.*

"Did you get a good night's sleep?" asked Stefan when he reappeared the next morning.

"Yes, thank you," Claire lied as she cleared away breakfast. "How about you? Did you sleep well?" She peeled a half-eaten slice of toast from the kitchen floor.

"No, not really." He picked up a pot of jam and screwed the lid back on.

"I expect it was the heat and a strange hotel room." She felt shy and self-conscious in his presence now, though he had made her feel so relaxed the day before.

"I've got a present for you."

"Oh?"

"Well, it's for both of us, really." He delved into the brown paper bag he had been carrying. "To share with a cup of tea."

He held out a small square cardboard box. It was tied with a mass of twirling ribbons and through its cellophane lid

Claire saw four fairy cakes exquisitely iced with pastel-colored swirls and flowers.

"Where did you get these?"

"That fancy patisserie shop you've got in town, next to the hotel. I thought they might appeal to you."

"I'll put the kettle on," she said, beginning to feel a little better.

"Let me give you a hand." Stefan lifted down two striped mugs from hooks which ran along the dresser shelves.

"I think your present calls for something more refined than mugs," said Claire, taking two cups and saucers from a glass-fronted cupboard on the wall. Delicate pink camellias decorated the fine white bone china, gold luster glinted on the cup rims and handles.

They sat once more on the wrought-iron chairs at the table in the garden, drinking tea and eating the iced cakes. Claire had put the phone to voice mail, the children were at school, and Ben was at nursery till lunchtime.

It was even hotter than the previous day. The air was heavy and still. Pale gray clouds started to appear on the horizon in front of them.

"I enjoyed last night," said Stefan, slowly unpeeling the paper cover from his second cake. Claire watched his long, sun-browned fingers. His hands were large; they looked strong. "William seems very proud of his home."

"Yes," Claire said, picking off a small corner of sponge and icing. "He is."

"I envy you both. You've got it all here."

"Have we?"

"The house in the country, the lovely children, the beautiful garden."

After a few seconds' pause, he added, "The perfect family."

Claire wasn't sure if he meant it as a question or not. She didn't answer.

They were silent for a moment. Claire took the last bite of her cake. Suddenly it tasted horrible, the pretty icing too sweet, the cloying sponge too difficult to swallow. She took a sip of tea to wash it away.

"Let's get on with the pictures, shall we?" she said, putting the cup back on its saucer. She moved too quickly, the cup tipped onto its side; she tried to right it and instead it toppled onto the stone flagstones with a heartbreaking smash. The sound seemed to echo out across the quiet valley. For a second Claire couldn't move.

Stefan bent down. "Maybe it can be mended." He started picking up the pieces. "Or maybe you can replace it?"

"I don't think that would be possible. It was my grandmother's," Claire said, taking a tiny shard of painted flower petal from his hand. "It was part of her favorite tea set. She was given it by a cousin who was a china decorator in Stoke-on-Trent; she painted it especially for my grandmother's wedding because camellias were her favorite flowers. It's unique, a one-off, I'll never get another." She felt so sad, as if a heavy weight had descended on top of her. Why was she always so clumsy, ruining things? "The tea set is the only thing I have that was my granny's and until now it was complete."

Stefan gently touched her arm. "I'm sorry," he said. "I wish there was something I could do."

"Don't worry. I'm being too sentimental. It's just a cup, I suppose. Right! Shall we get these pictures taken?"

"I'll get my camera," Stefan said. "I've left it in Claudia."

"Are you going to tell me why you call your car Claudia?" Claire said, trying to sound more cheerful.

Stefan smiled. "No. You'll have to wait for that." He walked away across the grass, which, Claire noticed, was turning brown from lack of rain.

Stefan was photographing Claire and William's bedroom. He worked quickly, moving easily around the room, taking pictures from as many different angles as possible. Claire watched him from the doorway.

He finished and looked back through the shots. "Come and have a look."

Standing beside him, she could smell sandalwood and lemons. She had a sudden desire to press her face against his chest, to breathe him in, to keep that smell inside her forever. She moved away slightly and peered at the screen on his camera.

"It looks beautiful."

"I'll just take a few close-ups of your cushions on the bed and then I'll be done in here. Any chance of another cup of tea?"

When Claire came back from the kitchen, she found Stefan looking at the photographs on top of the chest of drawers. In his hands, he held a picture taken on her wedding day.

"How long ago?" he asked.

"Eleven years. Just before we moved here."

"You looked very pretty."

"I looked awful." She took it from him. Claire hadn't looked at it properly for years. It was a family group. From behind the glass her mother-in-law stared back at her, tight-lipped and straight-backed, in a huge feather-trimmed hat that looked as ridiculous as Claire's dress. She was standing too close to her only son, her head inclined proprietarily toward his shoulder. Next to her, William's father laughed his usual jolly laugh toward the camera, as if oblivious to his sour-faced wife. Claire's own mother stood slightly apart from the group, husbandless, hatless, and looking dazed in an ill-fitting knitted skirt and matching jacket. Claire was clinging onto William's arm as if she might collapse into her huge, white, puffy skirt. Her face looked pale, her smile forced. She remembered how firmly William's mother had laced her into the tight satin corset.

"I hated that dress. I could hardly move in all that net and chiffon," Claire told Stefan.

"Not your choice?"

"I had bought a red crochet shift dress in Portobello Market—a Mary Quant original," she said, sighing. "I imagined I'd be wearing that and we'd get married in the Chelsea Register Office with a handful of friends."

"Very sixties rock chick." Stefan laughed. "I like it. I can imagine that wedding picture. You on the steps outside looking glamorous; your groom in a well-cut suit and dark glasses."

"Unfortunately William had other ideas. Or rather his mother did."

For a start it had to be a church wedding, and not just their local Battersea church, or the redbrick church of her mother's suburban parish, but a pretty country church like the one in the Cotswold village that William had been brought up in. It had to be a traditional wedding—as many guests as possible, champagne, a five-course meal, three-tiered cake, morning dress for all the men, a picturesque setting for the photographs.

So in the end, of course, it was held in William's parents' village, the ceremony taking place in the ancient church where he had been christened, and a marquee on his parents' lawn for the reception.

William's mother had put herself in charge of everything from the guest list to the flowers in Claire's hair, rendering her new daughter-in-law redundant. On that day Claire had felt like an overdressed guest instead of the bride.

She made a face at the picture in her hands.

Stefan laughed. "I take it you have a formidable mother-in-law."

"That's one way to describe her. I didn't know how to stand up to her. I'd always considered myself quite feisty, but somehow she just seemed to drain the spirit out of me. It was definitely not the kind of wedding I wanted."

"Oh, well," said Stefan, shrugging his shoulders. "There's always next time."

Claire looked at him and he grinned back at her and then they both burst out laughing.

All that was left to do were the pictures of Claire working. Stefan asked her to put on one of her Emily Love aprons— red gingham appliquéd with a bird whose wings were made of pearly buttons. He photographed her as if she were hard at work at the table in her makeshift workshop. He positioned piles of her vintage fabrics behind her so that the spare bed wasn't visible and asked her to look as if she was cutting out heart shapes with her big steel scissors. He put brightly colored reels of thread in front of her, draped ribbon across the table, and sprinkled buttons in between. Without the children and Babette, Claire felt silly posing for the camera.

"Can you relax a little?" asked Stefan as he looked through his lens. "As though I'm not here."

"I can't. I can see you. You're definitely here. I feel ridiculous pretending to work."

"Talk to me, then," he said. "Tell me about Emily Love. Where did the name come from?"

"I'd just started the business when I answered the phone one day, just as I was telling Emily to turn the television down. It turned out to be someone new who wanted to stock my work. When I answered the first thing they heard me saying was 'Emily, love,' so they thought that was my business name and it just sort of stuck."

"So it could just have easily have been called Turn That Bloody Racket Off?" said Stefan, looking at her through the lens.

Claire laughed and Stefan clicked and clicked.

"That's better," he said. "Now tell me where you get your vintage fabrics from."

"Oh, all over the place. I buy bundles from local auctions, cut up old clothes and curtains from charity shops; friends send me bits they find."

All the time he took pictures; from the side, from the front, moving to the other side of her.

"Now let me think. What else can I ask you?"

Would you like to kiss me? The words popped into Claire's head.

"Would you like . . ." Stefan began.

Yes please, said Bad Claire in her head, *I'll just take my apron off and I'm yours for the rest of the day.*

"Would you like to move somewhere else in the future, or would it be too difficult to leave such a lovely home?"

For a second Claire found it hard to process what he'd asked. She felt sure he'd notice a sudden flush on her cheeks and the disappointment in her expression.

"William would never want to leave," she managed to say, trying to banish Bad Claire to the outer reaches of her thoughts. "He adores the house."

"I'd imagine you could feel a little jealous," Stefan said.

"Of what?"

"Of the house."

She felt surprised and slightly annoyed by his comment. "William's put in a huge amount of work to give us such a beautiful place to live. I'm very lucky."

Stefan started to look back through the shots he'd taken. "You're also very photogenic."

"I bet you say that to all the women you photograph."

"No," he said, "I don't. You also have a very photogenic house and I think there's a lot more of your hard work and talent in this house than you give yourself credit for." Claire could feel him looking directly at her, even though she had her back to him as she took off her apron. "The colors, the furniture, the fabrics—they are all you, your choices, your taste. They're the things that make it such a special home. Not the holes drilled for the damp-proof course or the varnish on the hardwood floors." Claire turned around and was struck all over again by how beautiful he was, with his strong features and tanned skin. There were laughter lines around his chocolate-brown eyes but also a deep groove between his eyebrows that she hadn't noticed until now. "I'm sure you could make anywhere you lived lovely."

Claire didn't say anything but started tidying the table. She took a piece of scarlet ribbon and wound it round and round her fingers.

"It must be fantastic for your children growing up here," said Stefan. "The sort of home all children should have."

"William and I think it's important to give them a lovely environment to live in." She slipped the ribbon from her hand and put it neatly into a drawer. "And as much stability as possible."

"Yes, you're right," he said, slowly packing away his camera equipment. "My father left when I was nine. I came home from school one day and he was gone. I didn't see him again for six months. The house we lived in, the house I'd been born in, was sold; my mother married again. She married my piano teacher and took me and my sister to live with him miles away from anywhere I knew. It turned out that she'd been having an affair with the man for years, even before he was my piano teacher. That was why my father left. We had to go to a different school. My sister and I hated it, and we hated our stepfather, especially. I was so angry with my mother. Why did she have to make everything change?"

"What about your father?" asked Claire.

"He decided to relive his youth in a series of bachelor pads, with a series of very young, very blond girlfriends, so no time for us. He even bought himself a two-seater sports car, so no room to take us out either. Both my parents are dead now. My dad crashed his sports car into a semi-trailer on the M50 and my mother died when I was eighteen." He looked away out of the window. Outside it was beginning to rain. Drops of water ran down the windowpane.

"My dad left when I was thirteen," she said. "Suddenly everything I thought I knew had changed as well. He went to live in America with his new wife, got a job as a lecturer in European history at a college out there. I thought I'd be having long summer holidays in California, but apart from a few initial birthday cards I never heard from him again."

"That must have been very hard for you." Stefan had turned to face her. "But you haven't let it put you off marriage or having your own family. That shows how strong you must be—how resilient."

Claire shrugged. She'd never thought of herself like that before.

"In lots of ways my parents' divorce put me off getting married," Stefan continued. "I worry that history will repeat itself and I'll make a mess of it. My sister is the same."

"Frightened of commitment?"

"Just frightened of hurting other people. Frightened of being hurt."

Stefan's eyes were focused on hers, his face serious, the groove in his forehead deeper. Claire knew she should look away but she couldn't let go of his gaze.

"You'd never do that to your children," he said, as though it was a fact. "You'd never mess up their lives; spoil everything you and William have."

"No," she said. "I'd never do that."

Stefan looked away. "I'd better go."

As they started descending the stairs, Claire felt as if she were losing something with every step. Hope perhaps. But hope of what?

"Maybe you should stay until this rain stops," she suggested. "I could give you lunch."

"I'll be all right," said Stefan. "I've got to get back. I promised I wouldn't be late." *Who had he promised?*

At the bottom of the stairs he turned to Claire and smiled.

"It's been a lovely couple of days. Thank you." He said it with a formality that made her want to shake him. "It was nice to meet you."

In her head Bad Claire screamed, *Don't leave me here; take me with you.*

"It's been lovely meeting you too. I'll look forward to seeing the pictures in the magazine."

He leaned forward and kissed her cheek, a light brush with his lips, and then he opened the front door and went out into the rain. Claire stood in the doorway unable to move. She wanted to run out, run out to him and say . . . say what?

He was getting into the MG, waving through the rain. He had turned on the lights and windshield wipers. Claire stood and watched, waiting for the crunch of the wheels on the gravel, but suddenly he was out of the car again, lights and wipers still left on, but he was running back.

"I just thought," he said, standing dripping in the rain in front of her. "It's my sister's birthday next month. I think she'd love one of your aprons—like the one with the bird and buttons you had on today. She's not been well lately; I think it would cheer her up."

"Okay. But I don't know your address or even your phone number."

"I'll e-mail you," he said. "I'll e-mail you through your Web site."

He leaned forward and kissed her cheek again and ran back to the car. The sky lit up with a flash of lightning closely followed by thunder, then she heard the gravel crunch of wheels on stones, and the air filled with the smell of wet lavender as his car brushed by the bushes on the edge of the drive.

Claire stood in the doorway, staring at the empty drive, unable to move, the sensation of his kiss still on her cheek. At last she took a deep breath and looked at the watch on her wrist. Ben! She was late for Ben! She rushed into the house and ran around collecting keys, her purse, a raincoat from under the stairs, a raincoat for Ben.

In the car, she couldn't remember which pedal the clutch was. Her brain refused to work. It was as if she was trying so hard not to think of Stefan that she couldn't think at all.

Somehow she managed to drive through the heavy rain to

the nursery and to look interested while the nursery assistant read out a list of his morning activities.

"Making sand pictures, song and dance, toast and fruit at snack time; he only ate the toast again, I'm afraid. Two number ones in the toilet and one in his pants."

"How lovely," said Claire.

CHAPTER 8

*Wooden toys and games mix happily with
antique furniture and junk-shop finds. The children's
brightly colored artwork lines the walls alongside
Victorian paintings and contemporary prints.*

After picking up Ben, Claire went into town and bought sliced ham and cheese at the delicatessen. She didn't feel capable of cooking. She went into the patisserie where Stefan had bought the fairy cakes and bought two loaves of her favorite Parmesan bread with olives and one loaf of brown sourdough. Then she saw the compartment in the high glass counter with the last few remaining fairy cakes.

"I'll have all of those," she said to the shop assistant, pointing to them.

"I want one now," cried Ben, who she was awkwardly balancing on one hip.

"We'll have them for dessert."

Ten beautiful pastel-colored cakes were handed to her in two ribbon-tied boxes. Looking at the boxes, she felt as though she was prolonging something, holding on to a tiny part of the last two days.

The rain had stopped; the sky had cleared and was now a

bright Wedgwood blue. The air felt cool and fresh for the first time in weeks. When Claire arrived home she got Ben settled in front of the television, letting him watch any DVD he wanted. He chose one of Oliver's *Harry Potter* films, unable to believe his luck. She just wanted him to be quiet so that she could have some time to think.

What was happening to her? She felt as if she'd come down with some terrible illness; she couldn't concentrate, her heart was beating too fast, her stomach lurched. Above all, she couldn't get the image of Stefan's face out of her head. The desire to see him again was almost overwhelming. She felt as though she were falling, actually physically falling. She tried to think about other things.

I have a lovely husband and a beautiful home, she said to herself. The phrase went round and round in her head like a mantra.

"Who are you talking to, Mummy?"

Ben stood naked beside her in the kitchen. She hadn't realized that she was speaking out loud.

"Oh, no one, darling. Where are your clothes?"

She bent down and hugged him. How could she have feelings for anyone who was not the father of her children?

"I want one," said Ben, pointing to the box of cakes above him on the table.

"All right," she said, absentmindedly untying a box and handing Ben a cake before remembering that she hadn't given him any lunch. He quickly snatched the bun from her and immediately started licking off the pastel-colored icing, not bothering with the cake itself. As Ben trotted back to the living room with his prize, Claire made herself a cup of tea and wondered how she could have turned into the kind of mother who sat her naked three-year-old in front of unsuitable DVDs, with only yellow icing for lunch. She started to make him a hummus sandwich and cut up an apple, but she knew he'd never eat it—not now that he had had a taste of highly colored sugar.

She didn't want anything to eat herself; her appetite had disappeared. She ought to be unloading the dishwasher and putting washing away, or sitting watching *Harry Potter* with Ben to make sure he wasn't getting scared by the CGI monsters, but she felt unable to do anything but lean against the work surface, paralyzed by the thought of Stefan.

Ben appeared with the phone in his hand—still naked but with a purple feather boa of Emily's draped around his shoulders.

"Grandma," he said solemnly, handing the phone to Claire. She hadn't even heard it ring. She really had to pull herself together.

"Claire?" the clipped voice said curtly. It was William's mother. Claire sat down on a chair, suddenly feeling exhausted. "We'll come a little earlier this evening. My tennis tournament's been called off because of the storms, so we'll be with you by six, if not before."

"Today?" Claire was confused. She had no recollection of any plans for this weekend.

"Yes, of course today. You are expecting us, aren't you? William said you were looking forward to seeing us."

"No. I mean yes, yes of course I am. Lovely." Claire felt herself drooping at the thought of yet another weekend with William's parents.

"We were thrilled when William phoned us yesterday and asked us to come and see what he has planned for your new summerhouse," she went on. "A summerhouse, what fun!"

Claire tried to disguise a sigh. "Yes, it will be."

"We haven't seen the children for so long. I expect they'll have grown."

She wanted to shout: *It's only been three weeks since you were last here; they haven't changed at all!* But she resisted. "Yes, I'm sure you'll hardly recognize them," she said instead.

Claire hung up as soon as she politely could and tried to think of the best way to kill William for doing this to her. Why couldn't he have mentioned that his parents were coming to stay when he came home last night or as he left for work in the morning? No wonder he had been so keen on mowing the grass.

Gradually Claire's angry thoughts subsided. *Stefan.* Would he be back in London by now? She looked at the large round kitchen clock on the wall. She thought he could be. Maybe he'd already sent her an e-mail about the apron for his sister.

She went into the study to check, turning on the computer, aching with anticipation. She waited for it to hum to life. Nothing happened. It was dead. *The lightning,* she thought. The lightning flash as Stefan was leaving, it had knocked out the computer. The modem must have gone. *Of all the times for this to happen.* Claire wanted to wail. It would be Monday by the time she could get their local computer repairman round to mend it. There would be a whole weekend of not knowing if Stefan was trying to get in touch. Claire put her head in her hands.

What was she doing? What did it matter if he got in touch or not? He was just a man she had briefly met. She knew very little about him. He had been kind to her, but to him she was probably just another woman with a nice home that he was being paid to photograph. Just another lonely housewife dissatisfied with her lovely life.

Claire went into the living room and sat on the sofa in front of the television. She should have been clearing all her fabrics, sketches, and the sewing machine out of the spare room for her parents-in-law to sleep in. She should have been putting Ben into the car for a desperate rush to the supermarket— bread, cheese, and fairy cakes for supper would not be good enough for William's mother. Instead she pulled Ben onto her lap and cuddled him tightly. He smelled of Very Cherry shampoo and toast. She sighed.

"Why are you doing big breathing?" he asked from beneath her embrace.

"Just sighing, sweetheart."

"Silly sighing," said Ben. "Silly Mummy sighing."

"You are so right. Silly Mummy," she said, and Ben twisted round and put his arms around her neck.

"I kiss you all over," he said, planting big wet kisses over her face again and again and again.

This is what matters, she thought. *My little boy, my children, my family.*

CHAPTER 9

Scrubbed wooden floorboards and quarry tiles create a naturally rustic feel around the house.

The weekend passed in a daze of loading and unloading the dishwasher and running around servicing her parents-in-laws' many needs.

"Are you all right, dear?" Her mother-in-law asked her on Sunday morning. "You seem a bit distracted."

"Just tired," replied Claire, who had just burned a batch of croissants in the Aga.

"Maybe that little sewing business of yours is too much for you. You have got three children and a house to look after as well."

"I think I'm managing all right, thank you," said Claire, trying not to sound defensive. "Emily Love is doing very well and I still only work part-time, so I have lots of time for the children."

"It's a good thing that William has such a well-paid job he can support you all," she droned on. "And he's so good around the house—a real 'new man.' I always knew he'd make a lovely husband, even when he was a little boy."

"Did you?" asked Claire, taking a deep breath.

William appeared in the kitchen in a bathrobe, fresh from the shower.

"Ben is on the sofa rubbing toast and jam all over the cushions."

"Could you stop him and clean his hands?" she asked, putting more croissants in the Aga and giving William's father's porridge a stir.

"The poor boy has only just got up," said William's mother, patting her son affectionately on the shoulder. "Don't worry, darling. You have your coffee, I'll deal with Ben. I don't know why you let the children eat in the living room anyway."

"That's just what I always say," said William, joining his silent father at the table and sorting through a thick pile of Sunday papers. His mother returned to the kitchen carrying a very sticky Ben, who was wrestling in her grasp and resisting all attempts to wipe his hands and face.

"I want *Transformers*." His voice was muffled by a damp cloth.

"Ben! Behave." William barked from behind a giant wall of newspaper.

"Television at breakfast time can't be good for children," her mother-in-law observed as Ben escaped back into the living room. "William never saw any television before teatime when he was a child, let alone as soon as he got up."

"That's what I always say," said William.

"There *was* no television before teatime when William was a child," his father said drily, from behind his own wall of newsprint.

His wife ignored him. "The children should be in here having breakfast with us, not glued to those terrible Technicolor American cartoons."

"They will be in here having breakfast with us," said Claire, through gritted teeth. "As soon as I can get these croissants cooked and the table laid."

She looked briefly out of the kitchen window and thought of Stefan standing in the rain. Suddenly everything felt much better.

At lunchtime the tree surgeon came and by teatime the space where the yew trees had been was a clear view to the smudged horizon above the sea.

"That's better," said William's mother, looking up from a Sunday supplement magazine. "Those trees always gave me the shivers."

"I'll miss them," said Claire, putting down a cup of coffee beside her. "They were as old as the house, if not older. I've got a feeling the house won't be the same without them. Cutting down yew trees is supposed to bring bad luck."

Claire could see her mother-in-law's eyebrows rising above her large, gold-rimmed sunglasses. The cat jumped up onto her lap and was immediately pushed away.

"I hope you're not being superstitious, Claire. I can't stand superstition; it makes no sense at all. I usually find it's a sign of ignorance." Claire glanced at the four-leaf-clover pendant hanging from her mother-in-law's thin neck and said nothing.

The first time she met William's mother, Claire had immediately realized that she wasn't the sort of girl that William was meant to marry. It was obvious from the way his mother pursed her lips together when she looked at her and wrinkled up her nose as if finding her distasteful, like a nasty smell. She constantly asked questions about Claire's background—her parents, her grandparents, her childhood home—as if searching for something suitable about her. Or trying to find something bad enough to persuade her only son to give Claire up.

Their upbringings couldn't have been more different. Life had treated William kindly. He had grown up in a big house in a postcard-pretty Cotswold village. His father, also an accountant, played golf and his mother had been secretary of the local tennis club for over twenty years. Prep school, private school, university, and then into a safe and well-paid job. For four years he had been engaged to Vanessa, the daughter of his parents' next-door neighbor. Vanessa had been everything Claire's mother-in-law had ever wanted in a wife for her son; blond and bright with long tanned legs and the best backhand in the county. William's mother could never forgive Claire for breaking up the "perfect match" despite the fact that the relationship had ended before Claire and William met.

"If she hadn't snared him so fast, I just know that William and Vanessa would have gotten back together." Claire had overheard her mother-in-law talking to a relative in the restroom at her wedding reception. "They really were just right for each other. Vanessa understood William; this should have been their day." Claire resisted the urge to tear off her ridiculous dress and walk away from the marquee, from William, his mother, the whole charade of a day; instead she had squeezed her voluminous skirts out of the small cubicle, smiled brightly at her pink-faced mother-in-law and William's elderly aunt, commented on the rain that had started to fall, and returned to her new husband for the first dance.

For a long time Claire half envied and half despised William's background. It stood for so much she had been brought up to disapprove of by her mother.

Claire's mother had fought her way from a flat above the tiny Grantham florists to university, where she fervently threw herself into left-wing politics and peace marches. In 1968 she had traveled to Paris on the back of a moped with a bearded history student to join the riots in the burning streets.

Somewhere between her subsequent marriage to the bearded history student (who had become a history lecturer in a newly built polytechnic) and moving into a small, dark, two-bedroom flat as a struggling single mother, the fight had left her. A brief stint at Greenham Common (accompanied by a reluctant teenage Claire) had briefly reignited her passions, but the reality of the day-to-day lonely drudge of life left her despondent and depressed. Her fire had gone out but her principles still smoldered and she worked hard at instilling them into her daughter.

Claire knew she had been a disappointment to her mother. After a wasted youth making out with boys and mooching around in Top Shop, she had failed to shine academically, failed to find a worthy cause to fight for, and then failed to lead the independent, high-flying life her mother had hoped for.

Sometimes, in her darker moments, when she wondered why she had married William, she thought that he had been her act of rebellion, just as she had been his. His background seemed so tantalizingly different from Claire's: so middle class, so comfortable, so normal. She had been determined to show her mother how it should be done, show her that you could live happily ever after in the domestic dream.

Look at me now, Claire often thought: cooking, cleaning, making school runs, planting flowers, creating pretty things to sell in pretty shops, putting dinner on the table, sorting socks and placing them neatly folded in the drawers. This is all I ever wanted. But sometimes it all felt so ridiculous she wanted to laugh—or was it scream? Standing at the school gates in her Boden skirts, she knew she looked the part but inside she felt like a fraud.

The one person she suspected could see right through her was William's mother. She knew that underneath their politely strained exchanges her mother-in-law could tell it was all an act and was just waiting for her to fail.

A t last it was Monday morning and everyone was gone. The computer man had promised to come and put a new modem in by lunchtime. Claire felt tight with nerves and anticipation. Would Stefan's e-mail be there?

Until then she had to cut out fabric for a dozen cushion covers and decorate them with appliqué stars and buttons. She found it very hard to concentrate on choosing the mixture of fabrics. Flowers, checks, polka dots, and paisleys swam and blurred in front of her. The choices she made were random rather than considered as she cut and pinned each one together. All the time she could feel her heart beating beneath her blouse and her stomach ached. Repeatedly, she glanced to the window to see if she could spot the computer man's van coming down the lane.

It was time to pick up Ben and he still hadn't arrived. She had to go. Leaving the half-finished cushions, she went downstairs and picked up her car keys. She thought about leaving a note for the computer man and the door unlocked, but an image of William's face as she explained to him why the house had been burgled stopped her and she locked up and left.

The car was hot from the heat of the midday sun and she opened the windows to let the breeze blow in on her face. The smell of fresh-cut hay and honeysuckle swirled about her as she drove down the country roads and every song on the radio seemed to be about falling in love. She felt she could keep on driving and dreaming all day.

After Ben had been collected, Claire retraced her drive home. As she came up the hill she could see the computer man's small blue van turning out of her drive and pulling away. She speeded up dangerously, beeping her horn and flashing her lights until she was only a few feet behind him, desperate to get him to stop. At last he indicated to pull over and she drove up alongside him in the narrow lane.

"I'm sorry," she said through her open window. "I had to go and collect my son. I thought you were coming earlier."

"Running late," said the large bearded man gruffly. "I waited ten minutes for you. I've still got nine damaged modems to repair by five. That thunderstorm knocked out half your village."

"Please come back," she begged. "I'm trying to run a business and I really need to collect my e-mails today."

"I've got to get on. I can come back tomorrow morning," he said.

Claire could hardly bear it; she'd never be able to wait until tomorrow.

"Please," she begged. "I'll pay extra. I'll pay double."

"Well," he said dubiously. "And a cup of tea. Two sugars?"

"Yes. And cookies—homemade."

"You're on."

Fixed," said the computer man, emerging from the study twenty minutes later. "You did say double pay, didn't you?"

"Yes," said Claire. "Will a check be okay?"

"Fine. All your e-mails are downloaded now and your Internet's back on. Any chance of another one of those cookies?"

"Yes, all right," she said. "Money, cookie—there you are. Thank you so, so much."

He left, munching loudly. Claire tried to sit down calmly in front of the computer.

"I want to play a game," said Ben, his own cookie in his hand, half sucked and soggy.

"In a minute, darling," she replied absentmindedly as she scrolled down the list of e-mails. There were over a hundred. A handful of orders from her Web site, a few for William, an awful lot offering her penis enlargements, Viagra, or fantastic financial opportunities involving large deposits into foreign bank accounts. She quickly scanned the e-mail addresses and titles. Nothing. She checked one more time—definitely nothing.

With a sigh she hoisted Ben onto her knee and clicked onto the *CBeebies* Web site.

Over and over again they made penguins hop over rivers on icebergs and flew a brightly spotted airplane through clouds avoiding balloons. Claire felt rather like a deflated balloon herself. She had been so sure Stefan would have contacted her over the weekend.

Stupid woman, stupid woman. Of course he wouldn't have been in touch. He'd probably forgotten her by now.

As she drove through the hot dry lanes to pick up Oliver and Emily from school, she tried to work out what she had hoped for anyway. Some declaration of undying love? An

offer of an exciting new life, of endless adoration and affec-
tion? *Of course not,* she told herself, that would have terrified
her. A small acknowledgment that he had liked her, thought of
her, enjoyed their time together? Or an apron order? Just a gift
for his sister? That would be enough.

CHAPTER 10

Balancing motherhood and being a businesswoman comes so naturally to Claire.

The house seemed to glow in the late-afternoon sunlight. Claire and the children sat on a red checkered cloth on the lawn, eating a picnic tea. Macavity sat beside them, hopeful for any sandwich scraps. Claire stroked his head and remembered Stefan doing the same. She cleared away the last of the empty plates and, leaving the children with a large bowl of strawberries, went into the study to check her e-mails for the thousandth time that week.

Nine days had passed since she last saw Stefan. Claire kept busy making two hundred lavender hearts as favors for a wedding and tea cozies for her first London boutique. She methodically went through the routine of the days—breakfast, school run, shopping, sewing, school run—her mind only half engaged.

Now she sat again in front of the computer, just in case he'd sent something in the last half hour.

Viagra. Viagra. Genuine Cartier Watches. No More Male Pattern Hair Loss. Emily Love Order.

She scrolled down.

Celia Howard: Re article.

It took Claire a few seconds to recognize the journalist's name.

Dear Claire,

Stefan has shown me the pictures; they look fabulous. I need to come and interview you for the article. I have a very busy schedule but can come down on Wednesday about 1:00 pm. Please send directions.

Celia

Claire felt a flutter of excitement. Even if she hadn't heard from Stefan, at least she would be seeing someone who knew him. She replied to say that the day after tomorrow would be fine and gave her a list of directions from the highway.

The children's bedtime was the usual riot of squabbles, toothpaste, tears, and a vast array of excuses for not staying in bed.

Claire lay on Emily's paisley quilt reading aloud to her *What Katy Did*. She was finding it hard to keep track of what was going on in nineteenth-century small-town America. Katy didn't seem to actually do anything very much.

"Isn't there another book you'd like me to read?" she asked Emily.

"No, I like this story. Granny gave it to me."

Suddenly Claire remembered her mother. She hadn't heard from her for weeks. Somehow she had failed to notice the lack of her usual phone calls. Images of her mother lying unconscious (or worse) in her flat flashed through her mind. Maybe she'd had a fall, a stroke, a heart attack—all three! Claire immediately ran from the room, picked up the phone in the hall, and dialed Elizabeth's number.

"You haven't listened to me read yet," said Oliver, appearing with his schoolbook.

"Cuddle!" demanded Ben from his room.

"What about Katy?" Emily had gotten out of bed and was tugging at Claire's arm.

The phone rang and rang. Claire quickly made a plan in her head. She'd have to put the children into the car and drive the sixty miles to her mother's. Should she call an ambulance first? Should she call the police?

"Hello," said Elizabeth.

"Thank goodness," said Claire, "I thought something terrible had happened. I was worried about you."

"Why would you be worried about me?"

"You haven't phoned for ages."

"I can't be phoning you all the time, Claire. I have got a life to lead."

"Oh." Claire was surprised by her mother's tone. She sounded . . . different.

"Anyway, you haven't answered any of my texts."

"You've sent texts?"

"Lots of them," replied Elizabeth, "and you haven't answered a single one."

"I didn't know you had a cell phone." Her mother always shunned the idea whenever Claire had suggested it might be useful for her to have one.

"I bought it last week. I don't live in the Dark Ages, you know."

"Oh," said Claire again. "I haven't looked at my cell phone for days. It needs charging and I haven't gotten round to it."

"Sounds like you're the one living in the Dark Ages, Claire."

"Are you all right?" Claire asked. Her mother sounded unusually animated.

"I had a little accident in the car but everything is sorted out now," said Elizabeth.

"An accident? Are you okay?"

"Absolutely fine. Look, darling, I'm just going out, so I can't talk for long." Claire wondered where she could be going; she never went out in the evenings. "I texted you to ask if you would like to join me for a week in a cottage in Cornwall at the end of next month."

"Well," said Claire dubiously, "William is very busy. I don't think he'll have time to get away."

"When is William not busy?" said her mother blithely. "I mean you and the children. I've booked a lovely cottage online and I'll be going anyway."

"You've booked it online?" Elizabeth had always refused to have anything to do with computers; just another instrument of the capitalist male, she said.

"No need to sound so amazed. I bought a laptop when I got my new phone. It's wonderful. I've been surfing all over the Web. I'll send you an e-mail with the details. You can Google Map it. E-mail me back if you want to come. I must go now or I'll be late."

"Late for what?" she asked, but Elizabeth had already gone.

Claire stood looking into the receiver. What had happened to her mother? She even sounded happy.

CHAPTER 11

*Colorful handmade cushions
and woven wool throws casually adorn an abundance
of comfortable sofas and armchairs.*

"Oh, my dear, don't you live in the back of beyond. *Lovely* roses. Shame we couldn't have had a shot of them around the door, but it's not very Christmassy, is it?"

Celia Howard wafted into the hallway. Cool, white linen draped itself elegantly around her long limbs, large amber beads emphasized her slender neck. She seemed to tower above Claire despite her flat shoes. Her hair was a thick blond swirl, effortlessly pinned up on her head. Claire noted with envy her high cheekbones. It was hard to determine her age. Maybe in her late forties? Probably older.

"*Lovely, lovely, lovely,*" Celia exclaimed, following Claire and Ben through to the kitchen. "Stefan has captured its charm *so* perfectly. Oh, look at all the Emily Love cushions on the chairs. *Absolutely divine.*"

"Tea? Coffee?"

"Chamomile is perfect for me. Now we need to be quick. As I said, I'm on such a tight schedule."

Sunlight poured into the conservatory as Celia perched on

a Lloyd Loom chair beside a pot of white geraniums. Claire served the chamomile tea in porcelain cups with slabs of lemon cake.

Celia got out her tape recorder. "I want you to tell me your story: how you found the house, what it was like when you bought it, what you have done to it, where you've sourced your furnishings and paint, et cetera, and a little bit about Emily Love and how you got started."

She turned on the recorder and Claire began hesitantly. As she talked, she began to feel as though she were telling an imagined story, a fairy tale.

"It all sounds beautifully romantic." Celia sighed. "Just the kind of article our readers *love*. Young couple restores old falling-down house, fills it with gorgeous things and children, starts a small successful business using reclaimed vintage fabric. So 'in' right now, glamorous recycling. Perfect. Inspirational. *I love it.* Thank you so much again, you've been wonderful."

"I think I've made it sound much more romantic than it really was. It has been hard work," said Claire. "Miserable sometimes, if I'm honest."

"I'm sure it has been, but no one needs to know that." Celia squeezed Claire's hand across the table. "Lovely-looking lemon cake but I just can't at the moment." She patted her perfectly flat stomach.

Ben was sitting in the corner dressed only in a T-shirt, having removed his pants, shorts, and nappy. Lemon-cake crumbs were scattered around him and he was happily driving a toy fire engine backward and forward across them.

"Isn't he adorable?" said Celia doubtfully. "How do you manage to keep it clean?"

"The house?" asked Claire, not certain if she might have meant Ben. "It's a never-ending challenge."

"It really is heavenly. I can tell why Stefan was so enthu-siastic."

"Was he?" Claire felt her mouth go dry and her heart start to beat hard in her chest.

"Oh yes. He *loved* it, and you certainly seemed to make quite an impression on him too." A surge of excitement swept through Claire. Celia finished her tea. "Such a *delicious* man. I can't keep track of his love life, though. Different women all the time." She laughed. "Now I really must go."

Claire's heart felt as though it had sunk into the floor. *Different women all the time?* She tried to pull herself together. So he had a complicated love life? He had all but said the same to her. She had made an impression on him—wasn't that what she'd wanted to hear? She should be happy. Why did she feel so flat?

Closing the door behind Celia, she leaned against it, sud-denly tired.

"Mummy." Ben pulled her skirt.

Claire realized that Stefan probably never had any inten-tion of getting in touch with her. Why would he when he had so many women to choose from?

"Wee wee on the floor." Ben pulled harder.

How could she have been so naive? Of course he would never be interested in a scatty housewife heading for forty in the back of beyond.

"It's wet, Mummy."

Anyway she was married to William. She was perfectly happy.

"And poo."

It was time to forget Stefan. Move on. Get over it. What was Ben saying? She let him pull her back into the conservatory, where she immediately saw the puddle and the poo and the cake crumbs, all nicely smeared together by a little hand.

"Ben!"

The phone rang. Claire went into the study to answer it.

"Hi, it's Sally." She sounded as dejected as Claire felt.

"Are you okay?"

"I'm all right." Sally didn't sound all right at all. "I just wondered if you wanted to come back to mine for a cup of tea after we've picked up the children? I can only offer stale malted milk cookies and I've run out of milk."

"You're not doing a very good job of selling it to me, Sally."

"Stop being so fussy and tell me if you'll come round."

"I can't," Claire said. "I've just remembered the lumber for the summerhouse is being delivered at half-past four."

"Oh." Sally sounded crestfallen.

"Why don't you come here?" Claire absentmindedly clicked on send and receive on the computer beside her. At the *ping* of new e-mails she looked down at the screen.

"Are you sure you're not too busy?" asked Sally.

Dear Claire,

I'm sorry to have not been in touch sooner . . .

"Not at all," said Claire, excitement building as she spoke.

"To be honest, I've got myself into a bit of a state . . ." Claire tried to concentrate on what Sally was saying.

I was away for a few days.

" . . . I just need to talk to someone . . ."

Am I too late to order that apron for my sister? Can you send it or shall I pick it up?

Stefan

" . . . I don't know what to do."

P.S. I thought you'd like to see the attached photographs from the shoot.

"It's fine to come here, Sally. Could you do me a big favor and pick up Oliver and Emily as well? There's just something I need to do before you come."

As she put down the phone she wanted to laugh out loud. She was suddenly ridiculously happy. She picked up Ben and danced him around the study. He squealed with delight. That was all she had wanted, wasn't it? Just an e-mail; some indication that Stefan was thinking about her. Surely that was enough. What did it matter about the other women? It wasn't as if she wanted to have a relationship with him.

Something smelled horrible. Claire remembered the wee and poo in the conservatory. Ben's hand was covered in it and now it was all over her too. She quickly ran around collecting disinfectant and kitchen towels, washed Ben's hands, changed her clothes, and wiped up the mess. Then she went back into the study.

Taking a deep breath, she clicked on the paper clip at the top of the message. A little gasp of delight escaped from her as the attachment opened. The pictures were beautiful, the colors so intense and warm that each room looked as if it were bathed in a rosy glow. There was a lovely picture of the three children around the Christmas tree, all of them looking pleased with their elaborately wrapped empty boxes; a gorgeous one of Emily eating mince pies at the kitchen table. No one would ever believe it wasn't really Christmas. Claire's favorite was a wide shot with the fire glowing in the fireplace in one corner and the children creeping down the stairs, the Emily Love stockings, bulging with brightly wrapped presents, hanging above the mantelpiece.

The last one was of Claire in her workshop bending over the fabric, pretending to cut it out. She hardly recognized herself. Her hair hung heavily over one shoulder and her skin looked clear and soft and radiant. Lips slightly smiling, eyes just glancing to one side. Looking at the photographer. Looking at Stefan. Claire usually hated seeing pictures of herself. She always looked pale, her cheeks too chubby, her smile too big, or not there at all, but in this picture even she thought she looked beautiful. Stefan had made her look beautiful.

Claire pressed reply.

Dear Stefan,

Thank you for the pictures. They are wonderful. The apron could be ready by this weekend. I can send it or if you'd like to collect it you'd be very welcome.

Claire x

She hesitated, took away the *x* and then pressed send.

Minutes passed and Claire stared at the screen. Just as she was about to give up:

I'll try and rearrange my plans this weekend. It would be lovely to see you again.

S.

Lovely . . . She realized she was grinning to herself.

Just then Oliver banged on the window in front of her. The twins' freckled faces peered over his shoulder. Claire leaned forward and opened the window.

"When will tea be ready?" Oliver asked. "We're starving."

"Soon," she said. She hadn't even thought about what to make for tea.

"Can we eat apples from the tree?"

"No, they're not ripe yet."

"What will we do then?" he whined.

"There's lemon cake in the conservatory. Share it with the others. I just need to send an e-mail."

"Can we really eat cake?" he said, surprised. Claire was usually very strict about eating before tea.

"Yes, really." She was already sitting back down at the computer.

"You're the best mum in the world," he said, running off to get to the kitchen before she changed her mind.

"I love you too," she called after him without looking up. She quickly pressed reply. She could hear Sally in the kitchen.

Dear Stefan,

It would be lovely to see you too. I'll get the fairy cakes this time.

Claire

She hoped she didn't sound too eager. She pressed send. Sally appeared in the doorway looking tired, her face devoid of makeup, her wild cascade of hair uncharacteristically lank.

"Mission accomplished," she said, flopping onto William's wooden swivel chair. "Two children collected and delivered, apparently intact."

"Thank you," said Claire, swiftly turning the computer off and getting up. "Let's go and get that cup of tea and you can tell me why you sounded so down on the phone."

Sally didn't move. "I think Gareth's having an affair."

"What?" Claire sat back down. "Are you sure? How do you know?"

"I don't know for sure." Sally looked miserable. "I only suspect that he is."

"Why?"

"He's cut his ponytail off."

"I thought you hated his ponytail?"

"I did, but I want it back now. I hardly recognize him. He's had a proper haircut in a salon—not just from Tony, the retired barber from the pub."

"Maybe he wanted a change of image? Maybe he did it for you?" Claire suggested.

"No, he'd never bother doing it for me. I know this is for another woman. There have been other signs too. He bought a polo shirt last week and a pair of jeans. He never buys new clothes. He's happy to go to work in trousers with the crotch hanging out and his Iron Maiden T-shirt that he's had since 1987. I have to nag him to wear anything different, even if we're going to a wedding."

"Who do you think would have an affair with him?" Claire tried not to sound as if the idea of anyone wanting to have an affair with Gareth was completely implausible. Sally had chosen to marry him, after all.

"That's the bit I can't work out," Sally replied. "It's not as if he works with any women in his IT department and only regulars go the pub—Pru and Lou are well over seventy and surely the gorgeous Dawn behind the bar would be way out of his league?"

"I think you're getting this all out of proportion, Sally. Gareth wouldn't have an affair."

"I know what you're thinking," said Sally. "Too lazy."

"Well, no. I wasn't thinking that exactly."

"I always thought so too, but now I'm not so sure." Sally looked as though she was about to cry. "I don't want to lose him, Claire. I love him."

In all the years she had known her, she'd never heard Sally say anything good about Gareth, let alone declare her love for him. Claire got up and came and put her arms around her. She itched to go and check her e-mails, and then mentally chastised herself for being such a terrible friend.

"I think this calls for something a little stronger than tea," she said. "I've got a bottle of Jacob's Creek in the fridge."

The sudden beeping of a lorry reversing up the drive heralded the arrival of the summerhouse.

The wine and two bare-chested lorry drivers unloading the timber helped distract Sally. By the time she'd had her fourth glass of wine and finished the lemon cake, she started to smile again.

"I wouldn't mind them at the bottom of my garden," she slurred slightly, holding her hand up against the glare of the evening sun so that she could see the men as they carried the massive planks of wood down to the cement base William had already laid. "Better than fairies," she said, and doubled over laughing. "Do you get it, Claire? Fairies at the bottom of the garden." Her wine sloshed over the table. "You've got hunky men at the bottom of yours."

"I think you've had enough now," Claire said, putting the nearly empty bottle back in the fridge. "Let's have a cup of coffee and wait for William to drive you and the boys home."

Sally yawned. "I feel much better now. I don't know why I thought Gareth was having an affair. Only horrible people have affairs and Gareth is not a horrible person."

Claire felt suddenly cold. "You're right, Sally. Only horrible people have affairs."

"I've never understood how people could deceive their partners. I mean, if you're not happy with your marriage, you either work it out or get out. You don't go off doing goodness-knows-what with other people behind everybody else's back, do you?" Sally hiccuped.

"No, you don't." Guilt crept over Claire. It *was* only an e-mail or two.

M y favorite girls." William was home early. He kissed them both, filled with good humor at seeing his latest project taking shape. "What are we drinking to? The summerhouse—that lovely new gazebo of ours?" He started opening a bottle of red.

"Before you have a drink, could you drive Sally and the boys home?" asked Claire.

"Of course," he said. "Come along, my chariot awaits." He really was in a very good mood.

"Now, *you* are a very nice man." Sally giggled, getting up unsteadily from her chair and pointing a finger at William. "You would never have an affair, would you?"

"No, of course not. Why would I want to have an affair when I have such a lovely wife?" He smiled at Claire. She wondered why he never said things like that when they were alone. "Besides, I wouldn't want to risk being thrown out of my beautiful home." *That was more like it*, thought Claire crossly. William laughed and gave her a squeeze.

He left with Sally swaying on his arm and the two boys wrestling each other across the drive and into the car. Claire knew she ought to get the tea. Instead she poured herself the last bit of wine from the bottle, went into the study, and turned on the computer.

Dear Claire,

Glad you liked the pictures.

Stefan

p.s. Let me bring the cakes. Do you like chocolate?

Claire pressed reply.

I love chocolate!

Claire

Send.
One minute later:

I know a shop that sells the most delicious Devil's Food Cake—can I tempt you?

Reply.

Yes, go ahead and lead me astray.

C

Send.

I'd love to.

S

It was suddenly too much for Claire. Were they still talking about chocolate cake? She shut down the computer, went into the kitchen, and started to peel potatoes very fast.

"What's for tea?" asked Emily, coming in from the garden.

"I don't know," she replied.

"It must be potatoes, but what else?" said Emily.

"Whatever you like." Claire felt unable to think straight at all.

"Fish fingers?"

"Fine."

"No broccoli," said Emily hopefully. Claire always gave them broccoli, as it was the one green vegetable they would all grudgingly agree to eat.

"Okay. No broccoli."

"Sally's going to have a sore head in the morning." William walked into the kitchen. "What's all this about Gareth?"

"Sally thinks he might be having an affair," she whispered, checking that Emily was out of earshot.

"I can imagine him doing that." William poured his glass of wine.

"Can you?" said Claire, surprised.

"Oh yes. He seems the type who would."

"Is there a type?"

"I think so. You can always tell the ones who will and the ones who won't."

"Is that true for women too?" Claire carefully laid the fish fingers in two neat rows on the baking tray.

"Definitely. I could look at all the mothers in the school yard and tell you who would and wouldn't be unfaithful."

"That seems a bit of a sweeping statement."

William came up behind her as she slid the tray into the oven. "Trust me, I can tell," he said. He put his arms around her and kissed the back of her neck. "And I know that you, my darling, are one of the ones who wouldn't even dream of it."

CHAPTER 12

Colors flow tranquilly from room to room . . .

Claire had planned to show William the pictures that Stefan had sent but somehow there never seemed to be the time. He spent every evening working on the summerhouse, steadily erecting it with the help of a retired builder from the village. To Claire, the pictures were like a precious gift from Stefan, which she wanted to cherish and not share with anyone for a little while.

All week she felt jumpy and anxious. When she put on an old denim skirt on Thursday morning, it slid down low on her hips and she realized how little she had been eating. Her thoughts were constantly drifting to Stefan. Her sleep became sporadic and she spent many hours lying awake listening for the dawn, thinking of him.

She spent a long time making the apron for Stefan's sister, making sure every stitch was perfect, every detail of appliqué and embroidery exactly right, the pearl buttons in just the right position. When she had finished, she folded it carefully and slipped it into the cellophane packaging, positioning the "Emily Love" label in the middle. Perfect. It was ready. Now she just had to wait.

* * *

By Friday morning Claire could hardly bear to stay still. Anticipation, excitement, fear, guilt—a mass of contradictory emotions threatened to consume her. She longed for time to speed up. The weekend seemed to be taking forever to arrive.

It was impossible to concentrate on the twenty-five meters of bunting she was making for a customer's garden party. Her sewing was all over the place; she hoped it would be going up on a windy day so that no one would notice the crooked stitching. Suddenly she didn't feel sure she wanted to see Stefan at all. Their e-mail exchange had been exhilarating, but now she was frightened. She hadn't heard from him for a few days.

Claire had let herself imagine that she knew him much better than she really did. She realized that she didn't know him at all. Who was he, really? Beyond his kind, friendly manner and attractive exterior he might be cruel-hearted, masochistic, even. Celia's words about the many women in his life kept surfacing in her mind even though she'd rather not think about them. But, try as she might, she couldn't help imagining what it might be like to be in his arms, to feel his limbs entwined with hers, to let herself melt into his kiss.

In her more sensible moments she told herself that she was a happily married woman with three children and she had always vowed never to behave as her father had done. Adultery? No, she could never do that. So what was the point of seeing him again, stoking the fire inside her, stirring up emotions she was determined not to express? She couldn't remember ever feeling like this about any man before; a feeling so strong, so inappropriate, that it terrified her.

* * *

Somehow the bunting was finished and it was Friday afternoon. Through the open window in front of her, Claire
could see white clouds puffing up from behind the bare timber shell of the summerhouse. Ben was asleep beside her on
the study sofa. She was at the computer writing a reminder
letter to a shop about an unpaid invoice, trying to keep her
mind focused on business. Macavity sat purring beside her on
the desk. She determinedly ignored the sound of a new e-mail
arriving until she had finished her letter and printed it out. As
she searched for an envelope in a drawer with one hand, she
clicked onto her e-mails with the other.

Claire,

Sorry but something has come up and I can't come to collect the
apron this weekend. Could you send it to the following address
instead? Shall I send you a check or would you prefer cash? Let me
know.

Stefan

Claire felt her heart plummet. For all her fears about seeing
him again she had somehow never imagined that he wouldn't
come, and this e-mail was more formal, colder than the others.
She wondered if she should have been more complimentary
about his photographs, expounded on how much she had enjoyed her time with him, but she hadn't wanted to appear too
enthusiastic for fear he'd guess how she felt about him.

Claire tried to rationalize her thoughts. It was good that he wasn't coming. It would put an end to her ridiculous fantasies, an end to these feelings she had that were almost like an illness in their intensity. She would send the apron in the mail and that would be the end of it.

As she slid the apron and an invoice into the padded envelope, she noticed that her hands were shaking. Her head began to spin, the room tilting unnervingly. As she sat down on a chair tears started to stream from her eyes. For a few minutes she gave in to the sobbing and the feeling of despair that filled her. She could feel a real, physical pain in her heart. *Heartbroken,* she thought.

Rain was drumming down hard on the roof of the conservatory. Claire imagined what it would feel like to put her hand out of the window and let it pour over her palm, so cool and soothing.

Suddenly she had the idea of taking the apron to Stefan herself. *I could do that,* she thought. I could leave the children with Sally and go on the train tomorrow and find his flat. *And then what?* She closed her eyes tight to try to stop the images of him that still seemed to fill her mind. *This must stop,* she thought. *It's got to stop.*

She forced herself to take some very big deep breaths, stood up, and reached for a pen to write Stefan's address on the envelope. If she left now she'd catch the post office before she picked the children up from school.

CHAPTER 13

The delicate hues of antique quilts on pretty, painted, wrought-iron beds . . .

A week passed. Oliver and Emily couldn't wait for the start of the summer holidays. Claire tried to keep busy: sorting out orders, gardening, cleaning, taking Ben swimming. She bought a pale green halter-neck dress on sale and a pair of high-heeled sandals—thin green straps of soft suede that flattered her newly slim legs. The dress and sandals were an attempt to cheer herself up, but all she could think of was how much she'd like Stefan to see her wearing them.

The weather was cooler now. The heat wave of the last month seemed to have burned itself out, just in time for the holidays. It made Claire sad; the intense heat had seemed like a reminder of Stefan, and now she felt as if the light breeze that had blown all week was blowing him farther away from her. She heard nothing. No check in the mail. No e-mail of thanks for the parcel.

The last day of term was also Ben's third birthday. The red-and-blue gingham bunting Claire had made especially for the party flapped and twisted in the drizzly wind. A group of anxious mothers sipped tea, nibbled on homemade shortbread, and sheltered in the conservatory as their children jostled noisily on the bouncy castle on the lawn.

"Be careful, Oscar."

"Please be gentle with Ralph. He's only little."

"No, Tabitha. Don't do that. You'll hurt yourself, darling."

Claire and Sally watched the other mothers through the kitchen window.

"I hope my boys aren't being too rough," said Sally as she poured chips into a stripy plastic bowl.

"They're fine," said Claire. "Those mothers from the nursery are so neurotic. Wait till they have a few more children. They'll soon give up worrying, and poor little Ralph and Tabitha will have to fend for themselves."

Sally picked up a glass from a tray of untouched glasses.

"I can't believe that none of them wanted Cava," she said, taking a sip.

"That won't last long either," said Claire, laughing. "Give them a couple of years and they'll be downing sparkling rosé at lunchtime along with the rest of us." She took a glass off the tray and drank it in one go as if to illustrate her point. She picked up another glass, but could only manage the first quarter before she spluttered on the bubbles.

"Are you all right, Claire?" Sally checked. "I thought I was the only afternoon binge drinker around here."

Claire shrugged. "I can't quite match you yet. I feel sick now."

"You haven't seemed quite yourself lately," said Sally. "I'm sure there's less of you than there used to be. Have you been going to Weight Watchers behind my back?"

"I'm fine." She sliced up the obligatory cucumber and carrots.

"New dress?"

"I needed a little treat."

Sally gently turned her around for a better look. "Ooooh. Very Marilyn Monroe."

"I've got new shoes too, but I can't walk more than a few yards in them."

"Taxi shoes."

"What?"

"Oh, you know. Shoes that are so uncomfortable you can only wear them from the taxi to the entrance of the party. And I don't mean children's parties."

"They're the only kind of parties I get to go to these days," sighed Claire. "Is it sad to spend days planning what you're going to wear to sit in someone's living room watching Charlie Chuckles and his Dancing Chipmunk while you shovel cheesy balls down your throat?"

"Yes, Claire, that is sad," Sally said, giving her arm a kindly stroke. "We definitely need to get you out. Life does go on after *CBeebies Bedtime Hour*, you know."

"What about you?" asked Claire. "Are you still worried about Gareth?"

"Oh, that." Sally laughed. "I don't know why I thought he was having an affair. Poor man, it turned out he was up for promotion at work and so he felt he'd better smarten up his appearance."

"Did he get the promotion?"

"He hasn't heard yet. But you can imagine how guilty I felt. Poor Gareth. I didn't tell him that I was sure he had a bit on the side; he'd have thought I'd finally lost my mind. Anyway, I'm getting used to him without long hair. He looks quite sexy, actually."

"Can we play on the computer, Mum?" asked Oliver, red-faced and panting in the doorway. Behind him, Sally's twins looked similarly bounced out.

"Okay. I'll need to go and turn it on, though. Wait a minute. Sally, can you arrange these cakes on the cake stand?" Claire handed her friend a tin of miniature fairy cakes iced with ladybirds and bees. She'd made them the night before, staying up past midnight to postpone yet another sleepless night.

"Wow," said Sally, opening the tin. "You've surpassed yourself this time."

"Just some little things I knocked together last night," Claire called as she walked toward the study.

"No need to show off," called Sally from the kitchen.

Claire entered the study and turned on the computer. *A quick check of my e-mails while I'm here*, she thought. Through the open window she could hear the shrill squeals of children on the bouncy castle. Glancing up, she saw that, as usual, Ben had taken all his clothes off, despite the weather. She skimmed through the junk mail and some new orders from her Web site and then suddenly she saw Stefan's name.

"Come on, Mum," said Oliver behind her. "Hurry up. We're waiting to play my new game."

"Just a minute." She could hear her heart beating. Hardly daring to breathe, she clicked on the e-mail.

Dear Claire,

Thank you so much for the beautiful apron. I gave it to my sister last night and she loved it—I knew she would.

I still need to pay you. You didn't say if you wanted a check or cash.

Can I treat you to tea and cakes somewhere special to say thank you
and I could pay you then? What about next Tuesday afternoon?

Stefan

Claire wanted to leap on the bouncy castle and bounce up
and down for joy. *Next Tuesday. Somewhere special.* (That would
be innocent enough. Only tea and cakes with a friend; not
exactly breaking any marital vows.)

"At last," muttered Oliver as Claire turned round.

"It's all yours, boys," she said, an irrepressible smile across
her face.

Claire walked back into the kitchen as calmly as she
could.

"What are you grinning about?" Sally asked, her mouth
full. She was leaning against a counter, working her way
through a bowl of popcorn that had yet to reach the tea table.

For a second Claire thought she would tell Sally, but then
she remembered her friend's views on adultery and decided
she'd interpret an innocent afternoon tea in completely the
wrong way.

"Oh, nothing," she said. "I have a favor to ask. Can you look
after my three next Tuesday afternoon?"

"Yes. Why?"

"Something's come up," said Claire, busying herself with
opening a pack of Thomas the Tank Engine paper plates that
Ben had insisted on. "I've got to see a customer."

"Is it another shop? Is it local? I hope it's not competition
for the gallery."

"No, a private customer," said Claire, avoiding eye contact.

Sally looked at her inquisitively. "Another bulk order of
bunting?"

"Something like that."

Dear Stefan,

I am so glad your sister liked her apron. Check or cash is fine with me. Tea and cakes on Tuesday sounds lovely. Where did you have in mind? I'll meet you there.

Claire

———————

Dear Claire,

I thought you might like a ride in my car. I'll pick you up. 2ish okay with you?

S

———————

Dear Stefan,

Meet me in the parking lot in town. 2:30 pm is better for me.

C

———————

Dear Claire,

Meeting in the parking lot sounds a bit illicit! I'll be there at 2:30.

S

Claire thought about explaining to him that she would be in town anyway. It would be easier to meet him there—nothing illicit about it at all—but she knew this wouldn't be strictly true and so didn't answer, just waited for Tuesday. She would see him once, that was all. Just an innocent cup of tea.

CHAPTER 14

*Soft and pretty . . . Embroidered muslin curtains
filter shafts of dappled sunlight.*

"You look lovely," said Sally as Claire handed over the children. "It must be an important customer."

Claire couldn't look at her. She fumbled in her handbag for Ben's spare nappies and his favorite bear.

"Those new sandals really suit you." Sally looked her up and down. "And your hair looks fab. Have you been to the hair-dresser's today?"

"No, I just spent a bit of time blow-drying it for once. I had to blackmail the children with chocolate and a new DVD to leave me alone long enough to do it."

"And your makeup looks gorgeous. You really do look like a fifties film star."

The green halter-neck dress, worn with a short cropped jacket and her new strappy sandals, had made Claire feel glamorous as soon as she put them on.

"You look pretty," Emily had said before they left the house. "Like a princess. Daddy will like you when he comes home." Her words had made Claire wince with a sudden stab of guilt.

It's just an innocent cup of tea, she told herself for the hundredth time.

"Thank you so much for having them." Claire gave Sally a hug. "I hope Ben behaves for you."

"I'm sure he can't be as bad as my two." Sally looked behind her into the cottage's chaotic hall; trainers, bags, and coats littered the small space. In the living room Ben could be glimpsed rolling on a huge leather sofa, laughing with glee as the twins and Oliver tried to tie him up. "Anyway, the boys already seem to have him under control. I'd better go and stop them from strangling him."

"I'll be back by six. I promise," called Claire as she walked down the path to her car.

"Don't worry," called back Sally. "I hope it's a big order."

A wave of guilt washed over Claire again; it was awful to lie to her best friend. She got into the car determined to turn back up the hill, go home, tidy the house, do some washing, forget Stefan. Then she started the engine, and as though pulled by an irresistible force, she headed for town.

The day had started overcast. Dull clouds had hung low in the sky all morning, but as Claire drove through the town she realized the sky had changed and was now bright blue. The sun shone warmly through her car window. Temporary traffic lights on the High Street brought Claire's car to a halt just outside the gallery where Sally worked. Sally's boss, Anna, was in the window arranging a display of pottery and handmade baskets. Looking up, she waved through the glass. Claire moved off; Anna was still waving and Claire hoped she wouldn't notice her turning into the parking lot and wonder why she hadn't come in to say hello.

She was late. She saw the MG already there, standing out

among the muddy four-by-fours and small, dusty hatchbacks. Its top was up despite the warm afternoon. Claire was relieved; she would feel less exposed as they drove through town.

Stefan stood beside the car looking ridiculously glamorous in a white collarless shirt and dark blue jeans. He wore sunglasses and his unkempt wavy hair and summer tan made him look like a film star himself.

Self-consciously, Claire parked the car. Stefan watched her with a smile as she tried to negotiate the narrow space.

"I know it's not straight," she said as she climbed out.

"It looks fine to me." He walked up to her and lightly kissed her cheek. "I was worried that you wouldn't come," he said, standing back.

"Children, tractors, small roads. We're always late round here," said Claire. She felt shy and awkward.

"You look beautiful."

She shrugged and smiled, both pleased and embarrassed by the compliment.

"Shall we go?"

He opened the door for her and she slid into the passenger seat. The smooth red leather was warm against the back of her bare legs. The mahogany-and-chrome dashboard glinted in the sunlight. The smell instantly reminded her of the long car journeys she took as a child. She had a sudden memory of her parents together, laughing in the front seat of their car as she ate Tic Tacs in the back. Her father driving with one hand on her mother's knee. *Had they been happy then?* she wondered.

Stefan started to maneuver the car out of the parking lot.

"The only trouble with classic cars," he said, heaving round the steering wheel, "is no power-assisted steering. Still, I'm sure it keeps me fit. Now tell me what you've been up to lately."

In her nervousness, Claire found herself telling him about

the fool she'd made of herself at the Oakwood Primary School sports day by falling over in the mothers' race and revealing her very large and very ancient maternity pants to the entire mass of assembled parents and children. As the words came out she wished they hadn't. This was not the sort of captivating conversation she'd imagined herself having with Stefan.

He laughed. "Sounds like you were the highlight of the whole event."

"If only I'd known I was going to fall over, then I'd have worn some less substantial knickers with a bit of lace on," Claire went on, wishing she could just shut up. "I have a sparkly thong that Sally gave me as a joke once. Even that would have been better than my enormous Bridget Jones–style pair."

"Stop!" He was laughing. "I can't concentrate on my driving with you going on about lacy knickers and glitzy thongs."

Claire felt herself blushing. "Sorry."

"No need to apologize," Stefan said, flashing her a smile. "It's just I'm not used to picking up women in parking lots who then launch into descriptions of their underwear."

She cringed. "Sorry. Again. It's just I'm not used to being picked up in parking lots, and to tell you the truth I'm a bit nervous, and when I'm nervous I say the most ridiculous things."

"Well, if we're both being honest, I've been nervous about seeing you again too. But now that I'm with you it feels as comfortable as . . ." He paused while he thought of a description. "As comfortable as putting on my favorite sweater."

"Or a big old pair of knickers?" she offered, and they both burst out laughing. "Where are we going anyway?"

They were driving out of town in a direction Claire didn't often go in.

"Surprise," he said mysteriously.

"I feel as if I'm being kidnapped."

"Actually, I have the ransom note written already."

"Just tell me where we're going or I'll throw myself from the car at the next junction."

Stefan glanced at her. "I know you can't run. You've told me that. I'll just catch you and put you back in the car."

She laughed. "I knew I should never have told you about sports day."

The little car went surprisingly fast down the high-hedged lanes. Wild roses and cow parsley brushed against its cream paintwork and shiny chrome.

After a few minutes' silence he relented. "Okay. You've worn me down with your sophisticated interrogation techniques. We're going to a little place I photographed for a magazine feature a few months ago. It's a Jacobean mansion converted into a five-star hotel. They lay on the most fantastic afternoon tea."

"Sounds lovely."

The car stopped at a junction. Stefan looked at her and smiled. He arched an eyebrow. "They have the most delicious cakes."

They drove for another half an hour. The smell of freshly cut hay came in through the open windows and Claire started to relax. Stefan told her about a house he'd been photographing in Scotland the day before.

"It was a fortified house. A castle, really. Parts of it medieval. The old couple who live there are quite mad. They have fourteen Great Danes and a huge black goat with a big red collar that sleeps in a basket in front of the Aga."

"Makes a change from a cat, I suppose."

"Maybe William would agree to a goat instead of a dog?" Stefan threw her a fleeting look.

"It would keep the grass short too," Claire said, laughing, but she wished he hadn't mentioned William.

At last the car swung through stone gateposts and down a long drive. The hotel stood on the side of a steep hillside looking over a wooded valley below. Ancient weatherworn carvings adorned its walls. Stefan parked outside and they walked up wide stone steps into a cool, marble-floored foyer. Claire gazed around at the sofas and armchairs arranged in sociable groups around huge fireplaces. Elaborate floral arrangements filled vast urns.

"Stefan, how lovely to see you again."

A man in a pin-striped suit appeared and shook Stefan's hand enthusiastically.

"I've wanted to come back ever since we did the shoot here."

"Your pictures looked superb in the magazine. It did business no end of good." His accent was faintly European—French or Italian, maybe.

"This is my friend Claire," said Stefan. "I've told her about your fabulous cakes."

"Tea for two then? No problem," said the manager. "Would you like to sit on the terrace? It's a beautiful day."

He led them through a blood red dining room. Crystal glasses glinted on crisp white tablecloths and Venetian mirrors reflected back at each other into infinity. They came out through French windows onto a long terrace. The sunlight was bright after the cool darkness of the interior.

The manager seated them at a table looking out across the view. In the bottom of the valley Claire could see a river twisting between the trees.

"This is very nice," she said when the manager had left them alone.

"I knew you'd like it."

A smiling waitress dressed in black and white appeared and laid out plates and silver cutlery between them. There were other guests sitting around the terrace. They all looked extremely glamorous. Claire was sure she recognized a woman in a wide-brimmed hat and elegant cream trouser suit. Wasn't she someone on television? The older man sitting with her looked vaguely familiar too. Claire couldn't help but stare at them.

When she looked away from them, she realized that Stefan had been watching her.

"I can't work out where I've seen them before either," he said, nodding toward the couple.

The waitress appeared again with a tray of steaming teapots, jugs, cups, and saucers.

"I just wanted to say thank you," he said, when they were alone again. "For my sister's present."

"You don't need to thank me like this," said Claire. "A check in the post or a credit-card number is usually enough."

"I wanted to thank you for the lovely time I had photographing your house as well. I don't normally enjoy my job so much."

"Well, thank you for the thank-you," she said, suddenly feeling shy. With one hand she played with the corner of her napkin, rolling the stiff white hem between her finger and thumb.

"I've got your money here," he said, handing her an envelope. "And I got this for you as well." He produced a small gold-and-turquoise box from the pocket of his shirt. He held it out to Claire. She took it from his hand. Slowly she lifted the lid. Inside, coiled on a bed of pink tissue, was a delicate necklace, its silver links interspersed with opaque beads and tiny mother-of-pearl buttons. "When I saw it I immediately thought of you. The buttons. I had to get it for you."

Claire slowly lifted the necklace out of the box. It was very pretty.

"I can't accept this."

"I can't take it back," he said. "I bought it in a gallery when I was visiting my sister. She lives in Brussels. I'm not going back there for a while. Don't you like it?"

"Oh, yes," Claire said, examining the necklace in her hand. "It's beautiful. Just perfect. Thank you." She looked up at Stefan and smiled. "I'll try it on." Putting it up to her neck, she fumbled with the clasp. One end dropped; it slid into her cleavage. She fished it out and tried to do it up again, feeling self-conscious and clumsy.

"Let me help you."

Stefan got up and walked around behind her. She held up each end of the necklace to him. He lifted her hair, gently laying it across her shoulder before taking the necklace in his hands. For a second Claire could feel his fingers lightly on the back of her neck as he fastened the clasp. He sat back down and looked across the table at her, smiling.

"It suits you."

Claire touched it; it felt cool against her sun-warmed skin.

"Thank you." She smiled back at him.

The waitress reappeared with a three-tiered stand of cakes. Chocolate gâteaux, creamy éclairs, custard tarts, and fruit pastries. Butterfly buns, fruitcake, scones, and little cream-filled pink meringues. Claire had never seen so many cakes.

"Wow," she said, wide-eyed.

"You choose first. You look like you need feeding up. What can I tempt you with?" he asked, turning the cake stand around so that she could view the selection.

Claire took a slice of Victoria sponge oozing with jam and

cream. It tasted light and fluffy. She was suddenly starving after weeks of having no appetite at all.

"I wish I could make a sponge that tasted like this," she said, wiping crumbs from the corner of her mouth.

"Do you want to try a bit of this one? It's delicious." Stefan didn't wait for Claire's answer but held out a forkful across the table. The pile of chocolate sponge and mousse slipped sideways on the fork. "Quick!" he said, laughing. "It's going to fall off." Claire leaned forward and took it in her mouth. It felt delectably soft and silky, melting on her tongue.

"Do you want some of this?" She offered a forkful of her own sponge.

"That's really good."

"What shall we try next?" he said when their plates were empty.

"You've got jam on your chin," Claire told him, handing him his napkin.

The afternoon passed quickly in a blur of cake tasting and cups of tea on the sun-drenched terrace. Stefan was so funny it almost made Claire forget how gorgeous he was. He made her laugh, gently teasing her and telling her stories about his friends and the houses he had photographed. They talked about their favorite food, favorite music and artists; about novels they'd both enjoyed and films he'd seen that she would have liked to have seen, if going to the cinema to see grown-up films were still possible. Claire couldn't remember the last time she'd talked to anyone about these things—things that used to be so important to her before the children, before William, before the house.

Stefan told her about his ten years spent wandering the globe: India, Russia, China, America—north and south. For the first time Claire wished she'd listened to her mother's advice and seen the world before she settled down.

Stefan's ambition had once been to be a travel photographer.

"But somehow I got sucked into interiors. Wherever I went it seemed that I always ended up photographing houses until that's what I became known for, and no one cared about my shots of Kilimanjaro at dawn or street vendors in Beijing."

"It's not too late," she said. "Can't you have another go?"

He stared into the distance. "I don't know. Now that I'm back in Britain I feel like I'm stuck in this rut for good." He seemed lost in his own thoughts. Claire reached out and touched his hand; effortlessly their fingers entwined. For an exquisite moment they remained like that. Somewhere inside the hotel a clock struck six.

"I've got to go," she said. Stefan let her hand go. "I promised I'd be picking up the children now." She couldn't believe it had gotten so late.

"I wish we could stay."

Stay for what? Claire wondered. *More tea and cakes? Dinner? The night?*

"I've got to go," she said again, and stood up, taking her jacket from the back of the chair.

They walked back to the foyer. Stefan went to the large oak desk to pay.

"It's on the house," she heard the manager say. "Please come back soon."

"I will," said Stefan.

"Bring your lovely lady-friend again," the manager called as they went through the large double doors.

"I'll see if I can persuade her."

As they drove back Claire felt happy, full of cake and sleepy. She could still feel the touch of his fingers laced in hers. Stefan turned on the CD player.

She smiled. "Leonard Cohen; I haven't listened to him for years. I used to play his albums all the time when I was at college."

"I would have thought you'd have been more of a George Michael sort of girl."

"I have hidden depths beneath my frivolous facade," Claire said, turning the music up a fraction. Stefan looked at her with half a smile and raised his eyebrows.

"I saw an exhibition at the Royal Academy last week," he said. "*Matisse's Women*—paintings mostly, a few drawings and a little bit of his ceramics. You would really like it."

"I can't remember the last time I went to an exhibition."

"Lots of lovely use of pattern, beautiful colors, very vibrant. I think it's on for a while." He looked across at her and his deep brown eyes met hers. "I could take you to see it."

Claire didn't answer. She had deliberately put all thoughts of any future out of her mind, trying to enjoy each minute as it came.

"Do you think you could escape to London at all?" he asked.

"I don't know. Maybe."

Her mind raced. The school summer holidays were long. William would be working right through them. Could she possibly ask Sally to have the children again? It was hard enough to find time for Emily Love at this time of year.

"When?" she asked, looking straight ahead. On the horizon she could see an empty shell of a derelict house, ivy outlining its roofless walls.

"Next week? Is Tuesday a good day?"

"I'd need to work it out," she replied. "I could ask Sally to have the children again, but I don't want her to get suspicious."

"Suspicious of what?"

"I don't know. Nothing. I don't know." She felt flustered.

"There's nothing to be suspicious about, is there?" He looked at her.

"No, of course not. I just don't know what she'd think."

"Where does she think you are this afternoon?" His eyes were back on the road.

"With a customer."

"Well, I am a customer, aren't I?" Stefan asked innocently.

"Yes, I suppose you are," she said slowly.

"You could be with a customer again," he said.

"Yes, I suppose I could."

"Anyway, you'd find this exhibition inspirational, I'm sure, and so it would really be research for your work."

"I'll see," said Claire. "I'll e-mail you."

"Text me," he said, parking the car back in the lot. "My number's at the bottom of my e-mails."

Claire opened the car door and turned to Stefan.

"Thank you for a really lovely afternoon."

"Thank you. I've enjoyed it very much."

"And thank you for this," she said, touching the necklace around her neck. She got out of the car.

"Send me a text about next Tuesday," he said, and she closed the door and walked away. No good-bye kiss or hug. She didn't look back. As she started reversing her car from the parking space, she saw the little sports car drive away behind her. She could still hear Leonard Cohen's languorous voice in her head.

Her mind was a blur as she drove back to Sally's to collect the children. Of course she wanted to see him in London. How could she not? She'd only left him minutes earlier, but she was desperate to see him again, just one more time, just to be with him for a few more hours.

I have a huge favor to ask you," she said to Sally. "Is there any way you'd have the three of them again next Tuesday?"

"Of course," said Sally. "They're no trouble at all. I think they actually manage to instill a bit of calm into my boys. Where are you going?"

"I have to go to London." She could feel herself blushing with guilt.

"Oh," said her friend inquisitively. "To see another customer?"

"To see an exhibition," said Claire quickly. "Matisse at the Royal Academy. I really want to go. Inspiration for work. A business trip, really."

"I saw a bit of a program about that on BBC4, before Gareth changed the channel to watch rugby. I'd love to see it myself. Why don't we go at the weekend? It would be more fun together, a girlie day out in the city. A bit of shopping, lunch—maybe an afternoon gin and tonic at the Ritz. What do you think? We could ask the men if they'd look after the kids."

"Actually," said Claire, panicking. "I think it would be better on my own so I can concentrate properly. I might go look in that new shop I'm selling to as well."

"Okay," said Sally, shrugging her shoulders. "It was just a thought. Hey, I like your necklace. You didn't have that on earlier."

Claire touched it. She had meant to take if off before getting out of the car. In her flustered state she had forgotten.

"I just got it," she said. "In the gallery. Where I was this afternoon."

"I thought you went to a customer's house."

"It was next door to a nice gallery."

Sally looked quizzically at her face. "You look like you're having some sort of hot flash, Claire. Maybe you're going through an early menopause?"

When the children were in bed, and while William fiddled with wiring in the summerhouse, Claire took her cell phone into the study.

Sending texts wasn't something she did very often. In fact she didn't do it at all. She phoned her friends, e-mailed customers. The need to text had somehow passed her by.

Sitting at the computer, she managed to copy Stefan's phone number onto her phone but was suddenly blank about how to actually send a message. She couldn't seem to get the numbers to change to letters on the tiny screen.

"Can you tell me how to send a text?" she asked Sally on the phone.

"Send a text? You don't know how to send a text? I remember showing you years ago. You can't have forgotten."

"I've forgotten," admitted Claire.

"You artistic types are always so technologically behind." Sally laughed.

"I manage a whole business online, don't I?" Claire said crossly.

"Who do you need to send a text to anyway?"

"Customers," said Claire. "And my mother. She's just got her first cell phone. In fact she keeps sending me texts I don't know how to reply to."

Sally sighed. "I expect you still use a carpet beater and put the washing through a mangle."

"Okay," said Claire, annoyed with her friend. "Don't worry. I'll just go to a phone shop and humiliate myself in front of some spotty teenager by asking him to explain texting to me."

"Calm down," said Sally. "Let's go through this step-by-step. I'll talk slowly."

Thank you for this afternoon. Next Tuesday is ok. C

I'll meet you outside the exhibition. 2pm? S

CHAPTER 15

A palette of chalky-white shades, collections of weathered country furniture, and displays of unusual objects create a charming effect in the large living room.

Just once more, she repeated over and over in her head in time to the rattling of the train. The journey to London took an hour, but it seemed much longer. She'd bought a magazine at the station; it lay unread on her lap. She couldn't concentrate. Her eyes were constantly drawn to the countryside speeding by outside, willing it to go by faster.

She'd had another trip to the lovely clothes shop, bribing the three children with packs of chips to sit in the corner while she hastily tried on a mountain of outfits. She had bought a swirling raspberry-red skirt which she wore with a vintage lace blouse she'd had since her college days. It fit for the first time since the children had been born, and looked perfect with the necklace Stefan had given her.

"Looking gorgeous again," Sally had said as she dropped off the children. "Have fun in the big city."

From the station Claire took a taxi. She couldn't face the busy hustle of the Tube, the hot walks down long, tiled corridors, the jostling on crowded platforms. After a frustratingly slow crawl through London traffic the taxi drew up outside the imposing building of the Royal Academy of Arts. Long banners advertising the exhibition hung down the length of the stone facade. The street was crowded with fast-moving Londoners and loitering Japanese tourists. Fumbling in her purse for the fare, Claire was aware of buses beeping at her double-parked taxi. In her hurry, her change spilled onto the rutted rubber floor of the cab.

"Come on, darling," said the taxi driver as she scrabbled to pick up the coins. "I can't sit here all day waiting for you."

Flustered, Claire handed the driver a twenty-pound note.

"Haven't you got anything smaller?" More beeping came through the open window.

"Keep the change and what's on the floor," she said, opening the door to hot traffic fumes and the noisy street. She took a deep breath and wove her way across the dense crowd of people in front of her.

Walking into the sudden quiet of the large entrance courtyard, she could see Stefan sitting on the steps. Her heart was beating rapidly beneath the white lace of her shirt. As she walked toward him she straightened her skirt and checked that the buttons on her blouse weren't coming undone; they had a habit of popping open and revealing more than she intended. He hadn't seen her. As she got closer Claire realized he was on his phone. He was talking, looking down, running his hand through his hair, laughing. Only a few feet separated them now. Claire slowed down her steps, waiting for him to notice her.

"I miss you too," Claire heard him say, and then he laughed again, throwing back his head. Suddenly he saw her. "I've got to go."

He stood up smiling and slipped his phone into his pocket.

"It's great to see you," he said, taking both her hands in his and gently kissing her cheek. "Was the journey all right?"

"Fine," she said. "I haven't been on a train for ages."

"Do you need a cup of tea to recover?"

"No, let's see the exhibition first."

"Come on, then, I've bought the tickets already." Stefan touched her back lightly as he led her up the steps. "You look lovely," he said. "Nice necklace!"

Claire touched the smooth pearl buttons and smiled.

Inside the gallery they moved slowly around the hushed white rooms looking at the brightly colored paintings on the walls. Matisse's women stared out at them, serenely beautiful; their flat calm faces looked at Claire amid a riot of bold pattern and color. Sensual feline bodies silently reclined on sofas upholstered with chaotic patterns, or sat upright, waiting, on bright wooden chairs. In front of the figures fruit or flowers in decorated vases sat on sumptuously patterned tablecloths. In the last gallery the female figure was stripped down to cutout shapes of paper—so simple, yet strangely erotic. To Claire these women looked strong and confident, at ease with their bodies, happy in their eternal settings. It made her feel aware of her own body; conscious of herself, her limbs, the way she walked. She and Stefan didn't speak as they moved around the quiet rooms side by side, but Claire felt powerfully aware of him beside her, the inches between them charged with a magnetic energy drawing them together, pushing them apart. Her skin prickled with his proximity to her. They didn't speak until they were outside again, blinking in the bright August sun.

"Now what?" asked Stefan. "Tea? Coffee? Something stronger?"

"Tea would be good."

"Do you like champagne?"

"It's been a long time since I've had any real champagne," she admitted. "Cava and a bit of fizzy Australian is the closest I get to it these days."

"I'll take you to my favorite bar," he said. "They do great champagne cocktails. It's not far."

They walked out into the busy pavements of Piccadilly and up Regent Street. Claire caught tantalizing views of clothes in shop windows as Stefan led her quickly on down the side of Liberty's and into the narrow streets of Soho. Her feet began to sting in her high strappy sandals as they negotiated the fruit barrows of Berwick Street. Stefan obviously hadn't heard of "taxi shoes." He took her hand as she slowed down and lost pace with him.

"Nearly there." He smiled at her.

He kept hold of her hand. Claire forgot about her painful feet.

At last Stefan stopped outside a narrow doorway. A tall man in a black suit stood just inside the door, and Stefan said something she couldn't quite hear and signed a large, lined book, then together they passed into a darkly lit corridor. As she followed Stefan up a steep staircase, Claire felt nervous. She remembered that she didn't really know him at all. At the top of the stairs a door was open and light flooded out. Claire stepped into a huge, starkly modern room. Along its longest wall a bar stretched the entire length. It sparkled with every bottle of spirit imaginable, suspended, like glistening jewels, on the wall or lining glass shelves behind. Long windows looked out over a leafy square on one side and into a busy Soho street on another. Each wall was hung with large black-and-white abstract paintings. Pale suede sofas and low glass tables were arranged around the room. It was empty apart from a group of businessmen seated beside one window and an eccentrically dressed man with a beautiful woman, both reading magazines. She was surrounded by shopping bags. Moschino, Chanel, Donna Karan, Burberry. Serious shopping bags.

"What sort of bar is this?" she whispered to Stefan.

"It's a members' bar," he said, leading her to a cream-colored sofa looking out over the square.

"Like a private club?" He sat down beside her so that they were both facing the window.

"Sort of. For creative media types. Do you like it?"

"I don't know," she admitted. "It's a far cry from our local pub in the village."

He laughed. A waiter, young, blond, and chiseled, silently put down a bowl of olives on the table in front of them.

"Hello, Barney," Stefan said to the waiter. "Any luck with the auditions?"

"No, I never seem to get a break. Thanks for asking, though, Stefan. What can I get you?"

"Could we see the cocktail menu, please?"

In seconds the waiter reemerged and handed them both a long, cream-colored menu of champagne combinations that Claire had never even imagined.

"You choose," Stefan said to her. "For us both."

"I think the responsibility is too much." The list seemed to blur in front of her. She pointed her finger randomly. "Elder-flower liqueur and champagne sounds lovely."

"Two elderflowers," Stefan said to the waiter.

As they waited for their drinks they were silent. Stefan's phone rang and he apologized as he took the call. Claire stared out of the window at the chestnut trees in the square below; their leaves moved gently in a breeze. Couples lay splayed out on the grass relaxing in the summer weather. Office workers sat on benches drinking out of cardboard coffee cups or hurried down the narrow paths crisscrossing the square, eager to get to wherever they were going. After a few minutes a disheveled man staggered into the square shouting and waving a bottle shrouded in a crumpled shopping bag. A tangled mat of gray half hid his face. As Claire watched him he looked up. She felt as though he was looking at her, shouting at her.

Inside the long closed windows she couldn't hear the world outside, only the crisp clink of glass meeting glass and the hushed, low murmur of conversation. Below her the man was mouthing silent, angry words up toward her. Suddenly he sank down onto his knees, his face twisted as though in tears. The people in the square ignored him. Claire looked away as well. On the other side of the room the barman was mixing their drinks in tall champagne flutes. When she looked back down again, the man was shuffling away, hunched up beneath his thick layers of coats. He threw his empty bottle toward a bin. It missed and smashed silently onto the path.

Claire suddenly wished she was at home in her beautiful house, in her comfortable kitchen, cooking, cleaning, and weeding the garden, playing games with the children. She was a married woman, a mother of three, nearly forty years old. She didn't belong here. She had been wrong to come to London. Wrong to see Stefan again.

"Are you all right?" he asked, putting his phone away. "I'm so sorry about that. It was about a job I'm doing next week. I've turned my phone off now." He turned to face her, studying her with concern. "You look sad."

"This just doesn't feel right," said Claire.

"Here?" Stefan asked, looking around the room. "We could go somewhere else. Just a cup of tea in a café, if you like?"

"No. I mean I don't think I should have come to London at all."

"You didn't like the exhibition?" His expression looked hurt. Claire reached out and didn't quite touch his arm.

"No," she said. "I liked the exhibition very much, just like you thought I would. I mean I don't know what I'm doing here, with you. I'm not sure it's a very good idea."

"Being with me isn't a good idea?" he asked her slowly.

"Yes," she said, nodding, then shaking her head. "I mean, no, it's not a good idea."

The waiter appeared and placed two tall champagne glasses in front of them. Claire picked up her glass and took a sip; it was delicious, like a fizzy elderflower cordial. Stefan put down his glass and leaned forward. His hair fell forward across one eye and he pushed it back to look at Claire, his face serious.

"Do you want to go right now?" he asked.

"Yes. I think I ought to." She finished her drink much too quickly and stood up, reaching for her bag. Stefan watched her but he didn't move. Claire felt light-headed as she fumbled for her purse. "I'll just pay for the drinks before I go."

"It's all right; they just go on my bill. I settle up at the end of every month."

"Oh." Claire felt suddenly awkward. "I'll just leave, then. Thank you for taking me to the exhibition." She took a small step away from the sofa toward the door. Stefan didn't make any attempt to follow her or to ask her to stay. She stopped and looked down at his face for one last time. "If you ever need any more aprons or perhaps a cushion or some bunting or a Christmas stocking . . . You know my e-mail address, or text me, or, you know, just place an order on my Web site." Stefan stared up at her, a flicker of a smile playing on his lips. "I can make anything you like," she continued, unable to stop talking, unable to drag her gaze from his. "I'm sure I could do something more macho for your flat, if you want . . ." *Just walk away and stop making a fool of yourself,* she pleaded with herself.

"Claire," Stefan said, and reached for her hand. "I don't want any black leather cushions or whatever you have in mind for macho soft furnishings." He was laughing. "I just want you to sit down." In an instant Claire found herself sitting beside him again as though pulled by some irresistible force. He moved slightly nearer to her, his thigh nearly touching her own, his hand still holding hers. Claire looked into his soft, dark eyes as his thumb began to make slow, tiny circles around her palm.

"What are you doing?" she asked.

"What are we doing?" he replied.

"I don't know."

"Can I kiss you?" His face was already dangerously close, his breath warm on her cheek.

"Okay," she whispered.

He softly touched her lips with his. The sensation was so intense it almost hurt. He moved away, looked at her, and then kissed her again. Claire closed her eyes, but bright colors swirled in front of her. Her lips parted; he tasted of champagne. She felt dizzy. The kiss seemed to last forever. When Claire finally pulled away, she was amazed to find the room still there, the bottles still sparkling on the shelves, the other customers still talking and drinking at the tables, as if nothing had happened at all.

"Are we allowed to do this here?" she asked.

"I don't know," he said, and kissed her again.

After what seemed like a long time they sat side by side again, only their hands still entwined.

Stefan ordered more drinks. "Are you glad you didn't go?"

he asked, turning to Claire; he put his arm along the top of the
sofa and his fingers gently stroked the back of her neck.

Claire felt too dazed and happy to reply. "I've wanted to kiss
you since the moment I first saw you," Stefan continued. "When
I walked into your garden and found you, covered in flour,
making mince pies on a boiling day, I thought you were the
most gorgeous thing I'd ever seen."

Claire looked at him; she hardly dared to breathe. It was
impossible to think of anything to say, so she took a sip of the
champagne cocktail that Barney had placed in front of her.

"I can't explain it," he went on. "It was like an instant connection. I knew you at once. I recognized you as if we'd known
each other before. I knew how you would be; intelligent, kind,
funny, easy to talk to, beautiful. And you were all those things;
you are all those things and more."

Claire laughed. She wondered if she was asleep and
dreaming.

"This isn't sounding right," he said. "I sound ridiculous, I
know, but that's how I felt. How I feel. But I know you're married. I know it's impossible. I know it's wrong to ask to see you
at all. I'm sorry, Claire. I thought maybe we could just be
friends, but I can't. I can't pretend not to feel the way I do about
you." She felt Stefan looking at her, searching her face for a
response, waiting for her reaction. She looked back out over
the square below and took another sip of champagne.

"When I first saw you standing in my garden that day," she
said, without looking at him, "I expected you to be arrogant,
conceited; full of yourself, maybe. But within minutes I felt as
if I knew you too, as though you understood me. It was so easy.
Just being with you felt so easy. You're right; it was like an instant connection between us. When you left after the photo
shoot, I couldn't believe that you would go; I thought you

would come back . . . And then your sister's apron and you said you'd come and collect it, but then you didn't and your e-mail sounded cold and so detached."

"I couldn't come," interrupted Stefan. "I decided I couldn't see you again. It would be too difficult to hide the way I feel. I thought you'd send the apron and I hoped I'd be able to forget you."

"And I thought I'd send the apron and try to forget you."

"But I couldn't forget you. I needed to see you again. You were like an obsession."

"Like an illness."

"Yes."

"After you came to the house to take the pictures, I couldn't breathe properly for days," Claire told him. "I had to remind myself to breathe. I couldn't eat. I couldn't sleep. I was hardly safe to drive the car. You were in my head the whole time." She looked at him. It was a huge relief to confess it all to him.

He raised her hand to his lips and gently kissed the tip of each finger. "Are you very happily married?"

Claire laughed. "What do you think? Would I be doing this if I was?"

"I don't know," he said. "You tell me."

"No, I'm not happily married," she said. "I'm miserable. I don't think I realized how unhappy I was until I met you. I hardly recognize William anymore. He's obsessed with the house, with making it a perfect home."

"It is a perfect home."

"But what's the point of it if everything else is sacrificed? You said you thought I might be jealous of the house. I was cross with you for saying that at the time, but the more I think about it the more I think you were right. I have been jealous. The house has come between us. William changed when we moved there; he seemed to fall in love with the house and out of love with me. But since I met you, I'm not jealous anymore. Now I just don't care."

"How could he not love you?" Stefan asked, pulling her close to him again. After a little while he said, "You don't have to stay with him."

"It's all so complicated. I have three children to think of."

Stefan ordered another two champagne cocktails. Claire drank hers quickly.

"I feel like I've waited years for you," Stefan said quietly.

She gently touched his face. He took her in his arms again and kissed her cheek, her neck, her lips.

She pulled away from him. "I should go."

"I don't want to let you go," he said. "I need to be with you."

"And I need time to think." She looked out of the window into the square again. The shadows were long. She looked at her watch. "I really have got to go. I'll miss my train. It's at five-thirty."

"We'll never get there," he said, looking at his own watch. "You'll have to catch the next one."

"I'll be late for the children. Late for Sally again."

"Phone her," he said. "If we leave now, you'll definitely get the six-thirty."

As they stepped out into the street, Claire felt her head spin. She wasn't used to champagne in the afternoon, and she remembered that she hadn't eaten lunch. Stefan took her hand.

"Shall we get a cab?" he asked.

"You don't have to come too."

"I want to. I want to be with you for as long as possible."

The bright light and sounds of the London evening brought reality back to Claire like a blow.

"Do you smoke?" she asked suddenly as Stefan searched the street for a taxi.

"I gave up a year ago. Why, do you?"

"I gave up seventeen years ago, but I need a cigarette right now. I think it might help me think more clearly."

He laughed. "You are full of surprises. Do you really want a cigarette?"

"Yes," she said. "I do."

"Okay, let's buy some, then."

They walked to the square that they had been looking down on from the bar, bought a pack of cigarettes from a vendor, and sat on a bench. Claire took one from the pack. Stefan held out a lighter to her.

"I'll light it," she said, taking the lighter from his hand. As she breathed in she felt dizzy, but she also felt calmer.

"Nice?" he asked, putting one hand around her shoulder and lighting his own cigarette with the other.

"I'm sorry," she said. "I don't know what has come over me and now I've made you smoke again after giving up."

"One won't hurt," he said, smiling at her.

"I don't know how we got from fairy cakes and cups of tea to champagne and cigarettes so fast."

"Am I leading you astray?" he asked, and blew out a long stream of smoke.

She grinned at him. He kissed her. She didn't want the kiss to ever end. At last she pulled away.

Her blouse had come undone of its own accord. She hastily did it up before she exposed her bra to half of Soho.

Stefan laughed. "I had no idea it would be so easy to undress you."

"Look at me." Claire was laughing too. "Making out on

park benches, clothes falling off, illicit cigarettes. I feel about fifteen years old."

Stefan tenderly took her face between his hands and kissed her again.

"When can I see you next?" he asked

"I'm frightened," she said.

"Of what?"

"That you'll hurt me."

"I'll never do that."

"Promise?"

Their eyes met.

"I promise," he said, gently kissing the palm of her hand.

They were silent in the taxi to the station. Stefan held her close against him, his arm around her. He stroked her hair.

"Don't come with me," she said as the taxi stopped outside the entrance. "I don't think I can manage an emotional good-bye on the station platform."

"No *Brief Encounter* moment?"

"No," she said softly, gently cupping his face with her hands, pulling it to hers and kissing his lips.

"When can I see you?" he asked her again.

"Next week?"

"I'm going to New York next week," he said. "I'm doing a job there."

Claire raised her eyebrows. "Are you sure you want to be with me? I don't think I fit in with your sophisticated jet-set, bachelor life." She was only half joking.

"You are a beautiful, stylish, and talented woman," he said, kissing her briefly between each word. The he sat back from her and looked at her seriously. "I don't know if you really want to get involved with me. A lonely, middle-aged photographer who takes pictures of other people's happy lives instead of making one for himself."

The taxi driver looked over his shoulder from the driver's seat. "Are you getting out or what?"

"Will you be back by Friday?" She'd have to ask Sally again to mind the children. Or maybe she could ask her mother.

"Yes."

"Meet me at the hotel that you took me to?" said Claire, opening the taxi door. "Two o'clock."

She shut the door quickly and the rush-hour commuters absorbed her in seconds. Now she was late for the six-thirty train. She only just made it, running down the platform, getting on just as the whistle blew for the train's departure.

Trying to catch her breath, Claire flopped into a seat. She felt stunned. Wasn't this what she had longed for: a declaration of his feelings, an opportunity to express hers? Why did she feel so shocked? So terrified? As the train slowly pulled through London's suburbs, she felt calmer. She started to think back over the afternoon, remembering his kisses, his hands, the strong hard muscles of his back she had felt through his shirt. She remembered what he had said, how he had made her feel. Putting her hands to her cheeks, she felt her face flush with the memories.

She tried to think about something else. *Supper.* What to cook for supper? Pasta? Sally would have fed the children, so it would be just her and William. *William.* She felt a huge wave of guilt wash over her. How could she face him tonight? Her head began to ache. She felt sick. Too much champagne. That cigarette had been a mad idea. The whole afternoon had been mad. Spaghetti Bolognese? She thought again. Pork chops and baked potatoes with peas? Stir-fry and noodles? *Stefan lying on a bed.* How lovely it would be to be lying beside him.

She closed her eyes, and tried to get rid of the image. *Trifle,* there was still trifle left from Sunday lunch—that would do for dessert.

Her phone buzzed with the sound of an incoming text.

I can't stop thinking about you

She didn't reply, couldn't think how to reply.

She thought of the nice mothers at Ben's nursery, Mrs. Wenham the headmistress, her own mother—what would they think?

A re you all right?" said Sally, opening the door to her. "You look really pale."

"I've got a migraine," Claire replied. "I'm so sorry I'm late."

"It's fine. Everyone has been fine. We've had tea and Ben has had a bath after an accident with some spaghetti."

"Thank you so much," said Claire. "I owe you such a big favor."

"It's okay," said Sally again. "Are you sure you're all right? You really don't look well."

"I just need to get home."

"Tell William to put the children to bed."

"He said he'd be home late tonight."

"Well, you go to bed yourself as soon as you can," said Sally, looking concerned. "This is what happens when you go gallivanting in the city on your own. Next time take me!"

"I know," said Claire. "I think I could have done with a chaperone."

* * *

Bedtime seemed to take ages. Ben went to sleep in the car on the way home. She desperately hoped that he would stay asleep and she could just carry him to bed. No such luck. He started screaming as soon as she lifted him from the car seat and then wanted *The Gruffalo* read four times in a row to get him to stay in bed. Emily had left her Nintendo DS in Sally's house and demanded to be taken back to fetch it. When Claire said no she refused to get into her bed and locked herself in the bathroom.

"Why are you so mean, Mummy?" she shouted from behind the door.

Oliver was hungry and decided to pour himself a bowl of Rice Krispies, spilling half the box all over the kitchen floor, followed by a large splash of milk.

Claire was exhausted. At last they were all asleep. With great relief she was able to lie down in her own room. From her horizontal position on the bed she slipped off her skirt and blouse and slid between the cool sheets, still in her underwear. William wasn't home, and the house was blissfully dark and quiet. She lay with her head buried in her pillow, trying to smother the throbbing pain. Trying to go to sleep.

Somewhere downstairs she could hear a phone, her cell. It was the sound of a new text message. Could she wait until morning? She lay there feeling ill, but the thought of a text from Stefan gave her the strength to get up and go downstairs. Moonlight through the windows cast deep shadows in the hallway. Claire searched through her bag in the semidarkness for her phone.

Good night. I'll be dreaming of you.

Suddenly Claire heard the key turn in the lock of the front door. She was standing beside it. Quickly she turned her phone off and threw it into her bag; she dropped the bag onto the floor and kicked it into the corner.

The door opened. William walked in and switched on the light.

"What are you doing?" he asked, looking at Claire standing in her bra and panties in the middle of the hall.

She started to laugh, despite her headache, suddenly aware that this could look like some misjudged attempt at seduction.

"Why are you laughing?" he said crossly. "What's going on?"

"I thought I heard a noise," she said. "I've been in bed. I've got a really bad headache, but I heard something, so I came down to check."

"I've got a bit of a headache too," he said, rubbing his temples. "Though after the day I've had, I'm not surprised."

"Oh, dear," said Claire, trying to sound sympathetic, but starting to climb the stairs at the same time.

"Why were you in bed in your underwear?" he asked.

"Because I couldn't be bothered to take it off." She sighed, slowly climbing a few steps more.

"Is that a new necklace?"

"I've had it for years." She was nearly on the landing.

"What's for supper?" William called up after her as she made it through the bedroom door.

"There's leftover trifle," she replied, and collapsed back into bed.

Chapter 16

The overall effect is stunning.

Good morning. S.

Claire had waited until William had left for work before turning on her phone.

Good morning. C.

What are you doing?

Making breakfast. What are you doing?

Lying in bed remembering yesterday.

Nice memories?

Very.

I wish I was with you.

Claire was making pancakes. It was a breakfast treat usually reserved for Sundays, but she wanted to do something special for the children to make up for her day away from them. They were still asleep. In a minute she would wake them up.

Her phone buzzed again. She looked at the message, expecting it to be another from Stefan. But it was from her mother.

Hello darling. Are you coming to Cornwall? Love Mum x

Claire couldn't think about Cornwall. She couldn't think about the future at all. The next time she could see Stefan again was as far as she could go.

All day Claire felt as though her mind was whirling, her stomach tight with fear but also giddy with happiness. She went over and over the previous afternoon in her head, remembering every detail, every moment, every word.

I miss you, he sent as she walked down the aisles in Waitrose, trying to concentrate on what to buy and to stop Oliver and Emily from filling the trolley with sweets.

Thinking of your beautiful eyes, as she sat with a group of other mothers at a Play Barn birthday party, drinking a tasteless cappuccino and trying to keep Ben in sight as he careened down terrifying slides into a ball-filled enclosure.

This time yesterday you were in my arms, as she scraped ground-in Play-Doh from the coir matting on the stairs.

As she was making macaroni and cheese for tea, her mother phoned.

"Did you get my text?"

"Yes, Mum," said Claire, trying to stop Ben from climbing onto a chair beside the stove.

"And I sent an e-mail you haven't answered. I was ringing all day yesterday and you weren't there. Are you all right?"

"I'm fine, Mum. Just a bit busy."

"You sound odd."

"Thanks! Are you all right?"

"I'll tell you how I am when I see you," her mother replied mysteriously. "Can you get away for a few days to come to Cornwall?"

"I'm still not sure," said Claire, stirring pasta into the cheese sauce. "No. It's too hot!"

"Pardon?"

"Sorry, Mum. Ben is trying to steal bits of pasta from the saucepan."

"Just for three or four days. I'd love to see the children playing on the beach by the cottage. It looks beautiful on the Internet. The children will love it."

"Yes, I know," said Claire. "I'll try my best. Ben, get down and go and play with Emily."

"Do you have a webcam on your computer? I've just bought one. If you have one we could talk and I could see you at the same time."

"No, we don't have a webcam," Claire said, wondering what other pieces of technology her mother was about to embrace.

"Well, you'll have to get one. You've got to keep up, Claire."

"But what if I can't come to Cornwall? Can you cancel the cottage?"

"Oh, that doesn't matter; I'll be going there anyway."

"Are you sure you're all right?" asked Claire, suddenly worried about her mother, who sounded a little odd herself.

"Better than ever. Let me know if you can come. I'd love to see you."

"Would you be able to come and look after the children for me next Friday?" *Please say yes,* thought Claire.

"Sorry, I'll be busy next Friday. Is it something important?"

"Not really."

"Look, I must go. I'm running late."

Claire suddenly had a huge urge to confide in her mother. She took a deep breath. "Mum, I want to tell you something . . ." But her mother had already gone. Claire stood staring at the phone in her hand.

"It's probably for the best; I don't need to tell anyone. Just my little secret."

"Secret, secret," echoed Ben.

William was home early with flowers.

"What have I done to deserve these?" asked Claire, looking at the bunch of white lilies in his hand. She hesitated before taking them from him. Her grandmother had always told her that white lilies were for innocence and she felt drenched in guilt.

"I just thought I'd been neglecting you lately," he said. "When I saw you last night with your bad headache, looking so thin, I was worried about you. I wanted to let you know that even though I might work late or be busy building the summerhouse, I do think of you." He took her in his arms and hugged her. Claire hadn't expected this at all.

"I think you need a little treat," William said, still holding her.

"Do I?"

"I've booked a table for two, just you and me, at the Italian bistro in town for this Saturday night. I've asked my parents to come down to babysit."

"Oh, how lovely," she said, trying her best to sound enthusiastic.

"You deserve it, darling," he said. "I know how hard you work with the children and your little business." He lifted her chin and kissed her mouth; his lips felt dry and rough.

"Yuk," said Oliver, walking in the room. "That's disgusting. Stop it."

William let go of Claire and scooped Oliver up into a fireman's lift and ran with him around the room.

"Mum," Oliver called through breathless laughter. "Your phone was ringing." He held it out in his hand from his position over William's shoulder.

Claire grabbed it from him as they passed her.

I can still feel your lips on mine, more delicious than any cake or champagne.

She quickly turned off her phone and pushed it to the back of the tea-towel drawer. Then, lifting down the Poole Pottery jug from the dresser, she started to arrange the lilies.

"I do love you, Claire," said William, coming up behind her and encircling her in a tight embrace. She felt sure that he would feel her heart thumping through her shirt and wonder what was wrong, but he quickly released her and headed for the door.

"I'll just go down to the summerhouse and do a few things before supper. Call me when it's ready."

CHAPTER 17

"I know how lucky I am . . ." says Claire.

The lilies lasted a week. The air of the house hung thick with their sweet, heavy scent, making Claire feel slightly sick. In that time she had taken the children swimming three times, been to town to buy them new shoes, had two picnics with Sally and the children, four trips to the supermarket, two to the organic farm shop, had the car serviced, taken Macavity to the vet with a cut nose, received twelve orders online for cushions, aprons, and bunting, had two inquiries from new shops, sent out orders to an interiors shop in Glasgow and a small gallery in St. Ives, cut out and appliquéd twenty cushion covers (very late at night), entertained and fed her parents-in-law, and been out for a meal with William.

In that time she had also had forty-two texts from Stefan and she knew that he had photographed a converted windmill near Cambridge and a Gothic mansion in Yorkshire, got a plane from Heathrow to New York, photographed a Manhattan loft apartment, bought a new jacket, been to an opening at the Museum of Modern Art, had dinner with an actor friend, seen a play on Broadway, and at the time she was throwing the wilting lilies on the compost heap, he was somewhere above the Atlantic on his way home.

Two days left until she saw him again.

She had been nervous about the meal with William. She couldn't envisage them sitting across a table from each other with anything to say.

His parents had arrived later than arranged on Friday night, his mother showering the children with presents, cuddles, and games and then expecting Claire to get them into bed and asleep in time for the adults to eat at a reasonable hour.

"You should be much firmer with them," she said as Claire stopped stirring the risotto yet again to put Ben back to bed and to ask Emily and Oliver to get back into theirs.

"They're just very excited about your visit," said Claire through gritted teeth. "That's why they can't sleep."

"Lights out, door closed, no nonsense," said her mother-in-law. "That's how it was for William. He knew I meant it."

"Maybe you could go up and have a go, then, dear," suggested her father-in-law from behind his glass of whiskey.

"What a good idea," said Claire. "I'll get on with this risotto, or we'll never get to eat."

You look much too thin," said her mother-in-law as Claire came downstairs dressed in a simple black silk dress the following evening. "You girls and your ridiculous diets. I don't know why you can't accept that you should be filling out by the time you get to your age. You can't hold back time."

"I haven't been on a diet," protested Claire.

"It's probably running around after three children that keeps her so lovely and slim," said her father-in-law, smiling at her.

"I knew three would be too many for you to cope with," put

in her mother-in-law. "I told that to William before Ben was
born. He agreed with me. Said he'd only wanted two at the
most, but it was too late by then."

"I cope as well with three as I did with two," Claire insisted.

"And they're a credit to you," said her father-in-law kindly.

"Thank you," said Claire, wondering how he had managed
to live with his wife for so long.

"I'm only saying it's a strain on you both. Poor William,
working all hours to keep you all."

"I do contribute financially as well," said Claire, trying to
keep her voice steady.

"Well, maybe when Ben's in full-time school, you'll be able
to get a proper job again," her mother-in-law continued.

"Are you ready to go?" asked William, coming downstairs.

"Definitely," said Claire, stepping out of the door as quickly
as she could.

Claire needn't have worried that they would have nothing to
say to each other over dinner. From the moment they opened
the car doors William was talking about "Project House." As
they drove into town he was distracted by a site on which three
new houses were being built.

"I can't understand it. How did they ever get permission to
build those hideous eyesores here?"

"I like them," she said. "They look like nice family homes
with fair-size gardens too. It would be lovely to have a view of
the river and be so close to town."

"Modern monstrosities," said William with a shudder, and
then he started talking about their house again.

On and on he talked over the meal: worries about the roof;
windows that he wanted to replace; a plan to move the outside tap. By the time their desserts were served, Claire realized she had hardly said a word all night. She took a chance to

change the conversation when William stopped talking to take a large mouthful of chocolate cheesecake.

"I wonder if your mother's got the children into bed yet?"

"My parents are so good to come and look after them," he said. "It's a shame they don't live nearer."

"The children always seem to enjoy seeing them," said Claire, delicately cracking the sugar crust of her crème brûlée with her spoon. She was imagining what it would be like to be sharing a meal in this intimately lit restaurant with Stefan.

"I was thinking that if our guest room had an en suite bathroom . . ." said William, pausing to shovel in another mouthful of cheesecake.

"Good idea," she said, not really listening.

"It would be easier when my parents come to stay, and then we might tempt them to come more often."

"Actually, I think the guest room is fine as it is," she said, suddenly taking notice. "An en suite would never fit into that room."

"Emily's bedroom next door to it is a very good shape and size for an en suite." He took a pen from his shirt pocket and started drawing a sketch on a paper napkin. "Toilet here, sink unit, maybe a double one here, shower where the cupboard is. Knock a door into the guest room. Move the bed against this wall here."

Claire stopped him. "That's all very nice, but just where is Emily supposed to sleep?"

"Above the kitchen."

"There's nothing but air above the kitchen. It's only a single story."

"Yes," he said. "At the moment. But what if we build on top of it?"

"How?"

"I've planned it all out," he went on, drawing sketches on a separate napkin. "Lower the kitchen ceiling. Raise the roof so that it's more like a large attic space. There would be plenty of room to stand up in the middle. Cupboards down the sides, like this; a dormer window at the back. We'd need planning permission, of course. It could take time to win them round. They're all bloody control freaks in the local planning department. They let those horrible new houses go up, but I bet we'll have to fight for this."

"And it would all be so that your parents could have an en suite bathroom when they come to stay?" asked Claire, trying not to sound annoyed.

"Remember how good they have been to us, darling." Claire thought she could detect a slight edge in his voice that stopped her from going any further.

"It will be nice to see the summerhouse finished," she said, and then William, distracted by his new favorite project, started talking about the tongue and groove he was going to panel the inside walls with and the insulation he was going to put in the ceiling.

T hat was nice, wasn't it?" he said as they drove home, giving Claire's knee a squeeze with his hand.

"Yes, lovely. Thank you." Claire let herself daydream about Stefan as she stared out into the night.

"Couldn't believe the bill, though. We can't afford to be doing that sort of thing too much."

"No." She sighed.

"Not if we're doing this attic conversion and en suite."

She changed the conversation. "My mother wants us to go to Cornwall with her for a few days to a cottage."

"It's a bloody long way for a few days," he said. "I can't go. God knows, I've little enough time to get everything done as it is. I have to finish the summerhouse and I need to sand down the living room floor over the next few weeks. It's covered in scratches from Ben and his ride-on toys."

"I haven't noticed the scratches," she said, looking out into the darkness beyond the window.

"And there's still that stain you made with the raspberries. I'll have to rewax the whole floor. We won't be able to use it for a few days."

"Then maybe the best time to do it is when I'm in Cornwall with the children."

"What about me?" he asked. "Are you going to leave me on my own?"

"It's only for a few days. It will be nice for the children to have a bit of a holiday and I'd like to see my mother. I'm worried about her. Lately she hasn't sounded like herself at all."

"Thank God for that," he said. "I just hope she sounds like someone a bit more tolerable."

"William!"

"It was a joke, darling!" He squeezed her knee again.

"I was thinking about encouraging her to join something—an evening class or maybe a walking group."

"A walking group? They'd never put up with her. They'd probably all walk much faster trying to get away from her. They'd probably run!"

"I suppose that's another joke?" she said, looking at his silhouetted profile and deciding that sometimes she really didn't like her husband at all. "It's not funny. It's mean."

"You're being overly sensitive about her, as usual."

He swung the car into the drive and stopped with a jolt. The front door opened and the bright light of the hallway flooded out. William's mother stood on the porch in her peach-pink padded dressing gown. She put her hand up to wave. William got out of the car and went to greet her.

Chapter 18

Set among idyllic country scenery . . .

At last Friday arrived. Everything had been arranged. Sally had agreed to have the children, yet again. Claire hoped her friend had been joking when she made her promise to have the twins to stay for a week to pay her back.

Claire woke up early, not sure if she'd managed to sleep at all. Every bit of her ached with longing to see Stefan. The more days that went by since their last meeting, the more she yearned to be with him again. She knew he had returned home the day before.

Just touched down. Not long now! x

In the shower she rubbed moisturizing shower gel over her body, wondering how much of her Stefan would be touching later. She found herself speculating about the hotel having rooms available and felt shocked. Was it that sort of hotel? Was she ready to be that sort of woman? *Yes, yes, yes,* said Bad Claire in her head. *Maybe,* said the respectable housewife and mother she tried so hard to be.

The early morning dragged. She unloaded the dishwasher

and swept the floor. William got up and Claire made him coffee and set the table for his breakfast. The children woke up
and she sorted out the usual arguments about cereal. Her husband left for work and she checked her phone.

Counting the hours. x

I'm counting minutes, there are nearly too many to bear. x

She watered the red geraniums on the kitchen windowsill,
looking out at the bright blue sky which heralded a perfect day.
She heard a new text arriving and picked up her phone.

I can't wait to see you again . . .

Claire hadn't finished reading when suddenly the back
door was flung open and Sally's twins tore through the kitchen
shouting for Oliver and demanding games on the computer.
She barely had time to feel confused before Sally walked in
and threw herself down on a chair.

"I've chucked him out," she said.

"Who?" asked Claire. She still had the phone in her hand,
message half unread. She turned it off and slipped it into her
pocket.

"Who do you think?" Sally threw her arms up in exasperation. "That bastard husband of mine."

"Gareth?"

"I hope that he's the only bastard husband I have, otherwise I'm more unlucky than I thought. Yes, of course I mean
Gareth—the sneaky, no-good lump of pigs' crap."

"Oh, Sally," said Claire. "So, he has been having an affair
after all?"

"In his dreams he has." She got up and opened Claire's cookie tin. "He's having a virtual affair. I might have known he'd be too lazy to actually get off his backside and exert himself in some other woman's bed."

"What do you mean?"

"Even you must have heard of cybersex, Claire." Sally finished chewing a mouthful of cookie and took a deep breath. "The lying piece of shit got himself onto a dodgy Internet dating site calling himself 'Big Bad Bear' and has been sending dirty messages to some woman who goes by the name of 'Sweet Betty.'"

"He told you this?" Claire had to resist the urge to laugh at Gareth's cyber-name.

"Oh no." She took another cookie. "I found out for myself last night. He forgot to turn off the Web site before he went to the pub. I sat down to do my Tesco's shop online and found this message from Ms. Betty, or whoever she is, telling me that all she's wearing is a pair of crotchless knickers and an eight-foot boa constrictor—did I want to turn on the webcam to see her?"

Claire did laugh then; she couldn't help it. It seemed too ludicrous to believe. Sally shot her an angry look.

"I can tell you, Claire, there was nothing funny about reading the whole backlog of messages they've been sending back and forth for weeks. It was disgusting, tasteless, tacky stuff. No wonder Gareth started smartening himself up a bit—not to go and meet this woman but rather to sit in our back room while she ogled him on her computer. Probably while I'm upstairs checking our two nine-year-olds' heads for nits or in the living room with a pile of ironing."

"What did you do?"

"I turned on the webcam and told her where she could shove her bloody boa constrictor and what she could do with her crotchless knickers—and believe me, by the look on her scraggy face, I don't think it was what Gareth would have told her to do with them."

"Oh, Sally, this is awful." Claire gave her a hug. Sally's well-upholstered body felt tense, as if she were trying to keep herself from breaking down. "What did you say to Gareth when he came home?"

"There wasn't much to say." Sally moved back to the chair, sat down, and put her head in her hands, burying her fingers into her unbrushed mane of hair. "By the time Gareth came home, I'd put all his stuff in garbage bags and dumped it in the front garden, except for his Iron Maiden T-shirt, which I cut into little pieces and sprinkled up the path."

"What did he do?"

"He was upset about the T-shirt, but when I told him I'd found out about Sweet Betty, he just turned around and started loading the black bags into his car. Obviously it didn't all fit in—there's only so much of a man's life that can fit into a Ford Fiesta—so I expect he'll be back this morning to collect the rest. I didn't want to stay around to see him."

"Where do you think he's gone?"

"Absolutely no idea. And do you know what? I just don't care. I'm so angry."

"Is it that bad?" Claire asked. "It's not as if he actually met up with her. Couldn't you try and work things out together?"

"No way," said Sally. "It doesn't matter if he met her or not. It's what was going on in his head that counts." She sat up straight in the chair and tucked her shirt into her jeans in a businesslike manner. "He's not getting any second chances.

That's why I've made an appointment to see a solicitor at two o'clock this afternoon. I want to know where I stand when I divorce the cheating rat bag."

"Two o'clock?" Claire said quietly. "What about . . ." Her voice trailed off. Suddenly she realized what Big Bad Bear's cyber-infidelity meant for her: she wouldn't be able to see Stefan today.

Sally seemed oblivious. "Obviously I'd be entitled to the house. It's the twins' home and I reckon he'll have to pay quite a lot toward their upkeep. But what I'd really like to know is how often he legally has to have the boys to stay with him. I'm hoping it's every weekend at least. That reminds me, would you take the boys this afternoon while I see this solicitor? I know I said I'd have yours but the last thing I expected was this marital bomb going off. Do you think the gallery you were going to see will understand?"

"Don't worry," Claire said, sitting down beside Sally and taking her hand. "You do whatever you have to do and I'll help in any way I can." Inside, she wanted to weep with disappointment and frustration.

Sally stayed all morning drinking tea, eating cookies, and pouring out her fury and pain in a tirade of insults about Gareth and bravado about her future as a single woman.

After a couple of hours Claire managed to extricate herself with the excuse of needing the toilet. Once in the bathroom, she took her phone out of her pocket and sent a text.

So sorry. Something's come up. I can't make it today. x

After lunch Sally set off for the solicitor's office, leaving Claire to deal with the twins, who had somehow gotten up onto the roof of the summerhouse. Once she'd lured them inside with a bowl of microwave popcorn, put on a DVD, settled all the children in front of it, and locked the back door, she turned on her phone again. One new message.

Don't worry, it's fine. I understand.

Claire read it three times. She could have done with more regret, more disappointment.

What about tomorrow?

I've made plans. I'm free on Sunday afternoon.

Can we rearrange for Sunday then? x

Fine. 2pm?

Great, I'll look forward to seeing you. x

And that was it; no more. Claire spent the rest of the day trying to shake off a sense of unease, though it was hard to pinpoint exactly where it came from.

Sally came back from the solicitors full of determination to file for a divorce.

"Don't you think you should wait?" said Claire. "Let things settle. Talk to Gareth. What about counseling?"

"I'm not having some soft-spoken counselor tell me I should try and understand Gareth because he's still coming to terms with being weaned from his mother, or once found his father dressed in a twinset and pearls, or some other rubbish I no longer care about. I've decided. As far as I'm concerned, Sweet Betty and her overgrown grass snake are welcome to him."

CHAPTER 19

Vintage chic and contemporary essentials
are combined with style throughout.

"I need to go out on Sunday afternoon," said Claire as she sat opposite William at the kitchen table. She topped off his wine-glass and passed him another slice of *ciabatta*.

"Why?"

"I've had an inquiry from a shop a few miles away, a really good one, and I've said I'll go over and show them samples. They're too busy in the week, but the shop is closed on a Sunday, so they said that's the best time." The lie seemed to come so easily.

"I thought I might make a start on sanding the living room floor," he said.

"I thought you were going to do that when we're away?"

"I've got loads of other things to do as well. I want to re-paint the wall on the landing where Ben has scribbled in felt-tip pen and I'll have to mow the grass."

"Okay," said Claire, playing what she hoped would be her trump card. "I'll ask my mother to come over and look after the children."

"All right," he said. "I'll do it. But you won't be too long, will you?"

Leaving the children was like planning a military operation. Claire had given them all an early lunch and loaded and turned on the dishwasher. Oliver and Emily both had birthday parties to go to in opposite directions. She had presents wrapped, cards written, step-by-step instructions printed out on how to find each venue, with arrival and pickup times highlighted. The children were dressed—Oliver in a pirate costume and Emily in a pink T-shirt and tutu skirt with her brand-new school shoes, which she insisted on wearing. Claire left Play-Doh and a "magic water" painting book on the kitchen table to keep Ben occupied while he was on his own with William. The cookie tin had been refilled with homemade jam tarts and a big pan of tomato soup sat beside the Aga for the children's tea. The house was clean and tidy, Macavity fed, plants watered. Claire had hardly had a chance to think about where she was actually going.

It wasn't until she was in the car driving out of the village that she let herself remember what she was doing. In the twelve days since she had seen Stefan in London, her emotions had swung wildly from ecstatic joy to guilt, despair, terror, and back to joy again. For days she had been numb with indecision, completely unable to think of what to do or what she wanted, but in the last forty-eight hours she had emerged from a fog of confusion and the future seemed clearer. Maybe, just maybe, she could leave William—start again. The strength of her feelings for Stefan gave her the courage to imagine a life without William, a life without the house.

It was not impossible. *People do it all the time,* she told herself, thinking of Sally, who was behaving as if separating from Gareth was the best thing that ever happened to her. She had spent the whole of Saturday in Claire's kitchen extolling the joys of being a single woman.

"Good for her," William said to Claire after she left. "She deserves someone better than that layabout."

"I always liked Gareth," Claire said, ironing a dress she planned to wear the next day. "Remember all the help he gave me with the Emily Love Web site?"

William shrugged and flicked on the evening news.

Claire drove down the long, high-hedged roads too fast. She needed to be with Stefan as soon as possible. The weather had been dry all week; the bushes and trees looked parched and dusty. Most of the hedgerow flowers were spent and the hay was piled in neat blond blocks across the close-cropped fields. She hardly noticed the scenery. Her mind was focused on her destination and on the excitement of seeing Stefan again.

Claire needed to find out more about who he really was. He had spent two days with her, observed her daily life, seen her home in detail. He knew where she spent her working day: where she woke up, where she ate her meals, where she brushed her teeth. She had no idea what his flat was like, where or how he spent his time. She wanted to know about his friends, his sister, what he watched on television, his favorite beach, mountain, castle. All this information seemed somehow vitally important. But most of all she just wanted to be with him again, existing in his space, even if they didn't talk at all.

She had only had one text from him since Friday.

Might be held up. Could we make it 2:30?

As her car crunched onto the gravel parking area, Claire could see immediately that his car wasn't there. She looked at her watch. She was five minutes early. She got out and waited, leaning against the warm body of her car. She looked at her reflection in the tinted window of the Mercedes parked beside her.

Her hair was loosely caught up in a clasp at her neck; wisps fell down in curls onto her shoulders and blew gently on the light breeze. She had on a pale pink vintage dress that she hadn't worn for years. The fitted top had a row of tiny fabric-covered buttons ending at a belt at her waist; the short, capped sleeves showed off her smooth, sun-browned arms. The fit was perfect—lightly skimming her hips and flaring out into a swinging, calf-length skirt embroidered with white daisies. She had bought it from Portobello Market before any of the children were born. Teamed with her new sandals, a pair of large sunglasses, and the necklace Stefan had given her, she felt particularly pleased with how she looked.

She willed herself not to look at her watch. The designated time arrived, then passed. He was late. He hadn't been late for her before. She touched her necklace; the smooth, round buttons reassured her. He would surely come soon. After twenty minutes she decided to go into the hotel. The manager recognized her at once.

"You are Stefan's friend," he said, coming round from behind his desk to take her hand and shake it enthusiastically.

"I'm supposed to meet him here," she said.

"Yes, yes, he made a reservation. A table for two on the terrace," said the manager, consulting a big red book on his desk. "He should be here now. Come with me."

He took Claire by the arm and gently directed her through the dining room, onto the terrace and to a table beside the balustrade around the edge. White teacups and silver spoons were already set out neatly.

"Do you like it here, in the shade?" the manager asked her, pulling out a chair. "The shade is nice on a hot day like today."

"Yes, thank you. It's lovely," she said. *Where was he?*

"Don't worry. He will be here soon," said the manager, as if reading her mind. "I expect the traffic was bad getting out of London." He shrugged his shoulders. "Would you like a drink? Wine? Coffee?"

"Could I have a glass of water?" Her mouth felt dry, her stomach tight.

"Of course."

He left her on her own.

She tried not to watch the wide double doors leading out from the hotel's interior. Instead she looked at the other people seated on the terrace: families finishing their Sunday lunches, couples lingering over coffee, and the odd lone customer reading a paper or talking on the phone. They all looked so self-contained and happy.

Claire felt anxious. Supposing he'd had an accident or suddenly been taken ill? She noticed the single dark crimson rose in a small vase on the table. Dark red roses were for mourning. Now she really was counting the minutes. Each one seemed like an hour.

A waitress brought her a clinking glass of ice water. A thin sliver of lime floated among the ice cubes.

"Thank you," she said and took a sip. Then, at last, Stefan was walking toward her.

He looked beautiful in a pale cream linen jacket and white shirt—more tanned than when she had last seen him. She saw

a woman look away from her lunch companion to watch him
as he passed her table. Claire's heart soared as he approached,
suddenly excited. She had to resist the urge to get up and run
to him.

"I'm so sorry," he said, leaning over and kissing her cheek.
"My car wouldn't start. I ended up having to borrow a friend's."

"Oh, dear. The beautiful Claudia. Will she be all right?"

"Yes." He took off his jacket and draped it over the back of
his chair. "I know a very clever mechanic who does wonders
with old cars."

He sat down, and they were silent for a moment. There was
something about him that made Claire nervous. He seemed
detached from her; distant. The softness was missing from his
eyes. He wasn't smiling.

"I've missed you so much," she said, putting out her hand,
touching his. He didn't take it. She withdrew and took another
sip of her water.

"Claire." From his tone she knew he was beginning something she didn't want to hear. "This isn't going to work, is it?"

She was silent; she couldn't reply. She felt as if he had physically hit her. Part of her wanted to get up and walk away
immediately. Go home. But she sat very still and stared at him.

"You know it as well as I do, don't you?" he said, looking at
her across the table. He shrugged his shoulders slightly, as if
waiting for a response.

"Why?" she asked quietly.

He sighed. "Because it's an impossible situation, you and
me. You're married with children. You have a life with someone else. You don't want to hurt your children, to destroy your
home. So what are we doing?"

With her eyes she studied the lichen on the stone balustrade behind him, yellow and white and gray. It looked like a

landscape—trees, bushes, hills—as if someone had painted it on the stone for decoration.

"But I thought . . ." she said, but couldn't find the words to continue.

"What?"

"I don't know what I thought. I thought it could work, that I couldn't feel the way I feel about you and have it not work. I thought you felt the same. What you said when I met you in London? All your texts?"

"I know, I know," said Stefan, running his hand through the dark waves of his hair. "I meant what I said. About the way I felt about you."

"And now, suddenly, you don't feel like that?" she interrupted. "How can you have changed your mind so quickly? Did you see me again as you walked through the door and decide that actually I wasn't quite as attractive as you remembered, not quite so desirable?"

"No," said Stefan, taking her hand in his. "No. I walked through those doors and saw you and you looked more beautiful than ever, so lovely in that dress. I knew it was going to make it even harder to say this—to do this—but I have to. I've spent the last two days trying to decide what would be best."

"I don't understand," she said, looking at the cubes of ice melting in her glass.

"I can't destroy your life. I've seen it, photographed it. Your home. Your children. William. It's perfect. I can't destroy that. You'd never forgive me; I'd never forgive myself." He let go of her hand.

"But the things you said? The way you said you felt about me?" said Claire, still looking at her glass. "Why did you bother saying anything at all if this is how you feel?"

"I wasn't thinking properly. I was being selfish. I was only thinking about myself and how I felt about you; what *I* wanted. Now I realize how impossible this is. You don't really know me. You don't know what I can offer you. *I* don't know what I can offer you. You've got three children. I don't know anything about children. I can't even fit them in my car. What would it do to them if your marriage broke up? I know what my parents' divorce did to me and my sister. You told me how you felt when your father divorced your mother. You don't want to have an affair. I don't want you to have an affair—all the deceit, the lies, the guilt—so what would we do?" He sat back in his chair and looked at her.

Claire wondered if this was some kind of test.

"Would you like to order now?" a waitress appeared beside them.

"What would you like?" Stefan asked Claire. "A cup of tea? A glass of champagne?"

"No," she said. "I definitely don't feel like champagne." She looked at the waitress. "Could I have a gin and tonic, please?"

"A glass of white wine," he said. The waitress moved away.

"I still don't understand what made you change your mind so suddenly," said Claire, looking up at him.

"It was when I sensed your hesitancy. When you didn't answer my text, I knew that you felt uncomfortable. I'd pushed you too fast into something you obviously weren't happy about and—"

"Stop, stop!" She was staring at him. "What text didn't I answer? What wasn't I comfortable with?"

"My text on Friday," said Stefan. He looked slightly embarrassed and lowered his voice. "When I suggested that I book a room for us here."

"I never got a text about that." She thought back to the texts that they'd sent each other on Friday morning before Sally had come crashing in with her news. There had been the text she was reading when Sally arrived. Had she ever finished reading it?

"And then a few hours later you canceled the whole thing. I thought you'd decided it would be wrong to see me at all."

Claire took her phone out of her bag and checked back through all the texts. She hadn't been able to bear to delete any of them. There it was:

I can't wait to see you again . . .

That was as far as she had read before being interrupted. If Sally had entered a few seconds later, she would have had time to read:

. . . I'm so tempted to book a room for us. What do you think?

Claire let out a little groan of dismay.

"I never read this. I didn't cancel because I thought what you had suggested was inappropriate or too fast or whatever other reason you've been concocting in your head. I canceled because my best friend and nominated child minder for that day threw her husband out of their house for cheating with a woman with a boa constrictor."

"Hey, now it's your turn to stop." Stefan laughed for the first time that afternoon. "You're losing me. I'm not even going to ask about the boa constrictor, but you're saying that you never even saw that text?"

"I never saw the text. It had nothing to do with why I had to cancel. I had no one to look after the children and I just didn't think it was going to work if I brought them all with me—no matter how many boxes of crayons I had in my bag." Claire smiled at him. She wanted to reach out and touch his beautiful face, trace the laugh lines around his eyes with her fingertips. It had all been a misunderstanding. Now everything would be all right.

She put her arms out toward him on the table, willing him to lean forward. Instead he leaned back in his chair and stared out across the valley.

"I was so looking forward to seeing you. I was desperate to see you, longing for you all the time I was in New York," he said at last.

"And now?"

"On Friday, when you canceled, it was as if reality suddenly hit me. The bubble burst and I realized it would be wrong. I've spent two days thinking about this. Even now that I know you didn't see the text, I still know that it wouldn't work. The guilt would eat away at us, destroy us in the end."

"How can you be so sure?" she asked.

"I know how I would feel. I can't do it, Claire. I've met William. I can't do it to him. I'd feel awful."

"What about me?" she said, suddenly angry. "Are you thinking about me at all?"

"I'm sorry but I've made up my mind."

He took a pack of Marlboros from his pocket and lit one. He didn't offer one to Claire but left the pack and the lighter beside the vase in the middle of the table. After a few seconds Claire slid a cigarette from the box and lifted it to her lips. Stefan picked up the lighter and lit it for her. She inhaled deeply and then blew out a long stream of smoke. She felt a little better.

"You told me that you end relationships because you are

frightened of getting hurt," she said, touching his arm. "I think you're frightened now. You think I'll hurt you and you're getting out before that happens. Am I right?"

Stefan said nothing. His expression seemed impenetrable.

"To protect yourself," she went on, "you're hurting me first."

"No, Claire," he said, suddenly looking at her again. "I would never hurt you."

"That's what you said in London," said Claire. "That's what you promised. But you *are* hurting me. This hurts."

"I'm not saying it to hurt you," he said, looking upset. "I just think of everyone else that would be hurt. It's not what I want. I'm only being realistic."

"I can't decide if you're being realistic, honorable, or just a coward," she said angrily.

The waitress put their drinks on the table and quickly walked away.

"It's not as if I have some sort of idyllic marriage," Claire said, her fingertips touching the ice-cold glass in front of her.

"I know," he said. "I know you're not happy, but it's up to you to sort things out. You have to decide what happens between you and William."

"What if I decide to leave him?"

"That would be up to you," he replied. "I can't be involved in that."

"Would you wait for me to make a decision?" Claire asked.

"I don't know," he said. "I can't say yes or no. I just don't want to be involved."

"I see," she said. "Fine. I understand."

She stubbed her cigarette out in the ashtray, stood up, and picked up her bag.

"I'd better go."

"Don't," he said. "Don't go yet. You haven't even started your drink."

Claire stood still. She knew she should just turn and walk away across the terrace, get in her car, and leave. She sat down again and took a sip of her gin.

"This doesn't make me at all happy," he said, looking across at her.

"It doesn't make me happy either." She sighed, "I just don't know how you can suddenly be so detached from your emotions."

He shrugged. "You are so lovely, Claire," he said, taking her hand in his. "I want you to know this isn't easy for me. I feel awful about it."

"But you've made up your mind?" She looked at him; he had a look of resigned decision on his face that reminded her of a parent determined to not let a child have another cookie before dinnertime.

"Yes, I've made up my mind. I can't see you again."

Claire felt as if everything was crumbling in front of her. She didn't know how she could cope with this loss, this rejection. Despite the warmth of the afternoon she suddenly felt cold. She picked up her drink and took another sip.

"Are you all right?" he asked. "You're shivering."

"I'm fine. I think I'm just a bit shocked. I wasn't expecting this."

"Here." He took his jacket from behind his chair and came round the table to drape it over her shoulders. "A bit warmer now?"

"Thank you." She could smell him on the jacket. She breathed in; she wanted to capture the smell forever.

"There's something I haven't told you," said Stefan, lighting

another cigarette. "Something that might help you to understand me a bit better. Understand me or maybe even hate me."
He shrugged.

Claire took another cigarette as well. "Tell me."

"I've been in this situation before."

"What do you mean?"

"I mean I've been involved with a married woman before."

She looked at him and then past him, down the valley,
through the trees, and to the river sparkling through the thick
summer foliage. She wasn't sure she wanted to hear Stefan's
story after all. She imagined kicking off her high heels and
running across the hotel lawn, into the woods, and splashing
in the water.

"It was when I was in Australia." He took a drag on his cigarette.

"Go on," she said cautiously.

"She was the wife of a wealthy businessman—he'd made a
fortune buying up land around Sydney. He had a luxury yacht
that they lived on. I was asked to photograph it for a magazine.
That's how I met her."

"Oh," Claire said. "You really have done this before."

"No, it was different. I don't want you to think I make a
habit of picking up married women when I photograph their
homes."

"Only twice, then?" She gave him a quick, ironic smile.

"Yes, only twice."

Their drinks were finished. The waitress cleared the glasses
onto a tray.

"Two coffees," Stefan said to her. He glanced at Claire; she
nodded. The waitress seemed to melt away.

"So what happened?" Claire asked.

"She'd only been married a few months. Things weren't

working out the way she'd hoped. He'd made her leave her job, he was out all day. I suppose she was lonely when I met her. We had an affair."

"For how long?"

"Three years."

"Three years!" she repeated.

"She kept promising to leave her husband. We'd make a plan for the future and then she'd always back out at the last minute. My coming home to England was part of the last plan. I told her I'd had enough. I was going home and if she was serious about me we could meet at the airport and she could come with me. I remember sitting in the departure lounge and slowly realizing she wasn't going to show up. I so nearly walked out of the airport and went to find her."

"But instead you got on the plane?"

"Yes, I got on the plane, came home, found a flat, a job. I had a few short-lived relationships—"

"And here you are," said Claire. Jealousy, anger, hurt, betrayal; it all seemed to be filling her up, oozing out of every pore. What a fool she'd been.

"I don't want you to think that I still have any feelings for her," Stefan continued. "I realize now how shallow my relationship with her had been. How little we had had in common. I never felt the way I feel about you. It never felt so overpowering, so intense."

Claire said nothing.

"Do you despise me?"

The waitress appeared with their coffees. Claire slowly poured milk into hers.

"I don't despise you," she said, taking a sip from her cup. "I think differently about you, about the things you said to me. But I don't despise you."

She knew that now it was time to leave, but she felt unable to move, weighted to her chair by sadness.

"Do you understand why I don't want to get into that situation again?" asked Stefan, looking into her eyes.

"From your point of view I can, but what I can't understand is why you set off down that road at all. Why you got involved with me when you should have just walked away."

"I couldn't walk away," he said, taking her hand. "You were too important to leave behind." He leaned forward and kissed her lips. His mouth felt velvet soft. She wanted more, and kissed him back, unable to stop herself, then pulled away.

"I'm going home now," she said, slipping Stefan's jacket from her shoulders and handing it back to him.

She stood up and started to walk away. Stefan followed her.

With every step they took together across the terrace, through the hotel restaurant and lobby, Stefan became more distant. A barrier had come down between them.

By the time they reached the parking lot, Claire knew she had lost him completely.

"I'll be in touch," he said.

"No," she said. "Don't. I don't want any room for hope."

"Are you all right?"

"I'm fine."

"Good." He took his car keys from his pocket. "You'd better go now or you'll be late."

Claire turned and opened the door of her car. She looked back at him.

"You never told me why your car is called Claudia," she called.

He was already walking across the gravel to the small blue

hatchback parked on the other side of the parking lot. He stopped and walked back to her.

"Was that the name of the woman in Australia?" Claire couldn't stop herself from asking.

"No." He touched her cheek. "Claudia was one of my primary school teachers. Mrs. Casanovas. My very first love."

"So you were into married women even then," she said with a tight smile.

"This isn't about some married-women fetish." Stefan's face was serious. "I wish with all my heart that you were single." He turned and walked away.

Blinking back tears, Claire got into her car and quickly started the engine. She tried to make her mind blank, tried not to think about the ache that throbbed inside her as if she had been physically beaten.

Just drive, she told herself, and slowly pulled away across the parking lot. She didn't look at Stefan's car as she passed it, and she didn't look behind her as she made her way down the long drive back into the maze of country lanes that would take her home.

Ben turned the hose on and made a huge mud puddle in the flower bed," said Emily, running to the car as Claire opened the door.

Oliver ran after her. "Then he sat in it and rubbed himself all over with mud," he told her eagerly.

"All over his hair and everywhere," said Emily. "Daddy was really cross."

"Where is Ben now?" asked Claire.

"Over there," they chorused, pointing to a completely mud-encrusted Ben happily jumping up and down on a mini-trampoline. Bits of dried mud flew off him with every bounce.

"Where have you been?" William came through the front door wiping a large paintbrush with a spirit-soaked rag.

"I've only been as long as I said I'd be," said Claire defensively. "Why haven't you given Ben a bath? He's filthy."

"I've been trying to paint the wall on the landing. The last thing I need is him coming in and getting mud all over the wet paint."

"Has everyone had tea?" she asked. "Did you heat up the soup?"

"No, I told you I've been painting the wall."

Claire sighed. She wasn't capable of getting cross. She looked at Oliver and Emily and held out her arms to them. They cuddled into her, and she hugged them tightly.

"Was it worth it?" asked William sourly.

Claire looked up from the children. "Was what worth it?"

"The shop. Did they order anything?"

"Oh," she said. "I don't think I'll hear from them again."

"Complete waste of time, then," he said, stomping back inside.

"Yes," said Claire. "A complete waste of time."

CHAPTER 20

*The master bedroom reflects Claire's love
of simple country style. "I wanted this room to feel
as peaceful and tranquil as possible," she says.*

Dear Stefan.

It was four-thirty in the morning. Claire had lain awake all
night, her body physically aching with sadness and loss. At
about three o'clock, as William sweated and snored beside her,
she began to compose an e-mail to Stefan in her head. When
a thin line of gray appeared between the shutters she got up.
Silently, she went downstairs into the study. The computer
whirred into life at her touch. Claire sat down and started to
type.

Dear Stefan,

I feel so sad. I don't want to lose you from my life. I feel so sure we
could work things out. I don't think I can go on living with William,
especially not feeling the way I feel about you. I know it will be
painful and very difficult, but that will pass in time. If you could wait
for me to sort things out here, then we could see how things work out

between us—just take it slowly, no commitments, no guilt (leave that
to me). Surely the way we feel about each other is too precious to
throw away so easily? Please don't let this chance of happiness for
us both disappear. Maybe we could meet in the week to talk?

I miss you.

Claire x

She pressed send before she could change her mind and
went into the kitchen to make a cup of tea.

Claire stood outside, her feet bare on the damp grass. In
her hands she nursed her mug of steaming tea; in her heart
the sadness started to lift a little, to be replaced by hope. What
time would Stefan wake up? What time would he look at his
e-mails? How long would he take to answer? What would he
say?

She wondered if she'd sounded too desperate. Could she
really leave William? In the darkness of the bedroom she had
suddenly felt so sure she could, so sure she would, but now as
the sun started to rise behind her she thought of her children
and felt a stab of pain. To put them through this tangle of adult
emotions, adult complications and confusion, seemed cruel
and selfish. To make them divide their time and love between
her and William, to introduce a complete stranger into their
lives—how could she do that to them? But then she thought of
Stefan.

"Mummy, what are you doing?"

Emily was crossing the lawn toward her, sleepily rubbing
her eyes, her cotton nightdress creased and crumpled.

"Mummy!" A cry from the kitchen door as Ben appeared,

hair on end, his arms held up toward her. "Cuddle me," he pleaded.

Claire walked toward them. She hugged Emily and picked up Ben and squeezed him tightly.

"Would you like to go for a walk before breakfast?" Claire asked. "We could take some jam sandwiches and juice and have a picnic in the woods."

"Yes, please," said Emily excitedly. "Shall I wake up Oliver?"

Wild fuchsia and honeysuckle jostled for space in the shaggy hedgerows that lined the lane from their house. Bees and hoverflies buzzed above them. Claire walked holding Ben's hand as Emily and Oliver ran on ahead picking and blowing at dandelion heads in the early-morning sun. She had left William sleeping. The alarm clock hadn't yet gone off. In the kitchen she had laid his bowl and spoon on the table and beside them his breakfast cereal and a small glass of orange juice. In her mind, Claire formulated a plan of action. She would talk to William tonight; tell him she wasn't happy with their marriage. She would make an appointment to see the solicitor Sally had seen to find out exactly what would happen if they got divorced. She thought about the cottage. She couldn't deprive William of his beloved house. It was beautiful, but in so many ways it had never felt like hers. Could she move? She thought of the pretty Georgian houses in town. Some had lovely gardens.

She tried to think of herself and the children in a different environment. Meals in a different kitchen, the children getting used to different bedrooms. Not so much space. It would be a challenge. It could be fun, liberating, her own home—her and Stefan's home? What would Stefan want? They could buy something together, another house in the country, maybe.

She and Stefan decorating another house, furnishing it together, living in it together. Waking up every morning with
him. Her heart leaped at the thought. William would see the
children on weekends and holidays. She didn't think he'd want
much more than that, though the thought of spending time
without them made her sad. The children would be upset, of
course, but they'd soon get used to it. Lots of children did.
Maybe they could explain it all to them during the weekend.

Her mind raced on and on with plans and dreams, but at
the back of it there remained a nagging anxiety. How would
Stefan answer her e-mail?

When they got home, William had left for work, his breakfast bowl and glass and mug empty on the kitchen table. While
the children went out to play in the garden, Claire checked her
e-mails. Nothing. She went into the kitchen to tidy up. She
decided to make chocolate fairy cakes for a lunchtime treat. In
between greasing the tray, sifting flour, cracking eggs, and
melting chocolate, she went in and out of the study constantly
to check on the computer. She was just sliding the cakes into
the Aga when her cell phone buzzed. A text. Her heart jumped
as she picked up her cell.

Are you definitely coming to Cornwall? Love Mum x

Yes. Looking forward to seeing you soon. Love Claire.

She wondered what her situation would be by then. It was
two weeks away, yet her whole life could have changed. She
looked at the clock on the kitchen wall. It was only ten to eleven,
but she felt as if a full day had passed already. She went into the
study again. *One new message,* she read on the screen.

Dear Claire,

Thank you for your e-mail. As I said yesterday, I don't want to be
responsible for breaking up your marriage. You must make your own
decisions, I cannot be involved. I think it's best to end things
between us at this early stage. Thinking of you. Take care of yourself.

Stefan x

Claire read it again and then another time. She felt numb.
His words sounded so detached, so unemotional, so definite.
She stared ahead out of the window at the children playing on
the grass; she was unable to get up. Remembering all the plans
she'd made earlier that morning, she felt stupid and naive. She
sat motionless in front of the computer for a long time. Stefan's
message blurred and distorted on the screen. Emily tapped on
the window and asked for a drink.

In the kitchen she handed out three cups of orange juice,
then sat down at the table and was still again for another long
time. She stared blankly at the shelves of the dresser, cluttered
with an assortment of plates, mugs, photographs, LEGO blocks,
and children's paintings.

Emily came in.

"When are we having lunch?" She looked at the dirty bowls
waiting to be washed by the sink. "Have you made chocolate
cakes?" she asked, dipping her finger into the remnants of the
thick dark goo of sponge mixture and licking it.

Cakes. Claire had forgotten the cakes. She got up and opened
the Aga door. The hot smell of burning hit her. She pulled out
the cake tray and looked at the three rows of beautifully domed,
but blackened tops, cracked and gently smoldering.

"Oh, Mum. Why didn't you take them out before?"

Claire felt tears sliding down her cheeks. All she could do was stare down at the tray in her oven-gloved hands.

"Oh, Mummy." Emily wrapped her arms around Claire's waist. "Don't cry about the cakes. We can go to the shops and buy some more. It doesn't matter."

Oliver ran in. "Sally's here, Mum. She's just parking the car." He looked at his mother, surprised. "What's wrong?"

"She's burned the cakes," explained Emily, still with her arms around Claire.

"Oh," said Oliver, uncomfortably shifting from one leg to another and then quickly returning outside to play with the twins, who had just appeared in the garden.

Sally's voice came from outside the back door.

"I've only popped round for a minute," she called. "I just had to tell you what I've done this morning." She came through the door and stopped. "Claire, whatever is the matter?"

Claire stood shaking with sobs, tears dripping onto the burned cake crusts.

"It's the cakes," said Emily. "They're burned. Can I go out and play now, Mummy?"

Claire seemed unable to reply.

"Of course you can," said Sally. "I'll sort out Mummy's cakes. You go outside."

Sally gently took the cake tray from between Claire's hands, slid off the oven gloves, and steered her toward a chair.

"Never any good crying over burned cakes," she said. "Over burned anything, for that matter. Otherwise I'd be in tears most days in my kitchen." She wiped Claire's cheeks with the oven gloves, dabbing softly as though she were a child.

Claire didn't say anything, couldn't say anything. She put her head in her hands and continued to cry.

"Come on, love," said Sally kindly. "It can't be that bad." She rubbed Claire's back as she sat down beside her. "What is it?" she tried again. "The children all look well and happy. Is it your mum? Is your mum ill?"

Claire shook her head.

"Is it William?" asked Sally. "Is William all right?"

"He's fine," she said in a muffled voice.

"Has he done something to upset you?"

Claire cried harder. The oven gloves could no longer contain the flow of tears. Sally passed her a nearby tea towel. She buried her wet face in it and was unable to answer any questions.

Sally picked up a fairy cake from the tray and peeled off the thin paper cup around it.

"Look, they're fine on the bottom," she said, picking off a bit of soft sponge and putting it into her mouth. "Delicious! You see, sometimes things look disastrous, but it's only on the surface and everything is all right underneath." She put out her hand and stroked Claire's arm.

"Is it something William's done?" she asked. "Has he suggested one home improvement job too many? He's not having an affair, is he? William wouldn't do something like that. He's not like the devious skunk that I've been married to for far too long."

"He's not having an affair," sobbed Claire through her tea towel. "It's me. No, it's not. I'm not having an affair. I haven't had an affair. Well, I don't think I have. I don't know." She burst into another fit of sobbing.

"You don't know if you've had an affair? You're not making any sense."

Claire sighed and sat up, wiping her eyes. She didn't look at Sally but stared at the spots on the tablecloth.

"I fell in love with another man," she said quietly.

Sally gasped.

"I fell in love with another man and I think I would have left William, but now he doesn't want to see me anymore," Claire went on.

"Who doesn't want to see you anymore?"

"The other man. He says too many people would get hurt."

"He's got some sense, then," said Sally. "Who is he?"

"The photographer who took pictures of our house."

"You've been having an affair with the bloke who came to photograph your house and family?" Sally sounded incredulous. "Do you think the magazine knows he goes around destroying the lovely homes and lives he photographs?"

"I don't think he does go around destroying other people's lives."

"Only yours, then," said Sally. Claire decided not to tell her about the woman in Australia. "I can't believe you've been having an affair."

"I don't think I've had an affair with him, really," said Claire, wiping her eyes again. "I just liked him a lot and saw him a few times over the few weeks and kissed him a bit."

"And?" asked Sally. "Anything else?"

"No, not really."

"Mmm," said Sally suspiciously. "Big Bad Bear and Sweet Betty didn't even meet, but my solicitor says it could still be classed as adultery."

"Mum, we're starving."

Oliver and the twins stood at the door to the garden.

"You can have some chocolate cakes," said Sally.

"Yuck, they're all burned."

"I've brought different ones," said Sally. "You go on back and play, and we'll bring them out in a minute."

Reluctantly, the boys disappeared.

"Right, here's a knife," said Sally, handing it to Claire and taking out a brightly colored melamine plate from a cupboard. "If we just take them out of the paper cases and cut the burned tops off, they'll never recognize them." Sally smiled. "You see you're not the only one who can be deceitful here."

"I haven't been deceitful," Claire protested. She had stopped crying.

"You never told me what was going on." Claire wanted to wince at her reproachful tone. "And I'm your best friend. I'm presuming that you only pretended to be visiting galleries and seeing customers while I looked after your children. That's what I would call deceitful."

"I couldn't," Claire tried to explain. "I couldn't even admit how I was feeling to myself for a long time."

The round remnants of the fairy cakes looked quite appetizing, especially when Sally topped each one with a Smartie stuck on with a tiny spot of butter. The children fell on them as she took them into the garden.

"That should keep them happy for a while," she said, coming back in. "Are you feeling any better now?"

"A bit."

"I just can't believe it," said Sally, popping a charred cake top into her mouth. "I thought I was the one with the unhappy marriage. I thought you loved William. I thought you had the perfect marriage."

"All this is perfect," said Claire, waving her arm around the room. "The house, the garden, the stuff. But it doesn't feel real. It doesn't feel like part of me. Just because the home is perfect doesn't mean the marriage is."

"I know William loves you."

Claire shrugged. "I think he loves the house more."

"What are you going to do?"

"This morning I really thought I could leave William, get a new house with the children, start again. I thought, naively, that I could start again with Stefan. I had stupid fantasies about choosing furniture, having breakfast together."

"Your fantasies are a bit on the tame side," said Sally, laughing.

Claire ignored her. "Then I got his e-mail. I burned the cakes and you came in." She started sobbing all over again.

One cup of tea later, Claire took Sally into the study and showed her Stefan's e-mail.

"Sounds like he's made up his mind." Sally peered at the screen. "I think he's being very sensible. Think of those poor children out there in the garden. I think he's doing the right thing, putting a stop to it before innocent people get hurt."

"What about you?" asked Claire. "You've left your husband. What about *your* children?"

"For one thing, I didn't have much choice. The man was doing goodness knows what in front of a computer screen. Please don't tell me I should have just ignored it and carried on as before. I will never get the image of that barely dressed snake woman out of my head—I'm seriously traumatized. And secondly, I didn't have a home like this to deprive the twins of." Sally took Claire's face in her hands. "I'm sure you can make things work with William. He's the father of your children, you've lived with him for years, and you've made a lovely home together. It's not worth walking away from. You hardly know this Stefan man."

"It's all right," said Claire with a sigh. "I can feel all my determination seeping away. I'm not going anywhere."

"Good!" said Sally. "Now I want you to promise me one thing." She smiled at Claire. "Next time you don't really, sort of, have an affair and fall in love with another man, could you let me know sooner so it's not such a shock? Between you and Gareth I feel as if I've started living in a bloody soap opera."

"I can promise you now," said Claire. "There won't be a next time. I can't ever go through this again."

"Look at me being all domestic!" Sally took away the barely touched sandwich she had made Claire after she'd fed five children beans on toast. "I'll stay here this afternoon and watch the kids. You go to bed and get some sleep. You look exhausted. I promise you'll see everything more clearly by the time William gets home."

"Thank you," said Claire gratefully.

She felt so tired as she closed the shutters and slipped between the cool sheets of her bed, but her sleep was broken and short. Stefan drifted in and out of half dreams and she woke up repeatedly to cold, wet pillows soaked with tears. She could hear the children playing in the garden below her. After a few hours Sally came in with a cup of tea.

Claire sat up in the bed. "Can I just ask you something?" she said.

Sally sat down beside her on the embroidered quilt. "What?"

"Are you really as happy as you seem, now that you've separated from Gareth?"

"No," replied Sally. "It's been the worst weekend of my life. If I'm being honest, I'm heartbroken. I miss his lazy body lounging on the sofa. I miss his smelly clothes left lying all over the floor. I miss the way he always held me close to him in the night. I miss the greasy frying pan he always left on top of the stove. I suppose I just miss him. I keep finding bits of his Iron Maiden T-shirt all over the garden and holding them up to my face to see if I can catch his smell. I've been crying myself to sleep, the boys are acting up even more than usual, and Gareth keeps phoning me in tears. I love him. I don't want to live my life without him, but I'll never forgive him for what he put me through, for what he destroyed, so this is how it has to be."

Claire took Sally's hand in hers. She looked so sad.

Suddenly Sally pulled herself up and smiled. "I'm hoping this could be the start of a whole new me, though. Fitter, slimmer, more dynamic. I'm giving up sugar, I bought some running shoes this morning, and I'm going to sign up for a retail management course in September. I'll show Gareth that I don't need him anymore. Then he'll be so sorry."

"Good for you, Sally."

"Come on then, Madame Bovary. Time to get up." Sally flung back the sheets. "I've put a bottle of white in the freezer and I'm going to open that box of Thornton's chocolates I found in the back of your jam cupboard. The new me doesn't officially start until tomorrow."

CHAPTER 21

*Dark rooms were easily opened up
into light-filled living spaces.*

The week passed slowly, painfully. Claire cooked meals, took
the children to play at friends' houses, drove them to an endless stream of birthday parties, and pushed a shopping cart up
and down the aisles at Waitrose almost every day.

"You look peaky, dear," the woman on the checkout said.
"Summer cold?"

"Yes," said Claire, not meeting her eye.

She couldn't sleep. At night she sat for hours in the silence
of the house drinking tea in the kitchen, ironing, answering
Emily Love e-mails, sweeping the floor, and trying not to hope
for word from Stefan. Trying not to check her phone, not to
look for e-mails from him.

She wondered where he was, what he was doing. She had
nowhere to picture him. He knew exactly where she was. If he
thought of her, she would be in the house, the village, the town
that he had seen her in before. Trapped in her domesticity;
forever walking through rooms, down lanes, down pavements,
down aisles, while he could be anywhere in the whole world.

Two days after she had last seen Stefan, Claire had gone to

a run-down gas station on the other side of town. Guiltily, she asked the bored teenager behind the counter for a pack of cigarettes. As he fetched them down she looked out of the smeared glass window at her children waiting in the car on the forecourt and felt ashamed. She added three packages of chocolate buttons and hid the cigarettes in a zippered compartment in her bag.

At home she put on a video and while the children sat engrossed in front of it she went outside, stood behind the summerhouse, and smoked two cigarettes in quick succession. Briefly, the nicotine took away the pain.

As each day passed, she felt as though she was losing Stefan—losing him in her mind, in her memory. Bit by bit his face seemed to slip away until after a week it was a blur beneath the dark waves of his hair. She tried to recall their conversations. At one time she could remember so many things he'd said, but soon she doubted her ability to recollect and wasn't sure what things were real or simply hoped for. Sometimes a brief image would flash into her consciousness: his hand on a glass, the curve of his fingernail, a tiny brown mole on the side of his neck. Then the image would be gone and though she'd try she could not bring it back. As the memories drifted away, her heart seemed to ache more with the loss, until she wondered if one day she would be left with no memories, no recollections at all, only pain.

Cigarettes became a kind of refuge. Something to look forward to. Something that eased the pain, if only for a few minutes.

She smoked guiltily, secretly—round corners, crouched beneath windowsills, leaning against the back of the summerhouse. Instead of having an illicit affair with Stefan, she was having one with nicotine.

* * *

One rain-swept August afternoon, Claire slipped the button necklace into a padded envelope and wrote Stefan's address on the front. Before she could change her mind, she bundled the children into raincoats and walked them down to the village post box. They squabbled over who would post the envelope through the slit in the Victorian box in the churchyard wall. Finally it was Claire who put an end to the argument by posting it herself. Immediately she regretted it and wished there was some way of fishing it out; but it was done, the necklace was returned, a line drawn, a definite end. As Claire trudged the damp children back up the hill, she knew that returning the necklace made no difference. It couldn't end so easily, there was no simple cure for the aching in her heart.

Sally was kind, but there were only so many times that Claire could tell her that she missed Stefan, that she thought her heart was breaking. William seemed to notice nothing; he was too tied up with his own distractions, too tired to wake up to the sound of Claire's nocturnal wanderings, too engrossed with building the summerhouse to notice how silent she had become.

Cornwall was the last place Claire wanted to be. Every day she hoped that Stefan might just appear or text or e-mail or write or come in his lovely car and take her away. She didn't want to go too far from home, just in case. Cornwall seemed too many miles away for Stefan to find her if he changed his mind.

CHAPTER 22

Organized disorder has its own intrinsic charm . . .

With a sinking heart, Claire drove west; the children squabbling and then finally sleeping in the back of the car. Endless miles of highway gave way to dual carriageway, then smaller roads, threaded with villages and farms, then lanes, narrow and green with ferns and long grasses.

Claire stopped and consulted her mother's directions. She drove on, down tightly bending lanes. Occasional flashes of silver on the horizon reminded her that she was headed for the sea. She reached a holiday resort—little white apartments piled up the steep valley slopes and motor homes lined up along the cliffs in the distance. Her mother's directions took her out of this village through even smaller lanes until, just as she was sure she'd gone too far, she saw a sign for the cottage. She pulled onto a gravel drive lined with pots of scarlet geraniums. Claire looked around for her mother's brown Mini. All she could see was a bright red motorbike with a silver sidecar.

She hardly had time to wonder about the motorbike before her mother appeared in the doorway and ran toward Claire's car. As Claire got out, stiff after the long drive, her mother embraced her so enthusiastically that they almost toppled over together.

"Look at you," Elizabeth said, holding her daughter at arm's length. "You look terrible. Are you ill?"

"Just tired, Mum."

"Well, let me look after you now." Claire couldn't remember her mother saying anything so maternal for a long time. Gratefully, she let herself believe that her mother really meant it. The children woke up and were excited to see their grandmother—then, after a few moments, desperate to get to the beach.

"Where's your car? Whose motorbike is that?" Claire asked as Elizabeth herded them all toward the cottage.

"I'll tell you later," she replied. "Let's get these poor children onto the beach first."

Elizabeth led them into the small, neat cottage (faded dried flowers seemed to adorn every available surface) and then out through French windows at the back. They opened almost directly onto a tiny cove. Seaweed-covered rocks and pebbles lined the higher shore, but they gave way to the soft yellow sand of a completely empty beach. The children immediately took off their socks, shoes, and shorts and ran into the sea in their underpants and T-shirts, screaming with delight. Claire thought how cross William would be with her for not telling them to put on their swimming things first. She didn't care. He wasn't there.

"I'll bring you down a mug of tea," Elizabeth said, disappearing inside.

Claire stood on a large rock, watching the children. They were playing chase with the tide as it moved lazily up and down the flat wet sand. She looked up to the cliffs above the cove and could see the outline of a man and a dog walking on

the path. The man walked slowly, limping along with the help
of a stick. The dog seemed to be patiently keeping the same
slow pace, though every now and then he ran in front a few
yards before returning to his master's side again.

Elizabeth walked toward her with two large mugs of tea.
Claire noticed that she'd had her hair cut shorter. Her usually
severe gray bob had been layered softly around her face;
Claire thought she could detect some golden highlights
running through it. The new style made her look younger,
prettier. She had put on a little weight; it suited her. Her fuller
figure was flattered by a long linen tunic worn over jeans. Turquoise beads around her neck complemented her bright blue
eyes.

"You're looking well," said Claire as her mother handed
over her tea.

"I am well," said Elizabeth. "Very well."

"This is a lovely place you've found."

"It's even lovelier than it looked on the Web site," agreed
Elizabeth. "It's a shame we've only got it for a week."

"You know, we can only stay four nights," said Claire. "The
children start school again on Monday."

"I know, but we'll stay on and finish the week anyway."

"We?" said Claire, surprised.

"That's what I wanted to tell you," said Elizabeth, her cheeks
flushing pink.

Claire sat down on the rock she had been standing on.

"Yes, you might need to sit down, dear. Shove up and I'll
join you." Her mother sat down beside her.

"Well, go on, tell me then."

Elizabeth took a deep breath.

"I've met a man," she said. "A really nice man. Wonderful,
actually. Well, I think he's wonderful."

Claire stared at her mother, unable to think of what to say. After a few seconds, she managed: "Who is he? How did you meet him? Where is he?"

"He's called Brian," Elizabeth explained. "I met him two months ago. I've been longing to tell you but I wanted you to be able to meet him at the same time."

"How did you meet?"

"I ran him over." Elizabeth took a sip of tea.

"What?"

"I ran him over with my car." Elizabeth gave a short laugh. "I didn't mean to. It was an accident."

"You ran him over?"

"He was rather in the way," said her mother. "He should have been more careful where he put his easel. He admitted that right from the start."

"His easel?"

"Brian is an artist," Elizabeth explained. "He and his wife used to run painting courses from their house in France."

"He's got a wife!" Claire exclaimed.

"No. She died three years ago," said Elizabeth. "Breast cancer. Very sad. Poor Brian hadn't painted at all since she died and then the first time he decides to get his brushes out again I come along and plow into him." She laughed again.

"It doesn't sound funny, Mum."

"Obviously it was a terrible thing to happen, but there was a funny side to it too. When you meet him you'll realize it's very hard not to laugh around Brian."

"Did you hurt him?" asked Claire.

"He broke his ankle. I think he was quite lucky. It could have been so much worse. He'd just stood up to gauge the angle of the church tower he was painting when I reversed straight into him. I don't like to think what would have hap-

pened if he'd still been sitting down. I was trying to get out of
a very tight parking space in the parking lot. I was late for an
optician's appointment. I didn't realize he was painting just
behind me."

"Did you not see him in your mirrors?"

"Oh, no," Elizabeth assured her. "He was in my blind spot.
As I've said, it was a silly place to set up an easel."

"So you ran this man over, broke his ankle, and now you're
on holiday with him in Cornwall?"

"I know it sounds like an unlikely way to start a relationship." Her mother smiled. "I drove him to the hospital but I
didn't feel I could leave him waiting there on his own. We were
in the emergency room for three hours until he was seen and
then we had to wait another two hours before he was X-rayed
and his ankle put in a plaster cast. We never stopped talking.
He made me laugh. We found we had so much in common. It
felt as though we'd known each other for years. An immediate
connection. Do you know what I mean?"

"Yes," Claire replied. "I know exactly what you mean."

"I think I fell in love with Brian in that hospital waiting
room. Hard seats and weak coffee from a machine never seemed
more romantic." She giggled as if she were a young girl. "He
lives with three cats, two pigs, twelve ducks, and a dog called
Buster. He's good and kind and he makes me laugh. I'm so
happy. I can't believe it."

Claire put down her mug and gave her mother a hug.
"That's fantastic, wonderful."

"Do you really think so? I've been so nervous about telling
you."

"Why?" asked Claire. "I've always said you should find someone else."

"Have you?"

"I'm sure I have, loads of times. I know I'm always wishing you would find someone."

"Someone to take care of me in my old age?" Elizabeth raised her eyebrows. "So you don't need to worry about me so much?"

"Someone to have fun with while you're still young enough to enjoy it," said Claire. "You only live once, so you might as well make the best of it. Is that his motorbike?"

"Yes," replied Elizabeth. "Isn't it fabulous? Buster goes in the sidecar."

"Where do you go?" asked Claire.

"On the back, of course. I've bought some leathers and a helmet. You should see me. It'll make you laugh. Of course poor Brian hasn't been able to ride the bike for weeks because of his ankle. So coming here was his first long ride. It was my first time on the back of a bike since before you were born. It was wonderful. The wind on my face. It's like the good times with your father all over again."

"I didn't know there were any."

"Oh yes." Her mother looked out across the sea. "There were good times. That's why I couldn't understand why he always wanted other women. Why he wanted to leave." She was silent for a while and then turned to Claire and shrugged. "But that was all years ago. I think it's time I let him go now."

"Yes," said Claire, and took Elizabeth's hand in hers, squeezing it gently.

A dog barked, and looking up, Claire saw the man from the cliff walking stiffly down steep wooden steps toward them.

"Oh, here he is." Elizabeth got up and walked toward him. She kissed his cheek and Claire could see she was telling him something. They smiled at each other, an exchange so intimate that she had to look away. The children were digging a

hole for the tide to fill. They were surprised by the golden re-
triever running toward them. Ben screamed.

"Gently, Buster," the man called to the dog. "He won't hurt
you," he assured the children as the dog jumped into their
hole and started barking and turning in circles, brushing their
faces with his wagging tail. "He only wants to say hello."

Claire stood up and walked across the sand to meet her
mother and Brian. Her first impression was of someone solid:
wide-shouldered, medium height, his stomach gently rounded
over corduroy trousers pulled in with an ancient-looking
leather belt. His weather-beaten face was bearded, his gray
hair thick though somewhat wild. Deep lines fanned out on
each side of lively eyes. You could see that he had been a very
handsome young man—he was still a handsome man.

He held out his hand to Claire.

"It's lovely to meet you," he said, smiling warmly. His hand
felt smooth, his handshake firm.

"Mum has been telling me all about you," said Claire.

"Good things, I hope."

"Oh, yes."

"She has certainly made me a very happy man." Brian took
her mother's hand in his.

"I think it's time for a celebratory drink," said Elizabeth.
"It's well past five o'clock. Gin and tonics all round."

"Yes, please," Claire and Brian chorused, and they all
laughed.

"That's a shock too, Mum," said Claire. "You never drink."

"Well, you only live once, as you said yourself, dear."

Claire called to Ben, scooped him up, and walked with
Brian up to the cottage garden as her mother went inside to
fetch the drinks. From a wooden table they could still watch

Oliver and Emily running in and out of the waves with a very excited Buster bounding beside them.

Brian carefully stretched out his leg in front of him. He winced with pain.

"How is your ankle?" asked Claire, cuddling Ben close to her to keep him warm.

"Getting better, but I think getting back on the old bike and driving a hundred and fifty miles wasn't that great for it. It certainly feels stiffer today."

"It was an awful thing to happen," said Claire. "To get knocked down like that."

"No, not awful at all." Brian smiled. "It was the best thing that's ever happened to me."

"I'm sure there are easier ways to meet someone."

"Well, your mother certainly has an unusual way of getting a man's attention."

"She seems so happy," said Claire. "Quite changed. Would I be right to think you are responsible for dragging Mum into the twenty-first century?"

"If you mean introducing her to the wonders of the Internet, then yes, that was me. She's a fast learner. She's never off her laptop now."

Elizabeth returned with a tray of glasses, a bowl of cashew nuts, and a towel to wrap around Ben.

"Cheers," said Brian, raising his glass. "To a very happy future."

"To a happy future," mother and daughter echoed.

"So, you used to live in France?" Claire asked Brian. He was throwing nuts into the air to catch them with his mouth. Ben squealed with laughter at his display.

"I still live in France," he replied, handing Ben a square of chocolate that he had produced from the pocket of his denim shirt. "I have an old farmhouse that I renovated years ago. It's in the Dordogne. I had only come over here for a day or two to meet my son's new baby. My first grandchild. She's called Alice. I was painting them a picture of the church where Alice will be christened when I met your mother." He squeezed Elizabeth's hand across the table. "Now I've got my ankle out of plaster and I'm back on my wheels again, I need to get back home. The animals are being looked after by my neighbor but they'll be missing me. I also want to get the painting classes back up and running and"—he hesitated and exchanged a glance with Elizabeth—"I want to take your mother with me."

"For a holiday?" asked Claire.

"No," Elizabeth replied. "I'm going to move to France to be with Brian. To live there. My flat is on the market already."

"Wow!" said Claire. "That's a big life change."

Her mother looked at her, and smiled nervously. "Do you think it's too big?"

"No, it's not too big. Do it if you want to, Mum," said Claire. "You were a French teacher for thirty-five years—you speak fluent French. I remember how much you wanted to live in France when I was little, but Dad wouldn't even go there on holiday. It could be fantastic. Why not grab all the opportunities you can?"

"That's what I say," said Brian. "At our age you never know how long you've got left. You could get ill or have a heart attack or some madwoman in a brown Mini could run you over." Claire's mother swiped at him crossly. He caught her hand in his and kissed it. They both laughed and Claire couldn't help smiling.

"I thought you might not approve." Elizabeth's face was serious again. "It's not as if we've known each other very long."

"Two months is a long time if you love someone," Claire said.

"I thought you'd be upset about my leaving you and the children."

"We'll be over all the time," said Claire. "It will be a great excuse to have French holidays. The children will love it."

"I wonder what William will think," asked her mother.

Who cares? thought Claire. "Well, I expect he'll foresee all sorts of potential problems and pitfalls—you know how he worries. She touched her mother's hand across the table. "But I'm really happy for you." She looked at Brian. "For both of you."

"Can we put our swimsuits on now?" Emily shouted as she ran toward them, panties and T-shirt dripping. Oliver followed, equally soaked.

"I think it's a bit late for that!" Brian laughed. "You're already drenched."

"Who are you?" asked Emily, looking at the stranger suspiciously.

"I'm Brian," he said. "Your grandmother is a very special friend of mine."

Just then Buster ran up to the table and shook himself violently. Seawater sprayed out all over everyone.

"And this is my other special friend," said Brian, patting Buster's soggy coat. "Now, I should go in and make a start on supper. Any volunteers for giving a hungry dog his dinner?"

"Me, me, me!"

They ate looking over the little cove and beyond to a far-off headland. The setting sun was still warm and Claire began to feel herself relaxing for the first time in weeks. Brian made them large crêpes, which he served with melted cheese, ham, and fried eggs. He told Claire and the children that it was a traditional Dordogne specialty. Claire was suddenly ravenous in the fresh sea air; it had been a long time since she had enjoyed a meal so much.

Brian told the children about all the mischief Buster got into on their walks and let them feed the dog small treats from their plates. They laughed, delighted, at the big yellow dog pushing his nose around their toes looking for dropped food, his shaggy tail slapping against their bare thighs.

After the meal Brian suggested he take the children back to the beach, where he directed them in a scramble over the rocks and pebbles to search for driftwood for the cottage fire. He stood on the highest rock holding Ben's hand and pointing out with his stick branches for Oliver and Emily to collect.

"He's lovely, Mum," said Claire, watching them as she collected up their plates from the table.

"I think so."

"He's a big hit with the children," Claire added. "I think they're going to have a lot of fun with Buster too."

She could see Oliver and Emily climbing over the large flat rocks, Buster close beside them, sniffing in between the crevices. Ben was picking up pebbles from the foot of the rock he shared with Brian. He handed them with great importance one by one to Brian and watched in wonder as Brian skimmed each pebble across the incoming water, making them hop across the waves.

"Are you all right?" Elizabeth asked her. "I'm worried about you. You've lost so much weight." She came and put her arm around her daughter's shoulder. "You seem sad."

"I think I just need a bit of a rest," said Claire. "Don't worry about me. I'll be fine."

* * *

After Claire had put the three exhausted children to bed, Brian and Elizabeth showed her pictures of the house in France on Brian's laptop. It was a beautiful rectangular farmhouse with shuttered windows, ocher-colored walls, and an undulating terra-cotta roof. The garden was a wilderness of trees and flowers bordered by a wide, shallow river. A duck pond was fringed with irises and a painted wooden duck house sat on an island in the middle. They showed her pictures of the little medieval town nearby. Pretty golden buildings clustered on a steep hillside leading down to a medieval bridge.

"Proper shops there," Brian said. "Patisseries, boulangeries, hardware shops selling everything you'd ever need. The people are so friendly. I've know them all for years. They were so good to me when my wife died."

Brian made a fire as the late-summer chill set in and they sat around it drinking wine, telling Claire more of their plans for the future. Buster gently snored at Brian's feet.

"The children will love it over there," he said. "We'll soon have them fishing in our river and there are loads of fossils in the rocks around the house, and a lake nearby to swim in."

"We'll come as often as we can," said Claire, genuinely looking forward to it, though she couldn't help thinking how much Stefan would like it.

She found herself imagining being there with him: sitting drinking wine in the shady garden, watching the children playing in the river, walking down the narrow lanes of the town hand in hand, leaning over the bridge as the water flowed beneath it. She felt sure he would have gotten on well with Brian.

"You look miles away," her mother said, bringing her back

to reality. "You must be tired after your long drive. Don't let us keep you up with all our talking."

"It must all be a bit much to take in," said Brian kindly. "You didn't even know I existed until today and now I'm whisking your mother away to foreign parts."

"I know I should have told you before but I haven't seen you for so long," said her mother. "And I wanted to talk to you face-to-face, for you to meet Brian yourself."

"I wish you both lots of happiness."

"You're very generous," said Brian.

"No, not generous," said Claire. "I just think if you can find someone you want to be with and you can be with them, then you're very lucky." She got up. "I'd better go to bed; I suddenly feel exhausted. Must be the sea air." She kissed her mother's cheek. "Night, Mum," she said, and kissed Brian too. "It's so lovely to meet you." She smiled at them both and left the room.

In bed she could hear them quietly talking as they washed up, laughing together, whispering, so obviously happy in each other's company. She realized that there was only one other bedroom in the cottage. She remembered a patchwork-covered double bed she had glimpsed earlier and tried not to feel shocked.

Claire woke up early. Ben had gotten into her bed sometime in the night. She held his warm, soft body close to hers, feeling his gentle breathing on her cheek. After a little while she extricated herself from his embrace and got up and pulled on jeans and a sweater.

She left the children sleeping in their room and made herself a cup of tea in the silent kitchen. Taking it outside, she stood looking at the sea. The tide was high and the air crisp and cold. Gulls soared against another bright blue sky. The rhythmic sound of the waves rolling onto the shingle edge of the beach mixed with birdcalls high above her.

She walked up the steep cliff steps until she reached the top, looking down on the clear green water glistening in the morning sun. Sitting down on the short grass beside the coastal path, she took a cigarette from a box of ten in her pocket. As she lit it and inhaled, she thought of Stefan and wondered where he was. Waking up to the noise of London traffic, or somewhere hundreds of miles away in another country? Maybe he was on the other side of the large expanse of water in front of her. She gazed out across the sea and her heart ached with the longing that had become so familiar.

"Those things will kill you," said a voice. Brian and Buster appeared from the opposite direction. Claire jumped at being found out.

"Don't tell my mum," she said as he sat down beside her.

"You're a grown woman." He laughed. "Not a twelve-year-old behind a bike shed."

"I know," she said. "But I still think she'd be cross with me."

"Only worried about your health." Brian smiled at her. "But I'll keep your secret, don't worry. I'm sure you have your reasons. We all need the odd vice to make life worthwhile sometimes."

"Yes," said Claire, looking down onto the rough gray rocks of the cliff.

"I know I drank too much when my wife was ill," Brian went on. "The odd nightcap gradually turned into half a bottle before bed and then a couple of glasses of whiskey in the morning as soon as I'd made her breakfast. Whiskey with lunch, whiskey with tea and supper. I felt very guilty at the time but, looking back, I think it helped me through it. I needed something; otherwise I'd have gone mad."

"That must have been a terrible time for you," said Claire.

"I thought my life was ending too," he said. "Wished I could go with her when she died. Seriously thought about making that happen. It was a very bleak year, the year after her death."

"You must have loved her very much to feel so sad."

"I adored her; we'd been together since we were fifteen. I never imagined I could love another woman. But then I met your mother." He looked at Claire and smiled. "She's been like a gift for me, an unexpected gift. An explosion of light out of all the darkness of my grief. It just shows you—even if you think everything is lost and that only loneliness and despair remain, the most amazing things can happen. Never give up hope. If life has taught me anything, it's that things always get better."

"I hope you're right," she said, finishing her cigarette and stubbing it out in the short grass.

"Did your mother tell you that I've asked her to marry me?"

"No," said Claire, looking up at him, surprised. "What did she say?"

"She refused," said Brian. "She says she'll never get married again."

"Give her time. It was dreadful for her when my dad left. She was so upset, felt so betrayed and hurt. Does it matter to you if you're married or not?"

"I'd just like to show her how much she means to me," he said. "Show the world how I feel about her."

"Give her time," Claire said again. "It's not been long since she met you. She'll need to learn to trust again after all these years."

From where they sat she saw her mother and the children

on the beach below. Buster barked and got up to go and join them.

"Your mother is worried about you," said Brian. "She thinks you might be going through a rough patch."

"If what you said just now is right, then things will get better." Claire stood up and waved at the little group below.

"I can understand if you don't want to talk about it," said Brian. He stood up and put a hand on her arm. "But don't give up hope."

Together they slowly walked down the steps onto the sand. Ben ran over to Brian and threw his arms around his leg.

"I found a shell," he said proudly, holding out his hand.

"We saw a seal," shouted Oliver excitedly behind him.

"I saw two," called Emily.

Elizabeth gave Claire a hug. "It's so lovely having you all here."

"It's lovely to be here," said Claire, hugging her back.

The four days passed quickly: playing with the children on the beach; walking on the headland; drinking endless cups of tea, gin and tonics, and glasses of wine with Elizabeth and Brian on the terrace; laughing at Brian's funny stories. The children loved him. He gave them rides on his motorbike—Emily and Ben in the sidecar, Oliver proudly on the back. Brian drove them slowly up and down the lane while they called and waved to Claire and Elizabeth as though they were on an amusement-park ride. Ben was constantly demanding his attention and Brian was happy to give it to him. He took Oliver and Emily bird-watching on the cliff tops and they all went out on a boat trip, joined by a school of dolphins swimming along beside them in the waves.

Buster was an endless source of fun, never tiring of chasing a stick or jumping in and out of the tide, chasing the three children. Brian and Elizabeth cooked together in the evenings, slicing vegetables and stirring pots side by side, creating lovely meals "to fill you out a bit," as Elizabeth said to Claire.

Claire had never seen her mother so happy, so good-natured. Gone was the constant underlying note of bitterness in her voice; gone her unrelenting cynicism and suspicion of life. She was cheerful, lighter in her tone and attitude, relaxed and full of fun. She played cricket on the beach with the children and bedtime games of Monopoly with Oliver and Emily, cheating disgracefully, then denying it outrageously when found out.

To Claire it was like the family holidays she'd dreamed of as a child. Happy days together on a beach in the sun, rather than the quietly tense times the three of them had spent looking at prehistoric burial mounds or stone circles—her father's great passion. He would take endless photographs and measurements for a book he never even started to write. They rented rooms in musty guesthouses eating tinned grapefruit for breakfast and sleeping on scratchy nylon sheets.

As an adult, Claire could still feel mild depression sweep over her as they sped past Stonehenge on the A344. It always seemed strange that her father had settled in California, so far away from his beloved ancient British sites.

Claire felt sad as she and the children hugged Brian and Elizabeth good-bye at the end of their visit. The children begged her to let them stay until the end of the week and cried as she bundled them into the car. Claire felt like crying too. She longed to stay, but the thought of explaining to a pursed-lipped

Mrs. Wenham why Oliver and Emily were starting the new
school term late kept her firm in her resolve to head for home.

Claire got in the car and drove away, beeping the horn and
waving until the little cottage was out of sight.

She's doing what?" William exclaimed when Claire got home
and told him her mother was moving to France with Brian.
"Does she really know this man? He could be anyone!"

"He's lovely," said Claire, the happiness she'd found in
Cornwall slowly ebbing away as she faced her husband across
the kitchen.

"You hear about men like him, seducing old women, making them sell their houses, and then going off with all their
money."

"I don't think he's like that," she said, sighing. "He's just a
nice man. I could tell how happy they were together."

"Well, I wouldn't trust him," said William. "Just you wait
and see. She'll be left heartbroken and penniless. And what
about the children?"

"What about them?" asked Claire, trying not to get cross.

"What about their inheritance if it all disappears in your
mother's mad adventures?"

"Why do you have to be so cynical?"

"I'm not cynical," he replied. "It's you and your mother who
seem to be naively taken in by this complete stranger."

"You'll have to meet him and then you'll see how nice
he is."

"I hope your mother doesn't think we'll have the time or
money to be constantly going back and forth to France." He
noisily opened cupboards looking for a jar of coffee.

"We must have run out," said Claire, suddenly feeling tired after the long drive home.

"We're low on a lot of things," said William, making himself a cup of tea.

"Are we?" she said, inwardly fuming at William's inability to find time to shop himself while she was away. "The children liked him a lot."

"Who?"

"Brian."

"I hope you didn't leave them alone with him, Claire. As I said, you've no idea who he is."

Claire got up and decided to check her e-mails.

Already there were Christmas orders from shops wanting new Emily Love stock, a lot of Web-site mail orders, the usual junk, but nothing else. Claire stared blankly at the screen until William shouted from the kitchen that they were out of milk now too.

CHAPTER 23

A comfortable home that's always cozy.
Claire has created the perfect environment
for her family and friends to enjoy.

Oliver and Emily went back to school, returned to the competent care of Mrs. Wenham, and Ben went back to nursery to give Claire more time to work. She was exhaustingly busy, but even the hectic after-school schedules and the demands of Emily Love didn't stop her from thinking about Stefan.

Summer turned to autumn. The days grew shorter and the hedgerows started to turn brown, shed their leaves, and slowly rot. The new season made Claire even more depressed. The damp October cold made her summer memories seem remote. She put away her thin cotton skirts and dresses and got out sweaters, trousers, and long boots that Stefan had never seen her wear.

She bought new clothes to make herself feel better. Standing in changing rooms, she would look at her reflection and ask herself if Stefan would like what she was trying on, imagine places she might wear the top or skirt or coat, places she might go with Stefan. A new underwear shop opened in town and Claire let herself be measured and cosseted by the shop assistant, who brought her an endless succession of bras to try. The cheery woman talked on and on about the supportive benefits of each one, tightening, lifting, and adjusting.

"This one gives you the most fantastic cleavage. Your husband will love it!"

Claire looked in the mirror and wondered which one Stefan would most like to find as he slowly unbuttoned her shirt.

As she waited to pay for the bra she'd finally chosen, her fingers stroked the pale peach silk and delicate embroidery, a tiny tear of pearl nestled between the two softly padded cups. At the last minute she bought the matching knickers as well.

"Your husband will be pleased when he sees you in these," said the shop assistant as she wrapped them in crisp white tissue and slid them into a bag adorned with golden cherubs. The bra and knickers stayed unworn, still wrapped, in the back of Claire's underwear drawer for a long time.

What are we doing about your birthday?" asked Sally as they sat enjoying après-school-run cappuccinos in the hotel lounge in town. Sitting in front of a warm log fire, on soft suede sofas, they were flicking through the hotel's glossy magazines. Now that Sally had started her retail management course at the local college, Claire hardly ever saw her.

Although it was good to catch up, Claire was only half engaged in conversation. She was browsing through the latest copy of *Idyllic Home,* looking at the names of the photographers in the articles, searching for Stefan's name.

"Earth to Planet Claire?"

Sally was waving her hand in front of Claire's face.

"Sorry. What did you say?"

"I said, what are we doing about your birthday?" Sally repeated her words slowly.

"I don't feel like doing anything much." Claire knew she sounded flat, but these days she found it hard to summon enthusiasm for much of anything.

"Well, what about me? Don't I deserve a night out? I've worked really hard these first few months on my course and I've already lost nearly thirty pounds."

It was true that in the last two months Sally had transformed herself from a disheveled housewife and mother into a svelte and sexy mature student. Running and a strict diet regime had done wonders for her figure. Her toned thighs were now clad in skintight denim, tucked into a pair of knee-high black leather boots. A cashmere sweater showed off her newly discovered waist. Lately she'd started dating a blond and brooding twenty-two-year-old called Josh.

"I thought you were having enough nights out with your toy boy." Claire raised her eyebrows.

"I know," Sally said. "But I miss having a good old chat. There's only so much conversation you can have with someone fifteen years younger than you."

"I didn't think it was the conversation you were interested in."

"Well, I wouldn't like to waste too much time talking when there are so many other things to do with Josh." She winked at Claire and laughed. "If you know what I mean."

"You certainly didn't waste any time finding ways to fill those lonely nights when Gareth has the boys," Claire said. She couldn't help but feel slightly envious.

"I never realized there was so much fun to be had as a single woman. Maybe Sweet Betty did me a favor in the end." Sally hesitated and glanced at Claire. "But being married is good too—if it's not Gareth that you're married to, obviously. Things are all right now between you and William, aren't they?"

"Fine," Claire replied, looking back down at the magazine on her lap.

"Good," Sally said. "Now, what about your birthday? It's only three weeks away. Let's do something fun to celebrate. You're only thirty-eight once. We could book a table in a restaurant— get some of the other mums together as well."

Claire flicked absentmindedly through the pages of *Idyllic Home*. Suddenly there was Stefan's name blazing out at her from the glossy pages. She stopped breathing. A full-page photograph of a neatly proportioned Georgian house. *"An exquisitely renovated former rectory, elegantly furnished with period pieces with a modern twist."* She turned to the first page of the feature: a picture of a sumptuously decorated living room; all cream, beige, and chocolate. A long-limbed redhead sat on a chaise longue, one arm draped along its velvet back, her slim legs crossed, a cream silk shirt casually unbuttoned to reveal a hint of cleavage. She was smiling confidently at the camera. She was smiling at Stefan. Claire skimmed through the text.

"'This house is very special,' says Jilly, who combines the running of a four-star restaurant with a successful interior design business and life as a busy mother. 'We feel really at home living here.'"

Claire immediately hated Jilly. She wondered if Stefan had invited her to share cakes and champagne cocktails with him. She wondered if her unnaturally full lips had kissed Stefan's, if her slender arms had wrapped themselves around him, and if his hands had wandered underneath that luxurious shirt.

"Are you listening to me at all?"

Claire looked up to see Sally staring at her.

"If you would rather read magazines than organize your birthday party, that's fine. I'll just have to organize it for you."

Sally booked a table for eight at a new bistro for the night of Claire's birthday. Excitement fizzed among the mothers at the school gate. Outfits were planned, hairdresser's appointments booked. Claire bought a new olive-green silk dress and high-heeled gold shoes in an effort to get as excited as everyone else. The outfit would do for Christmas Day as well. Elizabeth and Brian had invited them for Christmas in France, but William had already arranged the usual visit from his parents.

Claire had to work most evenings after the children had gone to bed. She cut out cushions, aprons, lavender hearts, and bunting till the early hours of the morning. She packed up orders and wrote out invoices. The children needed to be taken to Cubs, swimming, ballet, judo, and violin classes after school. She endlessly tidied the house, cooked meals, and ironed clothes. She had so much to do that she felt as if she were wading through thick mud, struggling to get somewhere, but sinking deeper with every step.

"You'll wear yourself out if you don't stop," her mother told her, when she called from France. "I hope William is helping out with the children and doing his bit around the house."

"He's still working too hard," said Claire. "He's home late every night and he's finishing off the inside of his summerhouse on the weekends."

"Just try to make sure William realizes how hard you're working too. He's not the only one with a demanding job."

"I'll be fine," said Claire "It's only this mad rush up to Christmas."

Claire felt as though each day was hurtling her faster and faster toward her birthday. It wasn't being older that she dreaded, but the thought of so many more years to come. Years of school runs, cleaning, cooking, servicing William, looking after the house. She tried to remember if it had been enough for her before—before Stefan came and ripped opened the box where she had kept her needs and wants and emotions so neatly packed away. Now they were out and running wild, refusing to be put away again.

It was the Monday before Claire's birthday and she had woken to the first frost of the winter. The grass had been so white that Ben thought it must be snow and ran out to try to gather it up into snowballs. Claire had taken Oliver and Emily to school—where they delightedly slipped and slid across the icy yard—and then dropped off Ben at his warm, cozy nursery.

Once home, Claire made a cup of tea to recover from the chaos of the preschool rush. As her tea bag brewed, she picked up discarded pajamas and half-eaten bits of toast from around the house, loaded the dishwasher with cereal bowls, and stuffed a bundle of clothes into the washing machine. When her tea was made, she extracted a cigarette from the pack she kept hidden behind the tinfoil and went outside with her steaming mug to treat herself to a few self-indulgent moments. The garden looked beautiful encrusted in glittering frost, and the sun was bright. Claire felt happier than she had for a while and she began to look forward to her Friday-night birthday meal for the first time. She went back into the kitchen and checked her cell phone. It had become a habit she was trying to cut down on. It showed she had a text message. She opened it, expecting it to be from her mother, who was coming home from France that day to finalize the sale of her flat.

I thought you'd like to know your house has made the cover of the magazine. S

Claire stared at it. She looked at the time on the message. It had been sent minutes before. As she'd sat in the frosty garden, Stefan had been sending her a message. He had been thinking about her. She wasn't sure what to do. She started to write a text in reply, but then deleted it and went upstairs to cut out cushions. As she worked she went through a hundred different replies in her head; none of them seemed quite right. She had asked him not to contact her; she hadn't wanted any opportunity to hope. Why did he have to go and get in touch on the first day she'd felt better for months?

At lunchtime she sent:

Thank you for letting me know. How are you? C

He replied immediately.

I'm well, what about you? S

Thirty-eight on Friday—feeling old! C

I was 40 last month and have survived. S

Have you bought a cardigan yet? C

Slippers too and of course I need an afternoon nap now. S

I'm still too young for naps. C

You don't have to have them on your own! S

Claire didn't reply. She didn't know what to think. How could he be so suggestive now, after all he'd said when they last saw each other?

It was time to pick up the children. She hadn't gotten any work done all afternoon. As she drove to school, she tried to sort out her thoughts. She had spent nearly four months longing to hear from him, and now that she had, she was unsure of how she felt. He didn't get in touch again that day and Claire was determined not to reply to his last text, no matter how tempting it was.

The next morning their complimentary copy of *Idyllic Home* arrived with a thud on the doormat. William had already left for work. Claire was just about to leave for school with the children. On the cover SPECIAL CHRISTMAS ISSUE was picked out in dark red letters against a picture of their fireplace dressed with holly and candles. The Emily Love stockings hung down toward a blazing fire; tempting ribbon-wrapped boxes peeped out of each one. A list of smaller captions were printed beneath the title: *The Perfect Gift Guide, Fresh Ways with Seasonal Foliage, A Textile Artist's Inspirational Country House.* Claire took off the shiny plastic wrapping and flicked through until she found the article. The children jumped excitedly beside her. The pictures looked beautiful on the glossy A4 pages.

She took the magazine with her to show Sally as she dropped the children off at school.

"Did you really say this?" asked Sally as she started reading the text beside the pictures.

Claire hadn't had time to read it in her mad dash to get everyone out of the house.

Sally started to read out loud: *"Christmas is Claire's favorite time of the year; a time to gather her friends and family around her in her beautifully restored thatched farmhouse. She likes nothing better than to spend the weeks leading up to Christmas Day making heavenly handmade gifts for family and friends, each one uniquely crafted out of carefully sourced vintage fabrics and antique lace and buttons. When all her gifts are exquisitely wrapped beneath her tree, Claire can sit back and relax beside her open fire and reflect on the years of hard work that have made her house such a special place to be at Christmas."*

"Where have my heavenly handmade gifts been, then?" asked Sally. "And if you've got enough time to sit beside your fire and reflect at Christmas, you can come round and give me a hand instead."

"I never told the journalist any of that," said Claire, trying to get the magazine from her.

Sally turned away from her and read on in an exaggerated voice: *"On Christmas morning Claire enjoys preparing her festive feast in her pretty pastel-colored kitchen. Cooking her turkey slowly in her pale blue Aga the night before gives her and the children lots of time to welcome their many guests to their home and sit beside the tree exchanging presents and drinking mulled wine."*

"What?" exclaimed Claire. "What really happens is that I race round trying to tidy up all the early-morning present-opening carnage before William's parents arrive at nine, and then I remember I've completely forgotten to take the turkey out of the fridge. My mother arrives, William's mother upsets her and makes sarcastic comments about everything, William starts making shelves just as I ask him to help me prepare the vegetables, and I end up drinking a bottle of cheap Rioja—that I haven't had time to make into mulled wine—alone in the kitchen, trying not to cry."

"So you didn't tell any of this stuff to the journalist?"

"What do you think?" said Claire. "I told her about the house and what it had been like and all the work William did on it and about how I started my business."

"I hate to tell you this," said Sally, who had been finishing the article. "It doesn't actually mention William's hard work anywhere in this. In fact, it doesn't mention William at all."

William phoned at lunchtime.

"Did you know the magazine is out?" he asked as soon as Claire answered.

Claire felt herself inwardly bracing. "We got a copy sent to us in the post this morning after you'd left."

"Someone brought it in to work," William said. His voice was quiet.

"The house looks lovely, doesn't it?" she said hesitantly. There was silence on the other end of the phone. "The children were so excited. They've taken it in to show at school."

"Did you read it?" asked William. She could tell he was trying to control his voice.

"Yes, I did, but it's not . . ."

"Not what, Claire?" he asked. "Not my house, too?"

"I know but—"

"When you did the interview, did you just forget to mention that I live there as well? Did you just forget to mention your husband, who has worked so bloody hard turning it from a wreck to the sort of house they want to feature in their magazine?"

"I didn't forget, I—"

"I thought they hadn't even used the picture that photographer bloke took of us together, but then I realized that it's there after all. You're sitting on our kitchen sofa—and I've been airbrushed out."

"I hadn't noticed that. Oh, William, I'm so sorry."

"Don't you think people will wonder how you managed to do all that work on the house and produce three children all by yourself? A team of friendly builders and immaculate bloody conception?"

"I'm so sorry, William. I didn't know they were going to make it sound that way. Of course I told the journalist all about you and your amazing hard work. I don't know why she didn't mention you. I'm really upset as well."

He was silent again.

"William?" Claire wondered if he was still there. "I am sorry, but it's not my fault."

"They just used you and our children to fill their pages. Your naïveté in agreeing to do it amazes me, Claire."

"No, it's not like that," she said. "I've had over twenty orders on my mail-order Web site this morning and the phone hasn't stopped ringing with inquiries. It's been great free advertising for Emily Love."

William made a huffing noise and hung up the phone.

Claire stood with the receiver still in her hand for a long time. She felt awful. She could understand how hurt he must be.

As she made herself a cup of tea, the phone rang again. She let it ring. She'd spent all morning answering it and couldn't face talking to anyone else. After she'd had an illicit cigarette to recover from her conversation with William, she checked her phone messages. It had been William's mother.

Her voice barked out from the answering machine: "I saw the magazine today. My cleaner brought it with her. I was surprised, I hadn't realized that it was such a poor publication. What a dreadfully written article. Why didn't they mention

William or the help we gave you to buy the house in the first place? And you say that you found all your furniture in junk shops and local auctions, but what about that rosewood writing desk? We gave you that as a wedding present and that clock belonged to William's great-aunt Rosalind, it wasn't from a junkyard, and that watercolor painting in the hall was done by my great-grandfather, not found in a Dumpster! I hope you—" She was cut off by the bleep. Claire decided to have another cigarette.

By the time Claire realized she was late to collect the children from school, she was taking orders for delivery well after the New Year. The phone had rung and rung. Several shops had placed orders. There had been endless inquiries about one-off commissions. Her mother had sent an e-mail to say how lovely the pictures looked, but wasn't it a shame the article hadn't mentioned that all Claire's Cornishware had been inherited from her great-aunt, not bought in garage sales, as it seemed to imply.

Claire felt exhausted. It was wonderful to have so much interest in Emily Love, but the article was causing her a lot of trouble. She wished she had asked to see what had been written before publication.

The children came out of school—they were the only children left since Claire was so late. Mrs. Wenham, their headmistress, bustled behind them, holding a copy of the magazine.

"What lovely pictures," she called to Claire as she approached. "Oliver and Emily have been like celebrities for the day, haven't you?" She smiled at the two children, who looked as tired as Claire felt.

"It's just a pity," added Mrs. Wenham as Claire began to walk away with Oliver and Emily, "that they couldn't have been wearing their school uniforms in any of the pictures. You know, to give us a bit of a plug."

Claire thought she was going to scream. Instead she smiled brightly at Mrs. Wenham and led the children to the car.

She sat in the driver's seat and rested her head on the steering wheel. How many other people could the article possibly upset or disappoint? Perhaps William was right; she had been naive to agree to it in the first place. More naive than he could possibly imagine.

"Are you all right, Mummy?" asked Emily, from the back of the car.

"Great," lied Claire.

She picked up her cell phone.

I'm in so much trouble over the magazine article. Was it you who airbrushed William out?

By the time she got home, there was an e-mail.

I haven't seen the feature put together yet. I'm sorry if the article has upset you. Celia's writing always tends to verge on the fictional. It definitely wasn't me that airbrushed William out—the art department must have done that to fit the story. Is he very angry? I hope you don't regret doing it. S

I'm just annoyed. I wish you'd warned me about Celia and her flights of fantasy. I should have known that you can never trust the media. C

Does that include me?

Especially you.

Ouch. That hurt.

Good. While I'm feeling assertive I'd like to know why you've gotten back in touch with me when I asked you not to?

There was no response to that. All evening Claire checked her phone and e-mails but Stefan did not reply.

What a relief, thought Claire. Maybe he had gotten the message and would leave her alone. But that didn't stop her from getting up at three A.M. just to check that he hadn't been in touch.

CHAPTER 24

*Informal floor-length curtains introduce
a country feel to the upstairs rooms.*

William was still only speaking to her in reluctant monosyllables by the morning of her birthday. He grudgingly gave her a cup of tea in bed and handed her a small black box. Inside there was a pair of tiny pearl earrings, just like the ones his mother wore. Claire hadn't worn earrings for years.

"They're beautiful," she said, trying to sound grateful. She leaned over and gave him a hug. William grunted.

Oliver and Emily came in with pictures they'd got up early to draw for her. Oliver's was of Macavity engaged in some sort of battle with a fire-breathing robot dragon; fighter planes blasted them from overhead.

"Lovely," said Claire.

"This is you," said Emily, getting into bed beside Claire to explain her own brightly colored picture. "This is lots of Emily Love bunting and these are some Emily Love cushions, and this is your cake with loads and loads of candles, and here are your presents and some flowers and butterflies."

"They're fantastic pictures," said Claire, hugging the children. "I'll put them on the wall when I get up."

"Be careful what you use to put them up with," said William, who was getting dressed. "That sticky stuff you used before left marks and took out a chunk out of the paint." At least he was speaking normally to her again.

Ben tottered in with a large armful of his toys.

"For you," he said, dropping them on the bed on top of Claire before climbing in and snuggling down beside her.

"They're not proper presents," said Emily. "That's just your stuff, Ben. Mummy doesn't want toys and I bet you'll want it all back in a minute."

"It's very thoughtful," said Claire, and kissed the top of Ben's blond head.

Her mother and Brian had sent her a lovely 1950s silk scarf with a Paris street scene printed on it and a book about antique French fabric. William's mother sent a very expensive-looking jar of revitalizing eye cream (*"A unique mineral complex firms, lifts, and reduces the signs of aging"*) and a step-by-step cookbook (*"Simple recipes and instructions for those just starting out in the kitchen"*).

The phone started to ring with more inquiries and orders for Emily Love before Claire had even gotten the children to school. Somehow she managed to get them all dressed and out of the house before nine o'clock.

After a quick cup of coffee in the hotel with Sally, Claire went home to try to tackle all the orders that were still pouring in as a result of *Idyllic Home*'s article.

As she parked the car, she could see a square package wrapped in brown paper sitting beside the porch—something that had been too big for the postman to fit through the letter box. She picked it up and opened the door, pushing against a small pile of colorful envelopes that lay on the mat on the other side.

Claire made herself a cup of tea and forced herself to open her cards before the package like all good birthday girls ought to do.

After a few seconds she pushed the unopened envelopes to one side and picked up the parcel.

She started to tear at the brown paper, slicing through the packing tape with a jam-smeared knife left on the table from breakfast. Inside she found a neatly wrapped square cube. Claire tore away the wrapping. Cupcake-decorated paper covered a bright pink lidded box; she lifted the lid and pulled out huge quantities of marshmallow-colored tissue paper. At last she unearthed the present within—something wrapped in bubble wrap. Carefully she unwound the plastic and found herself holding a beautiful china cup. She gasped in surprise and sat down on a kitchen chair. She let her fingertips run lightly around the thin gold luster rim and trace over the delicately painted pink camellias that swirled around the fine white glaze. Her grandmother's teacup; an exact replica of the broken teacup from the set. Her heart quickened and she looked inside the box again. At the bottom she found a postcard of one of Matisse's paper cuts. On the back Claire read the neatly slanting handwriting:

> *I know a china painter who was able to copy your grandmother's teacup, I hope it's similar enough to complete your set again. I'm sorry if the magazine feature has made things difficult for you. I miss you. Happy Birthday. X*

It could only be from Stefan. He must have taken some of the broken pieces away with him on the day that she had inadvertently smashed it.

Claire sat looking at the cup for a long time until Macavity's

long, sleek body wound itself against her and brought her out
of her reverie. She took her phone from her handbag, typed
out a message, reread it several times, and finally pressed send.

Thank you so much for my cup. I miss you too. C

He didn't reply.

She loaded the washing machine, unloaded the dishwasher,
vacuumed the floor. She couldn't concentrate on work. It was
two hours before he replied.

I'm so glad you like it. I think about you all the time. S

I think about you all the time too. C

I can't forget the last time I saw you.

You made me so sad that day.

I've spent months regretting what I said to you.

Maybe you were right to end things the way you did.

The kitchen door opened. Claire jumped.

"Did I frighten you?" said Sally, standing in the doorway
with a purple sequined beret pulled down hard on her head.
"I know I look scary."

"Yes," said Claire, flustered, putting the phone down on the
table behind her. She laughed. "I mean no, you didn't frighten
me. Though you do look a bit odd in that hat."

"Odd? You mean I look awful." Sally sat down at the table
and buried her face in her hands.

"It's just a hat," said Claire, sitting down opposite her. "Surely you can take it off?"

Sally looked up, her face miserable, and slowly took off the beret.

Claire gasped. "Oh, Sally. What happened?"

"I know. It's awful, isn't it? How can I go out tonight?"

"It's not awful," said Claire. "It's just a bit . . ." She couldn't think of a tactful word.

"Clownlike?" Sally wailed.

"It's just a little bit . . . curly." Sally's hair, which for the last three months had been styled into a lovely, silky, straight bob, was now in large ringlet curls tight to her head. She reminded Claire of Shirley Temple, though she was careful not to say so.

"What am I going to do?" wailed Sally. "I wish I'd never gone to the hairdresser's."

"Can't you wash it?"

"I have." Sally pulled at one of the curls, which pinged back into a tight blond coil as soon as she let go. "Twice. Now I think it's worse than when I left the salon!"

"Why did you . . . ?" Claire's voice trailed off as she tried to phrase the question.

"Why did I ask them to make me look like one of the Marx Brothers?"

"Well, at least you haven't got a mustache and big cigar."

"No, not Groucho," said Sally exasperatedly. "The other one with the curly hair; was it Chico or Harpo?"

"It's not that bad," Claire tried to reassure her. "But I still don't understand what happened. I only left you a few hours ago and your hair was . . ."

"Straight? Beautiful? Sophisticated?"

"Yes, all of those."

"I went to the hairdresser's after I left you, so that I'd look gorgeous for tonight."

"Yes, I know. You said you were going for a trim," said Claire.

"The girl who cut it for me before had gone to collect her sick baby from nursery and so I had the only other person available—a man. Very handsome, very persuasive—very young. He said he could make it a bit wavy when he dried it."

"Oh . . ."

"A bit like Kylie Minogue, he said—just a bit of a change for tonight. Well, you know, I've always wanted to look like Kylie. How could I resist? Then he suggested a light perm so that it could be a bit wavy for longer."

"A light perm," Claire repeated slowly.

"Yes," said Sally, trying to smooth down her hair with her hands. "It seemed like a good idea at the time, but I think he left the stuff on for too long. Turned out he's only a student— a first year on the hair and beauty course at my college, and he's only been at the salon for a week. He didn't have a clue what he was doing."

"What did he say when he saw how it turned out?" asked Claire.

"That the curls would drop and become waves later."

"When later?" asked Claire.

"Over the next few weeks."

Claire thought Sally was about to cry.

"What am I going to do? What will Josh say? He won't want to be seen in the student bar with a middle-aged poodle."

Claire looked at her phone on the table. It had rung with a new text message. She couldn't look at it in front of Sally. She knew she wouldn't approve.

"Right," Claire said, standing up decisively and looking

at her watch. "We've got half an hour before we pick up the children. I'm going to get my straighteners and I'll see what I can do."

Claire came back and plugged in the tongs.

Sally asked: "What were you doing when I came in? Was I interrupting something?"

"Nothing much," said Claire, starting to pull the metal straighteners through a curly strand of hair. "Only opening some cards."

"You looked very guilty." Sally picked up the cup that still sat on the table amid the envelopes.

"I've always liked this tea set—were you about to treat yourself to a posh birthday cup of tea?" She picked up the postcard beside it. "Ooo, Matisse—you went to see a Matisse exhibition with your photographer man, didn't you?" She turned it over.

Claire snatched it from her. The straighteners slipped.

"Ow!" cried Sally. "You've burned my ear. Now I'll have clown hair and a red ear. Great!"

"Well, you shouldn't read other people's correspondence," said Claire crossly. "It's rude."

She picked up the postcard and the teacup and moved them to the dresser.

"Did I see you had your cell in your hand when I came in?"

Sally obviously wasn't going to let the subject drop.

"Maybe," said Claire innocently.

"Were you sending a text?"

"Remember who's holding the hot tongs," said Claire.

"Thanking people for birthday cards?"

"No."

Sally suddenly turned around and looked at Claire, her eyes narrowed.

"Careful!" said Claire, quickly moving the straighteners away.

"You're the one who needs to be careful," Sally said pointedly.

The phone rang again and Claire quickly pushed it far away across the table with the end of the straighteners, into the pile of birthday cards. Sally tried to grab it and missed. They both laughed.

Sally looked suddenly serious. "You're playing with fire, Claire."

"Voilà!" said Claire, unplugging the tongs and ignoring Sally's warning. She didn't want to be having the Stefan conversation with her. She didn't want her friend's disapproval to spoil the euphoria that she had been feeling for the last few hours. "I think your hair looks lovely now!" She had turned the curls into gently undulating waves around Sally's face. It really did look very pretty.

"Thank you," said Sally, getting up and looking in the small mirror beside the door. "What a relief. Now I can go to the ball!"

"But first we have five children to pick up from school, give tea, bathe, put in pajamas, get to bed—"

"And you've got a *husband* to feed."

"Okay," Claire said. "I get the message. Sending texts to other men is wrong." She picked up the phone and put it in a drawer of the dresser.

"And dangerous," Sally added. "Don't do anything to jeopardize the girls' night out. Otherwise the wrath of the Oakwood Primary mothers will come down upon you and you'll be very sorry." She picked up her car keys. "Are you coming, then, Birthday Babe?"

"You go on. I've just got to turn something off upstairs."

As soon as Sally's car had disappeared down the driveway, Claire retrieved the phone. Two text messages.

If it was right to stop seeing you why does it feel so wrong?

And then another half an hour later:

Are you busy celebrating? Happy birthday. x

By the time Claire parked the car outside school a third text had appeared.

Can I see you?

Claire put the phone away, got out of the car, and with a small smile forming on her lips, walked toward the school gates.

The children seemed determined not to let Claire get ready to go out. From the minute they had come home there had been fights for Claire to try to referee, and then Ben found a box of champagne truffles one of the other mothers had given her as a present. He ate them all and got sick all over Emily. Oliver said he had to make a model of a dinosaur for a school project and he needed to start that night so that the papier-mâché could dry. Emily had a ballet exam the next afternoon and wanted Claire to watch her practice her routine— over and over again.

At last they were all in their pajamas and sitting quietly in front of a DVD. Claire raced up the stairs to try to get ready.

In her mind she had envisioned a leisurely soak in a bubble bath, maybe a scented candle on the side, a glass of wine, gentle music wafting in from the bedroom. In reality, it was a quick shower with just enough time to randomly slap on a bit of body lotion afterward as a treat. She should have shaved her legs, she thought, but never mind, she'd be wearing tights.

Her phone rang as she went into the bedroom.

As I haven't had an answer from you I'm assuming you've been abducted by aliens?

She replied:

Yes, I have. Please come and rescue me.

She rubbed moisturizer into her face and began combing tangles from her wet hair.

I'd come right now but unfortunately Claudia doesn't do deep space.

Does that mean you're just going to leave me in their evil clutches?

I wish you were in my evil clutches.

What would you do with me?

"The DVD's finished. Oliver threw a cushion at Ben. He's crying."

Emily came in and sat down beside Claire.

"Who are you texting?" she asked.

"Just a friend," said Claire, putting the phone in her handbag to take with her later. "Let's go and sort those bad boys out."

Claire felt dizzy with excitement. Stefan's texts were the best birthday present she could have had. She didn't know where they were leading. At that moment she didn't care.

She went downstairs with Emily and tried to sort out a full-blown cushion fight that was going on between Oliver and Ben.

William walked in. "I've come home extra early so that you can go out."

"Thank you. I really do appreciate it." Claire tried to sound as grateful as she could. "Could you stay down here and sort out the children while I finish getting dressed?"

He followed her up the stairs. "I think I'll have to go back to the office over the weekend to finish what I was working on today."

"Okay," she said, sitting down at her dressing table.

"I've had a hell of a day," he said, sitting down on the bed.

As Claire applied her makeup and quickly dried her hair— no time for glamorous styling now—William told her in great detail about the problems of his day. Claire put in as many "oh dears" and "how awfuls" as she could and decided to wear her new underwear for the first time. She took it from the back of her drawer and put it on. William didn't seem to notice.

"I bought black paint to do the gate on the drive this weekend."

Claire stepped into her new dress, smoothing down the green silk over her waist and hips. After she had put on her gold high heels, she stood in front of the mirror to see her reflection. She wished she still had the button necklace; it would have looked just right with the neckline of the dress.

"How do I look?" she asked, turning to face William.

"Fine," he said, taking off his shoes and looking under the bed for his slippers.

"Just *fine*?"

"Very nice," he said, picking up a *Screw Fix* catalog from the bedside table and starting to read it.

"Do you think I look thirty-eight?" Claire asked, looking back in the mirror at the fine lines around her eyes.

"Yes," said William absentmindedly.

"Do you think I'd look better if I went out with a paper bag over my head and wearing an old sack?"

"Mmm," he said, engrossed in the magazine. "There's a power drill here reduced to half price. It's much better than the one I've got."

Emily burst into their room. "Sally's here to pick you up. She's got a big present for you."

Claire picked up her handbag.

"Will you get the children into bed now?" she asked William.

"Okay," he said, still reading.

"Your dinner just needs heating up in the Aga. It's on the side covered in foil."

"Mmm."

"I'll take a key. I don't know what time I'll be back." She went over and kissed the top of his head.

Claire left him on the bed.

"Get Ben and Oliver upstairs and into bed will you, sweetheart?" she said to Emily as she ran down the stairs.

"Wow, look at you," said Sally, standing by the front door, holding a large glittery pink box. "You look fantastic."

"Thank you," said Claire. "You look beautiful too. Nice hair!" She took the box in her hands and shook it speculatively.

Sally started undoing the ribbon. "Come on, I can't stand people who are into delayed gratification. Just open it now."

Inside was a beautiful red leather handbag that Claire had been admiring in the craft shop where Sally still worked on Saturdays.

"You've mentioned how much you like it every time you come in," said Sally. "I thought you must be trying to give me a hint."

"No." Claire laughed. "I never dreamed you'd get it for me. It cost a fortune."

"Let's just say Anna hasn't paid me for the last few Saturdays. I just wanted to give you something for all the support you've given me since Gareth and I split up. You've really been wonderful." Sally moved forward to give Claire a hug.

"You'll make me cry," Claire said, hugging her back. "Then my mascara will smudge and I'll look like one of the living dead. Come on. Let's go out and have some fun."

"Aren't you taking your new handbag?"

"Do you think it will go with my outfit?" asked Claire, looking down at her green dress and gold shoes. "If I add red I might look a bit like a Christmas decoration."

"You'll look like a lovely decoration—it's nearly December after all. Come on, hurry up. I can hear a gin and tonic calling to me from the bar."

"It's a good job we're getting a taxi home," said Claire, laughing as she started to transfer her things from her old bag to her new one.

Sally grabbed Claire's handbag from her and quickly tipped the contents into the red one. "There, you're ready. Let's go."

"Bye," shouted Claire as she closed the front door behind her. The two women teetered down the gravel drive.

"Climb in, madame," said Sally, opening her car door and bowing like a chauffeur. "I've managed to get most of the crushed Wotsits and half-sucked Haribo sweets off the seats."

"You really know how to spoil a girl," said Claire, getting in. She felt excited as Sally drove away, looking forward to a rare night out with her friends. She was also looking forward to another text from Stefan. She wondered when she could meet him. Could she get away over the weekend? Make up an excuse to leave the children with William for a few hours? Maybe Sally would have them. She longed to see Stefan again, so much it almost hurt. She had to force herself not to look at her phone.

In the restaurant bar the sound of unleashed mothers filled the air—laughing and talking excitedly, unwinding from the pressures of children, jobs, and ill-tempered husbands. Everyone was dressed up and looking glamorous, out of the usual jeans and sweaters and office suits. Sequins and satin and lip gloss flashed and shimmered in the subdued lighting of the room.

They were escorted to a large table, in a corner away from the other diners. This proved to be a sensible decision on the part of the restaurant manager, as the noise level from their group rose steadily throughout the evening. The food was delicious—three courses and then a surprise birthday cake with sparkling candles. Wine-fueled laughter and funny stories streamed out of them all evening.

As Claire talked and laughed and ate and drank, she thought of Stefan: a constant presence in her mind, a precious secret from them all.

"Any more texting today?" asked Sally, when they were alone together in the ladies' room.

Claire applied a new coat of lipstick in the mirror and smiled.

"Don't worry; I won't do anything to upset my marriage to the wonderful William." She blew a kiss at Sally's reflection and decided she wouldn't check her phone until she got home. A postparty treat for later.

CHAPTER 25

*A dark slate floor creates a dramatic
effect in the entrance hall.*

When the taxi drew up outside, Claire's house was shrouded
in darkness. Sally had already gotten out in the village, accompanied by Josh, who had somehow materialized in the restaurant at the end of the evening. The taxi waited while Claire
scrunched across the frosty gravel on the drive and unlocked
the front door. As she opened it, she turned and waved, and the
taxi pulled away.

The hall was inky dark. Claire fumbled for the light switch
on the wall and turned it on. As the hallway lit up she jumped.

William was sitting on the stairs in front of her.

"What are you doing? You gave me a fright," she said, putting down her handbag. He stared directly at her but didn't
speak. She noticed an empty whiskey tumbler at his feet and
then she saw the cell phone in his hand. Her phone.

"Did you forget something?" William's words slurred
slightly. He was drunk. She stepped forward to take the phone,
but he snatched it back.

"'Finders keepers' we used to say at school," he said, and

laughed. "I found it on the floor. I was just locking up to go to bed when I heard it ringing. I couldn't work out where it was at first, but then I looked down and there it was."

She remembered Sally emptying the contents of her bag into her new red one—her phone must have fallen on the floor in the rush.

Claire looked at him silently. She could hardly bear to hear what was coming next.

"I thought it might be important," William continued. "I thought it might be you trying to get through, maybe the taxi hadn't come, and maybe you needed a lift home. But no, it was a text. You don't often get texts, do you? Never send them either, so you say."

Claire felt frozen to the spot.

"I was curious. Who would send you a text at ten o'clock on a Friday night? A special offer from your provider? Your mother needing to be rescued from that man she's run off with?" He stood up and slowly swayed toward her. "No, those would be far too mundane, too humdrum, too boring for my lovely wife. Do you want to see what it said?" Claire shook her head mutely. "Do you want to see it, Claire?" He thrust the phone in front of her face, too close to read it properly. The words *touch* and *kiss* seemed to leap out at her. She tried to remember the last text she had sent to Stefan. They had been joking about her being abducted. Something about evil clutches—Stefan saying he wished she were in his.

What would you do with me? That was the last text she'd sent him. He must have told her.

"I've seen all the other texts he sent," said William. He didn't take his eyes from Claire. She hadn't deleted any of them; they went all the way back to the summer, all the way back to the beginning.

"Oh, God," she said, stepping back, sinking down against the wall. She covered her face with her hands.

"What's going on?" William sounded unnervingly calm, almost as if he was talking to a small child who'd scribbled on the furniture or thrown their food across the table.

"I don't know," whispered Claire, looking down at the floor.

"What do you mean, you don't know?" he asked, still calm, still patient.

Claire shrugged.

"Who is he?" She heard the crack in his voice.

"I can't tell you," she said, looking up. Their eyes met.

"I would very much like you to tell me, Claire." She could tell he was trying very hard to keep control. "'S' it says at the end of the texts." His voice rose. "'S' for what? Is it a Steve, Sean, Simon? I can't think. I can't think of anyone we know whose name begins with 'S.' What about Sally? Is it Sally?"

Claire laughed in disbelief, though inside all she felt was fear.

"Don't laugh at me!" William's voice was loud now.

"I'm sorry. It's not Sally." She took a deep breath. "The texts are from Stefan. The man who photographed the house for the magazine."

William sat down again. "The photographer," he said, running his hands through his hair. "The bloody photographer who photographed my house for an article that doesn't even mention me? I should have known. I should have worked that out!"

"It's not how it seems," said Claire quietly.

"I bet it's not. I'm sure it's much worse." It was William's turn to laugh now. "You've been committing adultery with a man who photographed your lovely bloody life, the life I made for you. How many years of hard work, all hours of the day and night working on this place for you? And this is how you repay me?" He stood up. "Well, thank you very bloody much."

Claire put her hands to her face and shook her head.

"I'm sorry, William. I haven't even seen him since the summer."

"It doesn't sound like that to me," he said, shaking the phone at her. He was shouting now. "It sounds like you've been having some seedy little affair with a second-rate photographer behind my back for months." He threw the phone down on the floor and its plastic casing flew apart. "Making a fool of me. Humiliating me. Contaminating everything we've ever had with your sordid, disgusting behavior." He got up and stamped hard onto the pieces of her phone, grinding them with his foot and kicking the debris across the floor.

Taking a step toward her, he leaned forward, his face inches from her own.

"Did you ever think about the children?" She could smell the whiskey on his breath. "Did you ever think about our poor children when you were doing God-knows-what with him?" He leaned in closer and hissed slowly in her ear. "Did you ever think of me and what I've done for you? You selfish bitch."

He moved back slightly and for a second Claire thought he was going to hit her, but instead he put his head in his hands and started to cry—huge sobs that shook his whole body.

"Just tell me why." He looked up at her, his voice thick with tears. "How could you do this to me?"

Claire knew she should do something, comfort him, put her arms around him, but she was unable to move.

"I didn't have an affair."

"No? Then why was he sending you texts like that?"

"I only saw him a few times. I haven't had anything to do with him for months." She kept looking at the floor; the uneven lines and cracks of the slate were like mountain ranges against a stormy sky. "I didn't sleep with him."

William suddenly sat back down, his head falling forward onto his knees. It was the position of a small, frightened child. His voice shook. "Do you want to leave me? Do you want to leave me for him?"

"I don't know."

She saw his shoulders shake with another huge sob.

"Do you love me?" he asked quietly.

Claire moved toward him and put her arms around him gently, rocking him as though he were one of the children. She kissed his hair and with one hand she lifted his head from his knees and kissed his wet face. "I'm so sorry."

"Don't do this to me." His eyes pleaded with her.

"I can't think," said Claire, tears beginning to fall from her own eyes. "I can't think what I want."

"I phoned him," William said, still looking at her. "I phoned him up when I saw the messages."

"What did you say?"

"I don't want to tell you what I said."

"Okay." At that moment she didn't want to know.

"I can't believe you could do this," he said, after they had been silent for a while. "I thought I could trust you. I thought you were happy. Happy with all this." His hand gestured around the room. "I thought I'd made you the home you wanted. It has all been for you, Claire."

"You've felt so detached for so long," she said, sitting down beside him, her hand still touching his bent head. "As soon as you come home from work, there's always something that you're doing at home, on the house, making plans for the next thing you want to do. Last summer it was all about the summerhouse. Now you're busy making plans for the extension over the kitchen. It never stops. I only wanted us to be together, to be a family together. I don't care about new guest rooms or summerhouses. I just want a house to live in, not some eternal project. I thought you didn't really care about me anymore."

William shook his head. "You know how busy it is at work at the moment," he said. "That's why I have to work so late. I thought you understood that."

"You're not listening." Claire sighed. "I'm not talking about your job. I'm talking about when you're here, when you're at home. You're obsessed with this house."

A movement above them caught Claire's eye. Oliver and Emily stood at the top of the stairs looking down at their parents on the hall floor.

"What's the matter?" asked Oliver.

"What's wrong with Dad?" Emily sounded frightened.

"He's fine," said Claire, getting up. "Don't worry, everything's fine."

She came up the stairs and gave them each a hug.

"Back into your beds now."

Looking down, she saw that William still sat crouched on the floor, his head on his knees, oblivious to Emily and Oliver.

"Come on," she said to the children. "Don't wake up Ben."

She got them back into bed. By the time she got back downstairs, William had disappeared from the hallway.

Claire went into the kitchen. He was sitting in the dark at the table, the whiskey bottle and a full glass beside him. When she turned on the light, she could see the bottle was three-quarters empty; he must have drunk a lot of it before she came home. William gulped the whiskey down in one go.

"Does that help?" she asked.

"Yes," he said, and got up and retched into the sink. Claire turned on the kettle. William was sitting down again, sobbing into his hands.

"I think you need to go to bed now," she said. "We can talk in the morning. Everything will seem clearer in the morning." She doubted this was true.

She helped him get up. He stumbled against the Aga and she steadied him and guided him, still sobbing, toward the stairs. He was too drunk to manage them, so she led him into the living room to lie down on the sofa.

"Just leave me alone," he mumbled thickly as she sat down beside him. "I don't want to look at you. I don't want to be with you. I hate you." Claire winced and left him on his own.

She made a cup of tea and sat at the kitchen table with it, trying to think. She couldn't believe that this had happened; could hardly bear to remember the texts William must have read. She knew how stupid she had been not to delete them.

"Stupid, stupid, stupid," she said out loud. She had tried so hard not to look at her phone all evening that she'd never thought to check that she actually had it with her. "Stupid," she said out loud again; so stupid for making this whole mess in the first place.

She wondered what William had said to Stefan on the phone. Pressing her aching eyes with her fingers, she thought about Stefan. What would he be thinking now?

William was asleep when Claire went back into the living room. He lay along the length of the sofa, a loose arm hanging down to the floor. In the fireplace the flames cast shifting shadows onto his openmouthed, unconscious face. Claire picked up a wool throw from an armchair and put it over him. For a while she stood looking down at him, watching his chest move slowly up and down with each breath he took. She was numb and unable to move, unable to think what to do next. The grandfather clock in the hall struck three, the last chime echoing in Claire's ears as the house became silent once more.

Still looking at her sleeping husband, she tried to form a plan in her head. She would drive to London to try to see Stefan, to ask him how he really felt. She could be there by dawn. But what about the children? William would be in no fit state to look after them when he woke up. Claire phoned Sally—it may have been the middle of the night, but it wasn't so long since they'd both returned from the restaurant, surely she was still awake. Sally might be able to pick up the kids first thing in the morning and take them home with her. But she didn't answer; no doubt busy entertaining Josh. Claire tried to think. She would leave a note through her door and ask Sally to come round as soon as she woke up. In the kitchen she quickly wrote the note.

As she folded it in half she glanced at the *Idyllic Home* magazine on the table beside her. Stefan's photograph of their decorated fireplace seemed to shine out at her from the cover. The scene looked fake and contrived. *Not such an idyllic home now,* she thought.

She crept upstairs and checked the children one by one. She longed to bend down to stroke their sleeping faces, but dared not risk waking them. She wondered what she was doing. Was she really going to tear their lives apart? Was she being selfish to try to grasp a chance of happiness? She thought of Stefan—how lovely he had been with the children. Maybe it was a chance of happiness for them all.

If William would agree to a divorce and was civilized about working things out, maybe it didn't have to be so traumatic for the children. She would definitely see a solicitor next week. She stopped herself. She was jumping ahead. She must see Stefan.

Glancing at William still sleeping heavily beside the dying embers of the fire, Claire quietly left the house.

CHAPTER 26

The family gathers around the glowing fire to exchange presents and wish one another a Happy Christmas.

Ice sparkled in the car's headlights as Claire drove carefully down the steep hill to Sally's house. It was pitch-black as she slipped the note through the brass letter box.

The larger roads had been salted the night before and Claire drove faster as she passed the town and headed for the highway. All she could think about was getting to Stefan, seeing him again. She was nervous. Her heart thumped in her chest, and she felt sick with anticipation, her stomach tight beneath her seat belt. She took a deep breath, trying to calm down and control her nerves.

Suddenly she wondered if she was over the alcohol limit for driving; it was only a few hours since she had left the restaurant . Claire slowed down; maybe she should stop. A sign to the first service station on the highway loomed up in front of her. Coffee. She needed strong coffee, food. And cigarettes.

Dawn was starting to spread as she began to drive again. By the time she approached the edge of London, it was nearly light. The gray sky gradually turned blue.

The traffic increased as Claire passed endless miles of low industrial units and out-of-town shops. Gradually LEGO-like housing developments appeared, then pebble-dashed terraces and tall, dreary blocks of apartment buildings, giving way to the glass towers of city offices and hotels. Claire had remembered Stefan's address by heart after she had sent him the apron for his sister; like a lovesick teenager, she had even looked it up on a map. When she hit the South Circular, she headed north, eventually turning into a high street lined with stalls setting up for a Saturday-morning market.

Everything looked bright and busy in the early-morning sun—primary colors, bold patterns, music blaring, and people everywhere. It was so different from the soft muted tones and quiet sounds of Claire's country life. Once she had been part of all this color and pattern and noise. Now it seemed so strange and unfamiliar to her.

She knew she was getting close. She turned off the main street into a square of brown-bricked Victorian houses, pulled over, and parked. This was near enough for her to collect her nerves and work out exactly where she was going. She took a street map from her glove compartment and got out of the car.

Lighting another cigarette, she looked up the street name in the book and, finding the page, traced the last stage of her journey with her finger. It was only a few blocks away.

Back in the car she wished she still had her cell phone and could call Sally to make sure that the children were all right. She glanced around for a phone booth. Nothing. She would phone from Stefan's.

Claire drove off again, slowly turning down a succession of roads until she found Stefan's street. It was quiet. A hodge-podge of Victorian houses, a mixture of terraced and detached, stood on pavements lined with pollarded lime trees. It seemed too staid and solid for Stefan—too dull. Just as she was about to check the street name on the street map, she saw the Art Deco building, startlingly white against the blue winter sky. It stood apart from the other buildings, a strip of smooth green lawn in front. Huge metal-framed windows curved elegantly around each side of the building with long balconies climbing up above each other to the fifth floor. She knew this was it even before she saw the large silver number on a set of double doors and the MG parked just up the road.

Claire found a gap between two cars directly opposite the building and managed to squeeze the cumbersome minivan into it. She knew Stefan lived on the ground floor, he had told her that. The ground-floor window on the left looked dark and lifeless behind the sweep of shining glass. The window on the right was shrouded in heavy curtains, still drawn. Claire looked at her watch. Eight o'clock. Still early on a Saturday morning if you didn't have children to wake you up.

The double doors swung open and a man wearing Lycra and mirrored sunglasses came out pulling a bike alongside him. As he bumped it down the short flight of steps, he reminded Claire of an ant dragging a heavy object, concentrating hard on its challenging task. Once on the road, the man cycled away and everything was quiet and still again. Claire took a deep breath. This was it; she couldn't sit here all day. She reached for the door handle of the car and stopped. She didn't even know if Stefan would be there; he had never told her where he was texting from. For all she knew, he could be anywhere—photographing seafront homes in California or icehouses in Greenland. She hadn't even thought about what she was going to say to him. Nothing she could think of sounded right. All she wanted to do was to feel his arms around her once more, touch him and be safe in his embrace again. He would know what to do. She felt sure he would.

She opened the car door and started to get out. Something made her glance across at the right-hand window. A movement—at first just slight. The curtains swayed then separated to leave a gap of a few feet. Claire hesitated and got back in the car. A figure appeared in the window. It was a woman, tall and thin, with long curls of tangled dark hair falling over her shoulders. She was wearing a large white T-shirt much too big for her, pale legs bare below it. She stood with her slender arms wrapped around herself as if she was cold. Claire realized that this couldn't be Stefan's flat. His must be the empty-looking flat on the other side of the front door, or maybe there were more flats at the back.

She watched the figure for a few seconds. The woman was very still. She looked deep in thought. Another figure moved toward her from the depths of the room. A man. He gently touched her shoulder and she turned into his opened arms. He hugged her, stroked her long hair. He was tall and dark too, with a bare torso. He glanced up briefly before taking the woman's face in his hands and tenderly kissing her cheek.

Claire felt a stab of pain go through her as she realized that the man was Stefan. He was with another woman—embracing another woman—someone he was clearly intimate with. Someone he must have spent the night with. Claire looked away, sick with hurt and confusion. How could he have been sending her texts the night before? Now he was with someone else. When Claire looked back, the figures at the window were gone; only an empty gap between the curtains was left where they had stood.

Claire desperately hoped she had been wrong. Maybe she

had imagined it? Could she be in the middle of a dream? In a minute she would wake up, in bed, with William asleep beside her. Everything would return to normal. Maybe there had been no magazine, no photographer, no other man, and she could go back to being the obedient wife and mother that she had been before. The good wife and mother who didn't leave her children in the middle of the night and didn't dream of being in the arms of someone other than her husband; who didn't smoke and send adulterous texts. The good wife who didn't let herself get into situations where she felt her life was falling apart. But Claire knew it wasn't a dream. Stefan did exist and it had been him with a woman at the window.

She didn't know what to do. She had an impulse to cross the road, ring his doorbell, and confront him, but something inside her kept her sitting in the car. She felt too shocked to move, too humiliated. Inside, her hopes and fantasies were collapsing painfully into nothing. She sat motionless, her hands limp in her lap, her eyes still fixed on the dark gap between the curtains. She didn't know how long she sat like that. The road started to come to life around her. People jogged and Rollerbladed, parents pushed strollers, smartly dressed men and women hurried past—all oblivious to her. The bright sunshine seemed to make things worse, belying her mood of despair and hopelessness.

Just as she began to think about summoning the strength to drive away, the front doors of the building swung open and Stefan and the woman emerged. Wrapped up in winter coats and long scarves, they began walking down the steps toward Claire's car. In panic, she slid down in her seat. With one hand she reached down on to the floor, scrabbling for any form of camouflage. Finding a red knitted hat of Oliver's, she put it on, pulling it down hard, until she could only just see the road outside. She pushed back her hair and put on a pair of old sunglasses she found in the glove compartment. She silently prayed they wouldn't see her and that Stefan wouldn't recognize her car, but he never even glanced in her direction.

At the bottom of the steps Stefan put his arm around the woman and they turned and walked down the street. Claire saw him say something to her, his mouth close to her ear. She laughed affectionately and pushed him with her elbow. He seemed to squeeze her harder and she laughed again. Stefan turned his face toward the woman, and from his profile Claire could see he was smiling, and then all she could see were their backs, their coats swinging out behind them as they walked away and disappeared from view.

Claire sat up and took off the sunglasses. Anger started to rise inside her. How could she have been so stupid? How could she ever have trusted him? She had meant nothing to him. She had only been a game. The texts a bit of extra fun, an extra bit of excitement in his life. What a fool she had been to have ever thought it could have been anything else. She wondered how long he had been with the woman. They looked close, as if they had been a couple for some time. Maybe they had been together all summer, even when Claire had first met him. Maybe they had been together for years. Maybe they were married. Maybe it was the woman from Australia. Claire felt sorry for her. She was probably completely unaware of how Stefan behaved; how he was with other women. He obviously didn't care about the consequences of his actions, for all his virtuous talk last summer. He had just destroyed her marriage, her family, her children's happiness, her life—yet he could walk away with someone else, oblivious to the pain he'd caused. Claire hit the steering wheel hard and she found herself crying, tears pouring down her face, dripping down her neck and onto the green silk dress she was still wearing from her birthday meal. She realized she hadn't even taken off her coat from the time she'd left the restaurant the night before.

Claire jumped at a sudden loud tap on the passenger-side window. She looked up to see a cross-faced elderly man wearing a tweed jacket and spotted blue cravat. Claire turned on the ignition and pushed the button to open the window.

"This is permit parking only," he said, a gray mustache twitching above his thin lips. "Have you not seen the signs?" He jabbed a finger toward a small sign on a pole just up the street.

"Oh," she said, sniffing. "Sorry, I didn't realize."

"You seem to think you can just sit here for hours and it won't matter," went on the man. "Other people could be trying to park."

"Sorry." She reached up to brush the tears away and realized she was still wearing Oliver's hat. She whipped it off quickly and used it to wipe her eyes. The damp wool stung her face. She felt ridiculous.

"I've been watching you," said the man, his voice raised. He seemed oblivious to Claire's distress. "Sitting there, no permit visible. I'm sure you've been there for more than an hour. What about the proper residents? You could be prosecuted. I've every right to call the authorities, you know. You should be fined."

"Oh, shut up," said Claire suddenly, and shut the window. The man was shouting at her, but she couldn't hear his words. She started the car and pulled away as quickly as she could.

As she looked in her rearview mirror, she could see the man still standing on the pavement, one hand cupped to his mouth. Two teenage girls walked past and stared at him and then at Claire's car as she maneuvered over the series of speed bumps faster than she should have.

She had stopped crying by the time she was driving on the highway. Her head seemed clearer, her pain already less, or at least more manageable. Now she knew the truth. At least she knew there was no point in hoping anymore. Stefan wasn't worth it. He had never been worth it. She had made a terrible mistake, she only had herself to blame, and now it was up to her to try to sort out the mess she had made. The car clock said it was still only ten o'clock. This time yesterday she had been coming home to find the parcel from Stefan on her doorstep. She couldn't believe that so much could happen in twenty-four hours.

She had a huge desire to be at home, to be sitting in her sunny kitchen with a cup of tea, to be with her children. She wanted to see William, to try to sort things out. To say how sorry she was.

The miles passed quickly but Claire longed for them to pass faster. William would be hungover, she was sure, maybe still asleep. Would he ever forgive her? Maybe this was the chance they needed to start really communicating with each other. Maybe he would begin to understand what she had been trying to say about the house and his obsession with it. They could both try harder, try to change things.

The country roads were still white with a thick hoarfrost as she drove toward the village. The branches on the trees glittered around her like they were part of a Christmas-card scene.

As she approached a thin mist fell, turning the sun into a

shrouded hazy ball. The mist grew thicker as she passed Sally's house. Claire decided to go home before picking up the children so that she could talk to William without the threat of interruptions. She needed to see him as soon as possible.

As she turned the corner to start the climb up the hill, she saw something out of place. At first she thought it was a cloud, a long black cloud, but then she realized that clouds were rarely vertical. Instead, a plume of thick black smoke stretched high into the sky and a spike of bright orange shot up through it, followed by another. Claire's heart clenched. Fear took over and she blindly accelerated upward, desperately hoping it was just a farmer in a nearby field burning tires.

By the time she was halfway up the hill, she knew it was her house.

Flames leaped up from the thatched roof and burst out of the windows as they shattered. Smoke rolled out behind the flames and poured down the walls. Most of the village seemed to be gathered at the end of Claire's drive and three fire engines filled the front garden. Men in yellow uniforms ran around the house pointing hoses in all directions. The crowd beside the drive parted as Claire's car screeched to a halt.

As she opened the door, heat, smoke, and noise hit her. Loud bangs and cracks like gunshots exploded out of the burning building and she could feel the intense heat on her face as she almost fell out of the car in her panic.

She could hear someone shouting hysterically, "The children, the children, where are the children?" and then she realized it was her own voice.

Looking around, she saw only horror and pity on her neighbors' faces. A fireman appeared and started to move back the throng of people.

"Is this your house?" he asked Claire.

"My children are in there," Claire screamed above the noise. She tried to push him toward the house. "Get them out! You've got to get them out!"

"It's all right," he said, taking her gently by the arm. "We've got them safe. They're up here." He led her to the orchard, where she could see Oliver and Emily huddled, frightened and shaking, next to Sally, who was holding a howling Ben. Beside her stood Josh, looking horrified, and on Sally's other side a soot-blackened Gareth, with his arms around the twins, who stood frozen and unmoving for once. They all looked gray as they stared at the burning scene.

With a surge of relief, Claire ran to them.

"Thank God. Thank God," she said over and over again. She gathered Emily and Oliver into her arms and clung to them. They were all crying, including Sally and Gareth. She took Ben from Sally and hugged him, burying her face into his neck to try to find the smell of him she loved so much. But all she could smell was smoke.

"You've got this chap here to thank for them being safe," the fireman said, pointing with his thumb at Gareth. "He saw them at an upstairs window and he somehow got them down. I can't think how—it's quite a drop. Climbed onto the porch he said."

"I didn't find your note till it was too late," said Sally through her tears. "I only found it when I came to the front door when I heard the fire engines go by. I don't know what would have happened if Gareth hadn't been driving past to bring the boys home. They'd been so dreadful with him that he decided to bring them back early."

Claire's stomach heaved; she fought back the urge to be

sick. She tried to force the thought of what could have happened into the back of her mind. It was too much to take in. The bad dream had turned into a nightmare now. When would she wake up? All she wanted to do was wake up.

She knew she'd brought this about herself, by her own selfish behavior. How could she have left the children?

"Is Dad with you?" Emily shouted to her above the noise.

"William?" she said, frantically looking around her. "Where's William? Have you seen him?"

Sally shook her head. "We thought he was with you."

Oliver lifted his face from the depths of Claire's coat.

"I couldn't find you, Mum," he said. "The smoke alarm was going off. It woke us up. I shouted and shouted. We looked in your bedroom but you weren't there. I thought Dad was with you. I thought you'd both gone out."

"I wouldn't have left you on your own." Claire could hardly bear to think of how the children must have felt, thinking they had been abandoned in a burning house. Nausea swept over her again with the realization that William must still be inside. Her head swam, and she clung harder to the children to stop herself from falling.

"Then Dad is still in there?" Oliver cried out. He tried to break away from Claire, as if to run toward the burning building. Sally held on to him. He struggled wildly, but Sally's arms were strong.

"There's someone in the building," the fireman spoke urgently into his walkie-talkie.

"Okay. We're going in," came the crackled reply.

"The fire was well established by the time we got here," the fireman said. "We think it must have started on the ground floor. We had no idea anyone was still in there."

"Dad!" Oliver was screaming again and again. "Dad, Dad!"
Emily started screaming his name too: "Daddy, Daddy!"
Their cries cut through Claire like knives. She couldn't bear it.

"I know where he is," she said. "I'm going to get him out." She
kicked off her gold high heels, thrust Ben into the fireman's
arms, and started to run.

"Claire, no!" Sally tried to grab her but she pulled away.

"Hey!" the fireman shouted behind her.

Suddenly everything was silent; smoky air rushed past her.
She found herself moving across the grass toward the house,
her legs running faster than they ever had. Heat seemed to
swallow her up. The burning house sucked her inside and then
it was dark—pitch-black. Hot, thick, poisonous air was all
around her. She pulled her coat up over her mouth as she
pushed through splintered shards of glass left in the French
windows. She knew her feet were being cut but she felt no pain.
Orange lights glowed and shifted in the darkness. It was very
quiet. Claire dropped to her knees, one hand over her mouth.
She daren't take a breath. Her eyes burned and she closed them
tightly, inching forward, trying to get her bearings. How far to
the sofa? Surely not so far? Her hand touched something soft
on the floor, she groped out farther. It was an arm, then a hand.
It must be William. She managed to get to her feet and started
to pull. He was heavy; much heavier than she had expected.

Come on, she said inside her head. *You're not going to do this
to me, William. You're getting out. I'm getting you out.* She heaved
and he moved an inch or two in her direction.

That's it, she thought. *You're coming with me. I'll not let you go
like this.* She heaved again.

A huge blast broke the silence, a bright white flash lighting
up the darkness. In an instant she was surrounded by crashing
and cracking. Tiny hot red stars fell like confetti around her

and then larger chunks of burning timber started cascading down on top of her. She inched William toward her again and then a colossal bang came from above. The ceiling was falling. Through squinted eyes she saw flames encircling her arm. Her coat was on fire. She heaved again and was filled with an overwhelming energy and strength.

She was at the door and dragging William's inert body over the threshold when a huge crash seemed to shake the entire structure of the house. She felt herself being pulled from behind. She wasn't holding William's arm anymore, she was gliding weightless, floating above the ground, flying over the burning house, up above the children, the crowd and fire engines, above the smoke and flames. A man was talking to her, touching her face softly.

"Stefan," she said, and opened her eyes.

"No, I'm Mike. I'm a paramedic," the man said. "I'm going to try to get you into the ambulance now."

Claire looked around. She was lying on the grass, her arm wrapped in something wet and cold. She tried to take a breath and immediately started coughing.

"Try to relax," the man said. "You've inhaled a lot of smoke." He put a mask over her face.

"That was quite some stunt you pulled." The fireman from before was squatting down beside her. "I never expected you to do that. One minute you were beside me, the next I had a baby in my arms and you were in there." He pointed in the direction of what had been the house. The thatched roof was completely gone, burning timbers caved into a gaping hole where the roof had been. "I never had such a shock in my life. Anyway, you got him out. He's alive." He smiled at her. "But promise you'll never try anything like that again. Leave it to the professionals next time." He looked down kindly at her.

Claire tried to say she hoped there would never be a next time, but she was overwhelmed with another bout of coughing.

"Your husband's in the ambulance," the paramedic said. "He's in a bad way—a lot of smoke inhalation, though, miraculously, only minor burns. We'll get him to the hospital now."

Claire tried to get up.

"Don't worry," said the paramedic soothingly. "We'll get you in there too. You can go to the hospital together."

"You must really love him to have risked your life like that," said the fireman, still smiling down at her. "Good luck to both of you." He got up and walked away.

In the ambulance, Claire sat beside William. The oxygen mask looked huge clamped over his smoke-blackened face. She didn't dare look out of the back of the window as they started to move slowly away down the hill. She couldn't stop shaking; her teeth chattered together, her arm throbbed.

William groaned and his hand pulled at the mask. Claire looked anxiously at the paramedic, but he was busy with a piece of apparatus.

"Don't worry," said Claire, stroking William's arm. "I'm here. You're safe. The children are safe. They're going to Sally's house now."

William managed to pull off the mask. His eyes opened; they looked wild and shining. He stared at her as if he didn't recognize her.

"It's all right," she said. "We'll be at the hospital soon. There was a fire in the house but everyone's all right."

"The magazine," he wheezed. "I wanted to burn the magazine, to burn that article. It went up so quickly. Too much paraffin. Everything started to catch fire." He took a deep rasping breath. "I didn't care. I wanted to get rid of it all. I didn't want any of it anymore." He started to cough and splutter alarmingly. The paramedic got up and put the mask back on. William's eyes closed as he lost consciousness again.

Claire sat numb with shock. William had started the fire. William had destroyed their home—the home he loved. He could have killed the children.

It was all her fault.

CHAPTER 27

Original features and modern luxuries . . .

William was in intensive care for a week before being transferred to an ordinary ward. The doctors said his lungs were damaged but he'd probably make a reasonable recovery in time.

Claire's arm was badly burned and her feet had been cut by splinters of glass from the French windows. She had to have twenty-two shards extracted under local anesthetic. The doctors gave her painkillers for her arm and feet and tranquilizers for her tears and distress. She lay between the cold hospital sheets and tried to make sense of the series of hazy, horrific images that swam through her mind. Drifting in and out of a sedated sleep, she woke from nightmares only to realize that reality was just as bad.

The children had stayed with Sally. William's mother came and offered to take them home with her to the Cotswolds, but they cried and begged to stay where they were. William's mother seemed relieved to have the time to stay at her son's bedside instead of taking care of three traumatized grandchildren.

"He'll be heartbroken, of course," she said as she stood beside Claire's hospital bed on a cursory visit to her daughter-in-law. "He put everything into that house, and now it's all gone." She took a tissue from inside her cardigan pocket and sniffed loudly.

"He's still got his family," Claire tried to say. "He's lucky—"

"One careless act and his life destroyed," her mother-in-law interrupted. "You must have left the iron on or let something burn on top of the Aga. I expect it's easy to forget when you're struggling to look after so many children."

Claire opened her mouth to protest but felt too weak. Anyway, the truth was so much worse, and she was more culpable than if she had simply made a domestic slip.

Elizabeth and Brian arrived while Claire was still in the hospital. Her mother held her hand and stroked her hair as if Claire were a little girl again. It made her feel guilty. She knew she didn't deserve sympathy or kindness.

Brian went to the house and found Macavity, frightened and hungry, hiding in the old woodshed. He left him there but took food and a box of blankets for him to sleep in.

"It's not a pretty sight up there," Claire overheard him say to her mother when they thought she was asleep. "There's not much left. Just a burned-out shell really."

"Come and stay with us in France until you sort yourselves out," said her mother when Claire opened her eyes. "We've room for all of you."

Claire shook her head. She needed to be close to William, even though he turned away whenever she approached the hospital bed where he lay linked up to oxygen by plastic tubes.

After three blurred days the doctor told her she could go home. Home? She smiled and thanked him, but she knew she no longer had a home to go back to.

Claire swapped her hospital bed for Sally's spare one and held Oliver, Emily, and Ben tightly to her through the long, awful nights. She couldn't sleep for fear of nightmares, but the thoughts that filled her head as the children breathed quietly beside her were horrifying in themselves. Guilt, horror, fear of what could have happened—it all seemed to pin her down like a heavy weight, crushing her, making her feel sick. When she closed her eyes, she could see the fire, the burning house, the terror on the children's faces. She could still feel the heat on her face. The smell of smoke was inescapable, as if the thick, black, acrid air had gotten inside her permanently. She couldn't bear the dark and kept the bedside lamp on all through the endless nights.

She wouldn't let herself think of Stefan or the texts or remember her early-morning drive to London or the woman with the long dark hair. She pushed the memories away into a painful corner of her mind.

Instead of school, the children sat on Sally's sofa watching television, wearing borrowed clothes. They were quiet; too quiet. Oliver's and Emily's eyes looked empty and hollow, dark shadows underneath them. Claire couldn't bear to think of the terror they must have felt as they tried to get out of the burning house. They didn't talk about what had happened, though every now and then Emily would remember a toy or book or piece of clothing that was lost forever and start to cry, and Oliver asked Claire repeatedly what they were going to do. Ben was confused; he wanted to go home. He clung to Claire, following her, climbing on her, crying when she disappeared from sight.

Gareth took the twins to stay with him in the room he rented above a newsagents in town so that the cottage wouldn't be too crowded. Every day he came to check that Claire

and the children were all right. He seemed nearly as traumatized as they were. It was as though he needed to reassure himself that the children were really there, that he really had
succeeded in getting them out of the burning house.

Sally didn't ask too many questions about what had happened after their night out. Every day she drove Claire to
the hospital to visit William and to the surgery to have the
dressings on her cuts and burns re-dressed. Only once did she
chastise her.

"If only you could have just forgotten about that photographer. I told you not to play with fire."

"Is that meant to be a joke?" asked Claire, flatly.

"I'm sorry," said Sally, changing gear as she approached the
hospital parking lot. "Bad choice of phrase. I meant I warned
you not to get involved with Stefan again. I know the fire was
an accident, but if only you'd been there at the time, it might
not have been so bad."

"I know." Tears welled in Claire's eyes and she searched in
her handbag for tissues. "I know I was stupid." Sally handed
her a tissue from the glove compartment. "And to make it
worse, when I got to London to see him, he was with another
woman."

Claire started to sob into the small white square. She
couldn't stop, tears kept on coming. She wiped them away with
her bandaged arm. It felt as if all the pain was pouring out, all
the remorse, the shame, the loss; it kept coming out in heaving sobs.

Sally took her in her arms and rocked her as though she
were a baby. She kissed her hair and stroked her back.

"It's all right. It's all right," Sally repeated until Claire was
able to sit up and compose herself enough to go and face William's silence again.

* * *

A fire officer phoned and made an appointment to discuss the results of their investigation into the cause of the fire. Claire could feel her hands shaking with fear as Sally showed him into the living room. They must have found out that it was started with paraffin. She hadn't told anyone about what William had told her in the ambulance, not even Sally; she could hardly bear to think it was true. What would she say when she was questioned? Would the police be involved? Could William go to prison for arson?

Claire could feel her heart beating fast. It seemed to bang in her ears as the fire officer exchanged pleasantries with Sally and accepted her offer of a cup of coffee.

When Sally had gone he ruffled through a sheaf of papers on a clipboard, breathing loudly, his bulky frame perched uncomfortably on the edge of Sally's sofa. Claire stared at his plump, shiny cheeks; they were mottled red and purple. She wondered if they were discolored from years of facing into flames and heat. The thought of fire made her want to be sick.

"Sorry to keep you," he said, looking up at her. "I'm just making sure I've got everything in order before I start." Claire had a terrible feeling she really was going to be sick.

Sally returned with coffee and a plate of bourbon cookies. The fire officer started talking to Sally about the diet he was meant to be on. Claire could hardly bear it and willed him to get on with what he had come for.

"Now then," he said when Sally had finally left the room. "We take cases like these extremely seriously and do everything we can to find the cause. We want to know how a fire has started and of course you want to know how it started."

Claire nodded silently.

"My team, my very experienced and conscientious team, has searched the scene extensively, using all methods of investigation available to them." He took a sip of coffee; the mug looked tiny in his large, fleshy hands.

Get on with it, thought Claire, *just tell me.*

The fire officer sighed. "But I'm afraid in this particular case we couldn't find a definite cause."

Claire could hardly believe it. She tried not to laugh.

"It was most likely a burning log that rolled out onto the rug in front of the fireplace," the fire officer continued, helping himself to his third cookie. "It's very common with open fires. Leave them unattended and *whoosh,* the whole house gone in no time." He illustrated the *whoosh* with his hands, spilling coffee onto his jacket. He didn't seem to notice. "And then once a fire gets its teeth into a thatched roof . . ." He took another bite of cookie. "Well, you've seen for yourself what happens." He shook his head and grimaced, then he smiled. "You can't beat a nice bourbon cream. Got to be in the top ten for cookies in my book." Putting the mug down, he stood up, revealing a white shirt straining across a sagging stomach. "We'll be passing our report on to your insurance company. There shouldn't be any problem there." He cleared his throat and looked down at Claire, who was dumb with relief. "I'd just like to express my condolences about the loss of your house," he said. "It must be a terrible time for you. My missus said she saw it in one of those fancy magazines—she reads them in the hairdresser's. Very pretty, she said it was. Such a shame." He held out his hand to Claire and she stood up to see him out.

As she closed the front door, she felt almost giddy. She didn't know if she wanted to laugh or cry. For nights she had lain awake with worry that they would find the container or do some test that would reveal a trace of paraffin, but the intense heat must have destroyed any evidence. Would they have been looking for it anyway? Who would suspect that a happy husband and father, living in the beautiful home he had worked so hard to create, would ever try to burn it down as his family slept upstairs? It could only have been a terrible accident.

A local newspaper ran a story on the fire and the irony that it was being featured in an interiors magazine at the time. A national newspaper picked up on it and tried to interview Claire. When she refused to talk to them over the phone, they came to Sally's house, camping outside on the village green, waiting for Claire to come out.

"How does it feel to have lost everything?" The reporter tried to shove a small microphone at Claire as she got into Sally's car. His cheap leather coat flapped around him in the wind. "What's it like to have your beautiful home burned to the ground?"

"What do you think it's like, you stupid man?" shouted Sally. "Piss off and leave her alone."

A short photographer with greasy hair took pictures, pushing his camera against the car window as Sally drove away with a screech of tires.

The next day the story appeared as a double-page spread with pictures of the burned-out shell beside the pictures from *Idyllic Homes*.

UP IN FLAMES. THE DREAM DESTROYED, screamed the headline. *Cushion-maker, 40, still in shock as her husband lies critically ill in the hospital.* There was an out-of-focus picture of Claire staring through the glass of the car window. She looked haggard and confused; her complexion ashen beneath her scraped-back hair, her bandaged arm raised as if to try to cover her face.

"*'She is devastated,' a close friend told us,*" it said underneath.

Claire carefully folded up the newspaper and put it on the table in front of her.

"I told you not to look at it," said Sally.

"I'm glad I saw it," said Claire. "At least I know what the house looks like now. It makes it easier to accept what has happened. It's made it real."

"If I were you, I'd ask them to print an apology for saying that you're forty."

A large bouquet of flowers arrived from Celia Hammond. She sent her condolences for "the terrible tragedy that you have suffered." Claire thought about Stefan. What must he be thinking? He must know about the fire; even if he hadn't seen the newspaper, surely Celia would have told him. She kept thinking he might try to get in touch, but days passed and she heard nothing. She told herself he was the last person she wanted to see, to even think about, but small bubbles of long-ing still seemed to burst through the disgust, anger, and shame that covered her feelings for him.

CHAPTER 28

An intriguing mix of old and new.

"I don't want to push you out," said Sally, the first morning that Oliver and Emily went back to school. Ben still seemed too clingy to return to nursery and he sat on Claire's lap playing with LEGO blocks while she tried to take sips from a steaming cup of tea. Sally reached out for Claire's hand across the table.

"You know you can stay here as long as you like, but have you thought at all about what you might do? Where you're going to live until the insurance claim is sorted out?"

Claire tried to focus her mind. She had been trying to think about the future for weeks, to work out some sort of plan for herself, for the children, for William when he came out of the hospital. But every time she tried to settle on a course of action, her mind seemed to fuzz.

"There's something I haven't told you yet," said Sally. "Gareth and I are getting back together."

"Oh, Sally, that's wonderful news! I do like Gareth; he's been so kind since the fire and of course everything he did that morning was amazing."

"I know." Sally grinned. "He's such a hero. It made me realize how much I miss him. How much I really love him. I know he messed things up with his cyber-flirtation stuff, but everyone makes mistakes. I can see now that temptation can lead anyone astray in even the strongest marriages, like yours."

Claire took a sip of her tea. "I'm glad something good has come out of the whole fiasco. I'm really pleased for you both."

"I can't wait to rekindle the old passion," said Sally wistfully. "It will be like when we first met." She sighed happily. "Though obviously not in the back of his dad's Ford Cortina."

"Doesn't Gareth mind about you and Josh?"

"Josh is long gone now. Apparently it all got too 'heavy' after the fire. It did me the world of good while it lasted, though, and jealousy was the best punishment for Gareth. Anyway, I've got some new tricks now that I'm longing to show him. He won't be interested in busty Bettys anymore!"

"Well, I can see you won't want us in your way when he comes back." Claire felt panic rising. Where could they go?

"Could you find somewhere to rent in town?" asked Sally gently. "I know there's probably not much to choose from, but I could make inquiries for you. Anna did say you could stay in the rooms above the gallery, but there isn't a proper kitchen and the heating is a bit hit-and-miss."

Claire stared out of the window; it looked out at gray December fields and a leafless wood of oak trees that climbed the steep hill to where her home had been, to what was left of it. She missed the view from the top of the hill. She missed the feeling of looking out across the valley to the distant sea beyond. Suddenly she longed to see the view again.

"What do you think?" said Sally. "Shall I phone up an estate agent for you? Shall I ask what rental properties they've got?"

Claire turned and looked at her friend. She smiled the first smile that she'd attempted for a long time.

"I know what I want to do," she said to Sally. "I think I've thought of the perfect place."

It was the first time Claire had driven since the fire. The cuts on her feet still hurt as she pressed down on the pedals and she was relieved that she only had to go a mile up the hill.

"I'll come with you," Sally had said.

"No," replied Claire. "This is something I need to do myself."

The air still smelled of charred wood as she opened the car door. Tentatively she got out into the gray winter rain and forced herself to look in front of her. Even though she'd seen the picture in the newspaper, the reality was hard to take in. She squinted her eyes so that the house became a hazy blur. That was easier. She could almost believe that the thatched roof was still there, glass still in the windows, walls still painted Dorset cream. Slowly she refocused and let herself take in the sagging blackened hole that gaped open, like a festered wound, where the roof had been. One chimney had partially collapsed and the walls were blackened and streaked with smoke stain. All around lay glass from the windows and bits of stone that had fallen from the chimney. One remaining black branch of rosebush outlined the doorless porch.

As Claire walked forward she heard the crunch of glass under her boots. Walking around to the back garden, she stumbled as her foot hit against a fallen beam. It lay across the path like a giant stick of charcoal. Claire put out her hand to steady herself on the wall beside her. When she looked down she saw each fingertip was black, as if she had been fingerprinted for a crime. She bent down and wiped her fingers on the damp grass before continuing on, away from the empty shell of the house, across the lawn toward the view, toward the summerhouse.

The summerhouse looked perfect; its pretty blue-and-white exterior untouched by flames or smoke. Standing in the entrance, Claire couldn't see the house at all. She realized that all the windows faced away from the house as well. From inside all they would see was the rolling view.

Claire pushed the door. She hadn't thought it would be open; she'd assumed that William, always so fanatical about security, would have kept it locked. Surprisingly, it opened to her touch and so she went inside. William had laid an extravagant solid oak floor, and the weekend before the fire, he had painted the wooden-paneled walls and ceiling white. It was empty apart from the little wood burner in one corner and a small enamel sink against a wall.

Claire flicked the light switch and the room lit up. It felt dry and warmer than the cold outside air. The smell of pine and paint was a welcome relief from the smell of burned house. It was clean and simple and full of possibilities.

She looked around the single room. It was large—much too large, she had thought when it had been erected, but now she was relieved at just how big it seemed.

Slowly she walked around. If they had a foldout sofa bed at one end, three small mattresses that could be put away in the daytime, there would still be room for a table and chairs at the other end and some sort of a cupboard that could be used as a work surface. She could buy a microwave, a small fridge, a kettle, and a single electric ring would be enough to cook on. She would need shelves and pegs on the walls for storage.

A surge of energy, almost happiness, filled Claire. She felt excited, determined, filled with a sense of purpose that she hadn't felt for a long time.

For the next week she was constantly busy. As she went back and forth to the summerhouse, she grew used to walking past the blackened hulk of the burned-out house. The pain and guilt on seeing it faded until it almost seemed that it had nothing to do with her at all, that her home was a distant memory, far away in a different time and place.

The first thing Claire bought was a power drill, followed by a box of screws, a tape measure, a spirit level, and several long packs of wooden shelving.

"I could get someone in to do this for you," said Sally as Claire marked out in pencil on the walls where the shelves would go, measuring between them and testing the straightness with the spirit level.

"No," replied Claire, concentrating on the numbers on the tape measure. "I'm determined to do this myself."

"Do you want a glass of Cava to give you courage?" asked Sally, sitting cross-legged on the floor of the summerhouse with a bottle and two plastic cups she had brought with her to toast Claire's first attempt at DIY.

"I'll wait until after I've finished," Claire said, plugging in the drill. "I think drinking and drilling may be a criminal offense."

"Are you sure you know what you're doing?" Sally asked. "It's not too late to see what houses are up for rent in . . ." Her words were drowned by the shriek of the electric drill. Sally put her hands over her ears.

"There!" Claire stood back to admire the triangular support she had just attached to the wall. "It's easy. I don't know why I've never tried it before. Come on, Sally, I need your help to hold one end of the shelf."

An hour and a half later three neat rows of shelves and several rows of pegs and hooks lined the room. The two women sat in the middle of the floor.

"To my new home," Claire said, raising the glass in her hand. Sally raised hers and they laughed as the plastic cups dented as they tried to clink them together.

"I'm beginning to feel quite excited about this," Claire said, taking a sip of fizzing wine. "I think it's going to be lovely in here. Really cozy. It's funny, but I don't miss the house nearly as much as I thought I would. I don't feel sad anymore. In fact, I feel strangely liberated. I don't miss our things, the furniture, the ornaments, my clothes. I feel like I've been freed."

"There'll be a lot less vacuuming and cleaning to do in here anyway," said Sally, laughing. "I would be happy to be freed from that."

"Now that the house has gone, maybe William and I can start again. A clean slate. We can do anything we like."

"I wonder what he'll think of this," said Sally, looking around the room.

"He was the one who wanted the summerhouse in the first place."

"I don't suppose he was ever planning for you all to live in it, though," said Sally uncertainly.

Over the next few days Claire put up more shelves and made pretty gingham curtains, cushions, and a long string of bunting on a sewing machine that she had found secondhand. She bought a sofa bed, a small pine table, and five mismatched wooden chairs at a local auction, along with a box of assorted crockery, cutlery, and a saucepan, and made a worktop out of short planks of leftover oak floorboards that she found on William's woodpile. She built a frame out of bricks to support it and curtained off the space underneath to make a long, shelved cupboard.

The toilet had been her biggest worry, but she bought a portable chemical one from an RV dealer and with Sally's help erected a small wooden shed, beside the summerhouse, to put it in.

"People survived with outside toilets for thousands of years," Claire said as Sally wrinkled up her nose at the thought of using it. "I'm sure we can survive with this until we decide what our long-term plans will be."

Claire waited until she had bought a television and DVD player, a radio and a selection of children's books and toys, and then she decided it was time to show the children their new home. She had strung a brightly colored length of bunting along one wall and put flowers in a small jug on the table. The wood burner in the corner cast a welcome heat around the room. Macavity lay curled up against a cushion on the sofa, purring softly, delighted with his new abode.

Emily cried as Claire pulled up in front of their old home. Oliver said nothing. He had been withdrawn and quiet ever since the fire and Claire worried about him most of all.

Claire led them round the side of the house into the garden carrying Ben, who hid his face in her shoulder, wailing that he wanted to go home to Sally's house.

"Can we make the house again?" asked Emily, tears pouring down her cheeks. "I want it to be the same. Will it be *exactly* the same?"

"Maybe," said Claire. "We'll see what Daddy wants to do when he gets better. But come and see where we're going to live until then."

The children stared around them as they stood silently in

the doorway of the summerhouse. Claire tried to read their faces.

"Wow!" Oliver said after a while. "It's cool. Like a den."

Claire smiled.

"Not a den," said Emily, wiping her eyes with her hand. "It's like a Wendy house. Can we really sleep in here?"

"I want to watch a DVD," said Ben, flinging himself on the sofa.

Claire gave them lemonade and Rice Krispie cakes and they all sat on the sofa with Macavity between them watching a film until it grew dark outside and they went back to Sally's for one last night.

You've made it gorgeous in here," Sally said as she filled Claire's teapot with boiling water. "It would make a lovely feature for a magazine."

"You are joking, aren't you?" asked Claire, joining her friend at the table and opening a box of mince pies, which Sally abstemiously declined.

"Sorry," said Sally. "I forgot. I was only trying to say how nice it is in here."

"Thank you for the compliment, but I think I've had enough of showing off in magazines."

"Been there, done that, got the burned-out shell and ruined marriage to prove it?" Sally gave a cheeky grin.

"Sally!" said Claire, laughing. "Though that just about sums it up. I just hope the marriage isn't as irreparable as the house."

Claire and the children had been living in the summerhouse for a week when William's parents appeared. Claire answered the knock on the door with an armful of dirty washing; she was preparing for a trip to the launderette in town. The remnants of breakfast still littered the table and she hadn't had a chance to put the children's beds away.

William's father hovered on the path behind his wife while she stood stiffly on the threshold, reluctant to come farther inside. She looked around her with disdain. She didn't even bother commenting on what Claire had done to the summer-house. Her look said it all.

"I'm trying to persuade William to come back home when he's released from the hospital," she said.

"This is his home," Claire said.

"I mean his proper home. Where he comes from. Where he belongs."

"This is where he belongs; with his family," Claire said. She could smell the children on the washing in her arms and it gave her the strength to stand up to her mother-in-law. "I know it's all a bit makeshift in here, but it's somewhere for us to live while we decide what's best for our future."

"Your future?" William's mother's laugh was mocking. "Do you really think you've got a future? William's told me all about your sordid little affair. I think that causes him almost as much pain as losing the house."

"My sordid little affair, as you put it, is all in the past." Claire could feel her face flushing with anger. She squeezed the bundle of washing tighter.

"It's not in the past for William. He's so upset."

"I know we've got a lot to sort out, but I'm determined to rebuild our lives together. He's my husband; we've got the children to think of and we'll get through this."

"At least William has had the support of old friends. Vanessa has been wonderful. I'm sure you know that she's been to visit him in the hospital."

Claire didn't know but she wasn't about to admit it. She smiled brightly and said, "I know, she's been so kind."

William's mother only briefly looked disconcerted and then her eyes narrowed. "I don't know why William's so surprised at your faithless behavior." She stepped forward into the room. She casually flicked some crumbs on the table in front of her onto the floor. "From the minute I first saw you I knew you couldn't be trusted. I recognized you for the flighty tart that you really are."

Claire couldn't help laughing. "Flighty tart! I like that." She looked at the bony, hard-faced woman in front of her and kept smiling as she spoke. "I think you've said all you came to say. This is my home now. The house you found behind my back and treated as though it was your own is gone; I no longer have to feel beholden to you. I no longer have to be your skivvy while you fawn all over your treasured son and find fault with me. William is not a little boy at prep school anymore. He's forty-three and he can decide for himself whether he wants to live with you or come back to me, but I've decided I've had enough of your condescending behavior and I'd really like you to leave."

"Well!" William's mother looked as though she was about to explode. Her long camel-hair coat seemed to visibly swell with rage. "I've never been spoken to so rudely. You really are an ungrateful little bitch." Behind her William's father gave Claire a small, weak smile. She turned around and started pushing the washing into a carrier bag.

"Watch out that you don't trip on the charred lintels as you leave."

When she looked up William's mother had vanished. The door had been left open, swinging on its hinges, letting in the icy December air.

CHAPTER 29

The perfect country Christmas.

The week before Christmas the doctors said that William could go home; he had refused his mother's pleas to go with her to be cosseted in the Cotswolds. Claire felt hopeful, even excited.

For days the children had been decorating the summerhouse with paper chains, twigs of holly, and ivy branches in preparation for Christmas and William's return. Claire had strung up swathes of twinkling fairy lights and made a pretty wreath of winter foliage for the front door. There wasn't room for a proper Christmas tree, so Emily had painted a glittery picture of one at school, which Claire pinned to the wall, putting a collection of wrapped presents on the floor underneath it. The children had made a banner that Sally helped them to string across the front of the summerhouse: WELCOME HOME DADDY in large cutout paper letters suspended from a long ribbon.

Claire parked the car in the hospital lot and hoped that this would be the last time that she saw the place. At last they could all be together as a family. She almost skipped toward the tall, stark building to get her husband.

William waited for her on a chair beside his bed. Looking at him through the glass window of the ward, Claire was shocked to see how loosely the new clothes she had bought for him hung on his body. She noticed for the first time that his hair, uncut and longer now, was turning gray. She put on a sunny smile before entering the room.

"Come on then, darling. Let's get you out of here."

Sitting beside Claire in the passenger seat, William was silent, staring blankly out of the window. She wished he didn't have to see the remains of the house when she parked the car beside it in the drive. As she turned off the engine, he gave a low-pitched gasp and then let out a noise that was somewhere between a wail and a sob. He looked away and kept looking away while Claire helped him from the car and led him to the summerhouse.

Sally had kept the wood burner well stoked so that it was warm and cozy when Claire opened the door and gently guided William through it.

"Daddy," the children shouted together, jumping up from the sofa to embrace him.

Silently he pushed them away, sat down on a chair beside the wooden table, and with his head in his hands, began to cry.

The days leading up to Christmas day were hard. William didn't speak to Claire or the children except to answer yes or no. At the beginning he spent most of his time sitting at the table looking out of the window at the bare trees and distant sea, not even bothering to get dressed. After a little while he started to go outside and walk around. Sometimes Claire would come out and look for him and find him standing, staring at the hollow shell, his face expressionless. She tried to reassure him.

"We can build another house here or move away. Or buy a new house; start again. We could go anywhere." The insurance company had assured her they would get the full rebuilding insurance, as it had been an accident.

William shrugged off her embraces and refused to talk.

The small stone outbuilding, which had many decades ago been used as a woodshed, had not been damaged by the fire. Claire was pleased when she found William cleaning it out on Christmas Eve. At least he was doing something, though she couldn't think why he wanted to move out all the gardening equipment and sacks of manure and compost and leave them in the rain.

"Do you remember suggesting that I use this shed as a workshop for Emily Love?" Claire asked him, tentatively touching his back. After getting no response, she continued, "I've been thinking about taking you up on your idea. I could get an electrician to rig up some lights and a power point for the sewing machine and a heater. It would be dry enough to store the fabric and a bit of stock." Still no response. "I know it would only be temporary, but I've got to start Emily Love again. I've come so far, I don't want to lose the business now. What do you think? Now you've started clearing it out, maybe I could paint the walls inside after Christmas? It would be a project for us after the children go back to school. Something to do together."

William heaved out another large sack of compost and dragged it over to the others. Wordlessly he bent down and picked up one of the many fallen stones that now littered the garden. For a few seconds he passed it from one hand to the other as if trying to calculate its weight. Suddenly he raised his arm and hurled the stone, hard, toward the burned-out house. It hit a window whose corner still held a jagged piece of glass. The smash seemed to ricochet around the valley and the remains of the glass disappeared. He walked back into the summerhouse. Claire stood in the December drizzle, her eyes closed tight, trying not to cry.

C laire was dreading Christmas Day. How different it was going to be from the hot day in July when they'd pretended to celebrate it for the magazine. She booked a table at the hotel in town for Christmas dinner to make a change from the meals squashed around the little table in the summerhouse; Claire trying to make jolly conversation, the children squabbling over elbow room, and William morosely pushing his food around the plate without really eating it.

William had shown no interest in accepting his mother's invitation to go to the Cotswolds for Christmas Day, which was a great relief to Claire. In fact he showed no interest in seeing his parents at all. She tried to talk to him about it, but was, of course, met with sullen silence.

On Christmas morning they woke up to a low, gray sky full of swirling snow. By lunchtime the snow was too thick to get the cars out of the drive.

"We'll just have to have a lovely Christmas dinner here," said Claire, in the cheerful voice she seemed to use most of the time now, as she peered into the little cupboard. "We've eggs and beans and spaghetti hoops. How does that sound?" She looked at William, knowing the chances of a response were slim.

"That's not a proper Christmas dinner," said Emily, who was dressed up in a sequined party dress that Elizabeth and Brian had given her especially for the meal at the hotel.

"Well, it's the best I can do, darling," Claire said through gritted teeth.

Just then there was a knock at the front door. Claire and the children looked at one another with surprise. Oliver, who was nearest, jumped up to open it and in walked Sally and Gareth followed by the twins, almost unrecognizable in layers of coats, scarves, and gloves. Gareth was wearing a flashing Santa hat and carrying a large steaming parcel covered in tinfoil.

"Ho, ho, ho," he boomed, stamping his boots on the doormat. "Glad tidings of great joy and all that."

Sally also had a Santa hat on and carried a bulging shopping basket in each hand. Despite her new fitness regime she was out of breath from the trudge up the snow-covered hill.

"We didn't reckon you'd make it in to town for your Christmas meal," she said, sitting down and shrugging off her coat. "And my parents couldn't get through to us for dinner as we'd planned, so we decided to bring our meal up here to share with you!"

Claire hugged her. "You're wonderful," she said. "It's a lovely surprise to have you here, but the biggest surprise is that you've cooked Christmas dinner. I thought your parents usually brought it with them?"

"Not this year," Gareth said, a big smile on his face. Sally put her arms around him.

"This year Gareth cooked it," she said proudly. "Since I've got into doing up the house, he's decided to take over in the kitchen."

"I got into cooking those few months I lived on my own,"

explained Gareth as he took out a succession of Tupperware containers from the bags. "I found I enjoyed it and bought a few cookbooks. But this has been my biggest challenge yet."

The children jumped around the small room. Oliver started examining the boxes of food.

"Peas, carrots, mmm . . . mashed potato—my favorite, roast potatoes—yum, brussels sprouts—ugh, parsnips—you like those, don't you, Dad?"

William gave a slight shrug and then nodded.

"Gravy, mince pies—yum, Christmas pudding, custard— lush, chocolates." Oliver continued piling everything up on the work surface.

"Oh, Gareth, you've brought the works!" Claire said, giving him a kiss on the cheek. "I bet this will be tastier than the meal we would have had at the hotel."

"But best of all, we brought this." Sally opened the door into the snow again and brought in a plastic bag that she had left on the path. "It needed to be left on ice," she said as she drew out a bottle of champagne followed by a carton of fresh orange juice. "Buck's fizz, anybody?"

"Yes please," Claire said, bringing out four brightly colored children's cups. She hadn't gotten round to buying proper glasses yet. William shook his head to the cup that Sally offered him and instead produced a half-drunk bottle of whiskey from his jacket pocket and poured a generous helping into a mug.

The adults ate at the little table while the children sat on the sofa and floor with plates perched precariously on their knees. Gareth's food was delicious; even the children finished everything on their plates. And asked for more. When the champagne was all gone, the adults drank a bottle of Brian's homemade rhubarb wine. He had brought it as a housewarming present when he and Elizabeth came over from France before Christmas. By the time they'd finished the Christmas pudding and started on a game of charades and a box of After Eight mints, Claire realized she was enjoying herself.

It was so much more fun than the usual stress of Christmas Day—the mad rush of trying to entertain at home or the tongue-biting awkwardness of having Christmas Day with William's parents.

Claire tried not to look at William through the meal. She could sense his taciturn expression as Gareth tried to engage him in conversation and Sally fussed round him, trying to coax him to have a little more to eat. He hardly touched his Christmas dinner, but Emily had put a paper crown on his head and he smiled a little at Oliver's attempts to act out *Charlie and the Chocolate Factory* in charades.

"Good night. Many thanks," William said as Sally, Gareth, and the boys set off into the moonlit night, to head for home. Claire almost jumped in surprise; it was so long since she'd heard him say a sentence she hardly recognized his voice.

She hoped this might be the start of his emergence from the grim despair that held him in its steely grasp. Perhaps he had begun to realize that they didn't need five bedrooms, three bathrooms, an Aga, and a conservatory to have a lovely family life together. Maybe he would agree to something simpler from now on.

She liked living in the summerhouse. It was easier to clean, for a start. She liked having the children around her, not scattered all over the house doing different things. It was cozy and warm, and though they had to go to Sally's for a shower and the outside toilet was like icy torture in the January mornings, she thought she couldn't remember being happier.

But then she'd look at William's tight, grim face, or the raised, red scars on her arm and the horror would return again. The horror of what had happened, what they had lost. The thought of what they could have lost was worse. Claire had stopped taking the tranquilizers a few weeks after the fire, but sometimes she felt the need to go and sit in the orchard where William couldn't see her and have a cigarette to calm the fears that still threatened to consume her.

Claire tried to talk to William. She wanted to start the dialogue that she hoped would end the uncomfortable limbo they were living in.

"I'm so sorry," she would whisper as they lay on the sofa bed, the children breathing gently in their sleep beside them. "I'm so sorry about everything that happened."

"Don't," William would say, and move away from her into the dark.

"We can start again," she'd say to break the silence as they ate their sandwiches for lunch. "We can design a new house, here, just the way we want it. Or we could go somewhere else. Whatever you like. We can make a perfect home again." She'd reach out and try to hold his hand, but it was always just out of reach.

The doctor diagnosed depression and signed William off work for another three months after he was physically fit enough to go back. Claire and William were together every day and she counted the hours until the children came home from school to fill the summerhouse with their classroom news and their noisy demands for food and help with games and homework. Their lively chatter and laughter, even their bickering and quarrels, were a welcome distraction from William's gloomy silence.

Time, Claire thought. *We just need time.*

* * *

In late January Claire came home from a trip to the supermarket to find William up a ladder in the garden stringing electric cables between posts from the summerhouse to the old pig shed.

"What are you doing?" she asked, putting down the shopping bags and looking up at him. The sky was a startling bright blue and she had to shield her eyes with her hand from the glare of the sun.

"Putting in electricity," he replied, without looking at her.

"Oh, William, thank you! You know how much I've been longing to get back to work," she said, thrilled that he was starting on the workshop for her. "I'll put the shopping inside and then I'll come and help you."

"It's not for you," he said. "I'm going to move in here myself."

"Why?"

"I need more space."

"Oh," she said, too bewildered to think of anything else to say. It was the longest conversation they had had since the night he found the text messages. She stood looking at him for a minute. "It's not that bad in the summerhouse, is it?" she said finally.

He turned and stared down at her. "It's a shed," he snarled. "It's just a bloody shed and you're behaving like it's some sort of Snow White cottage." He started climbing down the ladder. When he was at the bottom, he walked up to her. "I'm not going to play in your damn doll's house anymore. You've made us live in a shed, Claire, and now I'm moving out and getting a shed of my own." His face was close to hers. It was unshaven and gray; his breath smelled sour. It smelled of whiskey. She found herself recoiling, stepping back and stumbling among the plastic bags at her feet. Though he could have put out his hand to steady her, William made no attempt to stop her from falling and Claire found herself on the cold grass, her hands stinging from the contact with the frozen ground, as her husband stalked away.

William moved his few things—a pillow, blankets, his clothes—into the outbuilding that afternoon. When the children came home from school, Claire told them Daddy had been feeling squashed and needed a bit more room. Emily and Oliver wanted to spend the night in "Daddy's new house," but William wouldn't let them.

You could use the garage at the bottom of our garden," Sally said as she and Claire sat in the chaos of Sally's kitchen drinking coffee. A pile of dirty pans and bowls teetered precariously in the sink; though Gareth's culinary skills were developing fast, he had yet to master the art of washing up. Sally had half painted the kitchen ceiling the night before and Claire had had to negotiate the ladder and a floor strewn with dripping paint cans and brushes before finding a chair to sit on. "We never use the garage. I can never be bothered to put the car in there—I'd only have to take it out again." Sally was already searching through an assortment of bowls on the dresser, looking for the garage key. "It would make a perfect studio for you. There's loads of room. Ah, here it is."

They walked down a short cement path to Sally's garage. Sally opened it and flicked a light switch. Claire stared around her.

"How could you say there's loads of room in here? I've never seen so much stuff."

Piles of newspaper threatened to collapse onto glass bottles and jars that spilled from carrier bags onto the concrete floor. At least three mildewed double strollers in various stages of dilapidation leaned against the wall and plastic trikes, ride-on cars, and rusty scooters tangled together with a dartboard, assorted buckets and spades, a two-wheeled skateboard, and a pink doll's pram.

"I thought the boys needed to get in touch with their feminine side," Sally said, when Claire pointed at the pram and raised her eyebrows. "But instead they got in touch with their demon side and within a day they'd sat in it and taken turns to run it into the wall until it buckled and the wheels refused to go round anymore."

By picking-up time they calculated that between them they had made over twenty trips to the local dump. The garage was now a clean square space with nothing in it but a long workbench at one end and a set of metal shelves.

"This will be great," Claire said, brushing down her dusty clothes. She looked around her, smiling at the thought of getting back to work. "Are you sure you won't mind me being here every day?"

"Mind? Why would I mind? I'll be at college half the week, but I'll love having you here to come home to, and maybe you'll even let me help sometimes. My sewing would be good enough to sew on a few buttons and I'm sure I could manage to coordinate a roll of packing tape and an address label."

Over the next few weeks Sally went with her to local auctions and garage sales and Claire started to build up a new collection of vintage fabric, buttons, and lace. Some of the shops and customers who had made orders before the fire had been willing to wait, so she had plenty of work to make a start on.

It was a relief to get out every day, to go to work in another space where she didn't have to be in William's gloomy company. Even though he slept in the woodshed, he still spent his days in the summerhouse. He sat close to the wood burner, unshaven, no longer bothering to hide the bottle of whiskey he seemed to get through every day now. Claire tried to suggest counseling but was met with a withering look. She felt inadequate, incapable of helping her grieving husband. It was so much easier to think about buttons and ribbons and pretty combinations of fabric.

Claire worked hard and with a renewed enthusiasm for the business; she was filled with ideas and spent her evenings sketching designs at the little wooden table and answering inquiries on her newly acquired laptop. On the days that Sally wasn't at college she joined Claire in the garage, willingly following her instructions, genuinely enthusiastic about what Claire was doing. Her retail course gave her the confidence to suggest her own ideas about marketing the business and within a few months Emily Love was doing better than it ever had before.

Despite William's behavior, as spring approached Claire felt as if something heavy was being lifted from her. She felt an exhilarating lightness inside, an excitement about the future.

Crocuses, then celandines, speckled the lawn, as they always had done, and daffodils pushed their way through the rubble that had fallen on the flower beds. Surrounded by the flowers and bright new leaves, Claire thought the house looked like a romantic ruined castle from a fairy tale. The children played beside it, making up stories of witches and magic and enchanted princesses who lived inside the dark walls, where they were not allowed to go.

The insurance money came through, but William wouldn't

talk to her about what they were going to do with it. It sat in
their bank account. Claire asked two different architects to
come and give them some ideas. The first arrived, brimming
with optimism.

"It will be like a phoenix from the flames," he said. "Let's
make this tragedy into something positive for you. Let's rebuild your dream but give it a bit of edge, bring it up-to-date,
make it spectacular this time. I see glass, I see sheets of slate,
and I see sliding doors onto a cast-iron balcony."

William asked him to leave before he could unfold the
plans.

The second architect arrived with no plans but an idea to
build a bungalow on the original site of the house.

"I love bungalows," he said to William. "They give you the
peace of mind that you can stay in your home well into your
old age because, let's face it, neither of us are on the right side
of forty and the future is closer than we'd like to think."

Claire tried to be polite as she showed the architect to his
car. William had uttered an expletive and stomped away minutes before.

"I think we need a bit more time to think about what we
really want," she explained.

He looked perplexed.

"I tell you, it's true. You can never go wrong with a bungalow," he called from his car window as he pulled away.

At night Claire would lie on the sofa—now that she slept
on her own, she didn't bother to make it up into a double
bed—wondering what to do. The possibilities jumbled in her
head: rebuilding, moving house completely. Would another
renovation project be what William would want? Would it be

something Claire could bear? William refused to talk about the future and increasingly wasn't there at all. He had begun to disappear for long hours at a time, driving off at lunchtime and coming home late at night. He never told Claire where he had been. She felt that she had no right to ask.

The summer arrived in bursts of sunshine between days of showery rain and fresh breezes. On the first hot afternoon they had in June, Claire parked the car and noticed a haze of color around the charred remnants of the front door. The roses were in bloom. Despite the flames and smoke they had survived to flower again. The sight filled her with optimism. If the roses could survive, so could she. If they could struggle against the odds to grow and blossom, she could too. Claire saw the roses on the same day that William went back to work.

CHAPTER 30

Where the heart is . . .

At the end of July, Claire took the children to France to visit her mother and Brian. She had tried to persuade William to come with them, but he had scowled and walked away every time she mentioned it. In the end she piled the children into the car and drove away, feeling guilt for leaving him on his own and relief that she could have a week without his brooding silence.

After the longest journey Claire had ever done without William to share the driving, they finally arrived. The flat, yellow house in front of her glowed warmly in the sun; faded green shutters were closed at the windows to protect it from the heat of the Dordogne summer. There seemed to be no one about. Claire and the children unfurled themselves from the car, stiff after their long drive, and the large house welcomed them into its cool, quiet interior. The ancient walls and limestone floors soothed her as soon as she walked in. Suddenly a heavy oak door opened and a beaming Brian and Elizabeth and a barking Buster tumbled into the hallway in a rush to greet them.

"We weren't expecting you so soon," Elizabeth cried, flinging her arms around her daughter.

"We were in the kitchen preparing a feast for you," said Brian, wiping his hands on a stripy apron before giving Claire a kiss and ruffling the children's hair.

"You weren't able to persuade William to come at the last minute, then?" Elizabeth asked as she led them into a huge kitchen, lined with pine cabinets and glass-fronted cupboards. Rustic pottery and copper saucepans were piled on the shelves and bunches of dried herbs hung from hooks on the walls. The most wonderful smell emanated from a huge cast-iron range; Brian took up position in front of it, stirring the bubbling pan of venison stew.

"No, unfortunately he couldn't spare the time now that he's back at work." It was only partly true, but Claire didn't want to hurt her mother's feelings.

It felt good to be back in her mother and Brian's easy company again. They insisted on Claire resting in the garden with white wine while Brian brought in the bags and Elizabeth showed the children all the special hidden places in the house with Buster following, his thick tail wagging in a frenzy of delight.

On her first morning, waking up in a wrought-iron bed under a crisp white quilt, Claire felt as though she'd had the best night's sleep she'd had since the fire.

Long, lazy days merged into one another. Her mother and Brian fussed around their visitors, cooking lingering al fresco meals, which they ate in the dappled shade of a vine-covered trellis. Friendly neighbors came and went, joining meals, bringing produce from their gardens. Claire marveled at her mother's rapid French. She seemed to become more gregarious as she spoke the language that Claire could only partly understand, her eyes twinkling, her laughter easy. Like the French themselves, she used her hands as she spoke, gesticulating to get her point across. Claire felt sad that her mother had spent so many years only having bored adolescents with whom to share her love of France.

Buster was a constant presence, his coat as golden as the farmhouse. He followed the children in their games around the garden before collapsing with them, hot and panting, for afternoon naps in the shade. Dog and children tangled together in contented sleep.

Before lunch Claire liked to sketch or read on the patio while Brian taught the children how to fish in the stream that ran through the garden or look for fossils in the small quarry at the bottom of his land. In the late afternoon they walked to a nearby lake where they would swim from a little wooden jetty or drift around in Brian's dingy—Buster at the helm, Claire and her mother reclined on cushions, while the children trailed their hands in the water and took turns to try to row the boat with Brian.

Sometimes her mother and Brian's easy companionship and obvious adoration of each other gave Claire a pang of envy.

Her mother seemed radiant. She was a different person from the bitter woman Claire had shared her teenage years with in their dark, cramped flat. She had developed a passion for gardening and proudly showed off the new flower beds she had made. Tall yellow sunflowers swayed above jewel-colored geraniums and salvias.

"Brian laughs at me for planting sunflowers," she said as she straightened a bamboo support. Claire noticed how brown her mother's arms had become. "The fields round here are full of them—they're crops like corn or barley—but I love them. They make me cheerful."

"I don't think you need sunflowers to make you cheerful," Claire said gently. "Brian seems to do that very well himself."

Her mother smiled. "He keeps asking me to marry him."

"Well, why not?"

"I don't want to go there again. I've been married and it was a disaster. All that pain for so many years. I just want to stay as we are. Why spoil it?"

"Oh, Mum." Claire took her hand. "It wasn't being married that spoiled it the last time, it was the man. Brian's so different from Dad. I'm sure he'd never hurt you. He loves you. For him marriage is a way of showing you how much."

Her mother shrugged and bent down to pluck a weed from the dry soil. When she didn't get up, Claire crouched down beside her and saw that her mother was crying.

"Mum, what's wrong?" Claire put her arms around her.

"I'm sorry, darling." Her mother spoke through muffled sobs. "I just get overwhelmed by it all. I can't believe that this has happened to me: that I met Brian, that I've moved here to this beautiful house, and that I can share it with you and the children."

"But why are you crying?"

The older woman wiped her eyes and looked at her daughter with a smile.

"I'm crying because I'm just so happy."

All too soon the week had gone; it was time to go home. Claire felt a sense of dread as she thought of William. What welcome would he make for them back in the summerhouse? She had been phoning him with no success, but Sally had texted several times to say that she'd been up to see him and he was fine—he had eaten a curry that Gareth had made and she'd seen him drive through the village every morning on his way to work.

Claire knew that when she got home they had to make some serious plans. They couldn't stay living in the summer-house forever. She would have to get William to commit to some sort of decision before the winter came again. She felt sure that once they had a plan, William would be happier, life with him would get easier. It might even bring them closer to-gether again—closer than before the fire, maybe as close as they had once been long ago. As close as they had been before the house had come into their lives.

CHAPTER 31

Restoration can be so rewarding.

A huge white moon shone behind the craggy silhouette of the house. Claire parked the car next to William's. She gently shook Oliver and Emily awake and lifted the sleeping Ben from his car seat. The garden was pitch-black. Claire instructed Oliver to find the flashlight in the glove compartment and with its beam the little group picked their way across the lawn.

The summerhouse was in darkness; the old woodshed too. William must be asleep, thought Claire as she pushed open the door and turned on the light.

Inside, mess and chaos reigned. Dirty plates and mugs littered the table, newspapers lay strewn across the floor, clothes and papers were piled on every available surface. The tap in the sink dripped onto a stinking dishcloth. Macavity slunk out from behind the wood burner. He wound himself around Claire's legs asking for food. Was he thinner?

"Where's Daddy?" asked Emily.

"He's asleep," replied Claire. "It's very late." She put the still-sleeping Ben down on the sofa. "Find some pajamas in the clothes bag and get ready for bed." Inwardly she seethed—at least William could have put the beds out for the children. She started to clear a space on the floor for their camp beds.

The door opened and suddenly William stood unshaven and disheveled in the room. Claire immediately knew he had been drinking.

The children didn't run to greet him as they might once have done. They held back, shrinking into the shadows of the room.

"Are you all right?" Claire asked him. She could feel her heart beginning to beat faster. Could she possibly feel afraid of her own husband?

"I've got something to tell you," he said.

"Can't it wait until the morning? Or tomorrow night when you come home from work?"

"I'm not going to work. I'm never going to work again—I've left. Given up. Resigned." He laughed; his eyes looked wild. Claire found herself wondering if the kitchen knife was in the drawer. "I'm never going back, never slaving over other people's bloody columns of figures, filling out other people's bloody tax returns."

"Oh," she said. Her mind went blank; she couldn't think what else to say.

"There's no point working," he continued. "No point making any money. What's it for? There's nothing left anymore to make the money for."

"There's us. Your family. Your children," Claire said. "How will we survive financially?"

"You can make the money for once, instead of sponging off me—funding your little sewing hobby, funding your affairs with other men." William kicked a piece of newspaper on the floor. Claire looked at Oliver and Emily; they were wide-eyed watching their father. Ben was stirring on the sofa. Any minute he'd wake up and start crying.

"Enough," Claire said firmly. "You're frightening the children."

"Don't you dare tell me what to do." William's voice was raised. "You have no right to tell me to do anything."

"I'm asking you not to frighten our children. Your children. Please, William, go back to bed and sleep the whiskey off. We'll talk in the morning."

"I suppose you want a divorce," said William. He crossed his arms over his chest and looked defiant.

"No," replied Claire. Ben started to cry. She picked him up and stood rocking him, as much for her own comfort as for his. "I'd like us to start communicating again and work out how we're going to live, where we're going to live, what we are going to do. I want us to stay together and build a new life for ourselves."

"I can't imagine anyone I'd less like to build a new life with than you." William spat out the words, his face twisted with rage.

The room seemed to blur in front of her. She held Ben closer.

Suddenly William seemed calm, as though he'd miraculously sobered up.

"Well, I want to get a divorce. It's the most sensible thing to do now that we're separated."

"I didn't know we were separated," Claire said. It sounded like such a ridiculous thing to be saying to her husband.

"I moved out of here months ago, didn't I?"

"You moved your bed—to have a bit more space, I thought—but I didn't think that you sleeping fifty yards across the lawn meant that we were separated. It certainly didn't stop you making a mess of this place while I was away."

"Of course it means we're separated. I left you, Claire, and now I want a divorce."

Claire buried her face into Ben's hair, wishing this conversation wasn't happening, wishing especially that it wasn't happening in front of the children. She was suddenly filled with a desire to lie down and escape into sleep.

"You spoiled everything, Claire. You broke the vows we made to each other with your infidelity." William stepped nearer to her and the words were loud again. She could smell his breath. The alcohol fumes made her want to turn away. "You ruined everything we had, you and your pathetic boyfriend and his crummy magazine. You betrayed me after everything I did for you; you destroyed our home. The home I made for you. I can't even bear to face my parents. You have humiliated me in their eyes. I can't look at my mother without seeing her disappointment. We had everything, Claire, and you just wiped it all away."

"Please don't." Claire didn't want to argue. Ben had stopped crying and was watching his father intently.

"Look at what you've done." He waved his arms at the room. "Look at how you've made us live. Look at how you've made your children live. You did this with your own selfish behavior."

Claire suddenly felt furious. She'd had enough. She moved to within inches of her husband's face and whispered, hoping Oliver and Emily couldn't hear: "I wasn't the one who started the fire and burned down your precious house. Not to mention nearly killing our children."

William stared at her, his face reddening. His jawline twitched and his arm came up. Claire thought he was going to strike her and instinctively flinched. Instead he banged his fist down hard on the table. A discarded mug of tea jumped; cold liquid spattered out across the pine, pouring over the edge onto the floor. She reached for the dishcloth in the sink and then he hit her, slapping her hard across the face and catching the side of Ben's head as he did so. Claire reeled back with the force of it and fell onto the sofa with a thump. Her face stung. Ben was screaming, Oliver and Emily were crying.

"Get out," Claire said, as steadily as she could. William turned around and walked out the door.

Claire felt too numb to check the time when she heard William's car drive away. She knew it was early because the room was still dark. She let herself sleep after that, but Emily's crying woke her before dawn.

"I just want it to be how it used to be," sobbed Emily. "Like it was when we lived in the house."

"It will all work out in the end, darling." Claire pulled her daughter into bed with her and stroked her long hair. "It'll be fine. You'll see."

"Has Daddy gone?"

"Yes, I think he has."

"Where has he gone?"

"I think he's gone to find somewhere of his own to live. Living here made him sad."

"Did we make him sad, Mummy?"

"No, darling, you didn't make him sad. The fire made him sad. He misses the house."

"It was his favorite thing," Emily said simply.

Claire hugged her and squeezed back her own tears. Her cheek ached where William had hit her. Idly, she wondered if she had a bruise.

How had this happened? If someone had told her a year

ago that within twelve months she would become a single mother with a black eye, living in a space the size of a trailer, she would never have believed them. She tried to think how her clumsy, unconsummated mistake of a love affair could have had such dreadful consequences. Was it all because of Stefan or would it have happened anyway? Were she and William always destined to fail in the end?

She wasn't sure if she could carry on on her own. How would she cope? Then she realized that she'd been coping on her own for months. What was the point in falling apart now? She would simply go on coping, sort out her life, find a house, make enough money, and try to mend the damage that had been done to the children. It wasn't up to her to mend William anymore—that was up to him now. The realization felt like a relief.

Emily snored lightly; she had gone back to sleep. Claire got out of bed and quietly opened the door. A pink dawn spread across the horizon and a blackbird began to sing in a holly hedge beside her. It seemed to sing with its entire heart, pouring out its joy. Slowly, somewhere deep inside her, below the pain and sadness and regret, she realized that a tiny grain of happiness was forming. As she listened to the blackbird, the happiness seemed to grow until it became almost too much to bear and she wanted to run across the lawn and sing with all her heart as loudly as the bird. It felt as if she had been released. William had let her go and it didn't feel sad or frightening or painful. It just felt good.

ONE YEAR LATER

The warm spring sun shone down on Claire's back as she pushed her spade into the dark soil. Emily gathered up the rocks and stones that Claire brought to the surface and put them in a wheelbarrow that Oliver ferried back and forth to the bottom of the long rectangular-shaped garden. Squatting on the edge of the vegetable patch, Ben dug earnestly with a trowel.

"There are two big worms here, Mum."

"Great," said Claire. "We need them to make the earth good for all the vegetables we're going to grow."

"And sunflowers as well." Emily stood up straight and shielded her eyes from the bright spring sunshine. "I'm going to grow sunflowers as tall as Granny's ones in France."

Frank, their big black Labrador, sniffed around them, wagging his tail as he pushed his nose into the soil. Macavity's ginger tail twitched as he watched the dog from the safety of a high stone wall.

"I'm going to see if we've any eggs today," said Ben, running over to the wire enclosure in the corner where their three black-and-white-speckled hens, Polly, Molly, and Dolly, clucked and scratched at the warm earth.

The garden was at the back of the house; it was one of the

new houses that William had described as "modern monstrosities" when they were being built.

"I suppose you bought this just to annoy me," he had said
the first time he had picked the children up for a weekend visit
after they had moved in.

"No, William," Claire said patiently. "I bought it because I
like it. It's light and spacious. It needs no renovations. It's easy
to look after, economical to run, and it has a lovely view of the
river. It suits us just fine."

Claire had enjoyed painting the small, sunny rooms herself. There was no one to tell her she hadn't properly prepared
beforehand or that there were drips on the doors. In most of
the rooms she chose light pastel colors to complement her
Emily Love cushions and her new range of curtains and quilts.

In her bedroom, she had papered the walls with a pattern
of turquoise, pink, and gold birds of paradise; she knew William would have loathed it. She loved waking up in the brightly
colored room underneath a pale green satin quilt she'd bought
in France. Usually Frank and Macavity crept in beside her in
the night, and she'd wake to licks and nuzzles from Frank's
damp, soft nose and contented purring from Macavity.

She felt so happy in her new house. No one minded if the
doorknobs were sticky or if there were handprints on the walls.
No one fussed about the jumble of coats, shoes, and bags that
littered the hall, or shouted at the cat for scratching furniture,
or at the children for using felt-tipped pens in the living room.
It wasn't a show home; it was a house to be lived in. Claire felt
as though she could breathe again for the first time in years.

The children were happier too. The garden had a gate at
the far end which led to a quiet back lane where they could
congregate with local friends and ride their bikes. After school
the house was always full of other people's children. Claire

loved the lively chaos and the constant chatter, requests for hot chocolate and cookies or homemade lemonade.

Claire could walk Emily and Ben to and from their school in a matter of minutes—no more mad rushes in the car down narrow country lanes. No more late marks in Mrs. Wenham's big red book. Oliver waited for the bus to his secondary school with a great gang of friends on the High Street. In the evenings he spent a lot of time fishing on the river with Gareth and the twins while Claire and Emily and Ben took Frank for long walks along the riverbank.

William had disappeared for three months after the night he had left the summerhouse. Claire knew he was all right because regular letters from his lawyer arrived embarking on divorce proceedings. She had assumed he would go to his parents, but almost daily frantic phone calls from his mother, anxious and full of accusations, proved that they had not seen or heard from him either. When he eventually appeared he looked years older. Avoiding eye contact with Claire, he told her he had given up drinking and mumbled an apology for hitting her.

As time passed he even seemed quite affable as he picked the children up for holidays or weekend visits, even if his conversations usually started with a remark about the state of her lawn or a bit of fraying carpet in the hall.

The ruins of the house and land around it had been sold to a developer for more than she had expected, and with the money left over after she had bought the new house, Claire had taken on the lease of a small bay-windowed shop on the

High Street. It was bigger than it looked from the outside and there was space for a workshop at the back. A duck-egg-blue sign across the front had EMILY LOVE painted in white lettering along it, with little hearts and daisies at either end. In addition to her own stock, Claire carried a selection of antique French furniture and textiles.

Every few months she, the children, and Frank piled into her new blue "Emily Love"–emblazoned van and went to visit her mother and Brian in France. They spent happy days there; the children romping around the old farmhouse with the dogs, Claire touring junk shops and old-house sales, collecting pretty wrought-iron furniture, vintage floral quilts, scarves, and lace. She started buying enamel kitchen utensils and old tin storage jars, which sold very well in the shop. Sometimes Emily came with her; she was increasingly interested in the business that bore her name. And as Emily got older, Claire found herself valuing her daughter's opinion on what would sell well back home.

"Oh yes, Mummy, that will look lovely." Or, "It's too fancy," or, "It's too frilly," or, "That's horrible." And several times, to Claire's amusement: "Definitely not, it looks like something Grandma would have in her house in the Cotswolds!"

CHAPTER 32

Exquisite taste and an eye for old-world charm.

When Sally finished her retail management course, Claire offered her a job managing the shop so that she could spend more time developing new designs in the workshop. The things that Sally had learned at college proved invaluable and she was bursting with ideas for marketing and displays. Her windows had become a town attraction. She changed them every month and people came especially to see what she had done. For a Valentine's-themed window she hung giant lavender hearts from a huge branch she had painted white; the hearts were interspersed with papier-mâché doves that Sally had made herself at home. When Claire introduced a range of pottery decorated with her designs, Sally cut out silhouettes of cupcakes which she suspended above a display of the new jugs, cups, and teapots. At Christmas she made a life-size sleigh out of cardboard, sprayed it gold, and piled it with boxes wrapped up with vintage fabrics. Emily Love had won the town's best-dressed-window competition.

Just after Christmas, Claire and Sally sat drinking their postschool, pre-shop-opening cup of tea. They were perched on high stools around the large antique counter that Claire had saved from a Dumpster outside a chemist's shop that was being refurbished.

"Can I tempt you to a tiny triangle?" Claire took a large bar of duty-free Toblerone from her stash under the counter and waved it enticingly at Sally. Sally shook her head and virtuously produced an apple to accompany her tea.

"You know the café next door is closing soon," said Claire.

"It's a shame," said Sally, taking a sip from an Emily Love mug decorated with a pattern of polka dots and hearts. "This town needs a good café. It will probably end up as another empty shop. It won't look good next to us and where will I get my lunchtime salad roll now?"

"I've been thinking," Claire said. "I might take on the lease myself."

Sally nodded slowly as she munched on a mouthful of apple. "It is a bit bigger than this shop. More floor space for us. We could certainly do with it, but it seems a shame to have to move when we've got it looking so nice in here."

"I don't mean we'd leave here," said Claire. "We'd keep this as the shop and keep next door as a café. We could have the café as part of the shop."

"Knock through into next door, do you mean?"

"Yes," said Claire. "We could use the new Emily Love tableware and the matching napkins and tablecloths. We could promote what we have to sell in here."

"What sort of café?"

"Like a tea shop really. Cakes and scones, tarts; maybe quiche and soup at lunchtime."

"Claire, are you trying to torture me?" Sally wailed. "I'll never be able to concentrate on my job, let alone stick to my diet." Claire ignored her; she knew Sally had developed a will of steel when it came to maintaining her hard-won slender figure.

"We could find a really good bakery to supply it. I was even thinking about our own range of fairy cakes with pretty Emily Love–inspired designs in icing on the top."

"Coordinating cupcakes—what a fabulous idea." Sally clapped her hands. "Cushions and cakes—everything a woman could possibly want all in one place! My tutors in college would have been so impressed with you, Claire."

"But I'd need someone to run the café. We would never have enough time."

Sally laughed. "You definitely couldn't trust me. I might fall off the wagon and eat more than I'd sell."

"What about Gareth?" asked Claire. "He's so fantastic in the kitchen now and he's always saying he'd like to leave his IT job to work freelance as a Web designer."

Sally sat up straighter on her stool. "Go on," she said. "It's sounding interesting, but I can't see how the two things tie together."

"If he could manage the café through the mornings and at lunchtime—make the quiches, a few salads, maybe a selection of paninis—we could get a couple of waitresses to work with him and take over in the afternoon so that he could develop his Web-designing business at home."

"As long as the waitresses are elderly and toothless, I think it could be a very good idea. I wouldn't want Gareth working with any svelte young things in pinnies," Sally warned. "I still have to keep an eye on him, you know."

"Don't be silly." Claire laughed. "Gareth only has eyes for you, and no wonder—you look a million dollars in those tight jeans. The only place you haven't lost weight from is your bust and that makes you every man's fantasy wife. Gareth wouldn't be interested in waitresses—young or old."

Sally looked delighted at the compliment and at the idea of

working with Gareth. "What a team we could be!" she said. "Like the Three Musketeers. We'll work together to build the Emily Love Empire, conquering the retail world with tea cozies and fairy cakes. We'll be the British answer to IKEA—they've got sofas and meatballs, we'll have cushions and custard slices."

"Calm down," said Claire, laughing. "I don't plan on global expansion just yet."

"What do you want to call the café bit?" asked Sally. "It ought to have its own separate name."

"I have been thinking about a name," said Claire.

"Claire's Cupcakes?"

"Nice," she said, "but I think I've already found the one I like."

"I know, I know." Sally bounced excitedly on her seat. "What about 'the Flighty Tart'? Your mother-in-law would love that." Claire had told her what William's mother had called her on the last occasion they had ever met. The two women burst out laughing. Claire laughed so much she spilled her tea on the credit-card machine.

"That name is appealing," said Claire, popping the plastic cover off the machine and mopping at its internal mass of wires and chip pads, "but Emily has come up with a name for us. It's quite simple, but it seems to say it all: 'Emily Loves Cakes.'"

"That sounds great," said Sally. "As the wife of the potential café manager, I'd like to endorse that name and propose a toast." She raised her mug. "To Emily Loves Cakes."

The two women clinked their Emily Love mugs together with a cheer that startled the first customer of the day, who had just walked in.

CHAPTER 33

Teatime is always special in Claire's house.

The café had been an instant success. Claire's regular customers loved the excuse to have a cup of tea and a cake in lovely surroundings and those in search of refreshments alone were often lured into the shop to be tempted by the gorgeous stock after they had enjoyed their coffee and cakes.

When Claire first took over the lease, the café had been decorated with hacienda-style swirls of shiny yellow plaster and heavily varnished orange pine paneling. She ordered builders to hack off the lumpy plaster, and over one weekend, with the help of Sally, she painted the walls a soft cream and covered the varnished wood with palest duck-egg blue. She furnished it with a mixture of comfortable sofas and painted chairs grouped around tables covered with polka-dot tablecloths. The effect was fresh and pretty, the perfect backdrop for her cushions, tea cozies, and embroidered napkins.

Gareth had jumped at the chance of leaving his job and being able to cook every day. Two waitresses, vetted by Sally—not too young, too pretty, or too thin—wore brightly colored

Emily Love aprons over black tops and trousers as they served the pots of tea or freshly brewed coffee. Large glass domes on a wooden counter covered slices of moist sponge, rich fruit cake, lemon drizzle squares, and brownies. But most popular of all were the little cupcakes iced with tiny pink hearts and pretty birds and flowers in the distinctive Emily Love style.

Gareth kept lunch simple: homemade soup or fresh rolls with assorted fillings, which were advertised on a large chalk-board on the wall. His one stipulation on accepting the job was that he wouldn't make quiche.

"Real men and all that," he'd said. "I don't care if you call it a tart or a flan or a galette—I'll know it's a quiche and I just won't do it."

It had been Gareth's idea to clear the overgrown yard at the back to make it into an outdoor eating area for warmer weather. After he and a few friends from the pub had hacked back the nettles and brambles, Claire employed a builder to pave the area with reclaimed flagstones and make raised flower beds around the edge. She bought up a collection of pretty, wrought-iron chairs and tables from a French café that was closing down and hung old tin advertising signs and antique garden implements around the stone walls. Window boxes lined the windowsills and hanging baskets cascaded down either side of the doorway.

"Wow," Sally said as she and Claire looked around them at the finished effect. "I know where I'll be spending my lunch-times from now on."

Claire smiled. "It does look lovely. Well done, Gareth, for coming up with the idea!"

"Well done, you." Sally put her arm across Claire's shoulder. "You've come a long way from making yards of bunting in your spare room."

"I can hardly remember that time," said Claire. "It seems like someone else's life. I feel like a different person now."

The warm bank-holiday sun shone down on Claire as she planted a selection of herbs in the new café garden. The children were all at birthday parties and Claire was enjoying a few free hours to get jobs done at work. She hummed an Aretha Franklin tune to herself as she dug down into the soft moist soil.

"Claire."

Startled at the unexpected voice, she turned around to find William standing in front of her.

"Sorry, I didn't mean to make you jump." He wore a pink shirt, something he would never have worn in the past, but it suited him, complementing the deep suntan he'd acquired on a recent holiday abroad. "I just wanted to have a word without the children being about."

Claire stood up, shaking the dirt from her gardening gloves before taking them off.

"Sit down, then." She pulled out a chair from one of the tables, offered it to him, and sat down opposite, placing the gloves on the table in between them.

William looked around him at the little walled garden. "You've made this really lovely."

Surprised by the unexpected compliment, Claire smiled at her ex-husband. "You're looking well," she said.

"I am well." He smiled back at her. "I suppose that's what I want to talk to you about. I wanted you to hear this from me, not from the children or from"—he hesitated and looked down at his hands, clenched together, on the table in front of him—"or from my mother."

"You've met someone," Claire said, sure the only reason her ex-mother-in-law would ever get in touch with her would be to gloat.

"Yes," said William, still looking at his hands.

"That's great," said Claire, smiling. She felt genuinely pleased for him. "I knew you wouldn't have gone on a Mediterranean holiday alone. Who is she?"

"Vanessa."

"Vanessa." Claire repeated the name slowly, suddenly feeling her congeniality sinking. "Your old Vanessa, or have you found a new one?"

William looked irritated. "Please don't be flippant, Claire. I'm seeing Vanessa, my fiancée from before . . ." He paused.

"From before me," prompted Claire.

"Yes." His face turned slightly pink. Claire noticed that it clashed with his shirt. "She was very good to me after the . . ." Again a pause. Claire resisted the urge to prompt him this time. "After everything that happened," William finally said.

A hundred questions flew around Claire's head, but most seemed too futile to ask.

"Vanessa has helped me get myself together, really sort myself out. I'm starting a position in her brother's firm in Cheltenham. We're looking for a house to buy; I'm hoping we'll get married next summer."

They were silent for a while as Claire tried to work out why this news had made her feel so unsettled.

"It's not as if you and I were ever going to get back together or anything like that . . ." His voice trailed away as Claire looked at him.

"I'm sure your mother is delighted." She picked up a gardening glove and began to fiddle with its fingers, picking the crusty flakes of earth from the hardened suede. "Isn't this what she always wanted? Vanessa as her daughter-in-law, your life back on its proper track—detour via Claire terminated."

"I don't care what my mother thinks. It's about what I want and what Vanessa wants. She makes me very happy—I'm just pleased we found each other again."

"How romantic."

"Are you being sarcastic?"

Claire sighed. "No, I'm not. I'm glad you're happy and I wish you all the best for your future." And then she smiled at William as she suddenly realized she meant it.

He returned the smile with a look of relief, and shrugged his shoulders to indicate there was nothing more to say.

"Thank you for telling me," said Claire. William stood up.

"I must go. Vanessa and I are looking at a house this afternoon—a cottage in my parents' village. It needs quite a bit of work doing to it."

"Don't get too obsessive this time," Claire said, standing up as well.

"What do you mean?"

"Don't let a house take priority over people."

William looked cross. "What are you trying to say, Claire?"

"All I'm saying is that a house is only bricks and mortar. Remember to make time and space for the people you love; they'll be the things that really make it a home."

She reached up and gently kissed his cheek. He looked surprised and confused. As he walked out of the garden, Claire wondered if he would ever understand.

* * *

Do you really not mind?" Sally asked, arranging a new display of cushions on a painted dresser.

Claire leaned against the counter, opening the morning's mail.

"No, I don't. I'm pleased for William. The children met Vanessa over the weekend and they said she's nice. Ben loved her because she let him have two ice creams at the park, but he says her bottom's not as big as mine—I'm not sure if he thought that was good or bad! Emily made things better by telling me that Vanessa's hair is gray at the roots and that she thinks she's got a face like a Shetland pony."

"Good for Emily." Sally laughed. "I wish I had a daughter to be sensitive to my emotional needs. Now the twins are at secondary school, I think they've forgotten I even exist."

"Oliver is just the same; I'm just the person who keeps the fridge stocked as far as he's concerned."

"But what about you?" Sally stopped midway through slotting a polka-dot cushion in beside a row of patchwork ones. "When are you going to find yourself a man and start having a bit of fun?"

"I *am* having fun," she said, a little annoyed. She enjoyed the shop and the café; she loved her little house by the river, being with the children, the dog, the chickens. It was fun, wasn't it? "I don't need a man to make my life complete."

Sally raised her eyebrows and turned back to the cushions. After a little while she said, "I always hoped you'd get back together with William."

Claire laughed. "That was never very likely. I know you always thought that William was Mr. Wonderful, but looking back, I realize how unhappy I had become. I felt like a little girl playing in the perfect doll's house, but I never seemed to get the rules of the game right. He thought he'd done it all for me, but in the end he'd boxed me in. I couldn't breathe. I couldn't be myself."

Sally took all the cushions down and started rearranging them in a different order.

"Did you ever hear what happened to that photographer man?" she asked.

"No." Claire ripped open an envelope and, after staring at a brightly colored piece of junk mail, scrunched it up and threw it in the bin.

"Don't you ever wonder where he is?"

"No," said Claire again.

"But don't you ever think . . ."

"No, I don't." Claire started tidying up around her. She picked up a pile of leaflets about their summer sale and banged them down hard on the counter. "I don't know what happened to him. I don't know where he is. I don't think about him, and to be quite honest, I don't care."

"Okay," said Sally, holding up a cushion in defense. "I was only asking."

CHAPTER 34

Everything has been chosen with love.

After persistent proposals from Brian, Claire's mother had finally said yes. The wedding was to take place in France on a Saturday in September, with Claire and the children arriving two days early to help with the preparations and to make sure Elizabeth didn't get cold feet at the last minute.

The early-morning sky was clear and bright as Claire packed up her little van with things to take to the wedding. Sally helped her carry trays and boxes from the shop, filled with lace-edged tablecloths, embroidered napkins, and yards of floral bunting that she had made specially to decorate the garden. Claire had even had hundreds of tiny cupcakes made, all iced with red and pink hearts.

Inside the café the children watched their mother and Sally through the window as Gareth made them bacon muffins and strawberry smoothies for breakfast. Emily and Ben could hardly contain their excitement as they waited for Claire to finish so that they could finally set off. Oliver was trying to look nonchalant and bored, but Claire knew he was secretly just as excited as his siblings.

"I wish I could come with you." Sally sighed. "I love a wed-

ding. Any excuse for dressing up and having a bit of a bop."
She wiggled her hips in a little demonstration of her dancing
skills.

"Sorry, Cinderella, you've got a shop to run," said Claire as
she tried to squeeze the last box of bunting into the back of the
van. Together the two women banged the doors shut and
leaned back against them for a rest.

"I'll just have to wait for yours, then." Sally grinned at
Claire.

"Wait for my what?"

"Your wedding."

"You'll be waiting a long time," said Claire. "Like forever."

"Why don't you hitch up with that bloke from the butcher's?" Sally waved toward a shop on the other side of the street.
"I know he fancies you. He's always asking you to try his
specialty sausages. You could do worse—though it is a bit of a
shame about the wart on his chin and the dodgy comb-over.
Look, I can see him now, arranging his chops in the window.
Shall I go over and tell him you're desperate for a nibble on his
chipolata."

"Sally, stop it." Claire gave her friend a playful swipe.

"Or that man from the estate agents who comes in for his
sandwich every day. There are things you can do to cure hali-
tosis, you know. Just a few hints on your first date and he'd have
it all cleared up by the wedding day."

"Sally! I'm not marrying the butcher or the estate agent just
to give you the opportunity to show off your moves on the
dance floor—I'm sure Oliver would get you a ticket to the next
youth club disco if you're that desperate for a boogie."

"Don't worry, our invite to William and Vanessa's wedding
will be dropping through the letter box any day now."

Claire laughed. "Somehow I don't think you and Gareth

will be top of the guest list and I doubt that the Cotswold String Quartet will be taking requests for 'Dancing Queen.'"

"Sounds like it's going to be a barrel of laughs," said Sally, making a face. "Don't tell me—William's mother is in charge of the preparations."

"Of course. And from what Emily tells me, it's pretty much a rerun of mine and William's wedding, though with the right bride in the grotesque dress this time!"

"Are you sure you're all right about him getting married again?" Sally touched Claire's arm, her face genuinely concerned.

"I keep telling you. I'm fine about it. Anyway, William and Vanessa are made for each other, not to mention William's mother and Vanessa! William and I were never really meant to be. It's all in the past."

"Talking of the past," said Sally. "I went out running yesterday evening and happened to run past your old house. There was a car parked on the drive."

"Oh," said Claire. She opened the passenger door of the van and took out her jacket. "It's chillier than it looks this morning."

"A man got out," Sally went on. "A man I'd never seen before. Not local. Actually he was quite attractive." She raised one eyebrow and smiled. "And I haven't looked at another man in that way since I got back together with Gareth."

"What was he doing?" asked Claire.

"Nothing. He was just standing there looking at the house. Staring. I don't think he noticed me."

"Maybe he was from the firm of developers who bought it," said Claire. "I can't understand why they haven't done anything with it after all this time."

"He didn't have a developer's sort of car and he looked sort of shocked, as if he hadn't expected to see it looking like a ruin. Anyway he didn't stay there long. About five minutes later his car passed me going down the hill."

Claire shrugged her shoulders.

"I wonder who he was?" mused Sally.

"Well, it's not my house anymore," said Claire, collecting up the envelopes scattered around the table. "So if some mystery man wants to stand and stare at it, it's nothing to do with me."

A t last the little blue van pulled slowly away from the curb. "I hope it's a good wedding," Gareth called from the café doorway.

"Maybe you'll find a man in France," shouted Sally as Gareth placed his arm around her shoulder.

"I'm not interested," Claire called back.

"If you found a man, Mummy, would you have another baby?" Emily asked from the seat beside her mother.

"No, darling." Claire smiled, edging through the town's early-morning traffic. "I don't think I'll be providing you with any more brothers or sisters, man or no man."

"You're too old for a man now, Mummy, aren't you?" said Ben.

"Yes, Ben, and too busy. You lot are enough for me."

T he morning of the wedding was warm and cloudless. Claire got ready in the sun-drenched bedroom, carefully taking her dress down from its hanger on the hook behind the door. All the guests had been asked to dress in white and Claire had found a genuine Dior concoction of silk and satin and chiffon in an antiques market in Bergerac. It hung delicately from thin shoulder straps, and as she slipped into it she felt as though she was being surrounded by a gentle breeze. Looking into the mirror, she gathered her hair up loosely in a mother-of-pearl clasp and put on a softly crocheted silk cardigan to hide the ugly scars on her arm. There was a gentle tapping at the door and Claire's mother walked into the room. Claire smiled; her mother looked beautiful, almost regal, in flowing lavender with a lilac lace bolero jacket and a comb of yellow rosebuds in her hair. Her eyes shone brightly and her sun-browned skin looked radiant.

"Will I do?" Elizabeth asked.

"Oh, Mum, you will so much more than do! You look amazing."

"So do you," replied Elizabeth, taking her daughter's hand in hers. "You should be the one getting married; you look like the perfect bride. I'm too old for all this nonsense; this should be your day."

Claire laughed. "You're worse than Sally; she's been trying to marry me off to all sorts of ghastly men lately. I'm perfectly happy being a wedding guest, thank you."

Her mother picked up a pink camellia corsage from the little oak dressing table beside them and carefully pinned it to the bodice of Claire's dress.

"Your grandmother's favorite flower," she said, adjusting the petals against the spray of green leaves behind. "What is it they are meant to mean?"

"Longing," answered Claire, trying to banish the image of a painted teacup from her mind.

The door opened again and Emily appeared, looking like an angel in a simple white lace tunic, a bunch of loosely tied

pink roses in her hand. She stopped and gazed at her grandmother.

"Wow, Granny. I didn't know you were so pretty."

Elizabeth raised her eyebrows and smiled. "Thank you,
darling—I think that was a compliment."

Emily ceremoniously handed her grandmother the bouquet with a curtsy. "Here are your flowers and a message from
Brian; he says, 'Don't be late and don't change your mind.'"

"Do you know, I think I have changed my mind," Elizabeth
said as she took the flowers from Emily and let them hang
limply by her side. "I'm not sure this getting-married thing is
really such a good idea. I don't know why Brian wants to make
such a fuss. Let's just call the whole ceremony off and have a
jolly good party instead."

"Come on." Claire laughed, taking her mother firmly by
the arm. "Emily, you take the other side and don't let go of
her until we reach the town hall!"

Brian arrived at the ancient town hall by motorbike and
sidecar wearing a bright purple silk shirt, Buster beside
him with a large white bow tied onto his collar. Buster was allowed in especially for the ceremony; Oliver and Emily kept
him under control by bribing him with dog biscuits throughout the formalities. Elizabeth shakily got through her marriage vows while Brian anxiously waited for each response, but
as the mayor pronounced them man and wife, Elizabeth's
beaming smile betrayed her joy. As they stood on the steps of
the hall, being showered with rice and flower petals, a conta-
gious happiness radiated from them both.

Afterward it seemed as if the whole town gathered at the

old farmhouse for the reception. They stood amid a mass of flowers that Claire's mother had grown in the garden. Her sunflowers swayed like extra guests surveying the scene from their lofty heights, and window boxes overflowed with red and pink geraniums along the front of the house. A violinist friend of Brian's—the son of a Gypsy, so he claimed—wandered around playing music to the crowd as they drank tall glasses of Pimm's floating with cucumber and wild borage flowers. The children helped themselves to cloudy homemade lemonade from earthenware jugs that sat on a table in the shade of the vine-covered trellis.

Long tables stretched across the grass, clothed in white and interspersed with jam jars filled with lavender and late roses. Claire had scattered pink petals in between the plates and cutlery.

Assorted pies and two cold poached salmons waited in the cool kitchen to be brought out, along with a selection of fresh salads piled into huge, honey-colored bowls made by a local potter. Neighbors brought large wheels of cheese, home-cured hams, breads, and wonderful desserts and pastries to add to the feast.

The lunch was long and leisurely. Bottle after bottle of champagne was opened, toasts drunk, and touching speeches made. Brian's speech had even reduced the men in the party to tears as he declared his happiness at finding someone whom he loved so much to share his life. Then Claire's mother stood up. In French, she thanked everyone for coming and making the day so special. Then she turned to Brian, thanking him for transforming her life and bringing her such joy. As the newly married couple kissed to the guests' cheers, two local women appeared carrying a pyramid of *choux* buns covered with a delicate cobweb of spun sugar, a thick band of brightly colored marigolds and chrysanthemums at its base. Claire explained to the children that this was a traditional French wedding cake called a *croquembouche*, and they were delighted when a large silver sword was produced for the bride and groom to hit the top with, showering the guests with shards of splintered caramel.

At last the light began to fade and the evening party began. A group of local musicians played accordions and violins and the guests danced, young and old alike, on a dance floor Brian had made from wooden pallets and old floorboards.

Claire sat on the steps of the kitchen, watching from a distance. She had danced with various men: the local doctor, the potter, the baker's teenage son. After that she had accepted a dance from the town's mayor, who had performed the wedding ceremony that morning. By the time Claire danced with him, he was very drunk and his feet repeatedly stepped on hers as he spun her around enthusiastically. She didn't like the way he held her too close in his sweaty arms and she caught a glimpse of his wife watching them, her arms crossed over her large expanse of bosom.

At last Claire managed to escape. Leaving the dance floor, she found a glass of wine and a quiet space to watch the magical scene. Fairy lights crisscrossed their way between the trees. Glass lanterns hung, suspended from branches, their candle flames reflected in the inky water of the river. All around her fireflies darted back and forth in the warm air as though they were part of the evening's decorations too.

Claire sipped her wine and marveled at the complicated dance steps that the older local people seemed to know. She could see Oliver and Emily among a group of children at the river's edge, laughing and splashing their feet in the cool water as they tried, in their basic French, to join in with the children's conversations. They seemed almost luminous in their white clothes, bathed in the light of an enormous harvest moon that rose behind the wedding party, like a beautiful backdrop in a play.

Oliver and Emily were growing up so quickly. Claire felt a pang of sadness. They were on the brink of their teenage years already, their childhoods waning, their adult lives beckoning from an ever-decreasing distance.

She looked around for Ben; still her little boy. He was dancing in his typically exuberant style with an elderly lady. Her olive-skinned face revealed a bone structure that, even in old age, made her beautiful. She solemnly followed the steps of the dance, gracefully accommodating her partner's lack of stature and coordination.

Brian's son was there, dancing in a slightly embarrassed way on the edge of the dance floor, out of time to the music, with the glazed look of a man who had driven through the night and only just made it to his father's wedding on time. In his arms he jigged his daughter—the little girl who, as a baby, Brian had come to visit when Claire's mother had fatefully run him over. His wife sat on a nearby chair breast-feeding their second child, looking exhausted and hot. Claire thought she ought to offer her a glass of lemonade, but just as she was about to get up, her mother appeared. Sitting down beside her, she took Claire's hand in hers and squeezed it.

"Are you enjoying yourself, darling?" her mother asked.

"Yes," replied Claire. "It's just lovely."

"You certainly had no shortage of men wanting to dance with you." Her mother nodded toward the dance floor.

"I'd no idea what I was meant to be doing. The dances are so complicated."

"You looked like you were making a good job of it from where I was sitting." Her mother's eyes twinkled in amusement. "I think Jean-Paul, the potter, rather likes you. He hasn't taken his eyes off you since you had your dance with him. I thought he was going to come over and punch the mayor when he was flinging you around."

"Mum! Are you trying to play the matchmaker?" Claire asked in mock incredulity.

"No, I wouldn't dream of it. But it's been a while since you and William separated. Don't you ever think about finding someone else?"

"Look who's talking." Claire smiled. "You were on your own for twenty-five years before you met Brian."

"I was just a miserable, bitter old grump of a woman. Don't be like me, darling. Don't leave it so long. You have so much to offer." She put her arm around Claire's shoulder. "My beautiful, clever daughter. I only want to see you happy."

Claire sighed. "I am happy, Mum. I have my gorgeous children, my own business, a lovely home, my garden. I don't need anyone else when I've got so much to make me happy."

"You know I've never pried into your personal life. I've never asked what happened between you and William. Though, God knows, he would never have been my first choice for you. And his dreadful mother . . ." She shuddered and they both laughed. "It's just sometimes I see such sadness behind your eyes and I wonder if you've been hurt more than I realize."

"I'm fine, Mum," Claire said. "I think I hurt William more than he hurt me." She looked into the distance, beyond the dancers and the twinkling lights, into the darkness. "I can't imagine falling in love with anyone again, having those intense feelings for another man, the desire to share my life with anyone else. Maybe you only get one chance at love in your life and mine just slipped away." She took a sip of wine.

"I'm living proof that you *do* get another chance," said her mother. "This whole day is proof of that for me and for Brian." She gently stroked her daughter's face. "Go and ask François for another dance and make your old mother very happy."

"Mum," Claire warned. "I don't want to encourage him, or any other man. Anyway, tonight isn't about me. It's about you." She stood up. "Why don't you come and dance with me instead, and we can try to work out some of these crazy dance steps together?"

Claire and her mother walked hand in hand toward the dance floor. The music had grown louder. A robustly built woman with red hair piled in curls on her head began to sing.

"I hope you know how lovely you look," Claire said, above the sounds of the accordion and the woman's soulful voice.

"Yes," replied her mother, smiling. "I can't count the times Brian has told me today."

"He's a lucky man to have you."

"No, I'm the lucky one," Elizabeth said as she put her hand lightly on her daughter's waist to begin the dance. "And I believe that one day you'll be just as lucky too."

"May I cut in?"

The voice came from behind her, but Claire felt her heart lurch in recognition and she hardly dared to turn around. She registered her mother's curious face, her polite smile for the stranger.

"Yes, of course you can," Elizabeth said, and let go of her daughter, moving to one side to be swept up by Brian and waltzed away. Claire wondered if she was about to faint, but suddenly she felt strong arms take hold of her, starting to gently move her across the dance floor to the rhythm of the music. She forced herself to look up into the face of her dancing partner. It swam in front of her as she tied to focus, tried to comprehend, whom she was looking at.

"What are you doing here?" she whispered.

"Looking for you."

Stefan bent his head and kissed her softly on the lips. She felt as though she was melting. *This must be a dream,* she thought, and found herself kissing him back. It felt so easy, so delicious.

She pulled away abruptly.

"How on earth did you get here? Why are you here?"

She stopped, motionless in the middle of all the moving couples on the dance floor, and looked up at the face she had never expected to see again. His hair was shorter than she remembered and speckled with strands of gray. He wore a collarless white linen shirt and jeans. A fine layer of stubble covered the lower half of his tanned brown face.

"I'm sorry. I know this must be a total shock." He had to shout above the music. Other dance couples were staring at them, irritated that they were blocking the dance floor. "And I'm sorry for kissing you like that. I couldn't help it. You look so beautiful in white, like the day I first saw you in your garden. Do you remember?" He took her hand. "Can we go somewhere quieter to talk?"

Claire started to let him lead her from the dance floor, then suddenly reality came flooding back; the reality of what had happened, what Stefan had done to her, what he had done to her life. Anger swelled inside and she stopped and snatched her hand away.

"No, we can't talk. I never want to see you again, let alone talk to you." Stefan moved toward her and she stepped back. He looked upset.

"I've driven for hours to get here. Couldn't you at least give me a few minutes?"

Claire desperately tried to decide what to do. Force him to leave and try to forget he'd been there, or let him stay to re-open old wounds and memories so painful she hadn't even dared to think about them for three years?

"You do realize that you're gate-crashing my mother's wedding?" she said.

"I know. Sally said it would be all right."

Claire felt her head spinning; she wished she hadn't drunk so much wine.

"Sally told you where to find me? How do you know Sally? I'm sure she'd never have told you where I was."

"Could we go somewhere more private?" Stefan reached out and touched her arm.

"Don't touch me," she blurted out, pushing him away. "Don't think you have any right to touch me, or any right to be here at all. What do you want? Why have you come here?" Claire was shouting now. She was vaguely aware that the music and the singing had stopped, that the other guests were watching, listening; she could see Elizabeth and Brian, their faces alarmed. Claire didn't care. "How dare you walk into my life again after everything that happened? How dare you just appear like this from nowhere and expect me to want to talk to you? You ruined my life; you turned it upside down and destroyed everything in it—my home, my family, my heart. You did that and look at you now: standing here like nothing happened at all, remembering how we first met, asking me if I remember it too. Of course I remember it, and I wish it had never happened. I wish you'd never walked into my garden. I wish I'd never met you at all.

"You have no idea what I had to go through to get to where I am today—while you've been swanning around the world, no doubt seducing other naive women in their idyllic homes and then going home to your girlfriend. Or is she your wife?"

"I don't have a girlfriend or a wife."

"I saw you with her." Claire's voice was getting louder. "You lied to me. You led me on. You let me fall in love with you, risk everything for you, and all along you were seeing someone else."

"Claire, I . . ."

She wouldn't let Stefan interrupt; tears were rolling down her cheeks; she tried to brush them away with her fingers. "Do you know what happened? Do you know what William did to the house because of you—because of us?"

"I know," said Stefan. "Sally told me. I saw the house. It must have been terrible."

"Terrible!" shouted Claire. "Yes, of course it was terrible. The whole house up in flames, gone forever; all those rooms you photographed, gone. The children could have been killed." She pushed up the soft translucent sleeve of her cardigan and held up her arm in front of his face.

"Look at these scars. And these are only the scars on the outside. You hurt me, Stefan. You hurt me more than you'll ever know, and the last thing I ever want to do is see you again."

Brian stepped forward and put his arm protectively around her.

"Do you need help, Claire? Shall I ask this man to leave?"

Claire looked around her and suddenly felt embarrassed by her very public outburst.

"What's going on, darling?" her mother asked, coming to join Brian by Claire's side.

"If I could just have a chance to explain, to tell you what really happened." Stefan's dark eyes held Claire's own. Powerless to look away, she remembered how he made her feel. Emotions buried long ago came flooding back. Suddenly someone was pushing through the crowd of people.

"Sally, what on earth are you doing here?" Claire decided it really must be all a dream.

Sally's face was flushed; she sounded out of breath. "You've got to talk to him, Claire. Please give him a chance to explain what happened."

Claire looked into Stefan's eyes again; they seemed to plead with her.

"Please, Claire, he needs to talk to you." Sally gave her a hug and then a little shake. "I wouldn't have come all this way with someone who drove like a maniac and talked about nothing else but you for seven hundred miles if I didn't think that it was important for you to hear what he's got to say."

"I don't understand."

"For God's sake, just talk to the man." She practically pushed Claire and Stefan from the dance floor.

"Okay." Claire sighed.

Stefan followed as she led him away from the inquisitive eyes, out of sight, to the side of the house. An antique lantern cast a flickering light across the cobbled drive.

"Claudia!" Claire exclaimed as she saw the MG parked in front of her. The top was down. She reached out and touched the shiny hood; it felt hot.

"She's done really well," said Stefan, putting his hand beside hers on the car. "She's been locked up in a garage for years and then suddenly I'm driving her like a madman across France to get to see you. Do you want to get in?" he asked, opening the passenger door. Wordlessly Claire slipped onto the smooth red seat. Stefan got into the other side and they sat in silence for a while. The music in the garden had started up again.

"Are we going anywhere?" Claire asked tentatively.

"Do you mean in the car?"

"Of course. What else would I mean?"

"Something more allegorical?"

Claire said nothing.

"I like your shop and café," Stefan said after a few moments. "Nice fairy cakes."

"Thank you," she said, staring straight ahead of her, watching moths as they buffeted around the lantern.

"Are you still using locally sourced ants in your pies?"

"Sorry?"

"The squashed ants in your mincemeat. I never eat a mince pie without thinking of you."

Claire laughed; she couldn't help it. She stopped laughing and looked at him.

"What do you want, Stefan?"

"I'm so sorry about everything that's happened," he said, holding her gaze. "I've been abroad. I had no idea about what happened. I'm so sorry," he repeated. "It's all been such a mess."

Suddenly tears were falling from Claire's eyes again. Stefan reached across her and produced a large white handkerchief from the glove compartment. She wiped her eyes with it and she could smell Stefan on the cotton—lemons, sandalwood. It filled her with a longing to touch him. She resisted and tightly scrunched the damp handkerchief between both her hands.

"I don't know why you've come back," she said, looking out

across the garden. "I've spent so long trying not to think about you."

"I've spent so long thinking of little else but you," he said. He took a deep breath and sighed. After a few moments' silence he said, "You were wrong. She wasn't my girlfriend, or my wife—the woman you saw me with. She was my sister."

Claire looked at him.

"She came that night after your husband had found my texts and phoned me up."

"William told me that he had. I couldn't bear to ask him what he said."

"He told me that he loved you, that you were the most precious thing in his life." Stefan sighed before going on. "He said he'd made mistakes, that he hadn't appreciated you, and he begged me to leave you alone, to give him a chance to mend his marriage. He was sobbing; it was heartbreaking to listen to. He told me he was going to show you just how much he loved you."

"Is that what he was trying to do when he set fire to the house?" said Claire grimly.

Stefan shrugged. "He was in a terrible state. I promised him you wouldn't hear from me again." He put his head in his hands. "Only a few minutes after I had put the phone down, my sister arrived out of the blue from Brussels. She'd been diagnosed with cancer, a terrible, fast-growing kind of cancer. She had such a grim diagnosis; had been given just six months to live. She had no one else, no partner, our parents were dead. She had simply gotten on the first flight to London and come to see me. We were always close. It must have been her you saw at my flat the next day."

Claire looked at him; she thought about the tall dark

woman, tall and dark just like Stefan. She had been thin. Thin because she was so ill? Claire felt her head spinning again.

"I immediately gave up work and went back with her to Brussels," Stefan went on. "I nursed her as she got worse; until she went into a hospice. I stayed in Brussels until she died."

"Oh, Stefan," Claire gasped, "I'm so sorry." She put her hand on his arm and kept it there.

"Afterward, I didn't want to come back to England. I was grieving, I was on my own, lost—or at least trying to get lost. I rented out my flat. Put Claudia in a lockup. I hadn't heard anything from you. I had nothing left to come back for. I spent a few months in the States working for different magazines over there. Then I started just aimlessly traveling around, taking random pictures, trying to forget the last few years, trying to forget all about my sister's illness and death. Trying to forget you." He paused and looked straight at her and then laughed. "I wasn't very good at that, I'm afraid, but I started selling my pictures to travel publications instead of interiors magazines."

"Isn't that what you wanted?" Claire asked. "To be a travel photographer?"

"Yes. It's funny the way things happen. Life can end up going the way you wanted it to, but the way you get there can be a lot rougher than you'd like."

"I know exactly what you mean," she said.

"I only came back to England last week."

"What brought you back?" Claire asked.

"Oh, you know," said Stefan, "frosty mornings."

"Marmite," she said, with a small smile, remembering their long-ago conversation in the heat of a July afternoon.

"And you," he said. "I came to find you, to see if you were happy, if you and William had managed to make things work.

I went to your house. You can imagine how I felt seeing it derelict. Then I found your shop on the High Street and I met Sally. She's a feisty woman. She gave me quite a piece of her mind when I told her who I was."

"I can imagine." Claire laughed.

"I explained everything to her, told her how I feel about you, how important it was that I saw you, and before I knew it she'd agreed to bring me to you here."

"She'd use any excuse to get to a wedding," Claire said, smiling.

"On the way she told me everything that had happened to you. It's true what you said. I really did ruin your life."

"Maybe it's not really ruined," she said. "Just changed. You were like a catalyst that made things happen. I'm much happier now than I ever was in that big house with William and his endless home improvements. The business is good; the children are lovely. I've even got some chickens and a vegetable patch and a black Labrador."

Stefan laughed. "Just like you always wanted." Then he was serious. "If I had known, Claire, if I had known about the fire, about your divorce, I would have come to find you long ago. I've had to stop myself from contacting you so many times. If only I had."

"It sounds like you had enough to go through yourself," said Claire softly. She noticed he looked tired; she felt her heart contract. "Things haven't worked out so badly for me after all."

"What about us?" he asked.

Claire didn't reply. Stefan reached into the pocket of his shirt and brought out a length of silver chain interspersed with small pearl buttons. Claire remained silent as she stared at the familiar necklace.

"I've kept it with me wherever I've gone. I've always wanted to give it back to you." He reached out and took her hand and let the chain fall into her palm. He gently closed her fingers over it and sat back in his seat. Claire looked straight ahead at the shifting shadows of the lantern-lit drive. She noticed pale pink roses scrambling over a trellis in front of them. According to her grandmother, pale pink roses meant perfect happiness to come. She turned to Stefan.

"I vowed I'd never get involved with anyone again. I'm used to being on my own, and I've got the children to think of and . . ." Her voice trailed off. She looked into his soft brown eyes and found it hard to look away.

"We could take it very slowly," he said, looking back at her. She had to fight an urge to touch his face. "Just one day at a time. We could have a lovely life together."

"Please don't say it could be perfect," said Claire. She thought she saw a glimpse of Sally and her mother peeping round the corner of the house. Stefan was gradually moving toward her.

"Okay," he said. "It definitely won't be perfect." And he leaned across the red leather seat and gently kissed her lips.

A Perfect Home

Readers Guide

Discussion Questions

1. Why did it take Claire so long to realize she wasn't happy in her life?

2. Do you think Claire should have been more communicative with William about what she wanted from their life together, and for herself? If so, do you think it would have changed anything?

3. Do you think Claire lets life pass her by? Why is it important to her to stay in her marriage? Discuss your thoughts on her life and marriage before and after the fire.

4. Do you think that Claire's feelings about marriage have been influenced by her childhood and her parents' divorce? If so, how? Does the changing relationship between her and her mother influence the decision she makes about her marriage?

5. Stefan knew Claire was married, but was flirtatious just the same. Do you find this unacceptable, even though, as is mentioned later in the novel, Stefan felt something special that he couldn't deny?

6. Discuss the irony of the title. What do you think the author is trying to convey? Do you think there is such a thing as a "perfect home"? Why or why not?

7. Discuss and give examples of how the house fire is like Claire's life.

8. Emily Love was the reason that *Idyllic Home* wanted to photograph Claire and William's house, so when the article finally appears, why is no one happy with it, blaming Claire for omissions and editorial license? How does this parallel Claire's life?

9. After the fire, when Claire and the children travel back from France after their holiday, she's hopeful that William's demeanor has improved and that they'll be close again, "as close as they had been before the house had come into their lives." Discuss the use of the phrase "had come into their lives." Do you think the house really held all the power in their relationship? Why or why not?

10. Do you think Claire was careless about her phone so that her relationship with Stefan could be discovered? Why or why not?

11. Claire finally feels at home in her new cottage and in her new life. Why does she feel at home here when she didn't with William? Discuss the parallel with her marriage and any deeper meaning.